Remember that no man loses other life than that which he lives,
Nor lives other than that which he loses.
—Marcus Aurelius

To know beauty, one must live with it.
—Irish proverb

❧ I ❧

You must understand—I'm not the type who sees omens and portents in everything. Even though my Aunt Kizzie once snapped the face of Jesus in her Jell-O salad, I didn't see anything in the photograph but bits of fruit cocktail and swirled cream cheese where the beard should be. I'm what you might call a practical Christian. I'm kind to strangers, I'm prepared for heaven, and I try to be a good testimony on earth. I don't have visions, I don't jump around in church, yet there are times I hear the still, small Voice—not audible, but insistent all the same.

The last time I heard the Voice I was in Manhattan, standing on the corner of Sixth Avenue and Fifty-fourth Street. A heat wave lay over the city like a wool blanket, and I wanted nothing more than to reach the little air-conditioned restaurant where I could relax and enjoy a cool drink. The pedestrian light had just changed to walk, so the crowd around me surged forward. But the Voice inside me said *wait*.

Perched on the curb, I lowered the book I'd been flipping through and felt my stomach sway. All around me, businessmen, shoppers, teenagers, and tourists hurried in complete oblivion to cross the street. A musclebound guy in black jogging shorts nearly knocked me from the curb, then rushed on without even an "excuse me." My eyes followed him, certain that a crazed cab or some drunk driver was about to careen through the crowd and scatter people like rag dolls. Why else would the Voice of God stop me *now*, when I was starving and tired after a long day's work?

The pedestrian light blinked don't walk, and a white-haired grandma pushed past me like a lineman intent on sacking the opposing quarterback. I leaned back toward the curb, bracing for the screech of brakes and sudden screaming, but . . . nothing happened.

The light changed again. The waiting cars in front of me peeled away, scattering a couple of pedestrians on the far side of the street, but no one was injured.

Just a typical New York afternoon.

I glanced around, making sure I hadn't missed any other threatening situations, then lifted my book again and credited the Voice to my hyperactive imagination. I'd just found the spot where the hero rescues the heroine from a fate worse than death when someone tugged on my sleeve.

"Meghann McGreedy? I *love* her." A petite, strawberry blonde girl next to me nodded toward my book. "I read that one last week. Have you heard about the sequel? I think she's working on it now."

"You mean this isn't the end of Horace and Irene?" The pedestrian signal changed again, and this time I didn't even think about waiting. The girl stepped off the curb, and I went with her. "What else could possibly happen to those two?"

"Anything can happen!" The girl was shorter than me, so she lengthened her stride to keep up. "For one thing, I hear they find a way to get back to 1995. I don't want to give away the ending, but in the epilogue Horace suggests going back to Ireland, and Irene has to because—" She stopped, her blue eyes twinkling at me. "Well, I don't want to give the ending away."

"You can tell me." I closed the book and tucked it under my arm as we walked. "I don't know you, so how can I hold anything against you?"

The girl smiled. "I like your logic. All right, then. Irene is pregnant, and she decides to have the baby in contemporary Ireland, though why she'd want to do that I'll never know. So they have to manipulate their time machine, but the contraption falls into a desperate bad humor, and Horace has to leave Irene. That's how this book ends."

She threw up her hands in a gesture of helpless exasperation, and I stared at her, mystified. From my work in the bookstore, I knew lots of people loved the Meghann McGreedy's books, but I'd never met anyone quite so enthusiastic about them. And this blue-eyed girl spoke with a lilting accent that had to be Irish, which meant she might be able to explain some of the strange situations Horace and Irene had stumbled across in sixth-century Ireland.

We had reached the deli where I planned to eat dinner, so I stopped on the sidewalk and smiled at my new friend. "I never thought I'd find anyone as hooked on these books as I am."

"I never thought I would either." She grinned back at me. "But when I saw you standing on the curb with the book in your hands, I knew we had to be kindred spirits." A pretty blush mantled her cheeks. "I don't usually go around talking to strangers, if you're wondering about me being some kind of loony."

"That's okay, I don't usually answer strangers who talk to me." I hesitated a moment, then pointed to the entrance of the delicatessen. "I was just about to meet a friend for a sandwich. Would you like to join us? He's a reader, too. Though he's not wild about Meghann McGreedy as I am, he knows quite a bit about literature."

"I was just beginning to think about a bit of dinner." The girl glanced at the sign over the delicatessen, then looked back at me. "Sure, and why not? I'd love to join you."

"Let's go then." I opened the door and led the way into the restaurant. As we stood and waited for a table, I suddenly remembered the Voice. I'd been so certain that I waited on that curb to avoid being smacked by a car in the crosswalk. But instead, I'd found a new friend.

An unexpected blessing.

As we studied the menu and made small talk, I learned that my Irish friend was Maddie O'Neil, a twenty-two-year-old student majoring in humanities at New York City College. Like most humanities majors, she had no idea what she wanted to *do* with her degree, but she loved art, she loved music, and she loved people. When Taylor entered the deli, saw my wave, and headed toward our table, the light in Maddie's eye convinced me she could very well learn to love Taylor Morgan.

Taylor tossed his attaché case into the empty space on the table, then sank into his chair and looked at Maddie as if he'd never seen a cute, blue-eyed strawberry blonde before.

"Taylor, this is Maddie O'Neil," I offered, feeling invisible. "Maddie, this is my friend Taylor Morgan. He's an assistant professor at the college . . . and my friend."

"The name is Madeline, but you can call me Maddie." She thrust her small hand across the table and smiled so warmly that her earlier smiles seemed like mere grimaces in comparison. "Kathleen tells me you've a fondness for literature."

"I should hope so." One corner of his mouth turned up as he winked at me. "I can't get away from it. Besides my work in the English Department, Kathleen's kept me busy reading her manuscripts for the last year. But she's probably already told you about her project."

"Not really." Maddie dimpled. "We just met. I saw her looking through one of Meghann McGreedy's books on the sidewalk, and I couldn't resist speaking to her. One thing led to another, so we're going to have a bit of dinner together."

"Interesting." As the waitress appeared at Taylor's side and flipped open her order pad, he held up his hand. "How about three hot teas? Madeline, I imagine that you enjoy afternoon tea."

"Absolutely. Lovely." Maddie clapped as if hot tea and June heat went together like bread and butter, but I shook my head.

"Diet soda for me," I told the waitress. "With *lots* of ice."

Then I ordered my usual tuna sandwich while Maddie ordered a crab salad. Taylor asked for the crab salad, too, and as the waitress moved away, he turned to Maddie. "That is the *most* lovely Irish accent I've ever heard. Where is your home?"

I crossed my arms as Maddie began to tell us—or tell Taylor—that she had come to New York four years ago. Last month she earned her bachelor's degree, but she wanted to take additional literature classes before deciding whether she should look for a job or enter the master's program.

Resting my chin in my hand, I watched her and Taylor. I had known Taylor for over a year, and during the past several months we'd grown quite close—in fact, I'd have to say we were best friends. Though we never specifically talked about it, I had been thinking that someday we'd marry and settle down together. I could just see us—he with his books and me with mine, sitting in his-and-hers wing chairs before a roaring fire. Barkley, my mastiff, would stretch out on the floor between us and snore happily as Taylor asked my opinion about some student's paper or the latest *New York Times* bestseller. Not a very passionate marriage, perhaps, but certainly a happy one.

Taylor and I liked the same things and shared the same temperaments. For at least six months, we had been meeting in this deli every afternoon, eating matching tuna sandwiches and drinking diet soda, but Taylor had abruptly become a tea and salad man, while I faded to invisible. What happened?

The waitress brought our drinks, and I watched silently as Maddie poured sugar and cream into her tea, and Taylor methodically imitated her. She stirred; he stirred. She sipped; he sipped. She giggled; he laughed. And neither of them noticed me.

"You know," Taylor said, abruptly glancing up at me as if he'd read my thoughts, "Kathleen and I are Irish, too. Kathleen is a descendant of Cahira O'Connor, and she actually discovered my name in the O'Connor family tree."

Maddie's delicate brow wrinkled. "Cahira O'Connor? Sorry, never heard of her. But O'Connor is a common Irish name."

"Cahira was a thirteenth-century princess," Taylor went on, the charm of his smile echoing in his voice. "Apparently on her deathbed she prayed that her descendants would break out of their traditional roles and fight for right in the world. Amazingly enough, Kathleen has discovered that three other O'Connor women—four, if you count Kathleen herself—have fulfilled Cahira's deathbed prayer. Every two hundred years an O'Connor woman appears with a streak of white hair over the left temple, just like Kathleen's. Three of those women have done incredible things with their lives."

Maddie leaned forward and stared at the side of my head as if a third eye had just appeared there. "Ah, sure. 'Tis surely amazing."

"Kathleen has written three manuscripts—books, really—on each of the other three women," Taylor continued, stirring his tea again. "They're remarkable, and I keep telling her she's destined for greatness. But Kathy doesn't think she has it in her."

"I just don't think there's any unique calling for women knights, women explorers, or women soldiers today," I answered, suddenly irritated by the entire conversation. "Seriously, what isn't a woman today capable of? Any woman with ambition and intelligence can decide to cure diseases, run for office, even orbit in space. The time of women stepping into men's roles to accomplish the unthinkable is over. *Everything* is thinkable. I'm sure Flanna O'Connor was the last of the adventures." There. No more to say. "Now can we change the subject? Maddie and I came here to talk about Meghann McGreedy's books."

"But why would we want to bore the poor lad with that fluff and nonsense?" Maddie lifted her teacup to her perfectly pink lips and smiled at Taylor over the rim. "Your work must surely be fascinating. Tell me about your favorite author."

Taylor shifted in his chair, his face brightening as he turned to face Maddie. "Well, though some say no one will ever beat Shakespeare for sheer depth and originality, I have the highest regard for Rudyard Kipling. He has been vastly unappreciated, and too many of our freshmen students have never been invited to read his work. A few have heard of *The Jungle Book*, of course, but most of them are more familiar with Disney's version than Kipling's."

I sipped my soda, then swirled my straw in the glass, only half-listening to a conversation I'd already heard at least a dozen times. On and on Taylor continued, extolling Kipling's genius, while Maddie's face glowed in rapt attention.

Would it have been too much, I asked the Voice, *to use someone else to play matchmaker? You could have let them meet at the grocery or the college. They could have smacked into each other in a fender bender. You didn't have to use me to introduce my best friend to the love of his life.*

◌⁂◌

WHAT MAKES ONE PERSON FALL IN LOVE WITH ANOTHER? IN Meghann McGreedy's books, the spunky, beautiful heroine usually insults, disdains, or slaps the strong, handsome hero upon their first encounter. The befuddled fellow always walks away vowing never to speak to that particular piece of feminine baggage again, but you just *know* they're destined to end up together. Any two people who throw those kinds of sparks on their first meeting are bound to get together again—and permanently.

That's what struck me as strange about Taylor and Maddie. They were both as pleasant as could be that first afternoon in the delicatessen. Maddie didn't toss a single insult or lift as much as a brow in dispute, but sparks were flying nonetheless. I wasn't surprised to hear Taylor invite her to join us at the museum opening we had planned to attend Friday night, nor was I surprised when she accepted. What astonished me as we walked through the museum and studied the so-so paintings of an up-and-coming artist was the realization that Taylor preferred Maddie's company to mine. When a thought struck him, he pulled Maddie to his side to share it. When Maddie sighed in ecstasy over a painting, Taylor hurried forward to admire it. And when Maddie spilled her purse all over the marble floor, Taylor crawled on his hands and knees among a crowd of well-heeled museum patrons to retrieve every penny and lipstick. We're very close, but I don't think Taylor would have gone down on his hands and knees for me if I'd dropped my last dime.

On the way out of the museum, Taylor suggested that we go to a movie the next night. Maddie accepted instantly, but I made up a lame excuse about having to wash my hair. Amazingly, Taylor bought it.

So I spent that Saturday night alone in my apartment with Barkley, my 240-pound mastiff. Determined not to sit around feeling sorry for myself, I whipped up an oatmeal-and-egg facial masque and poured myself a tall iced tea, then carried my bowl and my glass into the bathroom. As I sat in front of the mirror slathering gritty goop on my face, I assured Barkley that most men were idiots. Taylor Morgan, my best friend, had fallen into a blue-eyed trap, and Maddie had been blowing smoke when she said she was staying in New York while she tried to decide what career to pursue. The girl had finished school without snagging an engagement ring, so hunting season had officially been extended. And my naive Taylor, bless his heart, was definitely the most attractive stag in this neck of the woods.

Pushing his bulky chest up from the floor, Barkley lifted his nose in my direction, sniffing the oatmeal masque. "They have absolutely nothing in common," I told him, drawing a line of goo across my forehead like war paint. "He's quiet; she's active. He's self-contained, and she's so out there it's scary. Taylor's a very private person, but Maddie would tell her secrets to a perfect stranger. Look how we met—she talked to me, a perfect stranger, then accepted an invitation to dinner. She's nuts, that one."

Barkley edged closer, still intent on the oatmeal, so I offered him my index finger for a lick.

"And she's Irish, for heaven's sake—and probably six months away from being an illegal alien. Who knows? She may be looking for an American husband so she can become a citizen and stay in this country. Taylor is altogether too inexperienced with women—those outside of his books, at any rate."

Barkley finished licking my finger, then lowered himself to the cool tile floor, his eyes alert. Mindful of the dog drool on my index finger, I used my middle finger to paint my face this time, then offered him another taste of masque. "The truth is, buddy, I always thought Taylor and I would get together at some point. We're alike. We're best friends. And even though there's no passionate love affair going on between us, that kind of thing fades after a while, doesn't it?"

Barkley tilted his head and gave my finger a final lick, then sat back and blessed me with one of his brightest doggie smiles. I stared wistfully at him for a long moment, then sighed and washed my hands. Dogs are great listeners, but terrible advice-givers.

I got up, tightened the belt of my bathrobe, and gave my gooey reflection a test smile. The masque had definitely tightened on my skin —either that, or just the thought of Taylor and Maddie made me feel tense and strained all over.

❧ 2 ☙

The next two weeks flew by in a blur. Since the college semester ended, my boss at the Tattered Leaves bookstore had moved me from part time to full time, so work filled my days from nine till five. I still went to the delicatessen after work, and Taylor still showed up to keep me company—with Maddie. I was actually considering a deli boycott until Taylor took the hint, but then a miracle happened: One afternoon she didn't appear. The sight of her empty chair cheered me tremendously until Taylor explained that Maddie had to work late.

"She got a job?"

"I found her a place at the college." Taylor crossed his arms and grinned like a proud papa. "Administrative assistant in the English Department. With her humanities background, I think she's perfect for the job."

On and on he blathered, ad nauseam. Maddie loved the arts, Maddie loved the English Department, Maddie even loved Kipling. Since meeting Taylor only two weeks ago, she had read *The Jungle Book*, *The Man Who Would be King*, and now she had begun to read *Kim*.

"She's quite the reader," I remarked, wondering why my tuna sandwich seemed dry and tasteless today. "I hear the love of literature is an Irish trait."

"Well, so many of the great writers are Irish," Taylor mumbled around his sandwich. "James Joyce, Frank McCourt, and W. B. Yeats just begin the list." He swallowed, then looked at me with amusement in his eyes. "Don't forget, Kathy—*you're* Irish. And you're a writer, too."

"It's Kathleen—and I *hope* to be a writer. We still have to see if someone will hire me when I finish school."

"You're already a writer—your work on the heirs of Cahira O'Connor proves it. So don't keep putting yourself down. I still think you ought to try and get those manuscripts published as soon as you finish. There's still Cahira's story to tell—and your own."

"I have no story, and you know it. I'm as ordinary as white paper, so stop pushing me to be something I'm not." Pretending to pout, I picked up a French fry and dabbed it in a puddle of catsup. My work on the heirs of Cahira O'Connor was a bit of a sore subject and Taylor knew it, but at least the conversation had shifted away from the wonders of Maddie O'Neil.

Taylor turned his smile up a notch. "Still afraid you're destined to do something heroic in the twenty-first century?"

I shrugged to hide my confusion. "Why do you ask? I've gathered the impression that you don't care one way or the other."

He sank back, his face sagging like a kicked dog's. "How could you say such a thing? Of course I care. I thought we were friends."

"Of course we're friends." I ran my fingernail over the plastic table-cloth and struggled to conquer my involuntary reactions to that gentle and concerned look of his. "It's just—well, you've been spending so much time with Maddie."

"I know. And I'm glad Maddie had to work today, because I wanted to talk to you privately. I've been trying to find some time where we could be alone."

An inexpressible feeling of happiness sprouted inside me. "You have?"

"Yes." Taylor shifted and hung one arm over the back of his chair. "I'm about to do something profound, Kathy, and I need your guidance. You've never given me bad advice."

My happiness blossomed and unfurled like an American beauty rose. Maddie O'Neil had turned his head, but when Taylor needed advice, he turned to his most trusted friend. Me.

I leaned forward and folded my hands on the table. "I'm here for you, Taylor. You can tell me anything." I studied his face, searching for some insight into his thoughts. "What's on your mind?"

His hand moved restlessly across the table, then he picked up his fork and planted it on the tablecloth, the tines pricking the plastic. "This isn't easy for me to talk about, so I'll just get to the point. Maddie's father has prostate cancer. He's been through radiation, chemo, and everything else they could do, but nothing helped. The doctors estimate he has less than a year to live."

A rush of sweet sympathy poured through my soul. "Oh, Taylor, that's awful."

Nodding, Taylor turned the fork upside down. "Maddie hasn't been able to afford the trip back to see him, but she's going to have to go soon."

My sympathetic smile froze into position. What followed could be good news or bad, depending upon whether Maddie would return to Ireland alone . . . or with Taylor.

"So, . . . she wants to go home?"

"She hasn't said so, but I know she'll want to go soon. The thing is —" He blew out his cheeks. "Honestly, I never dreamed it would be so hard to say this. I feel like I can tell you anything, Kathy, but I don't know how to tell you I want to take Maddie back to Ireland, marry her there, then bring her back to New York. And I want you to go with us so you can be in the wedding."

My breath caught in my throat. He wanted me to go to Ireland with him and Maddie? To be in their *wedding?*

Something automatic took over, and I think I managed to give him a strained smile. "I can't go with you to Ireland." My voice sounded false and unnaturally bright in my ears. "Haven't you ever heard that three's a crowd?"

He hauled his gaze from his fork and returned his attention to me. "Kathleen," a warning note lined his voice, "don't be silly. You're my friend, and you're Maddie's friend, so of course we want you in the wedding. You brought us together."

How blind men are! I lowered my arms to my lap so he couldn't see my hands clenching and unclenching beneath the table. "Have you asked Maddie about this? Most women like to plan their own weddings."

"I haven't asked her anything yet," his gaze fell to the tablecloth, "but I'm 99.9 percent sure she's going to say yes when I propose. And I know she'll want you in the wedding. She's been away from Ireland for a while, so I don't think she'll have many girlfriends for attendants, and she has no sisters, only a brother. But she wants a big Irish wedding, and I want you there even if I have to make you the best man."

An odd coldness settled upon me. My best friend was about to wreck his life, and he wanted me to witness the head-on collision.

"Taylor, you've only known Maddie two weeks. That's not nearly long enough to make a decision about marriage."

"I've thought of that, that's why I want to spend several weeks in Ireland confirming our feelings and getting to know Maddie's family. I was thinking we could leave as soon as our passports come through, and stay through October." He looked at me with dewy moisture in his beautiful blue eyes. "I thought it'd be nice to be married on October 16; Maddie has mentioned that's her father's birthday. Then we can honeymoon in Ireland and come back to New York in time for Christmas and the beginning of the winter semester."

Ripples of shock spread from an epicenter in my heart, sending waves of numbness to the crown of my head and the tips of my toes. Quickly I counted on my fingers. "You want me to go to Ireland for four *months?*"

I noted a familiar softness around his mouth and knew he was about to smile. "By the time we get our passports, it won't be that long. And Maddie and I will need a few weeks to arrange the wedding details."

I swallowed the scream of frustration that had risen at the back of my throat. "And what am I supposed to do all that time? I can't just go hang out in Ireland—"

"You can finish your work on Cahira." Taylor dropped his fork and leaned over the table, dangerously close to me. "Think of it, Kathleen —you'll be right *there*. Right where Cahira lived and died, on the same ground, beside the same hills, under the same skies. You can visit libraries and museums and look at ancient artifacts. You can soak up local color until you're as green as a shamrock." His blond brows arched mischievously. "Don't tell me you've never wanted to go to Ireland. I know better."

I shook my head as mixed feelings surged through me. "Sure, I've wanted to go, but that's just Cinderella talk, Taylor. You're talking about leaving in a few weeks—and staying away for months! I can't go. I have a job, I have a dog, I have school. I can't just walk away from my entire life."

"When else are you going to go?" A blue flame of defiance lit his eyes. "I know you, Kathleen. If you don't come with us, you'll stay here, finish school, marry the first guy who asks you, and settle down to raise the statistical average of 2.2 children while you write sweet little feature stories for the local paper. You'll drive a station wagon, shop for groceries three times a week, and volunteer for room mother at your kids' school. And every night you'll fall into bed too tired from doing the little things to even *dream* about the big things. Is that any kind of life for an heir of Cahira O'Connor?"

I drew a deep breath and flexed my fingers until the urge to slap him had passed. "That sounds like a pretty good life to me. Why should I want more than any woman I know? I'd be *thrilled* to raise two happy kids and write stories for the local paper, as long as I fell into bed at night with a wonderful husband! I don't *want* fame or danger or excitement. I don't need those things. But you must need them, Taylor. Why else would you want to go all the way to Ireland to marry a girl you barely know?"

Taylor's blue eyes darkened as he held my gaze. "Because I know I can't live without her. And I know her well enough to know she would want to be married with her family present, so that means Ireland. And I cherish *you* enough to want you with me."

I managed a choking laugh. "You cherish *me?*"

He nodded. "I do. And I know you, probably better than you know yourself. I know Ireland is your motherland, whether or not you want to claim it, and Cahira's legacy is yours, whether or not you want to acknowledge it. You need to come with us, Kathleen. My happiness wouldn't be complete without you at my wedding."

Then why don't you marry me, *you idiot?* I stared at him, thinking the words I didn't dare speak because I knew *him* as well as he knew me. He thought of me as a sister, a friend, even a confidant, but I had never been a lover. And I would never be his wife.

I tore my eyes from his and looked at the floor, pretending to search for my purse, then bent down to dash the wetness from my eyes. "I gotta go."

"But you'll think about it?"

I picked up my purse, then met his gaze again. "You haven't asked Maddie yet. She just might turn you down."

Taylor laughed as if sincerely amused. "I don't think so."

I shrugged and stood, then plucked a ten-dollar bill from my wallet and dropped it on the table. "Here's the money for my dinner, along with one free piece of advice—don't buy a plane ticket before you talk to the bride. You wouldn't be the first overconfident man to royally embarrass himself."

Laughter floated up from his throat again, and I joined in as I walked off, hoping that for once life would prove me right.

THE SHRILL RINGING OF MY BEDSIDE PHONE WOKE ME AT ONE A.M. Still enveloped in the thick haze of sleep, I reached out and fumbled with the receiver. The sound of Taylor's voice brought me awake.

"I win," he said simply. "Apply for your passport right away. The wedding is set for October 16."

Awareness hit me like a punch in the stomach. "She said yes?"

"Of course she did. Maddie's anxious to get home to her family, so I'm going down to the passport office Monday morning. I'd like you to go with me, if you can get some time off."

I sat up and dug my fingernails into my scalp. "Taylor, you can't be serious. I told you—I have a dog, a job, and classes."

"You can find someone to keep the dog, and you can take a leave of absence from your job. Maddie and I talked it all out. Her parents run a farmhouse bed and breakfast, and her mother has agreed to let you and I have two of the bedrooms. We can stay free until after the wedding—and best of all, Maddie says there's a little house on the property that you can use as a work room. The farm is only a couple of hours from the ancient home of the O'Connors, and there are museums and libraries in all the major cities."

I stared into the darkness, thinking that my future looked as vague and shadowy as my room at that moment. "You've thought it all out, haven't you?"

"Of course." His confidence poured over the telephone lines. "Now go back to sleep and dream of emerald hills. I'll call again Sunday night, and we'll set up a time to go to the passport office."

"Taylor, I can't—" The phone clicked, and I found myself talking to empty air.

I dropped the phone back into its cradle, then rested my elbows on my bent knees. The man had absolutely flipped. Taylor Morgan was the last person on earth I would have described as flighty or irresponsible, but his behavior in the past two weeks had shattered every opinion I'd ever held about him.

What happened to the quiet, aloof, objective man I knew? Taylor Morgan was positively the least sentimental man I knew. Yet in the last twenty-four hours something had reduced my rock of objectivity to a wavering mass of emotional gelatin.

Lying down, I turned onto my side and curled into a ball. Oblivious to my pain and confusion, Barkley snored from his place on the rug beside my bed.

Taylor knew how much I loved my dog, yet he wanted me to leave Barkley behind for August, September, and October—three months is *forever* in dog years. You just don't do that with a beloved pet, especially one that eats two quarts of kibble for breakfast.

And how could I skip another semester of school? Taylor kept forgetting that I had postponed my education once before, when my parents died. Already I was the oldest student in my classes, a twenty-seven-year-old junior, the grand dame of English majors. I suspected my professors were placing bets on whether or not I'd graduate by my thirtieth birthday. But if I took another semester off, I'd never finish. Taylor never had to work his way through school; he had no idea how stretching a four-year program into eight could tax a person's resources.

Taylor was living in a fog; he didn't realize *anything*. Though by now he certainly grasped the fact that I wasn't exactly turning cartwheels over his plans to marry Maddie, he still didn't understand women. No matter what Taylor said to the contrary, I knew Maddie would *not* be thrilled to have me along on the Ireland trip. She wouldn't want me living under her mother's roof, and she *definitely* wouldn't want me to be the "best man" at her wedding. Oh no. The Irish were staunchly traditional, even *I* knew that much, and she'd have to be as thick as a plank not to realize that I didn't approve of this marriage.

How could I possibly go to Ireland? I might as well buy a black dress and hat because I'd certainly be painted as a scheming witch before October 16 arrived. No woman wanted to share her fiancé with another woman, especially if the other woman claimed to be the man's best friend. No—Maddie would not want me in Ireland or in her wedding. Ditto for Maddie's mother, father, brother, cousins, and cows. I'd be the outsider, the interloper, the odd guest that must be endured.

I couldn't bear it. I couldn't bear watching Taylor make a mistake. And most of all, I couldn't bear watching him slip away from me. These last two weeks, as hard as they had been, would pale in comparison as time trudged on and dragged me with it. Taylor would spend more and more time with Maddie, falling more deeply into love or lust or whatever he called this indefinable emotional state, and I would be increasingly relegated to the sidelines. By the time October rolled around, he'd probably forget why he'd invited me.

My best friend would slip away, inch by inch, moment by moment, as he prepared to become someone else's husband.

I sat up, pounded my pillow, and yelled into the darkness. "I can't go."

Like the faithful guardian he is, Barkley lifted his head and woofed a warning bark at whatever had dared disturb his mistress. I managed a wobbly smile, cheered by the fact that at least someone loved me, but fresh tears sprang to my eyes when I remembered that Taylor wanted me to put Barkley away, too.

He wanted me to sacrifice everything . . . for *his* happiness.

I lay in the dark for a long time before I finally fell asleep.

❦

I SPENT SUNDAY IN A MUDDLE OF CONFUSION, BUT TAYLOR'S PHONE message jarred me back to reality. "I'll pick you up at the bookstore tomorrow around eleven thirty," he said, his voice chipper and enthusiastic. "We'll go together to the passport office, okay? Don't forget your birth certificate and your driver's license. You'll need them both."

"I'd like to forget," I snapped, my stare burning through the answering machine as if Taylor could see me on the other side. "I'd like to forget we ever met Maddie O'Neil."

But I couldn't forget. In obedience to that still small Voice, I had hesitated on that blasted curb and met Maddie. Instead of saving my life through a miracle, God chose to ruin it through a mishap.

Sinking into the chair by my small kitchen desk, I pulled out my address book and searched for Aunt Kizzie's phone number. Kizzie claimed to be Irish, and though I doubted she had ever traveled out of Boston, she still spoke with a bit of her mother's brogue. As a teenager, I thought her old and odd. Now I just thought of her as odd. But since my parents' death, she was the closest relative I had left.

I punched in the number and waited as the phone buzzed in my ear. On the fourth ring, a breathless woman answered. "Yes?"

I didn't recognize the voice. "Kizzie Ledbetter, please."

"This is she, child."

I'm not sure where they originated, but tears welled up within me, wetting my cheeks and wavering my voice. My fingers trembled around the phone. "Aunt Kizzie?"

"Kathleen, darlin', is that you?"

"Uh-huh."

She listened to my hiccuping sobs for a moment, then filled the phone with quiet shushings. "Whist now, don't cry. Gather your thoughts and tell me what's wrong."

And so I began. I told the story as well as I could, sticking to the facts of the matter. My best friend had met a pretty Irish girl and wanted to marry her. In Ireland. In four months. And he wanted me to leave my life, my dog, my job, and my school, and go applaud him while he ruined his life.

I sniffled and drew a deep breath. Telling the story had calmed me; the bald facts seemed even balder in the retelling. The answer was so obvious; she couldn't help but agree. "Isn't that the most unfair thing you've ever heard?" I asked, moving the phone from one ear to the other. "I ought to just wish him good riddance and watch him go."

"Ah, darlin'." Her voice broke with huskiness. "'Tis a terrible heartbreak to lose a friend, I know, for friends are the face of God in everyday life. But you're not losin' him. He sounds like a good fellow, so he'll always care for you."

"But—he wants me to leave everything. He keeps talking about Cahira O'Connor and my so-called legacy—"

"Don't be belittling what you cannot understand, child. I've read those stories of yours, and I'm apt to think the man has a point. You ought to finish, for there's Cahira herself to be heard from. And how do we know you won't find your future over on the Emerald Isle?"

I bit my lip, wishing it were polite to tell one's elderly aunt to shake her head and clear out the cobwebs. "I don't have a future, Aunt Kizzie."

"Then tell me this, child—what will happen if you *don't* go to Ireland?"

I blinked at the unexpected question. "Well—I'll just stay here and work, I suppose. In the fall I'll register for classes again, and I should finish college in eighteen months or so. Of course, Taylor and Maddie will be back in New York by then, but they'll be married, so I don't expect I'll see much of them. But I'll have new friends, I suppose—maybe I'll meet someone else at school, or at work."

"So—you'd prefer this bunch of supposings and guesses to an adventure in Ireland? Ah, Kathleen, when did the blinders fall over your eyes? You've a chance to go to *Ireland*, the land of magic and wee people and great writers. I'd give my right arm to spend a week there, yet someone is handing you the opportunity to spend *months!*"

My mind reeled with confusion. "I have responsibilities, Aunt Kizzie. There's my job, and my dog."

"I'll take the wee dog, you can drive him over one weekend before you go. And you can always find another job when you come back. You're a hard worker. Anyone would be happy to hire you."

Sighing, I rested my head on my hand. This conversation was not going at all the way I had expected. I wanted support and reinforcement, but my ally had gone over to the enemy's camp.

I faltered in the silence that engulfed us, then took a deep breath, and decided I had nothing to lose by being completely honest. "I just don't know if I can handle seeing Taylor with Maddie," I confessed. "My heart will break every time I look at them together."

Aunt Kizzie's voice softened. "Are you in love with him, then?"

"No, nothing like that. But we're friends. Very close. And that will all end soon, I know it will."

Aunt Kizzie's deep, warm, and rich laughter floated into my ear. "Kathleen, lass, 'tis lonely you are. You need to find a love of your own."

I snorted into the phone. "Love is for teenagers and romance novels, Aunt Kizzie. I'll be happy if I can just find a nice man to marry. Someone who would be like me, someone with whom I could share a nice little house and a couple of kids—"

"'Tis love you need, Kathleen, and I'll be prayin' you find it. Now—before you make up your mind, answer me this—you said you heard a wee voice right before you met this Maddie. Do you believe what you heard was the voice of God whispering in your ear?"

I considered the question. "Yes. I do."

"Then meeting Maddie was neither accident nor mistake. 'Twas meant to be, and what follows was meant to be as well. Listen for God's Voice, Maddie, and consider this—when you're an old woman like me and yearning to see Ireland and the emerald hills, will you be sorry for not going when you had the chance? Don't think for a moment that only Taylor or Maddie is inviting you, for Ireland herself is calling your name. If I were you, child, I'd go, even if I had only the wings of the morning under my feet."

Tightening my grip on the phone, I swam through a haze of desires and feelings. Aunt Kizzie certainly had the gift of gab; she could probably talk the IRS out of an audit. But all the sweet words in the world couldn't change the fact that I'd be setting myself up for a major heartbreak if I went with Taylor to Ireland.

I thanked her for her counsel, replied "you, too," to her "I love you," then hung up.

Pulling my calendar out of the desk drawer, I stared at the empty box for tomorrow's activities. I had no plans but work for any day this week, no plans for this year besides work and school. My life was an endless succession of blank boxes, and though that was true in some sense for everyone, my boxes were blanker than most because I no longer had parents or family to help me fill in the empty spaces.

Perhaps Aunt Kizzie was right, and Ireland herself was calling my name.

I picked up a pen, then filled tomorrow's box: *11:30. Meet Taylor at work—go to passport office.*

❧ 3 ❧

A s the unsmiling woman at the passport office took our applications, birth certificates, and personal checks, she told us it would take at least twenty-eight business days for our passports to be processed and issued. Taylor and I went next to his office and checked the Internet for flight schedules and fares. Allowing twenty-eight business days pushed our departure date well into August.

We decided—without asking Maddie, I might add—to leave New York on Monday, August 16. The travel agent reminded us that mid-August was the end of the tourist season. Three seats together would be difficult to arrange if we delayed the least bit, so Taylor went ahead and made reservations on British Airways. He charged three round-trip tickets and told the travel agent to leave the return dates open. I looked away, knowing that he and Maddie would return after their honeymoon, leaving me free to choose my own return date. Taylor did say I could return with them, but I assured him I wanted to come home as soon as possible after the wedding. "After all," I informed him, holding my head high, "I have someone waiting for me: Barkley."

That evening, as we met at our usual table at the delicatessen, I studied Maddie's face as Taylor explained the arrangements he'd made. "Kathy will fly over with us," he said, squeezing her hand so that her engagement diamond caught the light and sent bright sparkles flying across the ceiling. "That way we'll all be together when we meet your parents. I thought it appropriate, since she brought us together in the first place."

Maddie gave him a wintry smile. "How thoughtful of you."

"It'll be convenient, too, since your folks will only have to drive once to the airport. You said Shannon was quite a distance from the farm."

The cheek muscles in Maddie's dainty face tightened, turning her smile from a social grace to a grimace of necessity. "You're very considerate, Taylor."

Uh oh. I lowered my eyes and sipped my soda. Trouble in paradise. If she didn't let Taylor have it here, Maddie would certainly vent her feelings once they left me. Maybe it was for the best. Maybe he would begin to see that this marriage just wasn't going to work. Better to know it now than to fly all the way to Ireland and discover he was about to marry the wrong girl.

A plan began to form in my brain, a scheme born of desperation and an honest desire to prevent a friend from disaster. We'd be thrown together in Ireland from August through October, three people in a relationship designed only for two. Friction was as inevitable as death and taxes, so I might as well use these opportunities to demonstrate that opposites should not always attract.

I met Maddie's gaze head-on. "Taylor is thoughtful and considerate." My lips curved in a smile, but my tone was dead serious. "He will always be thoughtful because he values his friends."

There. Let her know what she's getting into. Taylor, poor misguided male, would think I was merely defending him, but Maddie would hear my unspoken message: *I am important to Taylor, and I plan on staying important. Deal with it.*

Maddie's answering smile looked like a wrinkle with teeth in it. "I know Taylor is thoughtful." A definite gleam of resentment entered her eyes. "That's just one of the things I love about him—and that's why *I'm* marrying him."

I resisted the urge to wince, then looked at Taylor.

Totally oblivious, he squeezed Maddie's hand again and kept his eyes on the menu. "Shall we have the crab salad tonight, love? Or would you rather try the chicken?"

֍

THE MONTH OF JULY FLEW BY IN A SWEATY HAZE. AS BARKLEY AND I sat on the floor eating ice cubes in my sweltering apartment, I thought about my life's impending disaster and consoled myself with one thought—Ireland boasts of balmy summer weather. My heart might break and my soul might suffer torments, but at least the weather would be nice.

I gave my notice at work and was thrilled beyond words when Miss Richardson, the bookstore manager, promised to rehire me for the Christmas rush. I locked my precious books and academic records in a trunk, then placed an ad to sublet my apartment from mid-August through October. Aunt Kizzie said I could stay with her and Barkley from my return until November so that whoever took my lease could enjoy two and a half full months in my tiny East Village apartment. I didn't care who rented the place, as long as they paid the rent and abstained from behaviors that might result in my eviction. And with the East Village the way it is, the only behaviors that might prove unacceptable were pyromania and street evangelism.

Maddie stopped meeting Taylor and me for dinner, then Taylor started coming up with excuses not to meet me at the delicatessen. I accepted his desertion calmly and with complete understanding. Taylor seemed unable to comprehend what most women know instinctively— we do not share well. Especially not our men.

I suspect Taylor initiated a major brouhaha with his beloved when he told Maddie he had promised to drive Barkley and me to Boston. Of course, I invited Maddie to come along, and she was probably half-inclined to accept if only to keep an eye on us. In the end, however, she declined. So one glorious August Saturday Taylor and I piled into his Mustang convertible, put the top down, and sailed out of the city with Barkley's ears extended like the wings of a 747.

Aunt Kizzie was delighted to see us. She loved on "the wee dog" (who weighed at least twice as much as she did), kissed Taylor on the cheek, and hugged me with every ounce of energy in her birdlike frame. We stayed for dinner, a delicious meal of puffy yeast rolls, fried shrimp, and clam chowder, and we were in the midst of a friendly debate about Massachusetts politics when I made the mistake of bringing up Marcy Anne Wilkerson and her latest book.

"According to Marcy Anne Wilkerson," I said, theatrically waving my fork to make a point, "people who have a passion for politics usually suffer from an unquenchable need for power or adoration. But if we find the power of God within us, we will satisfy those needs and leave our strivings for politics—and things political —behind."

Taylor popped a shrimp into his mouth while Aunt Kizzie gave me a warning look that put a damper on my high spirits. "The power of God *where?*" She spoke as if she were strangling on a repressed scream of frustration.

"Within us." I glanced at Taylor, hoping for reinforcement, but he just tossed another shrimp into his mouth and grinned at me.

"That's stuff and nonsense, girl, and you're a fool for reading it. I've heard about that Marcy Anne Wilkerson, that so-called minister, and I'm not buying a word she teaches."

Oops. Sorry that I'd tapped one of Aunt Kizzie's hot buttons, I tried to direct my attention back to my dinner, but she wasn't letting go of the subject—or of me, either.

"I can't believe you'd waste good money on one of that woman's books."

"I didn't waste money on it, Aunt Kizzie." I stopped buttering my bread long enough to give her a reassuring smile. "The store had a promo copy, so I read it. I'm *supposed* to read books on the best-seller list so I'll know what's hot. I'd be useless if I didn't know what was happening in the book world."

"It's not just the book world—it's *the* world." Kizzie nodded, the blue of her eyes like a cold wave that rushed at me. "Honey, the world is at odds with the Truth, and you've got to realize that. I don't mind you reading those kinds of books as long as you know enough to discern Truth from a lie. What worries me is that you seem to have swallowed this woman's prattle hook, line, and sinker."

I placed my knife and roll on my plate, then folded my hands, and looked directly at her. "Auntie, I was raised in a Christian home. I was practically born in Sunday school, and I know the Bible—pretty well, in fact. You don't have to worry about me following some modern guru. I just thought her insights were interesting."

"You know the Bible?" A wry but indulgent glint appeared in her eyes. "All right, lass, answer me this—is the book of Hezekiah in the Old or New Testament?"

Taylor tapped his fork against his water glass. "I know this one! It's the Old Testament!"

I glared at Taylor through half-closed lids, then reached out to pat Kizzie's hand. "It's neither, Auntie. Hezekiah isn't a book."

Taylor dropped his fork in mock disappointment, while Aunt Kizzie leaned back in her chair, crossed her arms, and gazed at me with speculation in her eyes. "Don't get overconfident with me, missy, because it's a sly world out there. Most lies come dressed in pretty packages, while the truth wears homespun. It bothers me to hear you babbling a bunch of lovely nonsense."

To my annoyance, I felt myself beginning to blush. "You don't need to worry about me. I know the Lord, and I know what I believe."

"I'm not worried about you, love, but thinking of the people you'll meet along life's way. Will you let the truth shine from your life or hide it under a bushel?"

Recoiling as though she had struck me, I stiffened in my chair. Good grief, I wasn't called to be a missionary or an evangelist. I was only a student, one who hoped to finish school and become a writer. Someday, when I had the chance, I'd write the truth in my stories. They'd touch people's lives and make a difference.

I opened my mouth to speak, but Aunt Kizzie cut me off. "Listen to me, Kathleen O'Connor," she said, a burning light in her eyes that any sapphire would have envied, "you'll not find God's truth in any book that promises your life will be easy. God will ask hard things of you. He will demand *real* sacrifice. Faith is hard, lass, and requires constant giving."

"I give," I mumbled, grateful that I was doing something right. "When I go to church, I always put an offering in the plate."

Kizzie drew her lips into a tight smile. "Giving money is easy, love. 'Tis giving your *life* that's hard. If you're walking close to the Savior, he'll demand more and more until your entire life is given over."

Well. Afraid even to glance at Taylor, I coughed softly and stared at my plate. If Taylor hadn't regretted coming along before this, he certainly regretted it now. I had forgotten to mention that my Aunt Kizzie was a little *assertive* in her views. In New York, you could be assertive about art, gay rights, abortion, politics, garbage collection, or rent control, but you couldn't be assertive about God without people looking at you strangely.

"The silliest ideas are being accepted and defended without any genuine courage or sacrifice demanded," Kizzie said, picking up her knife and fork. "People are saying God is an alien, we are gods, we are aliens—I've heard a bit of everything." She took a bite of shrimp and began chewing, but the food didn't slow her down. "'Tis a load of rubbish, and no doubt."

Somehow we made it through dinner, and night had fallen by the time Taylor and I began the long drive home. We tuned the radio to a golden oldies station and slanted from one lane to the next, dodging the casual weekend drivers. Taylor didn't mention Kizzie and her dinnertime sermon, so I didn't either.

As I tilted my head toward his shoulder and let my heavy eyelids droop, I couldn't help thinking how perfect it would be if Maddie's dazzling diamond were wrapped around *my* finger. I know I was coveting (my neighbor's ring, my neighbor's fiancé) and breaking a major Commandment, but I couldn't help myself from wishing. Taylor and I never argued, we never disagreed, and we liked the same things. What else could you want in a relationship?

Time would tell, I told myself as I nodded off to the hypnotic rhythm of a Temptations tune. In time, familiarity always bred contempt.

꘏ 4 ꘏

Despite my misgivings about traveling with Taylor and Maddie, part of me was terribly excited at the thought of visiting a foreign country. In my twenty-seven years, I had never traveled outside of the United States—unless you count the time my parents crossed the Canadian border so I could see Niagara Falls from a foreign perspective—which really didn't seem all that foreign. There were as many tourists and souvenir shops on the Canadian side as on the American.

So it was with a great sense of exhilaration that I stepped off the plane and into the open air of Ireland. For a moment I just stood on the tarmac with my eyes closed, breathing deeply as the wind blew off the sea and set my blouse to billowing above my jeans. I thought of Aunt Kizzie and all my friends in the English Department who'd give their eyeteeth to stand in my shoes. Ireland was mine to explore for two months, and I had my good friend Taylor to thank for it.

And thank you, Aunt Kizzie, for convincing me to come.

"Kathy, are you going to stand there all day?"

My eyes flew open at the sound of Taylor's voice, then I hurried to join him. Maddie's short legs were moving like pistons, and she and Taylor had almost reached the terminal already.

I ducked my head into the wind and hurried to catch them.

❦

BALLYSHANNON WAS A WORKING FARM, MADDIE INFORMED US WHEN she hung up the pay phone, and her dad wasn't able to take the time to fetch us from Shannon. So we would take a bus from Shannon to Ballinderry, where Maddie's parents would meet us.

I must confess, I was so entranced with the sights of Ireland and the Irish that I scarcely heard what Maddie was saying as we went through customs. I walked slowly through the airport, listening to snatches of delightful lilting conversation while smiling at fresh-faced youngsters, curly-haired men, and more shades of red hair than Clairol ever imagined.

On the bus, I took a seat across from Maddie and Taylor and didn't even think about intruding in their conversation. While Maddie pointed out landmarks, I sat facing the window, delighted by the unusual aspect of riding on the left side of the road. As traffic signs, other vehicles, and landscapes whizzed by, I wondered if everyone who came here felt like they had fallen asleep and awakened in some sort of parallel universe. Everything was similar—people wore pretty much the same kinds of clothes you'd see in rural America, and for the most part they spoke English—but everything seemed delightfully skewed.

Some of the traffic signs made me smile: Mind Your Windscreen, Road Calms Ahead, and Dead Slow Turn. I laughed aloud when I saw one that read Acute Bend Ahead, then leaned over the aisle to nudge Taylor. "Look at that," I pointed to the sign. "Do you think they'd point it out if it were an ugly bend?"

Taylor laughed, but Maddie only frowned in exasperation.

Shrugging, I left Taylor to explain the joke and turned back to the window. Irish roads are amazing—they twist and turn according to the impulsive lay of the land, and the native drivers plunge fearlessly over them with little regard for speed limits, turn signals, or right of way. We drove through small villages with colorful names like Bunratty, Castleconnell, and Birdhill, then we left the four-lane highway and moved out into even twistier narrow lanes that took us through the villages of Puckane and Borrisokane. We stopped in many of the settlements to accept or disgorge passengers, and finally the diesel bus churned and choked its way into Ballinderry.

I don't know how I got the impression that Maddie hailed from a bona fide city—perhaps from her sophistication and the carefree way she handled the challenges of New York. But Ballinderry was definitely a village. Two main streets intersected at the heart of the town, and two colorful pubs stood kitty-corner from one another. Stucco-faced buildings housing a food store, a bank, and a half-dozen homes crowded cheek by jowl together on what appeared to be the main street, and a black and white sign pointed the way toward St. Jerome's Church.

"We're home!" Maddie squealed in delight, threw her arms around Taylor's neck and kissed him, then practically pushed her way over him in her hurry to get off the bus. I waited to let Taylor gather their things, then I picked up my small bag and followed, amazed that Maddie O'Neil had found her way from this quaint village to the city that never sleeps.

I couldn't help but admire the picturesque town. Bright shades of green, blue, and red adorned the plastered buildings, and the streets were clean and swept, even if people tended to park their cars helter-skelter on both sides of the road, on the curbs, even on the sidewalk. Several faces peered through windows at us, and I felt the scrutiny of curious eyes as I collected my luggage from the belly of the bus and thanked the driver. He tipped his hat, murmured something too fast and fluid for my tourist's ear, then climbed back aboard the bus and left us standing in a blue-gray cloud of diesel fumes.

Maddie moved toward one of the pubs, her high heels clicking over the stone sidewalk. "I'll call Mum," she said, smiling at us over her shoulder. "She'll be but a minute—the farm's not far. I'll have you home and in my kitchen before you know it."

Taylor leaned toward her as if he would follow, then he thrust his hands in his pockets and looked out at the village. I waited until Maddie disappeared into the building, then I grinned up at him.

"Is it what you expected?"

Taylor drew a long, deep breath. "Well, she said it was small."

"It reminds me of EPCOT. I expect Mickey and Minnie Mouse to come around the corner at any minute singing 'It's a Small World after All.'"

Taylor shushed me as a pair of women approached from a small house. Overcome by an inexplicable wave of friendliness, I nodded at them and smiled. If I had been wearing a hat, I would have swept it off in greeting—not exactly a New York thing to do, but I was feeling a little giddy.

Did Ireland affect everyone this way?

The women nodded back and moved on without speaking. Taylor was still staring at the main street, probably wondering if he would be able to hang onto his sanity in this quiet place for two entire months.

"What did she tell you about the farm?" I asked, hoping to divert his dark thoughts. "Is it a big place?"

His watery eyes held absolutely no expression. "Ballyshannon is a hundred-acre dairy farm. Not big by Irish standards, really. Nothing but cows and hay and green hills."

I tilted my head. "Perhaps there's a library nearby. I'm sure there's one in Limerick, which isn't too far. And I read that Waterford and Cork are really big cities, and they're only a few hours' drive to the south."

Taylor sighed again, then gave me a rather sad smile. "I just hadn't realized it would be this . . . archaic. Maddie's been encouraging me to begin work on my doctoral thesis, but without a decent library at hand . . ."

He drifted off, and I gaped at him, surprised by this unexpected bit of information. Taylor had never mentioned getting his doctorate before. I had always thought he was content with his master's degree and his work at the college, but apparently Maddie had ambitions for him.

"Well, there's the Internet," I pointed out. "And I'll be going to lots of libraries to research my Cahira project. You're welcome to come along."

The line of his mouth tightened a fraction more. "I don't know if Maddie would exactly approve of that. You were right about one thing,

Kathy—she doesn't seem as enthusiastic about our friendship as she once did."

I looked away, not knowing how to respond. Part of me wanted to proclaim indignantly that Maddie was behaving like a jealous child, but another part of me knew I'd feel the same way if the situation was reversed.

"Well, let's not borrow trouble," I said as the pub door opened and Maddie made her way out into the sunshine. "Let's just take each day as it comes, okay?"

"Right."

᠙᠙᠙

FIVE MINUTES LATER, A SMALL BLUE SEDAN COASTED INTO TOWN, straddled the curb, then braked to a halt. Almost immediately three doors flew open and an enthusiastic trio fell upon Maddie en masse, welcoming her with bear hugs, tears, and squeals of congratulations.

James, Maddie's father, was the first to detach himself from his daughter's side and shake Taylor's hand. He was a short man with lively blue eyes, ruddy cheeks, and dark hair that gleamed in the sunlight. He greeted Taylor with sincere warmth, slapped him on the shoulder, and welcomed him to the family. He appeared to be in his middle-fifties, and though I looked for some sign of weakness caused by the cancer, I saw none. For a man who might soon be on his deathbed, James O'Neil looked surprisingly fit and trim.

Finally, he turned to me. "Sure, and you're the friend," he said. I put out my hand, intending to spare him the awkwardness men sometimes feel when first meeting a woman, and he shook my hand with gentle firmness. "I hear you're the one who brought these two together."

I gave him a careful smile. "Something like that."

"Well, you're a bonny thing yourself, so why didn't you nab him?"

Maddie turned on her father in a rush. "Dad, what a cheeky thing to say!"

The Irishman didn't apologize, but lifted a brow and grinned at me.

"Is he not your type, then? Or is there something wrong with the fellow?"

"James O'Neil, I'll thank you to keep a civil tongue in your head!" Maddie's mother whirled on her husband, then turned directly to me— a rather odd move, I thought, considering that so far she had ignored Taylor altogether. Her dark auburn curls were wind-blown, and her bright blue eyes stared out at me from the face of a determined middle-aged woman. "So, you're the lass who wanted to come to Ireland and work on a book. I think it's wonderful of you to come along with these two."

I murmured something like a thank you, then watched Mrs. O'Neil reach out and take Taylor's hand. "The name's Fiona, love, but you can call me Mum, just like Maddie does. 'Tis pleased and happy we are to welcome you to the family. We've been so eager to meet you."

Coloring fiercely, Taylor bent to accept the woman's embrace, and I stepped back, allowing more room for the intimate family scene. Standing across from the O'Neils, Maddie and Taylor endured a barrage of questions about the flight and the bus ride, while the third passenger in the car, a very pretty girl of seventeen or eighteen, stood aloof and silent.

I felt her eyes upon me even before I turned, and when I smiled at her she neither blushed nor looked away. As slim as a pleat and fragrant in her summer dress, the girl favored neither Mr. nor Mrs. O'Neil, but that wasn't surprising since Taylor had told me Maddie had no sisters, only a brother.

"Erin, 'tis good to see you." Maddie pulled out of the family clique and moved to embrace the willowy beauty. "Were you at the house when I called?"

"Of course." The girl gingerly accepted Maddie's hug, then stepped back, apparently as reluctant as I to intrude in the intimate family gathering. "Your dad said I could ride along."

"Want to see the new brother-in-law, aye?" Maddie grinned, and an answering smile found its way through the girl's mask of uncertainty. "Well, we'll be sure to find a place for you at the wedding. We can't have our favorite neighbor just sitting in the church when we could use you for something special."

Maddie slipped an arm around Erin's waist and drew her into the family circle. "Speaking of Erin, what's the latest word from Patrick? Is he coming home this weekend?"

Mr. O'Neil's mouth took on an unpleasant twist. "Not this weekend, love. He says he's working on a big project. But he'll come home to meet your Taylor, never you mind. We'll get him home if we have to send Erin to Limerick to fetch him back!"

A deep flush rose from the neckline of the girl's sundress, and Mrs. O'Neil turned on her husband. "Hush with that talk, James. We've had enough matchmaking for one day. Help us get these bags in the car, will you? There's no way we can take all this baggage at once, but we'll do what we can."

I had been wondering how six people plus luggage would fit into a sedan built for four, but within a minute Mrs. O'Neil turned me to me and announced her plan. "We'll take Maddie and Taylor first, then come back for you and Erin and the bags." An expression of pained tolerance crossed her face. "I hate to leave you here on the stoop, but there's Erin to keep you company. We'll just be a bit."

"I don't mind," I lied.

So while Maddie and Taylor slipped into the back seat of the car like a pair of newlyweds, Mr. O'Neil and I piled luggage into the trunk. Then I stood on the curb next to the silent Erin as the burdened car roared to life and rattled away.

I sank to the edge of the curb and rested my crossed arms on my knees.

"So," Erin said, gracefully lowering herself to the curb beside me, "have you a boyfriend in America? I hear American men are real dotes."

"I have no boyfriend." I propped my chin in my hand and gave her a benign smile. "And what's a dote?"

Erin's eyes widened in surprise. "Why, it's someone to dote upon, a real love."

"Oh." I looked down the road, where the sedan had just disappeared behind a tall hedge. "Well, some American men are dotes, I suppose. But the good ones are getting harder and harder to find."

BY THE TIME I REACHED THE FARM AND MY ASSIGNED BEDROOM, I felt completely drained. Knowing that Taylor and Maddie would want to spend some time alone with her parents, I locked the door, lowered the window blind, and stretched out beneath a spotless Irish counterpane to lose myself in sleep.

Sometime in the middle of the night I awoke, sat up, then convinced myself to go back to bed. All the travel guides had told me that the fastest way to combat jet lag was to acclimate as soon as possible to the new time zone, so I lay down and prayed I'd wake up at seven to a big breakfast featuring pots of coffee and caffeine-laced edibles.

"And though I'm not sure what I'm doing here, Lord," I whispered to the darkness, "I'd appreciate it if you'd guide my steps. Ireland may be an island of rock, but now I feel like I'm walking on quicksand. So guide my path and guard my tongue—and help me see why it was so terribly important that I come on this trip."

I heard no answer from the blackness and no inner Voice, only the moan of the wind over the night-blackened emerald hills.

W hen I opened my eyes again, bright summer light had highlighted the edges of my window blind. I looked at my watch—8:00 A.M. Time to get up and begin a new day.

I pushed myself upright and looked around the room that would be my home for the next few weeks. Last night I had been so tired I barely took notice of my surroundings, but sixteen hours of sleep had reenergized my body and awakened my curiosity. The room I slept in was small, neat, and clean, with a pair of faded floral prints on the wall over the bed and bureau. My suitcases occupied most of the available space in the center of the floor.

I climbed out of bed and walked around the suitcases to a tall wardrobe standing near the window. I opened the mirrored doors and found only a half dozen hangers on the rod inside.

If I hadn't already known, I might have guessed this was one of the rooms the O'Neils offered to their bed-and-breakfast guests. There wasn't a single personal memento, knickknack, or photograph in sight.

Sighing, I raised the window blind, then gasped at the sight of a window box brimming with bright flowers—bleeding hearts, petunias, and peonies. I leaned onto the windowsill and drank in the morning air. Aunt Kizzie would have loved this.

Beneath my window, a door opened and closed. A brown and white Jack Russell terrier ran out, barking as he sprinted toward a group of buildings beyond the house. Looking down, I saw Mr. O'Neil step forward, pause for a moment to light his pipe, then tuck his hands into his pockets, puffing on his pipe as he followed the dog.

A feeling of guilt swept over me as I leaned back into my room. If Mr. O'Neil was up and about already, chances were good and Maddie and Taylor were up, too. They'd think I was a layabout if I stayed in my room much longer.

I dug for the tiny luggage key that would unlock my suitcases, flung them open, and took a moment to hang a few wrinkled blouses in the wardrobe. I arranged them, from right to left, in the order I thought I'd wear them. One thing I learned from my mother is that a woman who wears a well-rotated wardrobe always seems to have more clothes than she actually does. And since I had limited myself to two suitcases for this two-month trip, I intended to rotate my few sweaters, blouses, and jeans extra-carefully.

I pulled clean underwear and a pair of jeans from the bottom of one bag, then plucked a summer sweater from my second suitcase. Cracking my bedroom door open, I glanced down the hall. The bathroom that served both bedrooms on this landing stood just to my right, and from the open door to the room next to mine, I guessed that I'd have the bathroom and shower to myself. I darted into the bathroom and locked the door.

After showering and dressing, I combed my wet hair, applied a light dusting of makeup, then pulled on my socks and hiking boots. I stepped out into the hall again and double-checked the room next to mine—as I suspected, it was unoccupied. I passed another hallway as I made my way to the staircase, and saw doors to my left and right, one open, one closed. Occupied? As I made my way downstairs I heard the rumble of voices, but there was no one in the sitting room to the right of the staircase or the dining room to the left. Not knowing where else to go, I followed a hallway off the foyer to a swinging door marked Private.

Taking a deep breath, I pushed it open and saw Mr. and Mrs.

O'Neil sitting at the kitchen table. They looked up, startled into silence by my approach.

"Um—good morning," I said, feeling more like an interloper than ever. "Am I early or late for breakfast?"

"Our guests eat at nine," Mrs. O'Neil said, pushing back her chair. "If you'll go into the dining room, I'll make your breakfast."

"Please don't go to any special trouble for me." I stepped closer to the table and let the door swing closed behind me. "I just wanted to say that I appreciate your allowing me to stay here. I know the bed and breakfast is your business, and I'm sure you'll lose some income by having me take up one of your bedrooms. So I'd like to help if I can. I can do my own cleaning, and I'd like to help with the cooking if you want me to."

Mrs. O'Neil averted her gaze as a shadow of annoyance crossed her face. I stepped back, knowing I had somehow offended her.

"I've been handling the B&B by myself for nearly ten years, so I think I know how to manage things." Her forcefully polite words rang in my ears like thunderclaps. "And I'd rather not have a stranger meddling in me kitchen. Maddie says you've come here to work on a project—"

"The O'Connor book," Mr. O'Neil interjected. "She said you'd be spending much of your time up in County Roscommon."

Totally bewildered by this frosty reception, I tried to smile but only flinched uncomfortably. "Well—yes, I will have to go up there to have a look around. But I was really planning on staying here every night. Maddie said everything I'd want to see was within a few hours drive of Ballinderry."

Mr. O'Neil looked at his wife, then both of them looked at me.

"All the same, today, you shall have your breakfast with the guests." Mrs. O'Neil's thin, dry lips curved in a fleeting smile. "Tomorrow—well, we'll see what happens tomorrow. But the other couple ordered breakfast at nine. They've come to Ireland for the riding."

She moved toward the stove, and Mr. O'Neil picked up his newspaper, both of them dismissing me. I turned toward the foyer and the public rooms, my mind spinning in confusion. Several things had just become apparent, and most obvious was the fact that the O'Neils didn't—and wouldn't—consider me family. They saw me as an outsider, a guest, and I would likely remain so until I left. They were hoping I wouldn't get in the way, and the more time I spent working on my book, the happier they'd be.

With half an hour to kill before breakfast, I crossed the foyer to the front door, then stepped out to do a bit of exploring. The farmhouse, which I'd barely glanced at yesterday afternoon, was a long rectangular structure, with a centered front door and four windows on each side, two on each of the first and second floors. Mounds of colorful flowers spilled from boxes at every window, and a thin beard of ivy covered the upper walls as high as the roof. A graveled parking lot led from the road to a small stone porch before the front door, but a soft, green lawn spread beyond the parking lot to a charming little creek that curved through the grass. The house and grounds were beautiful, but the walled garden at the side of the house took my breath away. Peering through the garden gate, I saw an actual orchard with clusters of apples and pears hanging in abundance.

I laughed in simple appreciation of the glorious sight. In my entire lifetime I couldn't recall ever actually seeing an apple hanging from a tree, much less a pear. Yet here they were, waiting to be plucked, as natural and pretty as you please.

There was no sign on the garden gate, so I assumed guests were free to wander in it. I opened the gate and stepped inside, marveling at the profusion of tropical plants and flowers. Somehow I'd imagined that Ireland would suffer hard winters—after all, the Irish were famous for sweaters—but these plants wouldn't be able to survive freezing temperatures for prolonged periods. I made a mental note to correct another of my misguided preconceptions.

The garden ended at an ivy-covered, four-foot-tall stone fence; beyond it I could see other stone fences that probably served as cattle pens. To my left lay a patchwork of green pastures, dotted with black and white cattle; the house stood to my right. Directly in front of me were barns, cattle pens, and a large open area of trampled brown earth.

I debated climbing over the wall for a little more exploration, then decided against it. If I wandered into a place where I wasn't welcome, my already-dour hostess would grow even sourer. And since I had to remain here for two months, I knew I'd better do all I could to keep the peace.

I turned instead toward the house. The rectangular building visible from the front concealed other structures that had been added onto the back, probably as generations of the O'Neil family grew. Maddie had mentioned that the main house was over two hundred years old, so these rear buildings had to be later additions. Several chimneys poked up from the tin roof, and by process of elimination I figured out which windows belonged to the roomy kitchen where I'd met the O'Neils this morning. Other rooms stretched out behind it, and lace fluttered from several of the windows. If the front house contained the public spaces used for guests of the B&B, these back rooms had to be where the O'Neil family actually lived. Taylor, I realized, stayed in a room in the *family* section of the house.

I checked my watch, saw that it was nearly nine, and moved back toward the front door. As I crossed the graveled lot, I saw the small house Taylor had mentioned as a place where I could work in privacy. Roses rambled over its yellow stucco walls, and fuchsia and lupine grew as high as the square front window. I walked up to the rough door, knocked softly, and when no one answered, I opened the door and peered inside. A couple of chairs sat in the center of the room, while a heavy oak desk squatted against the far wall. A daybed sat in the corner of the room, piled high with pillows and a white linen counterpane. Though the building's design was primitive, I saw electrical and telephone outlets on the wall, so Taylor was right—this would be a good place to work.

I reentered the house just as an older couple came down the staircase. The man and woman looked older than the O'Neils and seemed quite distinguished. Her shoulder-length silver hair was tied neatly at the nape of her neck, and she wore jodhpurs and a soft sweater. He, too, wore clothing that reeked of casual elegance, and suddenly Mrs. O'Neil's comment about the other guests and riding made sense. This couple had come to the country to ride *horses*. And since the O'Neils did not keep horses, these people would soon be heading out for the day.

I nodded good morning to them, then followed the man and his wife into the dining room. Mrs. O'Neil had set a beautiful table for three, with an elegant silver teapot occupying the center of the table. I moved to the empty place and sat down to eat with people I didn't know.

The silver-haired woman gave me a polite fellow-guest's smile as she picked up the teapot. "Shall I pour?"

"Please."

"We are Hans and Aleen Christoffels." The woman spoke in a careful, educated accent. "We are from the Netherlands. Are you American?"

"Yes." I accepted the cup, thanked her with another smile, then reached for the sugar bowl.

"We didn't hear you come in last night." Aleen clasped her hands below her chin. "We thought we were the only guests in the house."

"I'm sure I was already dead to the world when you came in." I sprinkled a teaspoon of sugar into my tea, then began to stir. "But I'm traveling with two friends—surely you saw them?"

"The young couple?" Hans accepted a cup of tea from his wife. "I thought they were part of the family. They stayed in the kitchen until after midnight, laughing and talking."

I tasted my tea, then stared down at my plate. "They are part of the family—at least she is. The young man is her fiancé. I'm just along for the ride."

The kitchen door creaked then, and we heard the sound of quick footsteps on the solid oak floors. Fiona O'Neil entered the dining room with a tray loaded with three steaming plates of eggs, bacon, sausages, fried cherry tomatoes, and some dark bits of something I wasn't sure I wanted to taste. She set our plates before us with an ease any waitress would have envied, then lowered her tray and breathlessly asked if we needed anything else.

Hans, Aleen, and I shook our heads and murmured our thanks.

Mrs. O'Neil nodded brusquely, then turned and hurried away, her footsteps thundering down the hall.

I looked down at my breakfast and saw more food than I usually ate for lunch and dinner combined. Fiona O'Neil had provided her best for her guests—the outsiders.

꧁꧂

I HAD NOT BEEN IN IRELAND TWENTY-FOUR HOURS BEFORE REALIZING that Cahira O'Connor might prove to be my salvation. Without her, I would have nothing to do but sit around the farm and feel useless. In the space of a morning Mrs. O'Neil had made it quite clear that I wasn't family, nor would they treated me as such. Even Mr. O'Neil, who had smiled warmly at me during our introduction, had neither the time nor the strength to entertain or guide a bored American tourist. Maddie was no help, either. Eager to introduce her American fiancé, she took Taylor off in the family car to make the circuit of friends and relatives. Even Hans and Aleen, with whom I'd had a remarkably pleasant conversation at breakfast, hopped into their rental car and drove off to find a riding academy.

I found myself alone.

Solitude had its pleasures, I'll admit. If not for the strange sense of disconnectedness that left me feeling confused, I might have enjoyed wandering through the fields and tramping down the country roads. But some irritating little voice kept whispering that I didn't belong here, that I had no purpose for coming.

After breakfast, I thumped up the wooden staircase to my room, then stared at my open suitcases and the bed's wrestled sheets. One thing was clear enough. Mrs. O'Neil may have considered me a guest at breakfast, but she certainly didn't when it came to cleaning my room. My wet towel still lay on the floor, and the still-rumpled bed meant no one had even entered my room.

I sat on the edge of the bed, wondering if I should unpack or call a travel agent for the next return flight home. A strange thought struck me: I could go where I wanted, when I wanted, and if I were to fall down dead in some peat bog, no one would miss me for hours, perhaps days. This aimless pace was so unlike my minute-to-minute New York existence . . .

"The thing you need is a plan," I told myself as I bent to unpack my suitcases. "Find the nearest library. Take your notebooks and your tape recorder and ask if you can borrow the family car. Soon Taylor will be ready for a break from Maddie's relatives, so he'll be glad to go with you and help navigate these country roads. You'll feel better once you're elbow-deep in note cards and history books."

The simple act of formulating a plan did brighten my outlook. I stacked my jeans and underwear in empty bureau drawers, tidied the bed, closed my suitcases, and pulled out a canvas bag of note cards and blank spiral notebooks. As I was pulling my laptop out of its protective case, the sound of voices drifted in through the open window. I looked out to see Taylor and Maddie walking up the drive, hand in hand. Maddie's cheeks were flushed with excitement, and the wind had blown Taylor's hair into the same tangled riot every rural farmer wore. If Maddie had dressed him in a sweater and knee-high boots, he'd look like an Irishman altogether.

I left my supplies on the bed and skipped down the stairs to greet my friends. "You two were up early this morning," I called, my boots crunching the graveled drive as I walked toward them. "And I heard you were up late, too."

"I guess so." Taylor smiled at Maddie as she leaned into him. "Fiona started telling stories about Maddie and her brother—"

"Whist now, that's enough," Maddie teased, her Irish accent deeper and more melodic now that we stood on her home turf. "You behave and keep my secrets, or I'll make you eat blood pudding every morning till you grow to like it." She stood on tiptoe, kissed Taylor on the cheek, then released his hand and moved toward the house. "Let me check on lunch. I'll call you directly."

Wearing an unusual expression of contentment, Taylor thrust his hands in his pockets and watched her go.

"Nice morning?" I asked, my voice dry.

"Yeah. We drove around to several farms. I've met so many O'Neils and Kellys and Murphys that I'll never keep them straight."

"That's nice." I folded my arms and looked toward the horizon as a heavy and uncomfortable silence fell between us. Taylor should have noticed it, but he kept his eyes focused on Maddie's retreating back.

"I ate breakfast with Hans and Aleen." I glanced at him, searching for any sign of comprehension. "They were interesting people from the Netherlands. Mrs. O'Neil said they were here for the riding, and I was thinking bicycles until I saw them in jodhpurs."

Maddie went into the house, and as the door closed, Taylor finally turned to look at me. "That's nice. Say—what are you going to do this afternoon?"

Relief struggled with irritation as I stared at him. He hadn't forgotten me, and he wouldn't leave me here alone . . . as long as Maddie wasn't around to interfere.

I slipped my hands into my jeans pockets and stepped in front of him, blocking his view of the front door. "I thought I'd ask to borrow the car and see if I can find a library nearby. I looked at the map, and Terryglass is a good-sized city just north of us. If they don't have a decent library, Birr is just a few miles to the northeast." I playfully punched him in the shoulder. "So—do you want to come with me, or do you have to stay and play house?"

The warmth of his smile sent shivers down my spine. "I'd *love* to find a library. Last night I gathered that Maddie and her mother want to do all sorts of female things together—they have to shop for dresses, plan the wedding flowers, make out the guest list, and that sort of thing. If I can find some good books, I might be able to catch up on my reading and do a little work on my thesis while we're here."

I exhaled a long sigh of contentment. "Great. Shall we ask for the car at lunch?"

Taylor pulled a set of keys from his pocket and dangled them in front of me. "No need. Fiona gave me the keys to James' car. He doesn't get out much anymore, so the car is ours for as long as we're here."

We began to walk into the house together, and I brought up a subject I didn't dare mention with any of the family around. "How bad is he, Taylor? He didn't look very sick yesterday."

"Fiona says he has good days and bad days. Yesterday was a good day, but he was probably running on adrenaline because he knew Maddie was coming home. But he's already struggling to manage the farm work, and they've had to hire a couple of guys when it's time to sell cattle. But James can still handle the milking by himself, and milk is the mainstay of this farm." His voice dropped in volume. "When things get bad, though, Fiona is going to ask Maddie's brother to move back home. I gather she isn't exactly looking forward to that."

"Why not? Pretty young Erin is besotted with what's-his-name."

Taylor's brows slanted in a frown. "His name is Patrick, and from what I can tell, he's sort of the family prodigal. He and James had a falling out years ago, and Patrick's been in Limerick ever since. Maddie hasn't seen him in four years."

We had reached the door, so I turned on the threshold to ask another question. "So, what does the guy do in Limerick?"

"Computers. Intel and several other major computer corporations have opened offices in Limerick and Dublin, and Patrick does free-lance work for most of them. Maddie says he's done very well for himself, but his success only irks James."

"So—" I put my hand on Taylor's wrist as he reached for the door-knob, "it's James and Fiona now, is it?"

"Well, it can't be mom and dad," he answered, grinning back at me. "At least not until after the wedding."

I didn't answer, but stepped into the house and shivered in the cool shadows of the spacious, spotless front rooms.

⚜

I WAS PLEASANTLY SURPRISED TO DISCOVER THAT MRS. O'NEIL SET A place for me at lunch. I suppose since her B&B did not serve lunch or dinner, she either had to feed me with the family or run the risk of allowing me to starve under her roof.

Her cherry red and white kitchen was the sort of place I would have naturally felt at home if given half a chance. A small television atop the refrigerator provided a background of noise, while a hodge-podge collection of photographs decorated the front of the fridge. Red and white gingham curtains fluttered from the window, and a matching tablecloth covered a long table with a bench at each side.

Taylor slid onto a bench next to Maddie, and I sat across from them. Fiona took a seat at the end of the table, then nodded toward the bowl of chicken salad in front of Taylor. "Eat up," she said, her voice warm as she smiled at him.

I felt myself begin to relax. She didn't know me, she was probably feeling pressure to be accepted by her future son-in-law, and of course she wanted to please Maddie. She probably didn't mean to treat me with coldness, and truthfully, she hadn't done anything to hurt me. She had just kept me at arm's length, but I probably would have done the same thing.

Though I wasn't hungry after that big breakfast, I smeared some chicken salad on a slice of brown bread and took small bites so I wouldn't offend my hostess. She ate quickly, talking about the farm and Maddie's relatives, and the room seemed to warm as she shared a funny story and we all laughed. The temperature plummeted, however, when Taylor announced that we wanted to drive to Terryglass or Birr to find a library.

"A what?" Fiona's face froze, her brows arched into neat little triangles.

"A library." Taylor helped himself to the bowl of chicken salad and began to make a second sandwich. "Kathy wants to begin work on her project, and I thought I'd pick up some books on Kipling." He smiled at Maddie. "I thought I might find some interesting texts that I can't find in the States. Besides," he winked at her, "I know you and your mother have lots of girl things to do."

Maddie's fell in disappointment. "You're leaving me?"

Nonplussed, Taylor froze with his knife in mid-air. "I'm only going to the library. We'll be back before dark."

Maddie nodded, but her blue eyes filled with water as she stared down at her plate. I pressed my lips together and studied my half-eaten sandwich, afraid of what was coming next.

"There's a nice historic library in Cashel." A nervous tremor filled Mrs. O'Neil's voice as she set a heavy bowl of potato chips in front of me. "And Cashel is a famous place—you ought to see it while you're here."

Maddie looked up, her lips screwed into a petulant pout. "*I* wanted to take him to Cashel, Mum."

"Then go to Terryglass, Taylor, and stick to the bloomin' library." Fiona flung up her hands, then leaned back in her chair, her eyes hot with reproach as she glared at her daughter. Careful not to make any sudden gestures that might call attention to myself, I picked up my fork and sliced a tiny sliver of bread and chicken salad.

"You promise you'll be back before five?" Maddie whispered, glancing at Taylor through lowered lashes. "I wanted to take you to meet Erin's parents. They're the next farm over, and they're our dearest friends."

Taylor looked at me and blinked hard. "What do you think, Kathy? Can we be back by five?"

I nodded slowly, not daring to object.

Taylor gave Maddie a reassuring smile, then squeezed her hand. "I promise we'll be back before too late. We'll leave right after lunch and make great time."

Mrs. O'Neil shoved the bowl of potato chips toward me. "Have some crisps," she said, looking at me as if I were the source of every trouble in Ireland.

◈

"YOU'RE IN TROUBLE, YOU KNOW." I LEANED BACK AND LET MY ARM fall out the car window, truly relaxing for the first time in days. Taylor sat beside me, wedged behind the wheel in a backward car. He muttered to himself as he punched the sluggish accelerator and tried to adjust to driving on the left side of the road.

"I can drive on the opposite side," he said, pulling out onto the main road that would lead us out of Ballyshannon, through Ballinderry, and to Terryglass. "It's no big deal. You've just got to remember to keep your body near the line in the center of the road."

"I wasn't talking about driving." I looked out the window and smiled at the passing scenery. Aunt Kizzie was right—Ireland was one of the most beautiful places on earth, if you liked green fields and pastoral surroundings. If not for the car we were driving, I could almost believe we had been zipped backward through time, like the characters in Meghann McGreedy's books. Tall hedgerows lined the narrow roads and separated one field from another, and the few fences I could see were of gray stone, not barbed wire.

"Good grief!" Taylor jerked the car to the left as an impatient driver blew past us on the right. "How can they drive so recklessly?"

"See that?" I pointed to a sign with the number forty-five in a circle. "I heard someone in the airport say those weren't speed limits, but speed *suggestions*. The general rule seems to be drive as fast as you dare."

Taylor relaxed his shoulders and settled into the seat. "Right now I'm not feeling very daring. The last thing Maddie needs is for me to crash the car. I'd be late for that shindig at her neighbor's, and she'd never forgive me."

I stared at him. A frown had puckered the skin between his eyes into fine wrinkles. He was quite serious.

I braced myself against the car door as I turned to face him. "You really love her, don't you? This isn't just a passing infatuation."

He took his eyes from the road long enough to give me a look of surprise. "Would I ask her to marry me if I were only infatuated?"

"I don't know. I've never seen you infatuated before." I turned to watch the road as a stream of unspoken thoughts and feelings rose to the surface of my heart. Taylor could sense and address any one of them, for we were alone and we had always been totally honest with each other.

A small smile tugged at his lips. "I was infatuated with you once."

My heart nearly stopped beating. "With me?"

"Yes. Right after you read me your manuscript about Aidan O'Connor. There was something in the story, and something in the way you told it—something in *you*, Kathleen. I saw it and was drawn to it, but you kept pushing me away. It was pretty clear you thought we could be nothing more than friends."

I stared at him, baffled, as a tumble of confused thoughts and feelings assailed me. I had fancied myself in love with Taylor during that time, but then school began and our schedules filled up—

"I didn't know," I said simply, studying his face. "I never meant to push you away. I always liked you. A lot."

Taylor smiled, but I thought I saw a faint flicker of hurt in his eyes. "I know that. We've always been great friends. But when I read what you wrote about Aidan's great love, I knew you could never settle for anything less. Then you wrote about Flanna and Alden and all they endured to be together. And gradually I came to accept the fact that though we have a great friendship, we don't have anything like the relationships you wrote about in your books."

"Flanna and Aidan lived in different times, Taylor." My voice sounded strangled in my ears. "They were larger than life. I don't think anyone finds that kind of love today."

Taylor continued as if he hadn't heard me. "Whenever I tried to remind you that you are an O'Connor, you resisted so strongly that I knew you didn't want to think of yourself—or of you and me—in such a romantic, dramatic light. It finally became clear that we were never meant to be together."

My tongue seemed to stick to the roof of my mouth, but I swallowed and forced the words out. "Taylor, those were novel manuscripts. Love stories. And I made half of it up! I took plain facts and wove stories around them—"

"That's how I knew what you wanted. Whether you will admit it or not, you want passion and love, Kathleen, and you've never found that with me." A trace of laughter filled his voice. "Frankly, I'm surprised anybody could find passion with dusty old me, but Maddie's so different. She brings something out in me that I never knew existed."

I propped my arm in the open window and reached for the roof, clinging to it as a wave of bitter emotion swept my illusions and intentions away. Taylor loved Maddie O'Neil. He needed her, and nothing I could do would ever change that. I could make trouble for him, I could make Maddie jealous, I could talk about their differences until my throat rasped with laryngitis, but I'd never change the fact that he felt a passion for her that he had never felt for me.

"Kathy?" Taylor prodded my shoulder. "You okay?"

"Fine—just a little queasy. The winding road, I guess." I kept my face toward the open window, afraid to let him see the look of sick realization on my face. I pressed my free hand over my mouth as a raw and primitive grief overwhelmed me.

I'd only be making trouble for myself if I persisted in my plan to keep them apart. Maddie had given Taylor something I didn't recognize, that I had pushed out of my own life. She'd brought him passion and purpose. She had encouraged him to pursue his doctorate, to travel half a world away, to surrender his life in partnership to a virtual stranger. Passion and purpose. I didn't even know what those words meant anymore.

"Are you sure you're okay?" Concerned lined Taylor's voice now. "We could go back if you're not feeling well."

"Keep going," I whispered, closing my eyes to the dizzying blur of the roadside. "There's no turning back now."

"YOUNG WOMAN, YOU HAVE BEEN TERRIBLY MISINFORMED." The librarian pulled her spectacles to the end of her nose, then stared at me over their gold-plated frames.

"But I read it on the Internet. Cahira O'Connor was a daughter of Rory O'Connor, Ireland's last great high king."

"You wouldn't be believing everything you read on the Internet, would you now?" The woman shook her head slightly, then slipped from her stool, and gestured for me to follow. "Sure, don't I know people are always mixing up the facts?"

I stood still and heard my heart break. All my work—three entire volumes—was based on the story of an Irish princess who prayed that her descendants would fight for right before she was killed in the Norman invasion. Did I have *everything* wrong?

I hurried forward to catch the librarian. "Cahira wasn't the daughter of Rory O'Connor?"

"No, lass." The woman walked to a huge volume on a wooden lectern, then flipped several pages. "A granddaughter, perhaps, or a great-granddaughter, but definitely not his child. Rory O'Connor died in 1198 at the ripe old age of eighty-two, mind you. He abdicated his throne in 1184, then retired to the monastery at Clonmacnois until his death. His throne went to his younger brother, Cathal. There was another brother, of course, but Rory had his eyes put out in order to prevent him from claiming the throne."

I braced myself against a table as the heroic image of Rory O'Connor, champion of my fantasies, wavered and vanished. "Rory O'Connor was . . . a bully?"

The librarian cock-a-doodled a laugh. "All the ancient kings were, my dear. 'Twas a horrible age in which to wear the crown, even the crown of a province." She bent forward and studied a page in the thick book. "Here we have it. Cathal, known as the Red-hand, died in 1224, after making a solid peace with King John of England. The throne of Connacht then passed to his son Aedh, but that unfortunate lad was murdered in Dublin—some say by agents of the English Crown. In May 1227 the land of Connacht was adjudged to a Norman, Richard de Burgo, but Felim O'Connor, Aedh's brother, ruled the province while de Burgo tried to determine how to enforce his property rights." Her fingernail tapped the page. "Ah! Here 'tis—Cahira O'Connor was Felim's daughter. She died in the Norman invasion of 1235, and her son, another Aedh, later scored a great victory over a Norman-English army led by Ralph d'Ufford."

I struggled to weave the threads of history back into something that resembled my vision. "So Cahira's legend is still true? She prayed her descendants would follow her example when she died in the Norman invasion?"

"What you must understand, love," the librarian lowered her glasses again and stared at me, "is that the Norman invasion was not a single event. The Normans first came to Ireland's shores in 1169, when that villain Dermont MacMurrough went abroad seeking help to secure his lost kingdom. The Normans helped him, all right, but they stayed and kept moving through the land, taking bits and pieces of territory as they could. The O'Connors dwelled safely in the province of Connacht as long as they remained true to the king of England, but once King John died and Henry III took his place, wicked men took advantage of the boy king's youth to further their own aims. The invasion that resulted in Cahira O'Connor's death was the Norman invasion of Connacht, which took place on a summer day in 1235."

I nodded as my hope sprouted anew. "Will I be able to find much information on Cahira? I've researched three of her descendants, and I've come to Ireland to discover more about the lady herself."

"I believe we can find something." The woman moved across the polished wooden floors with an almost soundless tread, and I followed, aware that the thumping of my hiking boots sounded like the stomping of elephants. I looked around for Taylor as we traversed the library and finally spied him in a carrel with a stack of books at his right hand. He'd be happy, I knew, for several hours—or until it looked as though we'd be late getting back to Ballyshannon.

The librarian led me into a small room where a sign proclaimed Rare Books—Not for Circulation, then she proceeded to tap on a computer keyboard. I hung back, breathing in the scents of dusty paper, dried leather, and age. I could spend all the weeks of my Ireland adventure in this room and let Maddie and Taylor have the freedom they needed to plan their wedding.

"Here's something." The librarian moved to one of the shelves, then pulled out a leather book heavily embossed with gold. The red leather binding glowed beneath the fluorescent overhead lights, and when we opened the cover, the beautiful portrait inside astounded me. Without being told, I knew I was looking at Cahira, a princess of Connacht. The artist had painted a slender beauty in a flowing gown, one hand holding a prayer book, the other gripping a small bow. A quiver of arrows lay at her feet, and the auburn hue of her flowing hair was marred by a rather obvious streak of white near the left temple . . . just like mine.

"Fancy that," the librarian whispered, cutting a glance from the book to me. "You look very much like her. Even to the wisp of white hair."

"I'm an O'Connor, too." My voice sounded ghostly in the room. "I'm one of four women who inherited that same white streak. I'm hoping I'll be able to discover what it all means."

The librarian stepped back, studied my face for a moment, then nodded. "Well, naturally you do. I would too."

She placed the book in my hands, then pointed to a chair and desk in the corner. "These books aren't allowed out of this protected room, but you're welcome to stay and make notes on whatever you like. This book is the history of the O'Connors ending with Cahira, and I can search for others if you're interested. Though we have a good collection of rare books, I can borrow volumes from the libraries in Dublin, Cork, and Limerick. I may even be able to find something of interest at Clonmacnois."

I picked up the book and gently hugged it to my chest. "I'd like to read everything you can find. I'm going to be in Ireland several weeks, so I have time."

"Well, then." The librarian's tight expression relaxed into a smile. "We may become fast friends, you and I. This sort of thing has always fascinated me." She thrust out her hand. "Abigail Sullivan's my name, and I'd be pleased if you'd call on me for help. My mother's maiden name was O'Connor."

I smiled back at her, feeling that I'd found a friend—maybe even a relative. "Thank you, Miss Sullivan."

"Call me Abby."

"Thank you, Abby." She left me alone then, the door closing soundlessly behind her, sealing me in a room rich with the scents of age and mystery and sorrow. As I opened the book on the O'Connors and began to read, the sights and sounds of the library faded and I found myself traveling back through time, to the hedgerows and rutted paths of ancient Connacht, ancestral home of the O'Connors.

❧ 6 ❧

F riday, September 22, 1234
      The Kingdom of Connacht, Éireann

MURCHADH STIFFENED AS THE KING'S LITTLE IMP SLIPPED THROUGH
the doorway and ducked behind a tapestry. He folded his arms and
tucked his hands into his armpits, horror snaking down his backbone
and coiling in his belly as the king continued to speak, oblivious to the
cheeky intruder. The girl was a bloomin' eejit, likely to find herself
hauled into the circle of her father's men and severely scolded . . . if
she was discovered.

When a moment passed and the tapestry did not move or tumble
from its fastenings, Murchadh slowly exhaled and forced his attention
back to the king.

The imp, he thought, watching as Felim O'Connor paced before
his chiefs and warriors, was naught but a burden to him, despite her
smiles and bold laugh and charming ways. At eighteen, the girl ought
to have been in the care of a husband, but no suitors had come calling
at Rathcroghan in months. Her mother credited Cahira's maidenhood
at so vast an age to the unsettled state of affairs in Connacht; her

father blamed the crown that had unexpectedly come to rest upon his head.

"I'm thinking my authority intimidates them," Felim had confided one afternoon when he and Murchadh stood watching the girl practice with her bow. "She might have married any decent lad in Connacht, but none want to inherit this crown or her royal position." And so, after outgrowing—*outlasting* was probably the better word—her nurses and tutors, Felim of the O'Connors placed his daughter in her uncle Murchadh's charge and care.

Murchadh leaned upon the arm of his chair and rubbed his beard. If any intimidation were being practiced in Cahira's courtship, it doubtless came from the lady herself. Her shockingly direct eyes looked up and through a man, seeing even those things he wanted to hide. It was as if she knew the secrets men shared in the garrison late at night and had scraped against them often enough to wear the blush off her cheek.

He felt heat steal into his own face as he glanced back at the tapestry. Perhaps she *had* heard all their secret stories. The ease with which she slipped into the room bespoke a familiarity with spying.

"Murchadh, my esteemed friend and brother by marriage, what say you?"

The warrior jerked at the sound of his name, then felt heat sear his cheeks again. "My king?"

"The Normans. Since they are encamped at Athlone, and with our cousin Philip, do we stand to gain more by ignoring their requests or by answering?"

Murchadh leaned forward and tented his hands, gathering his scattered thoughts. "I cannot help but believe Richard de Burgo hopes to claim Connacht for his own," he replied, hoping he was not treading over recently discussed ground. The king and his men had been debating the Norman issue for weeks, ever since Richard de Burgo left his family stronghold in Limerick and camped at Athlone, only an hour's ride from Felim's fortress. Some of the king's men believed that Richard had entered Connacht only to curry the good favor of the current Irish king; others archly insisted that the Norman baron's visit was nothing but a thinly disguised scouting mission. The latter idea had much to recommend it, for seven years ago the English court at Dublin had awarded "the land of Connacht" to the politically powerful baron. For their part, the native Irish ignored the court's judgment, and for many years it appeared that Richard had, too.

Until now.

The king's brows pulled into an affronted frown. "I'm not forgetting de Burgo's claim. But I'm wanting to know what you think of his recent letters inviting me to meet with him."

Murchadh shrugged, then froze as the tapestry undulated against the back wall. "I think," he said, averting his eyes and stumbling over his suddenly thick tongue, "that you are wise to maintain your course, Felim. The O'Connors have ruled Connacht without help for years, and you're not needing help now. Ignore the man, and think of your own people. Let the Norman wind blow all he wants; there's no strength in him."

Felim stared into the empty space in the center of the chamber. "Aye, but Philip reports there are more than twenty knights at Athlone alone. They spend their days practicing with the sword and bow and lance, cutting up his fields as they race at each other—"

"They are fools, then, and haven't I said so?" Murchadh looked around the room for any who would dispute him, then quickly brought his hand to his temple, shielding his eyes from the living lump in the tapestry. He could have sworn that the spy had given the wall hanging an emphatic thump.

Rian, the king's distant cousin, lifted his hand. "Richard's last letter," he said, his blue eyes shooting sparks in all directions, "invited the men of Rathcroghan to participate in tomorrow's tournament. I must confess, I am certainly of a mind to accept—"

"You'll do nothing of the kind," Felim interrupted, absolute finality in his voice. "Think you that we should go down there and *assure* Richard that we are not as skilled with the sword as his men?" He swept his audience with a piercing glance. "Faith, let us not deceive ourselves! We are mighty warriors all, men of valiant hearts, and I know full well that you would defend your homes and your king with your last breath. But you are Irishmen, born free to work the land God has given you, and 'tis not your fault the land demands your sweat and blood. Let these Normans and their knights spend the livelong day playing at swords and horses. We have more important things to do."

A sudden soft sneeze broke the stillness, and Murchadh drew himself up, swallowing to bring his heart down from his throat. The king would look toward the back of the room; he would see the mountain in the tapestry and know the imp had ventured into yet another place where she did not belong. . . . But Felim kept his eyes on the floor, his brow creased in concentration. More important things pressed on his mind; the noise escaped his notice entirely.

Murchadh glanced around the circle. None of the other men had noticed either. Perhaps only his nerves were attuned to such soft sounds. Sure, and none of the others had trained themselves to think like the imp, to be ready for anything, any time, any place.

He lifted his chin on the pretext of scratching the soft hair at his neck, then let his gaze drift toward the back wall. Below the tapestry's bottom edge, in full view of any man bold enough to turn and look, the mud-spattered hem of Cahira's gown was clearly visible, along with two feet, short and slender in their soft leather pampooties. Murchadh felt his stomach tighten when he saw one foot nervously tapping the stone floor.

Always moving, she was, continually darting from the garrison to the stable to the courtyard. Murchadh turned from the sight of her impatient foot and sank slightly in his chair. Though her father had never minded that Cahira did not keep to the house or the kitchen like a proper maiden, she would be the death of Murchadh if her father found her hiding in his council hall.

Utterly miserable, Murchadh closed his eyes and prayed that for once his niece would remember to keep still.

Pressed into the narrow space between the heavy tapestry and the wall, Cahira turned and leaned against the cool stone, hoping that her slipper-shod feet weren't *too* obvious. She wasn't likely to be discovered, for most of the men sat facing her father, and he seemed to have a firm grip on their attention.

His topic certainly gripped hers. For days now the men had done nothing but murmur about Richard's company of Norman knights, and Cahira's curiosity extended far beyond the horizon. She had never seen a Norman, had never heard French, their language, had never beheld one of their bloody tournaments. Her world at Rathcroghan, which consisted of the family rath and the hedge-bordered fields beyond, had never even had a Norman in it. But now a flock of them had descended upon Athlone!

Cahira crossed her hands behind her back and leaned upon them. Someone in the room beyond asked whether her father ought to attend the tournament on the morrow merely to appear interested in maintaining the peace with Richard, but her father immediately bellowed out his refusal.

She had learned many things from her father, but Cahira always found his indirect lessons far more meaningful than his demonstrations. He had taught her how to string a bow, nock an arrow, and hit a target, skills which she found useful when she went out to rid the fields of jackrabbits. But from him she had also learned that he who roars loudest wins the argument, and he who rushes unexpectedly with a sword usually lands an effective blow.

Imitating her father, last week she had surprised Murchadh with a sudden lunge while they were playing at swords. After wiping a stream of blood from his bare arm, the old warrior congratulated on her *audacity*.

"Audacity?" The word was English, and new to her.

"Bold courage," he explained in Gaelic. "Lorcan the brehon taught me."

Cahira smiled at the memory, knowing the brehon would certainly admire her *audacity* if he knew she was hiding ten feet behind his chair. Not even he, one of those revered personages who had absorbed the annals of Irish lore and law, royal genealogies, and a forbiddingly large number of magic spells and incantations, would dare to eavesdrop on a king's council meeting. Lorcan sat in the room now at the king's invitation.

Someone in the chamber beyond interrupted with a question about cattle, and Cahira let her head fall back to the stone wall. The tapestry sighed with her movement, then settled upon her forehead and the tip of her nose. She caught her breath, repressing another sneeze as the smoky scents of last winter's fires filled her nostrils.

The dull debate about cattle and the autumn slaughter continued, so she closed her eyes and allowed her thoughts to drift into more interesting channels. What were the Normans truly like? Some of the men said they were bloodthirsty savages; others claimed they were dreamy-eyed fools, compelled to honor a code of behavior that valued poetry and dancing and sighing for love from afar. The traveling poets, the *filid*, told of Normans riding huge horses that clanked with colorful and useless metal trappings. "They pray devoutly," one poet recently told Felim's household as he entertained after dinner, "though some say they are more loyal to their masters than to God."

Cahira lifted her eyes and studied the woven lining before her eyes. How much of her acquired knowledge about the Normans was false and how much true? She would never know unless she ventured to Athlone and studied them herself.

A tickle threatened her nostrils again, and Cahira automatically lifted her finger to her nose, accidentally batting the tapestry. As the fabric shuddered, she held her breath and prayed her father would not be distracted by the movement, then exhaled in a long, silent sigh as the heavy curtain came to rest.

Her father was a brave man, but apparently he lacked curiosity and *audacity*. The Normans had camped less than an hour's ride away, and yet her father had no desire to see them. Part of her brain marveled at his strange lack of interest, while another part entirely understood his reasons. Time and history had proven one fact over again: Bad things happened to O'Connors who ventured away from home.

Cahira's grandfather, the great Cathal O'Connor, had signed a treaty with King John of England guaranteeing the rights of the O'Connors to rule Connacht for as long as their line continued, but

Cathal had scarce been put in his grave before the English court at Dublin voided those rights. Richard de Burgo, who had long coveted the fertile fields to the west of the River Shannon, then claimed that the people of Connacht were no longer loyal to the English Crown, worn by a gangly seventeen-year-old Henry III. The charge was utterly baseless, for the people of Connacht had continued to send their tributes to England, but Richard de Burgo's uncle, Hubert, just happened to be young Henry's chief counselor. . . .

And so, on paper if not in practice, the O'Connors lost the royal position they had occupied since the beginning of recorded Irish history. Shortly after this unjust judgment, Aedh, Connacht's king and Cahira's uncle, was summoned to Dublin by agents of the English Crown and murdered in a so-called "petty dispute among gentlemen."

Few accurate details about Aedh's death ever reached Rathcroghan, and Cahira's father accepted the kingship reluctantly. Felim, who had never ventured far beyond the hilly fields of Rathcroghan, found himself responsible for defending a *tuath,* or kingdom, whose borders stretched to the sea. Though Cahira had been only eleven at the time, she was wise enough to realize that a family who claimed the kingship of Connacht involved itself in a mysterious and dangerous business.

Her father's voice, hearty and robust, echoed through the great chamber and thundered above Cahira's thoughts. "What do you mean he refuses to send tribute to the English king? Has he no honor? Has he no *sense?*"

Surely the man who had brought this unfortunate news quailed before the king's wrath. A small smile crept to Cahira's lips as she imagined the scene in the room beyond—someone, probably one of her uncles or some other kinsman—now stared at her father, his face bright with embarrassment. He had undoubtedly suggested that they withhold their tribute of cattle in light of Richard de Burgo's unwelcome presence, but her father would not hear of disloyalty. Despite the present English king's deficiency, the O'Connors of Connacht had been allies of the English crown ever since that fool Dermont MacMurrough brought the Anglo-Norman invaders to Ireland's southern shores. The O'Connors had kept their land because they kept the peace, but if one upstart freeman thought he could ignore his duty to send tribute to the English King—

"Have you forgotten that even now, at this very moment, Richard de Burgo covets our kingdom?" Her father's voice echoed through the stone chamber in a low rumble that was at once powerful and gentle. "Now that de Burgo is no longer the king's representative in Dublin, he may find himself able to possess Connacht. We must remain on good terms with the English king."

"Surely Richard would not move against us." Another man spoke up, and Cahira did not recognize the voice. She inched closer to the edge of the wall hanging, determined to peep out and see who spoke.

"Like you," the man continued, "Richard de Burgo is descended from an Irish king. He would not dispossess any of us from the lands we have held for generations."

Cahira slid one eye into the open, then squinted until she placed the man who had spoken. It was Rian's father, a wealthy, pleasant fellow who enjoyed a comfortable life on his family's rath.

Her father looked blandly at his kinsman, with only a slight twitch of the eye to indicate that the man was treading on shaky ground. "His father married the daughter of an Irish king, in truth, but the blood that flows through de Burgo's veins is more Norman than Gaelic," the king answered, a hair of irritation in his voice. "And Norman blood is ambitious. It seeks what it cannot own. It demands what it cannot use. It requires what it cannot afford. And yet, through the power of Norman steel, it obtains all it desires."

Cahira ducked behind the tapestry as an aged and quavering voice called for the king's attention. The chamber beyond the tapestry swelled with respectful silence as the venerable brehon began to speak.

"Felim of the O'Connors," Lorcan said, "we have not forgotten that your brother, Connacht's past king, was treacherously murdered and his claim to kingship denied. But look to the land and see what God teaches us through nature. A turtledove, which only appears in summer, can threaten the wood pigeon with every breath, but nothing can change the fact that the wood pigeon has the forest to himself nine months of the year. De

Burgo and his kind cannot possibly occupy this vast kingdom, nor will they. So let your heart be at peace, and think only of your people."

A flicker of apprehension coursed through Cahira. Though spoken in fondness and affection, the brehon's words were the closest thing to a rebuke her father had heard since becoming king.

"Thank you, learned Lorcan." Her father's tone was velvet, yet edged with steel. "I value your advice and wisdom. But I will be on guard against the Normans, nonetheless. I also look to nature, and I see that it is not wise to let the cat play with the canary. Though the cat may seem friendly and gentle, its avaricious nature will eventually reveal itself."

His chair creaked as he lowered himself into it. "You, Donal, will go to your reluctant brother and tell him to double his tribute. What was his due—two calves? See that he brings four by the next full moon, or I will send my men to see that he recalls his duty. We have had no trouble with the Normans in these parts, and I will do nothing to rouse their ire. See to it."

"My king." Another voice joined the conversation, and Cahira bit her lip as she recognized it. Her kinsman Rian spoke now, and she would have known without looking that he sat at her father's right hand. No one had officially confirmed her suspicion, but she strongly believed Rian saw himself as the most likely candidate to inherit her father's position.

"Rian." Her father's voice brimmed with affection. "What have you to say?"

Cahira heard the sound of wooden soles scraping the floor, and knew Rian had stood.

"My king, increasing numbers of these Norman knights have been encroaching upon our lands. We have heard reports of knights riding near Clonmacnois and Athlone, even near Tulsk."

"Have they harmed any of our people? Stolen our cattle?"

"No, Felim. But they grow as thick as flies around a dead man. As I journeyed here, I myself saw a pair of them riding north along the river."

A soft gasp escaped Cahira at this news. *Normans* here, near her father's own fortress?

"If they harbor no ill intent toward us, why should they not ride through our lands?" her father asked. "We will do nothing to displease them."

"But, my king!"

"They are the enemy!"

"Let us keep the peace!"

A dozen different voices lifted in entreaty, and Cahira inched toward the edge of the tapestry, ready to take flight. Her father would dismiss this gathering before pandemonium broke loose, and she did not want to be found anywhere near this chamber when the men scattered in all directions.

"Steaphan, you have not spoken."

Cahira paused as a mantle of silence fell upon the room. She would have to leave in the next hubbub; her father would be less likely to look up in a sea of confusion.

"My people have complaints, sir." Steaphen's voice, though quiet, rang with an ominous quality that lifted the hair at Cahira's neck. "Last week a father came to me in great distress for his daughter's sake. The girl was alone in the fields when a pair of Normans came upon her— apparently they were two of Richard's knights."

The silence thickened, and Cahira shuddered faintly, knowing all too well what had happened to the farmer's daughter. Any woman who ventured outside the walls of her home without an escort risked being affronted by a passing stranger, just as a horse allowed to roam the countryside would almost certainly be claimed by another. And if these Norman knights were as depraved as the naysayers said . . .

"Did the girl belong to your house?" Her father's voice deepened in concern. "And was she harmed?"

"She is naught but a *betagh,* a food provider. And she is none the worse for the encounter, though her father will have a hard time finding the girl a proper husband."

"Well," Cahira heard her father hesitate, then push through the thickness in his voice, "ofttimes these things cannot be helped. Have the girl work close to her father from now on, and bid your women keep to their homes. This is unfortunate, but these are perilous times. Nothing further need come of this."

Confusion reigned for a moment as others lifted their voices in protest and argument. Cahira leaned forward, ready to dart for the doorway, but a tiny premonition lifted the hairs at the nape of her neck. Her father's men were all brave warriors, yet they spoke of the Normans as if they were some breed apart, some race of warriors that would prove invincible should they choose to engage in battle.

Why were they so different?

She leaned forward, tuning her ears to follow the younger men's voices. "Sure, and I've never seen such heavy horses! One beast alone wore a king's ransom in silver!"

"How they fight in such rubbish, I could never guess. If you upended one in a bog, he'd surely sink to the bottom until spring."

Cahira jumped as her father brought his hands together in a sharp clap. The roar of absolute silence followed.

"Thank you for your service, my good lads." His voice echoed with regal dignity. "I thank you for your wisdom and your opinions, but I am resolute in this. As long as we are faithful in sending tribute to the English king, Richard cannot say we are disloyal. So I will not respond to Richard's requests for a meeting, nor will any of you provoke his knights. 'Twill be impossible for Richard to find fault with us if we deny him an opportunity to meet with us. This is my decision. Now I send you forth with the blessing of God."

As the family priest began the benediction, Cahira caught her breath and slipped from her hiding place, not daring to glance over her shoulder as she fled the room. Her father would doubtless be standing with his head bowed and eyes closed, but Murchadh, that wily old buzzard missed nothing. He'd scold her like the devil himself if he knew she'd been in the hall, but she had never feared her uncle's scoldings.

Safe outside the chamber, Cahira brushed the wrinkles from her gown, then bowed her head and followed the echoing words of the priest's prayer, adding a silent and heartfelt amen to the request for blessings upon the king and kingdom of Connacht. The brehon's belief that the Normans were no threat assured her somewhat, but the knowledge that her father was not completely at ease sent chilly tendrils of apprehension spiraling through her body.

She glanced up at the soft sound of a woman's footsteps. Her maid, Sorcha, came through the outer room, doubtless on a quest for her missing mistress. Despite the fact that the girls were the same age, she would soon be scolding Cahira like a cranky old biddy unless—

"There you are!" Cahira threw her hands in the air and sighed heavily in pretended frustration. "Did you remember my cloak?"

Sorcha's round face crinkled in confusion. "Your cloak, lass?"

"I'll need it if we're going out." Cahira placed one hand on her hip, then lifted a brow. "Don't tell me you want to stay in the house and work with my mother. I thought we might go for a walk, but unless my fingers and toes deceive me, the wind has grown cold enough for a mantle."

Sorcha's round, timid eyes grew larger. "Go for a walk? Can you be forgetting what has happened to old Brian?"

Cahira blew out her cheeks in exasperation. Brian, husband to Mags, the chief cook, had been missing since yestermorning. He had gone missing before, usually because he was altogether too fond of drink for his own good, but last month he had been overtaken on the road, beaten by thieves, and robbed of a pair of rabbits. The beating had left him hunched and timid, and it did not seem likely he could survive a second mishap.

"Brian is likely lying in a field somewhere, sleeping off his ale. So hurry, then, and fetch a cloak for each of us. Run, Sorcha, before my father dismisses his men!"

Cahira smothered a smile as Sorcha whirled and ran toward the stairs. Taking advantage of the solitude, she moved to the window and considered the opinions her father's men had expressed in the hall. If the Normans were untrustworthy, and if they were truly spying out the land, shouldn't someone go out and spy upon *them*? Sending one man or two would arouse Richard's suspicion no more than the two Normans riding along the river this morning had aroused her father's.

She lowered her gaze from the cloudless sky to the courtyard. She could not see the surrounding pastures and fields, for tall earthen embankments topped by imposing timber walls surrounded the compound of Rathcroghan. Her grandfather had built this fortress to keep invaders *out*, but her father seemed intent upon using the fortification to keep himself and his family *in*. He had not yet learned the meaning of *audacity*.

"Here you are, lass." Panting with every step, Sorcha plodded toward Cahira, two mantles draped over her arms. Cahira took the uppermost and threw it over her shoulders as she moved toward the door. Her father's voice still echoed from the chamber, but soon he would finish his concluding remarks. If his men discovered Cahira anywhere in the vicinity, she'd be greeted and embraced and praised within an inch of her life.

"We have to hurry," she called to Sorcha, tugging on the heavy oak door.

"But lass," a whining note filled the maid's voice, "your mother bids me tell you that you must remain nearby. She expects you to say your farewells to your father's men as they depart."

Cahira's lively anticipation shriveled to a heavy, sodden dullness. "You spoke to my mother?"

"She saw me taking the cloaks. She wanted to know where you were going."

Cahira closed her eyes as a familiar crown of gloom settled upon her head and shoulders. *You are the daughter of the king*, she could hear her mother saying. *As such, you have responsibilities. How can you be forgetting yourself?*

She would never forget herself as long as her mother lived to remind her of her duties.

But if she stood at the outermost gate to make her formal farewells, she might be able to slip away in the confusion without drawing attention. Sorcha would remain with her, of course, and they wouldn't have to walk far. Rian had reported seeing Normans riding north upon the river, and what went north had to come south . . . eventually.

"Come then, Sorcha." She waved aside the maid's hesitation, then blinked as she stepped out into the bright autumn sunshine. "We will bid our farewells at the outer gate." Cahira deliberately lightened her voice. "And when all the riders are away, we will take a walk into the country."

"A walk?" Sorcha's countenance rippled with alarm. "Are we going far?"

"Just to the river." Cahira lengthened her stride as she moved through the courtyard and scattered the chickens. "I want to see if anything interesting has washed up on the shore."

Positioning herself beside the wooden gates of the outer rampart, Cahira pulled her cloak more tightly around her and glanced toward the doors of the hall. Not a single man had yet appeared, so someone must have broached a new topic and set their tongues to wagging again. She wrapped her fingers in the edges of her cloak and turned her back to the wind, reminding herself to be patient.

The compound that housed Felim O'Connor and his family was nothing like the grand castles the Normans had erected in the southern kingdoms. The brehons and filid spoke of castles with tall stone walls and impregnable towers marked with slits through which an archer could shoot at approaching enemies without fear. Some Norman castles, the rumors reported, featured private water closets and pipes through which water could be brought from tanks on the roof.

The O'Connor stronghold, like all those of the Irish kings, had been built according to the ancient brehon laws. Erected by the king's lowest vassals, his *ceili giallnai,* in return for his protection, patronage, and prayers, the king's home was guarded by two ringed embankments of earth topped by spiked fences. Cahira suspected that the Normans would think the wattle and daub dwelling small and common, but its great hall was roomy enough to seat the heads of Connacht, and the two upstairs chambers provided sleeping space for her parents, herself, and ten female servants. Murchadh and his men slept in a small building next to the stable. In the ancient times of war, when the battle cry summoned members of the king's *ceili giallnai* to Rathcroghan, as many as two hundred men, women, and children had found shelter in the great hall.

The brehons spoke of the bloody and troubled times when Éireann's kings had continually battled one another, but Cahira had never known anything but peace. Though rumors of unrest hung over Connacht like the low gray rain clouds that blew in from the sea nearly every afternoon, Cahira could not imagine her life changing. So what if Richard de Burgo claimed to own Connacht—what could he possibly *do* with all of it? Each measured field would still answer to the farmer who plowed it; each cow and lamb would still depend upon an Irishman to care for it.

"You're certain your mother will approve us being out here?" Sorcha fretted aloud. "It seems most brazen and unseemly for a king's daughter. I'm thinking we'd be wise to go back to the house."

"I'm not a king's daughter."

Sorcha's eyes widened for a moment, then she snorted. "Ha! How you jest, lass! Of *course* you're a king's daughter, the whole of Connacht knows it."

"I wasn't jesting. What I meant to say—" Cahira lifted her chin and met her maid's wide gaze straight on, "—is I wasn't *born* a king's daughter. I don't want to be special."

Astonishment touched the maid's round face. "Not want—but how can you say that? We all are what God makes us. There's no denying where he puts us. He put a crown on your father's head, and he put me in your charge." A glow rose in the maid's face, as though she contained a candle that had just been lit. "Besides, I'm thinking that he created us all special. None are more special than others in his eyes."

Cahira gave her maid a black look, then lifted her gaze. The door to the hall had opened, and men were filling the courtyard, some moving toward the stable, others toward the kitchen.

"Hurry, please," she whispered, rhythmically bending her knees beneath her cloak. "I don't want to stand here all day."

"You'll give them a fright if you keep jumping like a haunt," Sorcha remarked, lifting a brow. "Stand still, lass, and smile at the gentlemen. One of them is bound to have a son of marriageable age."

Cahira gritted her teeth as the real reason for her mother's request became obvious. An unmarried eighteen-year-old daughter was no shame if the girl planned to enter a convent, but Cahira had never even considered a religious vocation. She'd be as out of place in a nunnery as a milk bucket under a bull.

"Good day to you, sir." Sorcha smiled prettily as the first pair of men approached on horseback. Aware of the maid's gaze upon her, Cahira managed a faint, graceless imitation of Sorcha's expression.

"Good day to you, lovely lass." One by one, her father's chieftains and warriors filed through the gate. Cahira smiled until her jaws ached, then turned her gaze toward the rolling hills beyond the trampled Rathcroghan road. Despite autumn's cooling breath, the pastures of Rathcroghan were green and vibrant, the cleared fields sloping gently toward the river a short distance away. With any luck, she and Sorcha could find a tree or a bit of brush in which to hide while they spied out the invaders.

She drew a deep breath and forbade herself to weaken. "When the last man is gone, we'll walk to the river," she announced, lifting her chin. "Rian told my father he saw Normans riding north along the river this morning. If they intend to sleep at Athlone tonight, they'll be returning soon."

Sorcha's blue eyes filled with distress. "Why would you want to see *Normans?* I'd sooner go off to meet the devil himself."

Cahira shushed her maid with a stern glance, then dipped her head toward two mounted men departing through the gate. They returned her salute with broad smiles, then spurred their horses. Sorcha fell silent as the last of the Connacht men rode away in a proud parade. The silence held as Lorcan, the revered brehon, slowly approached with a carved staff in his aged hand and his student by his side.

Lorcan paused before Cahira. His eyes, bright beams above skin as dried and dark as tanned leather, focused upon her face. "I dreamed of you last night, my child." A silken thread of warning lined his voice.

Cahira looked up, her silence inviting him to continue, but he only watched her, his sparkling black eyes sinking into nets of wrinkles as he smiled.

She gave him an uncertain nod. "I hope it was a good dream."

He looked away then, toward the eastern horizon, and Cahira shivered as the wings of shadowy foreboding brushed her spirit. Had he mentioned this dream to her father? If the dream bode ill, he would have spoken to the king, who placed a great deal of value on the brehon's opinions. If the dream contained a warning, Cahira's father might attempt to clip her wings.

She waited, tense and fearful, as the brehon continued to stare at the horizon. Finally he spoke again. "When God made time, he made plenty of it. All will not end in your lifetime, my dear, as it will not end in mine."

And then, without a backward glance, the brehon picked up his staff and moved away, gliding in that effortless step that always made Cahira wonder if he had wheels beneath the hem of his robe. His silent student followed, leaving Cahira mystified and Sorcha troubled.

"That's not good, lass. Surely that is not a good sign! Let us go tell your father what Lorcan said. Or perhaps your mother can make sense of it—"

"Sure, and when has Lorcan ever made sense?" Cahira's gaze followed the tall brehon down the trail, marveling that a man so thin could seem so strong. "But he smiled at us, did you not see? If he had wanted to bring bad tidings, he would not have greeted us so warmly."

She waited until the brehon and his student disappeared beyond a bend in the rutted boreen, then glanced over her shoulder. Outside the stable, Rian and her father stood beside a pregnant mare, probably discussing the fate of the unborn foal. "Ask for it, you eejit," she murmured, studying the young man's face. "You are his favorite; Father would give you anything you asked for."

After tossing one glance toward the upstairs window to be certain her mother was not peering out, Cahira pulled the hood of her cloak over her head. "Come, Sorcha." She stepped onto the beaten path and gestured toward the river trail. "We will not be gone long."

Sorcha mumbled and complained and groaned, but she followed, albeit a few steps behind. *She is probably as curious as I*, Cahira thought, scanning the trees ahead for any unusual signs of movement. *But she would never admit it.*

❂

SLANTED SUNLIGHT SHIMMERED OFF THE GLOWING GREEN FOLIAGE that lined the path; the afternoon was as sweet as a September afternoon could be. Despite the cool breath of the wind, the air was warm and burnished with sunlight. After ten minutes of brisk walking, Cahira felt her step grow lighter with the elation that always overcame her the moment she passed from view of the fortress's lookouts. In her younger days, before her father was king, she had often slipped away from her nursemaids, and neither of her parents had seemed particularly distressed when one of her father's men brought her home. Since she had grown a woman's body, however, her father frowned at the thought of Cahira's gallivants, and her mother went positively pale at the idea of her daughter wandering in the countryside like a common betagh.

But how wonderful it was to wander outside! A wealth of puffy clouds had blown in to decorate the sky, and the thick ragwort on the hills colored her father's pastures with a golden glow. A herd of cattle lazily lifted their heads as she approached, then went back to grazing with a distracted, diffident air.

Sorcha finally stopped complaining. As the pastures yielded to the thick trees that shadowed the river, the maid quickened her step until she walked by Cahira's side. Together the girls moved through the trees, and Cahira shivered as the treetops stirred with the whisper of a warning breeze.

"'Twill be cold tonight," Sorcha murmured, ducking beneath a branch that arched over the path. "I can feel winter's breath in the wind."

"The king's fire will keep you warm enough." Cahira's mouth twisted in a wry smile. "Doesn't it warm every soul at Rathcroghan?" She lifted her head as she caught sight of molten silver beyond the trees. "Here is the river. I only hope we are in time."

A tremor touched Sorcha's full lips. "In time for *what?*"

Not answering, Cahira lifted her skirts and ran to the line where the trail to Rathcroghan intersected the grassy riverbank. Half-hiding behind a tree, she stared down the hoof-pounded avenue until it blended into a copse of trees near the horizon. Nothing stirred along the riverbank but the tall grasses already crisp with autumn's approach. She saw no sign of life—no horses, no peasants, and absolutely no Normans.

"Are you content?" Sorcha demanded, panting heavily as she hurried to keep up. "There is nothing here. Shall we turn back now?"

"Not yet." Leaning against a tree, Cahira positioned herself behind a screen of leaves, then motioned for Sorcha to do the same. "The afternoon is young. Let us wait and see if the Normans will pass by again."

"They might return to Athlone by another way." Sorcha thrashed her way into the brush. "You don't know they will return along the river."

"They'll need to water their horses," Cahira answered, staring off into the distance. "And this clearing is a good place. If they noted it as they passed this morning, they might return here."

Sorcha snorted in disbelief, then eased back into the forest shadows. With great particularity, she lifted her skirt a few inches, nudged a few twigs out of the way with the dainty toe of her slippers, and then sank to the ground in a billowing cloud of fabric.

Cahira turned and watched the river, determined to wait until sunset if necessary. From this vantage point she could see a good distance toward the north, for the drovers had cleared the riverbank here in order to water her father's cattle. A bend in the river itself obstructed the southern view, but the Normans, if Rian had spoken the truth, would most certainly be coming from the north.

Why were they canvassing her father's kingdom? Richard's claim to

Connacht was old and irrelevant news; he and his kind had been entrenched in Éireann for nearly seventy years. Before their arrival, the seagoing Norsemen had invaded settlements on the coast, and today no one worried one whit about them. The land was rich, fertile, and abundant—why couldn't these Normans be happy and content in their castles?

Apparently theirs was a bloody and violent heritage. Cahira had heard of Norman armies ousting the rightful Irish kings and using the native Irish to work their fields and herd their cattle. They were an arrogant and haughty lot, Rian once told her, with strange ideas and customs that separated people into groups that did not mix. "The masters," Rian had said, "live in castles built by the others, and they dress in fine clothes and ride magnificent horses while their people wear rough rags and live in mud huts. At dinner, the masters sit alone or with their wives only, at huge tables laden with more food than they could ever eat. The masters—the aristocracy, they call themselves— make odd gestures with their heads and hats; they bow and nod and wave their hands in strange signals that apparently convey a great deal of meaning. The lesser people must bow to the masters in just the proper way or pay a great price for their ignorance."

"Aristocracy." Cahira tried the word out on her tongue, then cut her gaze back to the riverbank. Were the two Normans she sought part of the aristocracy? Or were they from the group that had to bow and wave their hands before their master?

She moved around the tree trunk, relieving her left hip from the bite of the tree's rough bark. The daughter of an English king—*the* English king—must certainly be part of the aristocracy. While she, the daughter of an Irish king who openly paid tribute to the English king, must be what? In Éireann , she certainly belonged to the ruling group, for she and her family were part of the educated *aes dana* that included clergymen, poets, brehons, and kings. Uneducated craftspeople— smiths, physicians, and harpists—belonged to the *saer*. People who possessed no skills but farming were the betagh, and they belonged to the land and whoever possessed it.

But the groups were fluid, and any man could move from one group to a higher one if he studied and worked to improve himself. Moreover, there were no outward distinctions between the groups. A king of the *aes dana* might be better dressed than his betagh, but he would certainly not require his servant to bend and bow and slap his cap every time he passed by. Why should he? The Irish right of kingship could be granted to any man within a previous king's extended family, and whoever owned the title also bore the responsibility of protecting his people. He did not make the laws or serve as a judge. The brehons embodied Irish law; they dispensed justice.

To a Norman accustomed to English ideas about aristocracy, Cahira decided, she would be little better than a betagh. She felt a ripple of mirth at the thought.

Sorcha's strained voice broke into her reverie. "Please, lass, my throat is parched. Do you think we could step down to the river for a drink?"

Cahira swallowed, suddenly appreciating her own thirst. A chill had settled into their shady hiding place, and the sunshine on the tall river grasses beckoned irresistibly. She glanced up and down the river and noted that the riverbank stood as empty as before. Not a single Norman—common or aristocratic—in sight.

"Sure, and why shouldn't we go to the water?" After unpinning her cloak, she tossed it over a bent tree branch, then lumbered forward, disappointment making her feet heavy. "After that, I suppose we should turn back. Rian must have been wrong about seeing the Normans in this area, or they have already departed."

A fly swooped down from the sky to buzz around Cahira's ear. She swatted it away, then stepped out onto the grass and leaned backward, resisting the bank's steep slope. Within a moment she and Sorcha were kneeling on the soft muddy bank by the river's edge, their hands cupped in the cool water.

"Och, and that's cold!" Sorcha shivered dramatically as she slurped a long draught of the sparkling water. Then she reached for another handful and squealed when her pass caught a small minnow.

"Hush your screaming, or you'll scare the wee bugs from their hiding places." Cahira pressed her wet hand to the warm place at the nape of her neck. Her waist-long hair, remarkable for the white streak that began at her left temple and zagged like a lightning bolt through the red plait, hung in a single wrist-thick braid. Cahira often thought she would never be properly cool as long as the weight of a lifelong braid pressed upon the back of her neck.

"Are you warm, then?" Sorcha's eyes widened.

"A little."

A mischievous light filled the maid's eye. "Well, perhaps a little cooling off will do you good!"

Before Cahira realized her peril, Sorcha ran her cupped hand through the water again, sending a spray of silver drops in Cahira's direction. Stuttering in surprise, Cahira responded with a fervor Sorcha did not expect. Giggling and laughing, the girls waded into knee-deep water and splashed each other with abandon, the chilly water stinging their sun-warmed faces.

As Sorcha threw up her hands and splashed toward the shore in a noisy retreat, Cahira stooped to wipe a smear of mud from her cheek. She smiled, grateful that Sorcha was no longer miffed about leaving the fortress, but her skin chilled when Sorcha let out a fearful squeak. "Cahira! Do you hear?"

Cahira froze in the water, her ears straining for whatever sound had spooked her maid. A jangling sound came to her on the wind, accompanied by the steady, rhythmic clop of horses' hooves.

She felt a cold panic prickle down her spine. The riders were coming from the north, which meant they *could* be Irish, but that jingle was a foreign sound, signifying harness and armor no Gael would wear.

Normans! At least a pair of them, coming from the north. And close enough that they would see the girls if they tried to flee the river.

Sorcha realized the truth, too. The maid's face, sheened with water, had gone dead white.

"Go deep into the water." Cahira turned and gestured toward the bank of reeds growing near the shore. "Get into the reeds. Crouch in the water just there, among the rushes, but move carefully. Do not make a sound."

Sorcha opened her mouth as if to protest, but Cahira grasped her arms and pulled her into the water. The girl moved woodenly, as if her spirit had fled and left only a clumsy doll in its place, but Cahira had no qualms about propelling the doll into the thickest growth of the reeds. Once she was certain Sorcha had found stable footing, Cahira knelt in the water beside her, blocking the girl's escape. Lowering herself into water that seemed much colder than it had only a moment ago, she tried hard not to think about what might be lurking beneath the surface—and thanked God that St. Patrick had banished all snakes from Ireland long ago.

As long as Sorcha did not panic and scream, the thick reeds would be more than adequate camouflage. Cahira settled herself in the water, sinking until the river lapped at her chin, then felt her heart contract in a paroxysm of mingled anticipation and fear when the Normans drew up and stopped at the clearing. She had wanted to see Normans, and she could not have chosen a better hiding place—or a riskier one —than the river itself.

These men were warriors—knights, she supposed, for each wore the peculiar metal tunic she had heard her father's men describe as mail armor. Over the mail they wore brightly-colored sleeveless garments of bright blue, emblazoned with a white cross. The pewter-colored mail, however, covered their arms, legs and apparently even their bodies, for the air filled with a faintly metallic sound when they dismounted and led their horses toward the river. Sharp metal spurs protruded from the backs of their heels and tore at the long grass, while a sword hung from a belt at each man's waist and slapped against their muscled thighs. Upon their heads, Cahira noted as she lifted her gaze, each man wore a dull silver helmet. *An odd choice for headgear*, she thought, shrinking further into the reeds as the men led their horses down the sloping bank. *'Tis shaped altogether too much like a milking bucket to inspire fear in an enemy*.

At first glance the knights seemed as alike as twins, but then she studied their faces and discovered a world of difference. Though the first knight appeared compact and muscular beneath his strange costume, the face that turned toward Cahira was fleshy and pock-marked. As his horse began to drink, he removed his helmet and pushed the mail hood off his hair, then noisily splashed his face, as comfortable in the water as a pup.

His companion seemed more cautious. He led his horse into the water as well, but stopped on the bank and dipped his strange helmet into the stream. While his companion frolicked, the second knight dipped his hand into his helmet, then pressed the cool water to his cheeks, neck, and forehead. Only after several minutes did he push back his mail coif and allow Cahira to see dark and lustrous hair, with copper highlights that sparked in the sun. He was a good-sized man, tall and broad through the shoulder. The strange coat of mail became him.

They were roughly of the same age, Cahira guessed, about thirty years. They rode well, they carried themselves with confidence, and the second man's countenance was particularly well formed and pleasant. She saw no scars upon either man, no evidence of plunder hanging from their saddles, no blood dripping from their gloves or their swords.

Faith, these Normans weren't viscous marauders—they were rather handsome men!

She was about to give them her complete and utter approval until the free-splashing one began to speak in a melodic language she had never heard.

❧ 8 ❧

I 'll say this for the ignorant Gaels," Oswald said, shaking his head so that water flew, "they certainly have a lovely land. Fine-looking horses, too—and the women! That flaming-haired wench upriver was a treat for these weary eyes."

Colton lifted a brow. "The Irish say that if you meet a red-haired woman on a journey, you'd be wise to turn back."

"Turn back to her house, perhaps." Oswald's mouth twisted in something not quite a smile.

Colton sighed heavily, feeling as weary as a father who has spent too much time with an active child. "Make me a promise, *s'il vous plaît*. The next time you feel compelled to wink at a comely woman, take pains to be certain her husband isn't standing right beside her."

"You're no fun at all." Oswald thrashed his way up the bank, then swatted his horse to send the animal further into the water. "Why shouldn't we take our pleasure from these barbarians? It wasn't as if I tried to take her on the spot—"

Colton glared at his friend. "You know Lord Richard wants us to maintain the peace here. You will make them hate us."

"It matters not." Oswald lowered himself to the grassy bank, then leaned back on his elbows, and lifted his face to the warming rays of the sun. "The sun seems remarkably gentle in this land, have you noticed? When our Lord Richard rules here, I think I'll build a small castle right on this spot."

Colton drew his breath through his teeth in exasperation, then moved toward his saddle, where a generous loaf of Irish bread and a lump of cheese rested in a bag. His comrades, to a man, saw Ireland as a fertile land of happy fools. In their month at Philip's rath at Athlone, they had twittered at stories of fairies and mocked the Irish belief in leprechauns and changelings. But while they had been quick to ridicule a culture as old as their own, they had not noticed the particular gifts of the Gaelic inhabitants—their delightfully different music, their skill with metalwork, their plump and handsome livestock.

And yes, their host had assured Colton one night after dinner, though the Gaelic Irish had no knights per se, Éireann was famous for its warriors. "Look here," Philip said, pulling a book from a shelf in his hall, "a quote from the Greek geographer Strabo, who visited us in the first century."

He ran his finger over a beautifully inscribed page that glimmered with traces of gold. "Here." Philip's finger stabbed the parchment, and his voice softened to a reverent whisper as he translated the words into English: "At any time or place, you will find the Gaels ready to face danger, even if they have nothing on their side but their own strength and courage."

Philip lifted his gaze, his eyes burning like the clear, true blue that burns in the heart of a flame. Colton did not no doubt that if he had drawn his sword at that moment, Philip would have struck him down or died in the attempt.

The memory brought a wry smile to his face. Let Oswald and the others dream of the estates and castles they would build on these river-banks. Those dreams would fade to the clear light of reality the first time they faced a Gael's sharpened battle-ax.

He opened the bag on his saddle, withdrew the loaf of bread, broke it, and threw half to Oswald.

Oswald caught the bread with a saucy grin. "What about you,

Colton? You could find some pretty Gaelic wench to warm your nights and a proper English lady to attend to your house—"

"I'm not making any plans about the morrow, 'tis too uncertain." Colton eased himself down on the grass and bent his legs before him, his eyes following his horse. The animal had stepped further into the mud, seeking the clearer water that moved past the shoreline. The beast could swim, but the wooden saddle and a heavy blanket weighted him down. If the gelding got into deep water, he might lose his balance and be pulled under.

"Don't know what you want?" Oswald crinkled his nose. "The great captain Colton has not made plans? Surely you intend to ask for Richard's daughter in marriage, with some handsome Irish estate as her dowry." He lowered his voice, as if the trees themselves might be listening. "I hear Lord Richard plans to take possession of this very soil before too long. Connacht is rightfully his—the Crown says so, and Richard will have it before he dies."

Colton chewed a stubborn mouthful of the dark bread, then swallowed. "I want nothing of Richard's but his favor."

One of Oswald's brows lifted in amused contempt. "Come now! We knights have nothing except that which our lord sees fit to bestow upon us, and neither of us is growing younger. In the space of three years, mayhap four, you will want to have a little house where you can train younger knights—"

Colton had been about to take another bite, but the bread stopped just short of his mouth. "I know," he said, speaking slowly in order to make certain his meaning penetrated Oswald's thick intellect, "that our Lord Richard is ambitious. I cannot fault him for it. He is as God created him, and he is an honorable man. But ambition has no place in the heart of a knight. We live to serve God and our masters. We have no higher calling."

He lifted a brow and stared at Oswald, whose expression had gone blank with astonishment. For a moment silence reigned, then Oswald threw back his head and rocked with laughter.

Colton clenched his mouth tight and plucked a spot of mold out of his bread, then tossed the offending bit over his shoulder. "I don't know what you find so funny."

Oswald's mirth died away—a few last whoops, then he wiped tears from his cheek. "*You* are funny, my friend. You say you are not ambitious, yet you fought to become captain of Richard's knights."

"I believe in excellence. I want to be the best because I owe my master no less."

Oswald looked at Colton with amused wonder. "So be a knight, friend, for as long as you can. Mayhap your ambition will awaken when you find you have no skills and no master. The day is coming, for already your reflexes are slowing. Your aim is off, too."

"Only in your imagination."

Oswald rolled onto his side and grinned up at Colton with a speculative gaze. "Care to make a wager? I'll bet I can defeat you in any field of combat—"

"A dangerous wager. You must be more specific."

"All right, then." Oswald's smile narrowed. "At the tournament—let us wager about the outcome of . . . the archery contest." He picked up an imaginary bow, nocked an invisible arrow, then squinted and sent it winging over the river. "Let's see if your eye is as clear as it used to be."

Colton's heart thumped against his rib cage. He had a true aim, certainly, as well as a steady hand and quick eye. But he had not shot a bow in months. "The wager?"

Oswald's eyes flicked momentarily toward the horses, and Colton felt his throat tighten. His Percheron gelding was an exceptionally fine animal, deep-chested and broad, fast and yet undemanding. Oswald had often expressed his admiration for the beast.

He looked at Colton again, and leaned forward in a casual, friendly posture. "The wager is this: If I defeat you, your horse becomes mine. If you defeat me, my horse becomes yours."

"But we are on a cavalcade through Connacht. The loser will have to ride *something.*"

Oswald shrugged. "Then the winner will not take possession of the animal until we arrive back at Castleconnell."

Colton looked away, his gaze roving over the water as he considered the proposition. It would be a cruel blow to lose his mount. He'd have to find a way to win another unless Lord Richard should feel generous and agree to give his captain another beast. And it would be embarrassing to explain how he, a sworn knight of over fifteen years, had no destrier to ride into battle. But his honor had been challenged. And if he expected to continue to lead his men, he could not back down.

"I agree to your wager and its conditions." He emphasized his decision with an assertive nod. "No matter who wins the tournament at Athlone, the other shall ride until we return to Castleconnell."

"Wonderful." Oswald took a bite of his bread and smacked it in delight. "Now, friend, why don't we seal our bargain with a drink from your wineskin? And don't you have cheese as well? All this Irish beauty has awakened my appetite."

Colton stood and splashed into the shallows where his horse browsed the river grass. Colton affectionately patted the animal's neck as he reached for the wineskin hanging from his saddle.

He couldn't lose the gelding. The beast was only a tool, as necessary as a knight's sword and armor, but this was a *good* animal, an uncomplaining beast that had carried Colton unscathed through many a tournament and joust.

He slung the wineskin over his shoulder, then pulled the cheese from his bag. Setting it atop the wooden saddle for a moment, he cut two generous hunks with the tip of his dagger.

He was just about to sheathe his dagger when the gelding abruptly jerked his head toward a tall stand of brown reeds. The horse whickered softly, his ears flicking forward in interest. Something in the reeds had piqued his curiosity, possibly even incited his alarm.

Were they not alone? Memories of Philip's tales passed over him, shivering Colton's skin like the touch of fabled fairy. Irish warriors were foolhardy, Philip said, often flinging themselves into battle with no more armor than a helmet and belt, and no more deadly weapon than a short stabbing sword. And yet they won battles by virtue of unbridled courage—by surprise and stealth they overcame better-prepared enemies.

Were there Irishmen nearby? Hiding behind the reeds, perhaps, or beyond the curtain of trees that edged the riverbank?

Colton wrapped his fingers around the handle of the dagger, then reached for the horse's bridle. Clucking softly with his tongue, he maneuvered the animal so the gelding's massive bulk stood between him and the stand of fading reeds. Once he was safely sheltered, he peered over the top of the saddle and studied the water's edge.

The gelding tossed its great head in agitation, but still Colton saw nothing but tall withered reeds, flies buzzing over the fading stalks, and a duck paddling against the river's current. Farther away, dark against the blue sky, a sparrow hawk circled over the opposite shore, looking for prey. A constellation of water bugs speckled the surface of the water, dimpling its smooth surface . . . and just beyond, a pair of great green eyes stared at him from the thickest part of the reeds.

His throat went dry as his feeling of uneasiness suddenly turned into a deeper and much more immediate fear. Philip's myths about monsters and fairies who dwelled in lakes and bogs and mists took on a sinister aspect, and Colton felt his heart leap into the back of his throat. He was a Christian, a God-fearing knight sworn to obey the Lord, but perhaps the fathers of the church had not yet cast all the demons and devils out of Ireland.

Unable to tear his gaze from the riveting sight of those bewitching eyes, he instinctively crossed himself. The dark-lashed orbs blinked and widened slightly, and in that instant Colton realized that the river creature was as frightened to be discovered as Colton was to discover it.

Not a monster, then. Not a demon, fairy, or ghost, but human.

"Colton?" Oswald's voice broke the stillness. "Are you coming with that cheese?"

"In a moment."

Colton kept his gaze fixed to the eavesdropper, afraid the stranger would submerge himself and vanish if he looked away. Oswald's mount moved lazily through the shallows, drinking his own reflection from the river, sending a wave of ripples among the reeds. As the tall stalks swayed in the slight disturbance, he caught a glimpse of a fair forehead and a flash of red hair.

A woman. Colton resisted the urge to slap the side of his head and wilt from embarrassment. A girl had just scared him speechless! A bashful one, too, by the looks of her, a shy creature who had undoubtedly scurried into hiding as they approached.

Struck by the realization that his curiosity had to be making the girl uncomfortable, he abruptly lowered his gaze. Oswald would think it great sport to entice the maiden out of her hiding place, but Oswald also found it sporting to toss kittens into the air to see if they'd land on their feet. This girl had probably heard of their arrival at Athlone, and might be terrified . . . or wise.

He looked toward the reeds again, afraid she might have moved away, but the emerald eyes waited there still, as wide and round as his own had been a moment before. He nodded in an unspoken promise of discretion, then pulled the hunks of cheese from his saddle. "Eat quickly, will you, Oswald?" he called in English, hoping the girl would understand. "The hour grows late, and I want to reach Athlone in time for a proper dinner."

He glanced toward the reeds once again as he led his horse out of the water, but the girl with the green eyes had disappeared.

⚜

CAHIRA THOUGHT HER BLOOD WOULD FREEZE WHEN THE KNIGHT'S eyes met hers. Her temper, which had boiled hot at the casual, proprietary way the knights lounged upon her father's riverbank, chilled in the instant his dark eyes met hers. Her heart skipped a beat as they stared at each other, and the scalp of her head tingled at the thought that momentarily he would be hauling her out of the water.

But his face had tightened with fear, and for a moment she wondered if he had seen some truly terrifying thing behind her—a bear, perhaps? Then one moment moved seamlessly into the next, the fear faded from his face, and still they remained in their places, frozen like statues. An array of emotions flitted over his handsome face— alarm, distress, and curiosity—then he lowered his eyes to his saddle.

Cahira was tempted to catch her breath and duck under the water, but a blush burned his cheekbones.

The blush spoke volumes. He knew! He had surmised she was a woman, and he knew why she was hiding. Indeed, what man would not?

But the blush also spoke of shame, which implied decency, which meant that *this* man, surely one among hundreds, would not reveal her hiding place. The next moments confirmed her supposition, for the knight merely led his horse out of the water and told the other—in careful English—to hurry and eat. And before Cahira could have murmured an Our Father, the two Norman knights had mounted and ridden away.

She stared after them as she pulled her heavy garments out of the water and made her way to shore. She hadn't understood a word of the knights' conversation in French, but she had caught Richard's name several times. And the other man's arrogant, self-assured attitude needed no translation.

Behind her, Sorcha's teeth were chattering. "Sure, and don't I know we were about to die? Saints preserve us, but God was good! We could have been dragged up from the water and kidnapped, leaving your poor father with no choice but to go to war to redeem us!"

Cahira slipped in the mud and nearly fell, then regained her footing, and slogged up the bank. Once she reached the top, she dropped the heavy hem of her gown and followed the winding trail of the river with her eyes. She could see the two riders, each leaning back in the saddle, the foolish one making wide gestures toward the river on one hand, the trees on the other.

The fool was probably talking about what Richard would do with the land when he owned it. But as long as she lived, Richard would not possess a single corner of Connacht.

"What strange men! I was so frightened!" Sorcha was sobbing in earnest now, her fears pouring out in a flood of tears. "Sure, didn't I tell you we shouldn't be wanting to see Normans? And didn't I say we shouldn't be leaving the house without a guard? Your father will be in a desperate bad humor to hear of this. He will rant and rave and storm about—"

"Then don't tell him." The figures of the two knights blended into the woods and disappeared. All Cahira could see now was the winding length of the Shannon.

She turned to her maid and fixed her in a steely gaze. "We were splashing in the water, and we got wet. That is the truth, and it's as much as my father needs know."

"But the Normans! They are evil!"

"You don't know that. You couldn't understand them any more than I could. And while they might be arrogant and wear buckets on their heads, they committed no evil in our sight." Her thoughts turned toward the dark-eyed knight who had discovered her. *He* was not evil; she'd stake her life on it.

Sorcha stopped weeping and rubbed her arms.

"They weren't both arrogant." Cahira turned toward the woods to look for her cloak. "One was—well, he seemed a lovely man."

Sorcha squeaked in surprise. "Lovely?"

Cahira turned back to her maid. "He saw me, Sorcha. He could have found us both, but he said nothing."

Sorcha merely stared, tongue-tied, as Cahira reached out and took her arm. "We'll walk back slowly, so the sun will dry us a bit," she whispered, squeezing the girl's wrist. "And as we walk, we'll pray that God will bless the Normans' visit to Connacht with peace and safety. My father will not trouble Richard. So as long as Richard does not trouble my father, all will be well."

The girls found their cloaks and used them to dry off as best they could, then linked arms, and began to walk along the trail to Rathcroghan. Cahira lowered her lids and kept her gaze on the ground, not wanting to talk. Sorcha took the hint and followed quietly, the silence broken only by the sound of her occasional sniffle.

They had just reached the first hedgerows when a hoarse whisper broke the silence. "By all the saints, have you any idea what worry you've caused me today, imp?"

Murchadh stepped out from behind a tree, his hands on his hips and his countenance as troubled as a stormy sky. "Your mother has been frantic with worrying for half the day, and your father gone to his knees in the chapel. And I've been tearing up the fields looking for you—"

"And now you've found me." Cahira threw her arm around Sorcha's shoulder and gave Murchadh her sweetest smile. "We went for a walk to the river, that's all."

"And why would you be as wet as drowned rats?"

"We splashed about. 'Twas terrible hot in the sun." Cahira released her trembling maid and stepped closer to Murchadh. "At least that's what we'll tell Father. 'Tis a reasonable story, don't you think?"

Murchadh sighed, then rubbed the back of his neck as though it ached under the strain of guardianship. "Tell me the real story, lass, and let me decide what needs telling to the king. Were you really at the river?"

She tipped her head back and looked at him. She had to tell Murchadh the truth. It was part of their pact—he taught her, guided her, and indulged her in return for nothing but honesty. Long ago he had declared that keeping track of her was challenge enough for one man; he couldn't be expected to weigh truth from lies as well. So she was honest with him about her escapades, and Murchadh never told her father more than was absolutely necessary.

She looked him straight in the eye and gave him a clean answer: "Yes. We went to the river."

"By heaven above, why?"

"Because Rian said he saw Normans there."

Murchadh had been irritated before, now a wave of red-hot anger flooded his face. "You went to see *Normans?* What kind of eejit have we raised?"

"I'm not an eejit, and I was careful. They didn't—" She was about to say *see me*, but that wouldn't be exactly true, and she had never lied to Murchadh. The red in his face faded to a dull pink, and Cahira knew that duty wrestled with pride and curiosity behind his mask of disapproval. Finally one bushy brow lifted. "Did you, um—did you see them?"

"Yes." She grasped his arm. "They were extraordinary, Murchadh. Dressed all in metal from head to toe, with the funniest helmets I have ever seen. They wore swords and daggers at their belts, and their huge horses walked on hooves wider than your hand!"

Murchadh lifted his hand and studied it as if he'd never seen it before.

"They also spoke a language I've never heard—I suppose it was French. Though when they left, one of them did speak English to the other."

"Why?"

"I think—because he wanted me to understand him. He saw me when I was hiding in the reeds."

Murchadh drew in his breath, then gave her a swift head-to-toe glance as if mentally cataloguing her limbs.

"I'm not harmed." Cahira folded her arms. "And he did not reveal my presence to the other. He just mounted his horse and rode away."

"Faith, 'tis good he did." Murchadh reached out, smoothed the frizzed hair at her temple, then dropped his hand to his side. "Your father won't admit it, but the Normans at Athlone have frightfully unnerved him."

"I don't understand." Cahira linked her hand through Murchadh's arm as the three of them turned and began to walk up the road. "He said he wants nothing to do with Richard. And, like you always say, it takes two men to raise a quarrel."

"'Tis not a quarrel Richard has in mind, 'tis conquest. And while your father is right in avoiding conflict, Richard might get the idea that the men of Connacht have no stomach for battle. Your father worries—even I worry—that the knights encamped at Athlone will think us cowards."

Cahira shook her head. "Philip is our kinsman. He would not let those people think ill of us."

"Philip is in an awkward position, for he has a prowling wolf outside his door. He will do what he can to keep the wolf at bay, but sooner or later the hungry wolf will strike someone, perhaps even Philip himself." Murchadh fell silent as a shadow passed over them and a hawk screeched overhead. "And no matter what Philip decides," he finished, his voice low and troubled, "he does not speak for the O'Connors."

Cahira turned the situation over in her mind. "If there were only some way to prove ourselves," she murmured, her eyes lifting toward the towers of her father's fortress. "If we could show them that our warriors are as skilled as their knights."

Murchadh snorted. "We can't, lass. Our men aren't trained with their weapons. We use the battle-ax; they use lances and broadswords."

A guard in the tower stopped and waved a salute to the trio in the road. Cahira and Murchadh waved in reply, and as the man turned to survey the horizon in the opposite direction, Cahira noted the quiver on his back.

"We both use archers." The thought froze in her brain as an image came back to her. The arrogant knight with the scarred face had pretended to shoot an *arrow* over the river.

She whirled around to face her keeper. "Murchadh, we both use *archers!* And there is a tournament on the morrow. We could send a man to Athlone. He could enter the contest and prove we are as able, as courageous, as skillful as any Norman knight!"

His mouth quirked with humor. "By the saints above, how are we to do that? Your father has forbidden us to go to Athlone."

"I heard him forbid his men to participate as a group." Cahira shrugged away the shame of her eavesdropping. "One man could go, though, and not give his name unless pressed for it. And if he shoots well, the Normans will know we are neither cowards nor clumsy farmers."

Murchadh's eyes warmed slightly, and the hint of a smile acknowledged the merit of Cahira's idea. "So," she pressed on. "Who is my father's best archer? Coinneach?"

"No." Sorcha spoke up, startling both Cahira and Murchadh with her interest in the conversation. "Murchadh is far better than that bumbler."

Murchadh smiled at the compliment. "Olaghair, then."

Cahira frowned. "He's good with an ax and strong as a bull, but he's no archer."

Sorcha snapped her fingers. "Gillebard is very skilled with a bow and arrow."

"Bah." Murchadh spat the word. "We'd be lucky to get him sober before the morrow. Besides, Cahira is a better shot than that beslubbering fly-bitten minnow."

Cahira tilted her head toward her mentor. "What about you?"

The warrior considered the question, then shook his head. "I shouldn't do it. I'm your father's chief man, and everyone knows it. Philip would assume I was representing Felim of the O'Connors, and the Normans would agree. And if I failed . . ." His voice drifted off into empty air. "Faith, if they bested me, the Normans would lose all respect for us."

Sorcha waved her hand in dismissal. "We have no archer, then. 'Twas a good idea, but if no one is fit to compete—"

Cahira stopped in the trail, her mind and body coming to an abrupt halt.

"Lass?" Murchadh's eyes darkened with worry. "Is something amiss?"

Cahira lifted her gaze and gave her maid a slow smile. "I could go," she whispered, the realization blooming in her brain.

Sorcha's mouth twisted in a wry grimace. "Sure, you're a better shot than any man around. You could wear a short tunic and hose and put your braid in a cap."

"I could."

Sorcha gasped, the blood draining from her face. "I was only jesting!"

"Och, and have you both lost your minds?" Murchadh took two angry steps forward, then spun on his heel in the path. "Have you no sense at all, lass? You can't go among the Normans, not as a maid, and certainly not as a man. Your father would never allow it, and your wee mother would perish at the thought. You ought to stay home with the other women folk; you ought to be home right now. You are nothing but a troublesome imp, haven't I said so? The devil himself has put this idea into your brain."

"Would you have the Normans mock us?" The last traces of Cahira's doubt had fled, replaced by a glorious rage. "Would you have them think they can drive us from our homes and hitch us to their plows? That is what the Normans have done in the south! Even the great kings of Ireland have been set to working in the fields, and the brehons are not allowed to dispense law and justice where the Normans rule."

Murchadh's mouth dipped into an even deeper frown. "How do you know this?"

"Lorcan told me. Rather than evict the people from the lands they took, the Normans retained them to work the soil."

"But the betaghs," Sorcha protested, "have always worked the soil!"

"Before the Normans came they worked the soil for the Irish kings, who fought for them," Cahira explained, her voice hoarse with frustration. "How many of the Norman barons will fight for their betaghs? Lorcan says freemen and even those of noble blood have either had to submit to the Normans or flee from their homes. The blood that has flowed in freedom from of old has been reduced to slavery!"

Murchadh gave Cahira a look that said his brain was working to solve a completely different set of problems. "Even so," he said finally, "you cannot change anything by going to Athlone in a man's clothes. You know Richard wants an audience with your father. What if he decides to detain you for his own purposes?"

"Richard need not know we are present. Philip may be intimidated by Richard, but he is our kinsman, and he would not betray us to the Normans."

"Still, you will take a very great risk—and what will you gain for it?"

Cahira answered with quiet, desperate firmness. "I'll prove that the Irish will not give up easily. I'll be an example to the men of our *deirbfhine*, all the O'Connors, who will no doubt be watching and wondering what the Normans intend by this invasion. I'll give my father's people the will to resist; I'll show them that the blood which has flowed in freedom from of old will not be defeated!"

Flushed with determination, she lifted her chin, daring her confidantes to challenge her. Sorcha, however, lifted her hands and covered her ears. "I'll hear no more of this! You speak with your father's persuasion, so I cannot resist you. But this idea is madness! You are no less an eejit for all your convincing talk."

Murchadh looked at Cahira with an odd mingling of wariness and amusement in his eyes. "Faith, I should not allow you to do this."

Cahira drew herself up to her full height. "I will do it, Uncle, with or without you. Would you rather spent the morrow helping me or guarding my room? For I will go, if I have to sneak out a window and crawl out through the drainpipes. And then you'll have to search for me, and you'll find yourself at Athlone anyway, but in a terrible bad humor."

"You are a saucy, tickle-brained harpy," Murchadh answered, crossing both arms over his chest, "and your father will have me hide for even discussing this with you. But you raise a valid point, and your aim is as sure as any man's. We're not likely to be having this chance again, and I believe we should be happy while we're living—for we're a long time dead."

He stroked his beard. "What if I traveled with you to Athlone?" He let the question fall like a pebble into a quiet pool, then proceeded to answer it. "I can ask your father if I may escort you and Sorcha to visit your kinsman, Philip. Richard will not know us from any other Gaels in these parts. And even if he does learn of our presence, he'd be a fool to try and detain us with Philip's men ready to defend your father's honor."

"We'll travel together—just the three of us?" The idea seemed to deepen the color of Sorcha's cheeks, and Cahira knew the girl's thoughts had shifted from worry to love. Murchadh was the king's best man, and, despite his age, one of the most handsome. Sorcha had quietly adored him for years.

Murchadh frowned. "I'll have to pack your quiver and bow on my mount. 'Twould not be seemly for you to travel armed."

"But no one would question a warrior traveling with weapons." Cahira laughed in sheer joy, amazed at how easily her plan had fallen into place.

A reluctant grin tugged at the warrior's mouth. "Sure, and you'll be in a desperate bad humor if I refuse this thing."

She returned his smile in full measure. "You know the devil himself can't stop me from doing the thing I've made up me mind to do."

"Well, naturally," Murchadh answered, leaving the two girls at the gate. He turned and winked at Sorcha as he walked toward the stables, then pointed a stubby index finger at Cahira. "Take care of your part, and trust me to speak to your father tonight."

A stray sunbeam shot through the oilskin-covered window and touched Cahira's eyelid, bringing her as wide awake as if Sorcha had just screamed in her ear. She sat bolt upright in her bed and looked around the chamber, trying to see what had needled her awake.

The room was chilly in the weepy gray light, and all the other sleepers—Sorcha, the kitchen maids, and Brigit, her mother's maid, lay curled up like cats beneath their covers. The window glowed softly with the advent of morning, and through a pinhole crack a single sunbeam shone bright enough to make Cahira squint when her eyes met it.

The sound of hooves on the gravel outside snapped her back to reality. The tournament! At this moment Murchadh was probably preparing their horses, and soon they would be on their way to Athlone.

She swung her legs off her low bed, then pulled her blanket around her shoulders. Taking advantage of the silence, she padded to the trunk in the corner of the room and opened it. She cringed when the heavy wooden lid thudded against the wall, but none of the others stirred.

Cahira knelt and quickly rummaged through the stacks of clothing

—gowns, aprons, workday caps, and sleeves. Finally, at the bottom of the trunk she found some cast-off garments her father had worn before the dignity of kingship required him to dress in finer tunics. She picked up one *léine*, a traditional linen tunic, and fitted it against her shoulders. The shapeless blue garment fell to her knees, the perfect length for a young Irish archer.

She dropped the tunic to the floor, then pulled out a pair of woolen hose, garters, and a woven belt. Sitting back on her heels, she mentally ticked off the garments she would need. All she lacked was headgear, and she absolutely had to cover her head. Not many Irishmen, not even the roughest, wore their hair in a waist-length braid.

Seeking a cap large enough to cover a coiled braid, she riffled through the trunk again, then flattened herself on the floor to peek under the sleeping girls' beds. A gray mouse stared at her with bright eyes, then turned and darted through a hole in the wall. Cahira made a face and sat up. She'd have to take one of the stable boy's caps when she went to the barn. This room had nothing to offer but dainty woolen hats and wimples.

She rolled the garments into a ball, laid it on the bed, and reached for the gown she had worn the day before. The dress was still damp from the river and smelled slightly sour, but it certainly would not get any cleaner on the journey to Athlone. The laundress could have it after they had returned from the day's business.

She slipped the gown over her chemise, then took a quick glance in the looking glass. Her face seemed narrow and pale in the gray light, and again she wondered why her father often praised her beauty. His compliments probably sprang from his increasingly urgent desire to find her a husband.

She stood in the corner of the room and picked up a brush. With one hand holding the looking glass, she ran the bristles over the crown of her head, just enough to smooth the flame-colored frizz that haloed her face. Murchadh had never called her beautiful, for he always spoke the truth. And in truth, the face that stared back at her now was an imp's face. Cahira's mother had tried to impress the marks of education and gentility upon her daughter, but the mask of refinement rarely concealed the sprite who had never asked to be a king's daughter.

Sighing, she lay the mirror on the table and glanced at Sorcha's sleeping figure. While her fingers automatically subdivided the heavy mass of her hair, she reviewed the plan she and Sorcha had devised during the night. The girls would attend prayers at her mother's knee as they did every morning, then they would hie themselves out to the stable to meet Murchadh.

Before going upstairs to bed last night, she caught Murchadh's eye and saw his chin dip in a barely discernable nod—*all is well*. Cahira took a deep breath as a dozen different emotions collided in her heart. Her father had given permission for them to visit Athlone—probably hoping Cahira would pick up a suitor among the men at Philip's rath— and their daring plan would proceed.

An hour later she knelt before the wooden cross in the small room that served as the family's chapel and bowed her head as her father began the morning prayer. As his rich baritone filled the room, she clasped her hands and leaned upon the altar railing, then lifted her gaze in a disobedient glance. A slight crease marred her mother's smooth forehead, and Cahira knew she worried about old Brian, who was still missing. Cahira closed her eyes and lifted her heart in a silent prayer that Brian would be soon and safely returned.

Her father's voice, quiet and reverent, echoed in the chapel. "One thing I have asked of the Lord, this is what I seek: That I may dwell in the house of the Lord all the days of my life; to behold the beauty of the Lord and to seek him in his temple. Who is it that you seek?"

Cahira was so caught up in her thoughts that she nearly forgot to make the proper response: "We seek the Lord our God."

"Do you seek him with all your heart?"

She pitched her voice so that it blended perfectly with her mother's. "Amen. Lord, have mercy."

"Do you seek him with all your soul?"

"Amen. Lord, have mercy."

"Do you seek him with all your mind?"

"Amen. Lord have mercy."

"Do you seek him with all your strength?"

Yes, Cahira thought, even as her lips replied, "Amen. Christ, have mercy." *Give me strength today to shoot well, to show these Normans we are not ignorant savages or ignoble peasants. The fierce blood of the Gaels flows in our veins, and we are free.*

She pressed her hands more tightly together in an attempt to stop the spasmodic trembling that rose from within her. In less than an hour, she, Sorcha, and Murchadh would be on the road to Athlone, where Cahira would don the most *audacious* disguise of her life. Sure, and wasn't their plan purely brazen? In all the winding length of her life she had never met another woman who would even consider entering a men's contest, nor had she met another man who would have allowed her to do so.

A chiding voice rose in her mind, whispering that a king's daughter belonged within her father's walls, behind the guards who had sworn to protect her. But Cahira had never found the role of royal daughter a comfortable fit, and in assigning her care to Murchadh, her father had only strengthened her obstinate heart, for the gruff old warrior had never been able to refuse her anything.

"May the peace of the Lord Christ go with you, wherever he may send you." The king's voice gentled as he concluded the morning prayer, and Cahira knew he was thinking of the journey she would take today. She opened her eyes and caught her father's gaze as he concluded the morning office. "May he guide you through the wilderness, protect you through the storm. May he bring you home rejoicing at the wonders he has shown you. May he bring you home rejoicing once again into our doors."

"Amen," Cahira echoed, returning her father's smile.

⊙⧉⊙

THEY DEPARTED IMMEDIATELY AFTER BREAKFAST. CAHIRA WAS SOON grateful for Murchadh's company, for he engaged Sorcha in conversation, thus preventing the maid from trying to divert Cahira from her purposed course of action. Though it would have been proper for

Murchadh to ride next to Cahira, nothing moved on the trail ahead. So with a great show of nonchalance, Cahira invited Sorcha to ride next to Murchadh. She followed behind them like a servant, much happier without Murchadh at her elbow. She wanted time to think, to consider repercussions of her victory or loss to the Normans.

If she lost the archery competition, no one need know that Felim O'Connor's daughter had participated as a nameless Irish archer. But if she won, how delightful it would be to rip off her cap and allow her braid to tumble down her back! She would proclaim her identity, and her kinsman Philip would lift a toast in her honor. And, having been defeated by a woman, the Normans would slink back to whatever castle they had recently vacated.

Cahira sighed in satisfaction, warmed as much by the colors of late autumn as by the prospect of a bloodless victory. She dropped her horse's reins and let the animal follow the others, her own thoughts wandering to the memory of the men she had spied upon at the river. The one fellow was an overconfident fool, of certain, but the other had proven himself polite and tactfully incurious.

Or had he? In that moment when their eyes met she had been certain he saw her, but perhaps her over heightened senses had fooled her into imagining his notice. With all she had heard about demanding Norman knights, it was difficult to believe that any one of them could have seen her and left her safely alone.

The man could not be the gentleman she supposed, then. Her heart had been gripped with the thrill of the unknown, her eyes bedazzled by his striking good looks and the glint of his sword. He had been staring at his reflection, perhaps, but he could not have seen her.

Today she could not afford to be distracted by romantic notions. The Normans were a vicious lot, and she would take pleasure in humiliating them.

PHILIP'S RATH AT ATHLONE WAS NOT AS IMPRESSIVE AS Rathcroghan, but Cahira felt her pulse quicken when the walled embankments rose into view. She leaned forward and urged her horse into a slow trot, aware that Murchadh had straightened in his saddle and done the same. In the blink of an eye he transformed himself from a relaxed man out on a pleasant ride to captain of the king's guard and guardian of the king's only daughter.

Sorcha held her horse in check until Cahira rode beside her, then she cast her mistress a questioning look. "I haven't change me mind, if that's what you're thinking," Cahira said in a voice loud enough for Murchadh to hear. "Once we are inside, why don't you see if you can find us something to drink. I will find Philip and convey my father's greetings."

"I'll be staying with you," Murchadh called over his shoulder. "The place is crawling with strangers; see how many horses are in the field! You will remain with me until I have stabled our beasts."

Cahira lifted her chin, determined to show him how unconcerned she was. "I am not a child, Murchadh, that you should oversee my every move. I am perfectly capable of greeting a kinsman. Besides—I have my dagger with me."

"Aye, you do." Murchadh twisted on his horse and slowed until the two girls caught up, then he gave Cahira a one-sided smile. "And that is why I say I should remain with you. Either you wait for me, or you promise not to flash your blade at any lad who happens to waggle his brows in your direction."

"No one's going to waggle at me." Cahira's lips puckered with annoyance. "All right, then. I promise not to pull out the dagger unless I have need."

"*Real* need, mind you. Which means you can't be challenging Philip's sons to a tossing contest."

"Really, Murchadh." Cahira lifted her brows in pretend horror. "Can you be thinking I would do such a thing? 'Twould be rude." She him a slight smile of defiance. "Besides, Philip's sons couldn't beat me if they tried."

Murchadh lifted his hand in supplication and looked to the sky. "Heaven, hear her!"

"I'll help you stable the horses, Murchadh," Sorcha offered, giving Cahira a quick glance. "If you could use the help."

Cahira resisted the urge to laugh aloud. Her love-struck maid knew nothing about horses, but it was obvious she'd do anything to spend time with a certain warrior. "And would you be leaving me all alone, then?" She caught Sorcha's eye and winked. "Leave me then, Sorcha, but be sure to find me soon. I'll be needing your help."

A betraying blush brightened the girl's face, but Murchadh took no note of it. "You'll have to change into your disguise as soon as they call for the archers." He lowered his voice to a deeper tone. "If you can find a quiet corner, I'll stand guard while the maid helps you dress."

Cahira nodded and absently bent to pat her horse's neck. The animal stopped, for they had reached the fields where the horses were penned. She slipped from the animal's bare back, then smoothed the fabric of her skirt with one hand while she held the reins with the other.

"Thank you, Murchadh," she said, leading her mount to him. "And be quick with the horses, I beg you."

His eyes twinkled with mischief and a hint of concern. "Are you feeling a little nervous, then?"

"I'll be fine." She smiled at her maid. "Sorcha, if you can tear yourself away from Murchadh, I could use a drink of water."

Murchadh went pale at this unexpected comment, then a deep, bright red washed up from his throat and into his face. Cahira walked away, grinning.

PHILIP HAD ARRANGED FOR THE CONTESTS TO BE HELD IN A PASTURE south of the fortified compound, and benches lined both sides of the field to afford every spectator a decent view. After Cahira greeted her kinsman and his family, Philip's wife invited her to view the contests by her side. Cahira smiled and replied that Murchadh would fall into a fierce temper if she did not remain within his sight at all times. A tournament so populated with Normans, she pointed out, greatly troubled his mind.

The lady lifted her brows at this explanation but did not protest, so Cahira slipped away from her host and hostess and went to look for Sorcha. She found the girl at the well beside the kitchen building. Though occasionally servants would run in from the fields to fill their water buckets, now the area was deserted. Not a Norman was in sight, but Murchadh stood in the empty courtyard, his hands on his hips.

Cahira and Sorcha moved to the far side of the stone kitchen, away from any prying eyes. Philip's servants had been roasting and baking for nearly two days, and the succulent scents of roasting lamb and pork made Cahira's stomach growl. She shoved all thoughts of hunger from her mind, though, and focused on her task. Lifting her eyes to meet Sorcha's, she pressed her lips together and put out her hand.

"Saints preserve us!" Sorcha whispered, a glint of wonder in her eyes. "Are you still intending to go through with it, then?"

"I am."

"Then God be with you." Sorcha pulled the bundle of men's clothing from the sack she carried and handed it to Cahira, who spread the garments on the low wall of the cistern. While Sorcha helplessly hovered nearby, Cahira pulled her gown over her head, then unrolled the bundle of clothing she had taken from the trunk.

"Truth to tell, I prayed all night that you'd change your mind about this crazy thing," Sorcha whimpered, wringing her hands as she swayed on her feet. "We could have a lovely time with Philip and his wife, sitting on the benches and just watching the men."

"I'm not changing my mind." Cahira tossed her gown to Sorcha, then slipped the short tunic over her chemise. At least four inches of white linen hung beneath the tunic's hem, but Cahira gathered up the excess fabric and caught it in the belt at her waist.

"You *are* only going for the archery, aren't you?" Sorcha worried aloud. "I can't see you lifting a sword against those other fellows. And I'll run screaming to Philip if you're thinking of riding with a lance."

"I'm not going to lift a sword, an ax, or mount a horse." Cahira pulled one of the knitted stockings over her white legs and tied it above her knee with a garter. "I'm no fool, Sorcha."

"Y'are sometimes." The girl's eyes filled with water. "A darling eejit, to be sure, but an eejit all the same. What if they recognize you? What if they find out I knew? Your father will beat the life out of me, and he'll never trust Murchadh again."

"My father has never beaten a servant before, and I can't believe he'll be starting now." Cahira finished tying the other garter, then slipped her feet into her leather pampooties. Her legs looked strangely thin beneath the short edge of the tunic—almost insubstantial. How would they look when she walked onto the field and a hundred eyes compared her to those mail-clad *monsters?*

"Well, then." Cahira wiped her damp palms on her tunic. "That settles it, but for the hat I took from the barn. Help me wind my hair beneath this cap, Sorcha."

The maid tried her best, but after a moment it became clear that the length of Cahira's braid simply would not fit into the snug hat. "It's a boy's cap, and no doubt." Sorcha folded her arms as she stepped back to survey the impossible situation. "So it cannot be done. Let's get you properly dressed again, and we will join Philip and his wife—"

"I'm not giving up." Cahira reached back and pulled the heavy braid over her shoulder, then stared at it. She had never considered cutting her hair, not even when that strange white streak appeared above her left temple shortly after her father became king. Her mother had been horrified by its appearance, seeing it as an evil omen, but her father only laughed and said God had set Cahira aside for some special purpose. An invisible saint's kiss had painted the hair white, he suggested, or an angel had bent down and touched her with the blessing of hair as rich as rubies cooled by the breath of snow.

Blessing or not, the hair was now a liability. Without another thought, Cahira pulled her little dagger from her belt and began to hack at the braid.

Sorcha's eyes bulged. "Saints preserve us, you've gone truly mad."

"A wee bit, perhaps." Cahira kept cutting. "But hair will grow. And opportunities like this do not present themselves every day."

Sorcha closed her eyes and pressed her hand to her chest. "I'll be wanting to die when I see your mother again. She'll want to know why I let you destroy your one true beauty, and what answer can I be giving her? 'Twas bad enough when you decided to play at this charade, and unthinkable that Murchadh would come down with the same lunacy. But you could have done it quiet like, without speaking of it, but now she'll know for certain that you were up to mischief. There'll be no hiding this."

Cahira tilted her head, tugging at the braid with one hand while she sliced with the other. "I'll take the blame," she muttered between her clenched teeth. "When I beat the Normans, Father will be so proud that my foolish hair won't matter one whit."

The braid now hung by a wisp. Sorcha covered her face and moaned until Cahira's knife bit through the last strands. When the braid fell away, Cahira offered it to Sorcha.

"Save this for my mother. She's always liked it more than I have."

Peeping through the splayed fingers of one hand, Sorcha gingerly accepted the shorn braid, handling it as if it were a dead mouse. Laughing, Cahira ran her fingers through the shorn edges of her hair, marveling at the cool breath of the wind upon her neck. "I should have done this years ago," she said, picking up the stable boy's cap. It slid easily over her head.

"Now," Cahira fixed her maid in a stern gaze, "hide all these things in some safe place while I go with Murchadh to fetch my bow and quiver."

Sorcha pressed her lips together in a sign of disapproval, but she gathered Cahira's castoff clothes into her arms and turned away to do as she was told.

❦ 10 ❦

fter unseating Oswald and two other challengers in a jousting competition, Colton slurped from a dipper at a water station, then sniffed in appreciation as the aroma of roasted pork wafted over the area where the merchants had set up their booths. The carefree atmosphere pervading the tournament grounds reminded him of the fairs he had known as a child in Normandy. Merchants from all over France traveled to his province to set up booths and hawk their wares, while the common people from miles around came to visit neighbors, greet kinfolk, and be awed by the great variety of goods available from lands across the sea.

He dropped the dipper back into the bucket and wiped his sweaty brow with a kerchief. He'd been so young in those days—and so innocent. But the innocence vanished when the fever took his father, leaving his penniless mother with no choice but to offer ten-year-old Colton to the first passing knight who could find use for a squire. Fortunately—for Colton later learned that not all young boys escaped childhood as unscarred as he—the traveling English baron who accepted Colton was a truly honorable man. Lord William Archbold had vowed to spend his life honoring God, his king, and the chivalric ideals of loyalty, honor, and obedience. Before he had spent five years in England, Colton had passed the tests of knighthood, and that knowledge brought a smile to his dying patron's lips.

Lord William had been felled by an accident—or a curse, depending upon how an observer interpreted the simple wound that crusted and bled and sent red streaks shooting up the aristocrat's arm. After a fever set in, Lord William's affected limb swelled to twice its normal size. Despite the physician's attempts to purge the poisonous evil from his body, the kindly baron died, leaving Colton free to take an oath of fealty to Lord William's nearest relative, Lord Hubert de Burgo.

Attending his new master, Colton spent some months in the English courts where the boy king Henry III pretended to rule. Courtly duties bored him (and the king as well, it must be noted), and it was Colton's turn to pretend when Lord Hubert regretfully announced that he was sending all his newly acquired men to Ireland. Like the others, Colton frowned and made a great show of being reluctant to depart, but every man's heart lightened when their ship set sail. Their new master was Hubert's nephew, Lord Richard de Burgo, who was seeking to raise an army in order to claim lands he had lawfully won.

Colton enjoyed his months at Richard's castle on the River Shannon, but his mind immediately focused on the proposed cavalcade into Connacht. Expecting to see armed camps upon every hilltop, his nerves were strung as tight as a bow as they rode into the disputed territory. But in the six weeks he had traveled in Athlone and the surrounding areas, he met nothing but peaceful people, pleasant folk who were quick to smile at him once he assured them that he meant to harm.

Why did Richard need an army?

It wouldn't take much to overwhelm the Irish, Colton thought, watching the people as he walked through the merchant booths. The people of this so-called emerald isle were not adventurers by nature. They tended to remain home caring for kith and kin while the Vikings, the Normans, and the English plundered and settled their shorelines. The Norse Vikings, invaders of generations past, had entrenched themselves into the southern seaports and now seemed as Irish as the Gaels themselves, while many of the Normans in the southland evidenced the same disposition.

"Excuse me, sir—would you like some ale?" A pretty Irish maid stopped before Colton and timidly offered up a gourd. Colton gave her an indulgent smile, then slipped his hand around the gourd and drank deeply. When he finished, he noticed that the girl's flush had deepened to crimson.

So, it was like that. So many of the Irish girls had been bedazzled by the sight of his men. Colton tried not to encourage them, for he and his knights were in the country to serve Lord Richard, not Lady Love.

"Thank you, lass," he said, pressing the gourd back into her hand. "Now shouldn't you be getting back to your mother?"

The girl gave him a quick, jerky nod, then spun on her heel and moved away through the crowd. Colton locked his hand behind his back and continued his walk, his mind racing with a thousand thoughts.

Once he asked his master the reason for their advance into Connacht, and for an answer received only a peevish look. When Colton persisted, reminding his master that they had come a great distance and remained over a month in Athlone without once spying an enemy, Richard finally grunted out a reply. "The enemy are the O'Connors, and they are all around you, Sir Knight." His eyes flashed a warning. "We are here to fight not with swords, but with strength. They will see our power, and they will know we are superior. When the time is right, we will force them to realize they cannot resist us."

Colton halted as Richard approached now, with one arm draped loosely over Philip's shoulder and a cup of ale in the other. He had ingratiated himself with this kinsman of the O'Connors, promising friendship and benefits in return for Philip's influence with Felim O'Connor. Richard wanted an audience with the king of Connacht in which he could press his claim, but thus far neither Philip's entreaties nor the excitement of a tournament had worked to entice the king out of his fortress.

Colton bowed deeply to both men, then straightened himself as they and their retinue passed by. The Irish king must be as wily as a fox, he thought, moving through the crowd again. In truth, he would not like to raise his sword against any of these charming people. In a brief time, he had learned that the Gaels were easy-going to a fault, most of them, unless you toyed with their crops, their cattle, or their daughters.

A familiar voice caught his attention, and he glanced up to see Oswald trying to charm an English merchant's daughter. He leaned on a table in her booth, his eyes raking her form in a manner that seemed highly indecent. Curious to discover what Oswald found so appealing, Colton glanced at the girl. She was well-rounded and comely, but her mouth was decidedly thin and her eyes a bit narrow, nothing like the wide green eyes Colton had glimpsed among the shadows of the river reeds.

He opened his mouth to rebuke Oswald, then thought the better of it. It was a festival, after all, and as long as Oswald was talking and not touching, the girl would remain safe. There were too many strong arms and sharp eyes about for Oswald to get into true trouble.

Turning from the annoying antics of his friend, Colton directed his attention to a boisterous game wreaking havoc among the path separating the merchants' tents. Someone had offered a boar's bladder to a group of freckle-faced boys who, having inflated the organ, were now indulging themselves in a vicious game of kick-away. Colton followed the progress of the bladder, grinning as a wave of bittersweet nostalgia tugged at his heart. If he were not thirty years old, a knight, and a Norman, he might actually join in this game.

The bladder sailed in Colton's direction, and a sandy-haired youngster raced to intercept it. The boy pulled back his foot and kicked, but the wooden sole of his shoe only grazed the organ, leaving it spinning in the sand. While the boys hooted and cheered, the whirling bladder came to rest only inches from Colton's boot.

A flutter of alarm ran through the observant group. "He won't give it back!" one boy shouted, but a flood of reproachful shushing drowned the unflattering opinion.

Colton stared down at the bladder, then saw the tips of two small shoes shuffle forward. He looked up and found himself facing a wide-eyed lad of not more than seven or eight. The boy said nothing, but stared with owl eyes at Colton's mail, the armor, and the sword. He backed away, too cowed to speak.

Colton swallowed hard, feeling his own cheeks blaze with embarrassment. What rumors had these children heard that they should retreat from him in fear?

"Wait!" He held out his hand, and exhaled in relief when the little boy met his gaze.

Colton stepped forward, about to bend and toss the bladder back to the boys, but an irrational notion overtook him. Meeting the boy's eye, he flashed a winning smile, then brought his leg forward in a snap kick, launching the bladder in a high arc that would have impressed his own childhood friends.

The boy opened his mouth and gaped, following the sight of the inflated bladder as it flew over the baker's booth, the spice merchant's, and the silk importer's, then fell like a star toward the earth—and struck a young man directly in the face.

Colton cringed as his ears caught the sharp smacking sound. The boys scattered like the wind, and the offended youth stood still, his eyes lowered, one hand floating up toward his face as if he wanted to be certain the flesh remained attached to his head. A young woman standing next to the lad shrieked in horror, and a grizzled Irish warrior reached for his dagger as he fixed Colton in a blue-eyed vise.

Instinctively, Colton's hand moved toward the hilt of his sword. Though the assaulted youth did not appear to be armed, Colton had seen men come to blows over more trivial insults than this. He hesitated, then advanced with long strides, eager to make amends or defend his honor, whichever would be necessary.

"I do beg and pray you to forgive the accident," he began, ignoring both the warrior and the trembling maid. He spoke to the cap on the youth's head, all that was visible from his height. "I only meant to return the game to the boys. They seemed unwilling to play with the bladder in my vicinity."

"You goatish beef-witted barnacle!"

The warrior growled and took a step in Colton's direction, but the youth put out a pale, restraining hand. "Arrogant show off."

The whispered words barely reached Colton's ear, but he could not deny the venom in the voice. He rested his palm on the hilt of his blade, sending an unmistakable message to the bearded behemoth whose eyes glittered with challenge.

"I have asked for your forgiveness," he said, finding himself inexplicably uncomfortable facing an opponent who would not meet his eye. "If you will not give it, perhaps you would like to defend your honor on the field." He stopped and took a half-step back, bowing in a courtly gesture. "I am at your disposal, sir."

The head lifted then, and the Irish eyes beneath the brim of the cap were narrow with fury. "I will defend my honor, but not for this offense. I will readily pardon an accident, but offenses to one's home and family are not so easily forgiven."

Colton frowned, confused by the youth's words and his tone. "Offenses? Forgive my ignorance, but I do not take your meaning. I've been in this province only six weeks, hardly long enough to commit any offenses toward your people."

"You will take my meaning soon enough." With that, the youth lowered his head, spun on his heel, and stalked away through the merchants' tents, drawing his odd companions after him.

⁂

CAHIRA KEPT HER EYES DOWN AS SHE HURRIED AWAY, AFRAID THAT at any moment she might shriek or cry or scream. Him! Of all people, she had encountered *him*, and Murchadh had drawn his dagger and nearly skewered him! The knight seemed charming enough at first, rushing up to apologize for nearly knocking her senseless with that foul-smelling pig part, but he also been quick to suggest that if she didn't feel forgiving, she should have the feeling carved into her on the field of contest.

Conceited Norman knight! How she would enjoy defeating him!

And after she had done so, she would tell him that she spied upon him at the river, that she saw his eyes fill with fear when he thought he heard a noise in the reeds. He was no warrior—he was a man, and a rather silly one at that. Her father would never be caught playing kick-away with a band of boys, and Murchadh would never apologize for accidentally striking a passerby.

Sorcha called out to her, begging her to slow down, but Cahira kept up her quick pace, resentment beating a bitter cadence in her heart as she marched toward the field where the men were setting up targets for the archery competition. Half a dozen Irishmen and as many Norman knights lazed about outside the circle, each group remaining a careful distance from the other and occasionally eyeing the competition with suspicion. *If Philip arranged this tournament to help the two groups get along,* Cahira reasoned, *thus far he has made little progress.*

She walked toward the opening that led to the archery field, then halted as Murchadh grabbed her arm and spun her to face him. "Wee imp," his burning eyes holding her still, "I am beginning to think I was wrong. These are not our people you're shooting against; they are strangers."

"They are *big*," Sorcha added, her eyes squeezed closed so tight that her whole face seemed to collapse in on itself.

Murchadh relaxed his grip, but his eyes remained serious. "If it were a contest between our own people, I wouldn't be minding at all. But these are not our kind, lass, and I don't know what they will think if you defeat them. You saw the pride in the one we addressed a moment ago—such pride does not handle defeat with good grace."

Cahira stared at her beloved mentor, then felt her anger and determination drain away in a rush of insecurity. What was she *thinking?* To her left stood the huddle of Gaels, many of who would recognize her if she stood among them and tried to make conversation. To her right stood the Norman knights, and even at this distance they seemed inhumanly enormous. They had to wear some sort of padding beneath all that mail, she thought, squinting toward them, or the effort of carrying around so many extra pounds added unnatural layers of muscle. She heard them joking with each other in the strangely nasal language she recognized as French. To her left, the Irishmen laughed and hailed each other in Gaelic.

In the center of the field, poor Philip stood next to a smaller man clothed in a crimson fur-trimmed tunic. This man, Cahira realized instinctively, had to be Richard de Burgo, her father's enemy and the master of these knights. If she withdrew from the competition now, not only would she pass up the opportunity to humiliate these egotistical bullies, but she would also miss her chance to thumb her nose at the lord who kept her father pacing the floors at night.

Her mouth tipped in a faint smile. "You're right, Murchadh. Pride does not accept defeat easily, but I am proud, too. And I will do my best today."

The blare of a trumpet suddenly lanced the confusion, piercing Cahira's heart with its brittle blast.

Philip stepped forward and lifted his arms to welcome his guests. "Come one, come all." He spoke in a stilted, inflectionless English. "In honor of my guest, Lord Richard de Burgo, we will now begin the archery contest. Come, my friends and kin, and let us sharpen our skills as we toast each other."

"Go then," Murchadh's broad hand came to rest on Cahira's shoulder, then gave her a gentle shove. "And prove that these Norman have not yet seen what the free blood of Éireann can do."

Both groups of contestants had begun to move forward. With Murchadh's words ringing in her ears, Cahira walked at the edge of the Irishmen and kept her head down. The newly-cut hay crunched under her feet, which seemed ridiculously small compared to the huge boots marching around her.

"You'll be needing a right sharp eye to win with that thing." The man next to her had spoken, and Cahira was confused until she glanced up and saw him looking at her bow. He carried a regular hunting bow, a long instrument that required a man's muscled arm. Her short bow, which Murchadh had carved especially for her, required far less strength.

"My eye is sharp enough," she muttered, taking pains to pitch her voice low. "'Tis sharper than any of those Normans, truth be told."

The man cackled in appreciation of her bravado, then the group halted at a plowed line in the earth. As the group dispersed along the line, Cahira saw that Philip's men had set several upright posts on the far side of the field. Upon each post rested a single, small, unremarkable apple.

She closed her eyes. Hitting an apple would be easy enough, for she had hit smaller targets. But the distance was another matter—the men around her, including the Normans, would use bows with far more power. She could compensate by over-pulling, but if she drew the bowstring too far, the stress might cause the bow to wobble, sending the arrow careening over the grass. She had come to win, not to humiliate herself.

"The first round of the competition is simple enough," Philip explained, glancing down the row of competitors. "Each man to hit an apple will move into the next round, where the stakes and the difficulty will rise. Those who do not hit the apple are dismissed, and may God grant you better luck in the next contest!"

The competitors around Cahira twittered with nervous laughter, then shed cloaks and quivers and sword belts as they prepared to string their bows. Cahira kept her eyes downcast as she stepped between her bow and its string, then expertly pressed the bow's lower curve against her foot and slid the string to the upper notch.

"Faith, I haven't shot at an apple in years," the man next to her said as he adjusted his bowstring. "If they'd run a rabbit across this field, *then* we'd have some sport."

Cahira made a soft sound of agreement as she picked up her bow and pulled, testing the tension. She had not practiced in more than a week, but the skills involved in archery had always come naturally to her. *Too* naturally, Murchadh always said. Ladies should be skilled with a needle and thread, not weapons.

"Nock your arrows at your leisure," Philip called again, clasping his hands at his waist. "But hold until you hear the order to let the arrows fly."

Cahira ran her fingers over the string, testing its strength, then slipped her quiver from her shoulder and let it fall to the ground. She withdrew an arrow, completely aware that a sudden silence had fallen over the line of contestants as each man nocked his arrow for the one shot that would spell victory or defeat. Holding the bow in a horizontal position, she placed the notched end of her arrow onto the reinforced center of the bowstring, gripped the bow with her left hand, and rested three fingers of her right hand upon the string.

"Ready?" Philip called. "Take your aim!"

Like the others, Cahira turned her bow, extended her left arm, then pointed the tip of the arrow toward the target. In one steady movement, she pulled the bowstring with her three center fingers, then locked her right thumb under the bone at the junction of her jaw and earlobe.

"Release!"

Closing her left eye, Cahira centered on the target, then opened the three fingers of her right hand. The arrows flew out in a whistling cloud, and Cahira held her breath as *her* arrow, flying straight and true, struck the apple and knocked it from the post.

A ferocious cheer erupted from the crowd, and for an instant Cahira felt as though the clamor of approval rose for her alone. The men on her immediate right and left had completely missed their targets, one man's arrow flying far beyond his post, and the other burying itself in the hay stubble not twenty feet away.

Her cheeks reddened when she glanced down the line and saw that only one other, no, *two* other apples were missing from their posts. And both of those were on the Norman side of the field.

Shock rippled along her nerves when a crowd of burly Irishmen surrounded her. "Sure, and didn't I know the wee one would show all of us how 'tis done," the man next to her said, his broad hand pounding her back. "Thanks be to God, lad, that he sent a David among the Goliaths. For a moment I thought the Normans would take the day."

A pack of small boys ran behind the targets to fetch the pierced apples, and Cahira saw one lad triumphantly lift hers, her colorful arrow piercing it as neatly as a pin. Her pleasure turned to dismay, however, when she saw two other boys holding aloft the Normans' apples—or what *remained* of the Normans' apples. Both knights not only struck their targets, but their arrows hit the fruit with such force that nothing but weepy pulp remained.

She felt her smile freeze on her face.

"Och, can you just imagine what one of those arrows would do to a man's skull?" One of the lads in the Gaelic crowd voiced every man's thought. "What are they made of, steel?"

"'Tis the length of their bows," another man countered. "I've heard stories of them—Welsh longbows, they call them. They say an arrow fired from such a bow can strike a man and pin him to the ground."

A moment of heavy uneasiness followed, then a hand tightened around Cahira's arm. "Ah, lad, you wouldn't be letting such things worry you, would you now? This is a contest for accuracy, and you've got that to spare. You'll do fine, we're sure of it."

And then she was swept up in a surge of Irish masculinity and pushed, prodded, and fairly propelled toward the two Normans who stepped out of the line. Her dismay turned to outright horror when she realized that the two archers in front of her were the same two knights she had encountered by the river—*him* and the other.

God help me.

⚜

WATCHING IN INTEREST AND APPROVAL, COLTON CHUCKLED WHEN the Irishmen herded their wee champion forward. So, the lad with the hot temper had a sure aim as well! It was a miracle he had managed the distance with that dainty bow, but the young man had obviously been well-schooled in the art of archery. The lad wore plain clothing, so he was no one of significance, but even the common folk often had to shoot their supper.

Oswald exploded in a loud guffaw as the boy came forward. "What is a stripling doing on a tournament field? He ought to be home minding his mother."

Colton ignored Oswald's jibe and stepped forward. "Congratulations, lad. 'Twas a good shot."

For an instant the boy lifted his head, and from the angry glitter in those green eyes Colton thought his compliment would be repaid with another insult. But Lord Richard had stepped forward, and at the sound of the nobleman's voice the Irish lad lowered his gaze and turned away.

Oswald lifted a brow in an unspoken question, and Colton shrugged.

"This next round of competition will be most interesting," Lord Richard was saying, his gaze roving over the mixed crowd of Norman and Irish. "And I must congratulate our three champions. I recognize two of them as my own loyal men, my captain, Sir Colton, and Sir Oswald. My congratulations to you both."

Colton stepped forward to acknowledge the compliment, then he and Oswald bowed as tradition and honor demanded. The Irish lad, he noted as he turned to wave at the cheering crowd, neither bowed nor smiled. He had planted his bow in the soft ground, and stood with his hands resting atop it, looking out at the world with an intense but secret expression on his striking face.

"I'm afraid I cannot introduce yonder youth," Lord Richard said, gesturing to Philip. "Know you his name or his father's name?"

The balding Irishman stepped forward and squinted in the youth's direction, then shook his head. "Who are you, lad?"

Colton turned. The boy's face went pale above his bow and his fingers trembled, but his eyes flashed as he lifted his head and called out, "I am one with those whose blood has flowed in freedom from of old! A descendent of the great Brian Boru, an offspring from Éireann's last high king, Rory O'Connor!" The Irish in the crowd went wild with glee, and Colton blinked in surprise when the boy looked directly at him . . .and smiled.

The Irishmen behind the lad tossed their caps in a frenzied cheer, obviously finding more significance in the boy's words than Colton had. Philip flushed deeply, then stepped back to Richard's side.

Colton couldn't help grinning back at the boy. While the lad of certain lacked tact, he possessed an admirable overabundance of boldness. Judging by his clear speech, he had also benefited from education. Pride lay in the set of his pointed chin and fierce determination shone from those green eyes—there was no denying the lad was as Irish as yonder green hills.

Lord Richard held up his hand, quieting the crowd's enthusiastic roar. "For the next round of this competition," he began, "we will test not only your skill, but your nerves. We have a criminal in our custody, a man caught yesterday in a brazen act of theft. The apple will not rest upon a post this time, but upon the head of a man accused of stealing from our host, Philip."

The knights behind Richard parted ranks, and two Irish guards led a stumbling old man out of a storage shed and into the bright sunlight. The criminal, stooped and shriveled with age, pressed his hands to his eyes and walked slowly despite being yanked along by the guards' ropes. The fringe of white hair that crowned his head lifted in the faint breeze, and he seemed to proceed almost willingly, though his head remained lowered in shame. A dull rumble began amongst the Irish crowd, and Colton dimly noted it.

"We will begin by placing a melon on this thief's head," Lord Richard explained as the guards stood the prisoner beside one of the target posts and began to lash him to it. "If all three of you successfully pierce the melon, we will then move to a gourd, and finally to an apple. We will continue in the rounds, each man taking his turn, until two of the three men fail to hit the target. The remaining archer will be our champion."

Oswald withdrew an arrow from his quiver and began to whistle a cheerful tune. Colton withdrew one of his arrows and picked up his bow, wishing he could block the annoying sound of Oswald's whistling from his ears. From the corner of his eye he saw that the Irish lad had not moved.

"Lord Richard will probably want you to go first, lad." He held the arrow before his face and scanned it critically, searching for a loose feather. Even a tiny break in the gluing could send an arrow danger-ously off course. "But you'll have to be ready when he calls for you. His lordship is not a patient man."

Still the boy did not move. Colton lowered the arrow. The lad had gone pale; his eyes glittered like emeralds set on bleached parchment.

He was staring at the target—no, at the old man—in fixed concentration.

Colton leaned toward the young man. "Something wrong, lad?"

His mouth dropped open when the boy whirled on him. "Don't do it. I beg of you, don't do it. Raise a protest, join your voice with mine, and surely Philip and this Lord Richard will heed us."

Colton snapped his mouth shut, stunned by the boy's sudden ferocity. "Why shouldn't we follow our orders? The man *is* a criminal." Colton frowned, unable to understand the lad's passion. "Surely you Irish have laws. If a man is found guilty of a crime, he deserves whatever punishment the lord of the land decides to mete out."

The lad glared at Colton with burning, reproachful eyes. "Aye, we have laws. But this man is no thief, for he has a home, and with the king of Connacht. He is no more guilty of this crime than I!"

Colton pressed his lips together, resisting the urge to smile. "And how do I know you are not a thief?"

"You know, sir," the lad answered, his voice quavering with conviction, "because I give you my word!"

❧ 11 ❧

Trembling in the silence, Cahira allowed herself to cast a withering stare in the knight's direction. He seemed to think a man could be used for target practice as casually as a horse could be harnessed and ridden, but the thought of shooting at poor Brian sent a shiver of revulsion through her.

What sort of barbarians were these men? She'd heard rumors that the Norman lords ignored the basic rights of life and liberty in pursuit of their goals, but she had never thought she'd discover the truth in those rumors on a field of contest. Apparently the life of an old and poor man was useful only for pleasuring a crowd, for adding a bit of excitement to an otherwise dull and boring competition.

The knight, Sir Colton, was staring at her, his bow in one hand and his arrow in the other. He lifted the hand holding the arrow and wiped sweat from his forehead with the back of his hand, then squinted toward the post where Brian had been bound. The other knight, who had already nocked his arrow, turned and stared at his competitors.

"What's this?" he asked, his English pinched and nasal. "Have you lost your courage or your skill? Let me remind you, Colton, we have a wager riding on this event." His smile deepened into laughter. "*Riding on this*—I've just made a little joke. How clever of me to remind you that you're about to lose that grand horse of yours."

"Please." Cahira scarcely recognized the quavering voice as her own. "Let us agree to protest the use of a human target. 'Tis unjust, for though we are skilled with a bow, the winds are unstable and anything could happen—"

"You gutless Irish." The one called Oswald spoke again, his voice dry and biting. "What, are you afraid you'll nick the old man? His ghost won't have the strength to haunt you, laddie, nor are his heirs likely to come after you."

"Please!" Perilously close to tears, Cahira clenched her fist and stared at the more reasonable knight. She could explain that old Brian was part of her household, one of her father's own men, but doing so would reveal her identity and possibly expose Brian to worse danger. If Richard was truly looking for a means to move her father to action, shooting poor old Brian might be just the way to do it.

Girding herself with resolve, Cahira dropped her bow to the ground, then crossed her arms. "I won't shoot at him, and I won't let you shoot at him, either."

Sir Oswald threw back his head and roared with laughter. "How, now, listen to the twig threaten us!"

From his observation post, Lord Richard bellowed for their attention. "Fie on this delay, gentlemen! What seems to be the trouble?"

Oswald grinned and wiped his mouth with his sleeve, then looked from Cahira to Colton. She followed his gaze, instinctively knowing that Colton would settle the matter. Something about him demanded deference, and perhaps Lord Richard would respect him enough to grant his request for another target, if she had convinced him to spare Brian.

"Lord Richard!" Colton's voice, strong and resonant, rang out over the assembly. "It has been brought to my attention that in Ireland the crime of theft does not warrant a death sentence."

Richard's mouth curved in an expression that hardly deserved to be called a smile. "The old man is not Philip's prisoner; he is mine. Furthermore, Sir Knight, if your aim is true, the sentence will not be death. Hit the melon, and the old man is spared."

Cahira stepped toward Colton, her shadow blending with the

Norman knight's. "Then, sir," she called, "if you have such confidence in your knights, let me replace the old man. Release him to his kinsmen, and let me stand in his place."

COLTON STOOD THERE, BLANK, AMAZED, AND SHAKEN AS THE LAD bellowed out his solution to the dilemma. The *boy* would stand in the old man's stead? Such loyalty was rare even among knights; he had not expected to find it anywhere in Ireland. The lad was probably confident of his and Oswald's ability; still, this was a contest to the finish. At least one arrow would have to miss the mark in order for a winner to take the prize.

Aye, the lad possessed boldness aplenty. No tact, not much wisdom, but loyalty and impudence enough to equip a king's garrison.

"Let me propose an alternative." Colton dropped his bow and arrow in the grass and moved two steps forward, distancing himself from the lad. "Why have two knights competing against one another, when all the land wants to see a contest between the natives and the newcomers? Let me stand as the target, my lord, and let the lad compete against Oswald. Release the old man, and let the target rest upon *my* head."

Richard stood immobile, shock flickering over his face like heat lightning, but Philip clapped in loud approval. "A lovely idea!" the Irishman shouted, turning to share his glee with the members of his household. "Norman against Gael! And the old man goes free!"

As the crowd thundered its approval, Colton began to walk forward, knowing Richard could not now deny his request. To do so would seem dishonorable, and Richard valued nothing so much as the appearance of honor.

He felt the light touch of a hand on his sleeve and turned to see the Irish lad trotting beside him, his eyes wide. "Why?" the boy asked, his brows drawn together in bewilderment. "The old man means nothing to you."

"But he means a great deal to you," Colton answered, stopping.

"And no man loves life like him that's growing old. So get you back to your bow and remember—I'm growing older myself and am rather fond of living. I place my life in your hands."

The boy released him, and Colton continued walking toward the post, where a pair of his own comrades waited to bind him. One of Philip's guards was leading the old man away, and the poor old soul stopped to gibber a few words of gratitude before the guard yanked on his rope.

Some dim recess of Colton's mind, not occupied with immediate survival, speculated upon the boy's relationship to the old man. The lad bore little resemblance to the old fool, but Colton could have sworn that the boy's eyes flashed with recognition, even affection, when he saw the old fellow. If they were related, then, or even if they were friends, Colton had done the right thing.

He walked to the post and leaned back against it, then thrust his hands behind him. The knight standing there snickered as he bound Colton's wrists. "Is the sun getting to you today, Captain? Or have these Irish bewitched you? Oswald will shoot first, you know, you can take pleasure in that. He'll not miss, but that little Irish lad doesn't look like he has strength enough to get the arrow across this field. I'm thinking that his arrow will fall and strike you—" The fellow stopped knotting the rope long enough to step forward and tap Colton squarely in the center of his chest—"Right about there." The knave gave Colton a humorless smile. "Too bad mail armor won't stop an arrow. You may regret your actions here today, Captain."

Colton didn't answer, but lifted his gaze toward the sky. *"Thou shall not be afraid for the terror by night; nor for the arrow that flieth by day."*

Another man pulled a black hood from his belt.

"What's that?" Colton asked, uncomfortably suspicious.

"So you won't flinch," the knight answered, his fat face melting into a buttery smile. "That would be messy, wouldn't it? With this over your head, you won't know what's coming till it's all over."

Colton closed his eyes as the black cloth descended and blocked out the world. The crowd grumbled and hooted until someone balanced the melon upon his head. He stiffened his spine and held his breath, afraid he'd send the melon toppling and misdirect the archers.

Silence sifted down like a snowfall. In his mind's eye he could see Oswald picking up his bow and nocking the arrow.

God, if ever you steadied Oswald's arm, please do so now.

A TIDE OF GOOSEFLESH RIPPLED UP EACH OF CAHIRA'S ARMS AND raced across her shoulders as the arrogant knight lifted his bow and drew back. She closed her eyes as his fingers released the string, not daring to open them until she heard a solid thwack and the crowd's approving roar. The insolent Norman had succeeded, and now everyone waited for her.

How could she shoot at the man who had just saved her friend?

She couldn't. But neither could she withdraw from the contest, for doing so would mark her as a coward. Her withdrawal would shame Éireann, disgrace her father, and dishonor the memory of Brian Boru and Rory O'Connor, the kings she had just touted as her ancestors. Leaving the field of contest now would reinforce every supposition and prejudice the Normans had formed about her people.

She picked up her bow. Given only two choices, shooting at a Norman knight was by far the lesser evil. He had proven himself a steady target when Oswald took his shot, so if he didn't quaver, if the wind didn't gust, and if her arrow didn't dislodge a feather, she wouldn't miss.

The noise of the crowd diminished as she nocked her arrow. Waves of silence began from the men behind her and flowed across the field. The silence did not touch her, though, for her ears rang with the banging of her blood.

The figure of the hood-shrouded man seemed to retreat as she lifted her bow, pointed the tip of the arrow squarely at his head, then nudged it a fraction upward. Inhaling deeply, she drew back, locked the bowstring, and closed her eyes.

Father God, guide my arrow!

Opening her right eye just the barest bit, she released the string . . . and heard the crowd sigh like a bellows, then break into exuberant applause.

Oswald had already withdrawn another arrow, preparing to shoot again, but Cahira knew she could not continue. By the grace of God, she had proven the O'Connors' bravery and demonstrated Gaelic skill. She would not allow the gallant knight who had saved Brian to suffer harm.

Slipping her bow over her shoulder, with long strides she walked across the field and called to the masters of the games. "Lord Richard! Philip of Athlone! I have a message for you!"

Richard stood from his chair and scowled at the irregularity. "Why are you not preparing to take your next shot?"

"I am done with shooting, sir." She turned to Philip and doffed her cap, lowering herself in an extravagant imitation of the bow she'd seen the knights perform. "Philip, I have won for you today on behalf of Rathcroghan and your kinsman, Felim of the O'Connors."

"Felim?" Philip was on his feet in an instant, his large blue eyes vivid and questioning. "But Felim sent no representative to the games."

"He sent his daughter." Cahira straightened herself, then gave the Irish chieftain a cocky grin. "And it is she who addresses you now, pleased to report that her arm is as steady as any Norman knight's."

A wry smile gathered up the wrinkles by Philip's mouth. "*Céad míle fáilte*, Cahira." The warmth of his smile echoed in his voice. "A hundred thousand welcomes to you. You have honored my house today."

❦

BEHIND HIS HOOD, COLTON HEARD THE ROARING CROWD AND KNEW something out of the ordinary had occurred. He strained at his bonds and bellowed for release, and a moment later his comrade yanked the hood from his head.

Colton stared in amazement. The Irish spectators had spilled onto the grass, and all semblance of order had vanished from the field. His young opponent was whipping through the crowd in some sort of mad jig, cavorting before Richard and Philip with more than a dozen of his countrymen. In the twinkling of an eye the field of competition had been transformed from a somber place of testing to a riotous celebration.

"What has happened?" he asked, tugging uselessly on the ropes that still held his wrists. "Has the world gone mad?"

"She's a girl," the knight replied, his voice heavy with disbelief, "a bloomin' Irish princess. Be glad you didn't compete against her, Captain. What glory lies in victory over a wench?"

A girl? Colton's gaze ran over the archer's short tunic, taking in the unstitched hem, the slender legs, the dainty leather shoes. No wonder she had used such a slender bow!

He felt the corner of his mouth twist in a half-smile. No wonder she had felt compassion for the old man. Women were naturally more tenderhearted than men; most women would have dissolved into tears at the thought of even picking up a weapon. But this girl was different —and a king's daughter! He knew little about Irish royalty, but it was clear from this girl's example that Irish princesses did not lounge around their castles as decorative bric-a-brac.

Joy blossomed on every Irish face. From out of nowhere, someone produced a harp and pipe, and the lively sounds of an Irish gig filled the air.

The knight cut his wrists free, and Colton rubbed the chafed skin as he watched a juggler toss an endless circle of apples into the air. There would be no more contests today. The ale would begin to flow freely, and the knights who weren't disposed to dance would be so affronted by the frivolity they'd take themselves away. And Oswald, who had only equaled a *girl*, would certainly not object to ending the tournament.

Colton's smile turned to a chuckle. The girl, the Lord be praised, had just saved him from forfeiting what would have been a costly wager. He'd have to thank her.

His eyes searched for her, but found Oswald instead, standing alone at the edge of the merrymakers. He stood with his hand resting upon his sword belt, his dark eyes intent as he followed the surging crowd.

His mouth twitched in a grim little grin as he nodded to a pair of dancers who slipped from the mob.

Colton swung his arms forward, easing his tense shoulder muscles, and considered his friend's situation. It was no great shame to be bested by another knight, but to be matched by a *woman*. Such a thing would be inconceivable in Normandy or England. Women in those countries knew their places; they did not dress in rags and compete with men. True, England's Queen Matilda had once donned armor and led her knights into battle, but she never cast aside the dignity of her position. And yet the Irish stripling who had pleaded for the life of the used-up old man was the daughter of a king!

Colton moved into the crowd, anxious to find the girl. After jostling amid the dancers for what seemed an interminable length of time, he found his little competitor pressed against a rail fence, hemmed in by a broad-shouldered warrior and a nervous-looking maiden in simple garb. He recalled seeing the odd pair earlier, when he had smacked the disguised princess with the pig's bladder. No wonder the grizzled guardian had been insulted!

"Sure, now, and your father will have me hide," the bearded man was saying, his face the color of an overripe apple. "Why couldn't you have told me you were planning to start a riot?"

The girl crossed her arms across her chest. "I didn't start anything."

The warrior fixed worried eyes upon the other woman. "Sorcha, what are we to do? News of this will reach Rathcroghan soon, perhaps even before we do."

"Leave Sorcha alone." The princess flung herself into the maid's defense as passionately as she had fought for the old man. "'Tis my doing, and I'll take responsibility for it. Murchadh, you can say you knew nothing."

"I'll not be lying to your father." The color in the man's face deepened, and droplets of sweat ran down his jaw. "What sort of devil possessed us to do this thing?"

Stepping forward, Colton thrust his way into the conversation. "I was wondering the same thing myself."

All three jerked at the sound of his voice. Colton extended his hand in a sweeping and graceful gesture, eager to make peace and the proper introductions. He bowed to the besieged princess, then offered a lesser bow to the man and the maid. When he looked up, he thought he saw a smile play briefly on the princess's lips.

"Congratulations, Your Highness. You are an excellent archer."

She gave him a brief, amused glance. "There's no need for such titles with me; I care not a whit about my father's position. But I thank you all the same."

Painfully aware of a protective gleam in the warrior's blue eyes, Colton thrust his hands behind his back and tried on a pleasant smile. "But you have not answered their questions . . . or mine. Why would a king's daughter want to participate in an archery contest? In my country, archery is not a suitable avocation for young ladies."

"This is not your country." One of her brows lifted to emphasize the point. "I came here—*we* came here—because we want you Normans to know that Éireann's people are not unskilled or foolish or ignorant. We are different than you, sure, that much is painfully obvious. But we will not sit still and let your horses and your swords and your lances carve up our lands."

Her well-spoken answer seemed to satisfy the warrior, at least, for he turned and planted his feet before Colton, a satisfied smile curving his lips as he crossed his arms.

"I would be remiss if I did not thank you for taking the old man's place," she continued, lowering her gaze as a soft blush lit her cheeks. "He belongs to my father's house and, unfortunately, he wanders when he drinks." She looked up and gave him a heart-stopping smile. "Your gesture was most valiant. I will be certain to tell Brian's wife which knight redeemed him today."

Colton stared, totally entranced. "Thank you for not killing me."

"One small favor deserves another."

She smiled up at him then, her green-gold eyes sparkling with pleasure, and Colton resisted the urge to laugh aloud. By heaven, where had this girl come from? He had never known such boldness in England or Normandy. Such beauty, either. Though her wind-blown hair fell only to her shoulders, he could tell it was silky soft, a rich, silver-streaked river his fingers would love to explore.

"May I know your name?" he asked, aware that the man and the maid both stared at him with narrowed, suspicious eyes. "It would give me great pleasure to be able to pray for you."

Her red lips parted in surprise. "Am I in great need of prayer?"

"Surely every human soul benefits from a kindly word whispered in the Lord's ear."

She gave him a look of faint amusement, then startled him by reaching out and taking his hand. "I am Cahira of Rathcroghan, the land where you and your companion rode yesterday. I am pleased to make your acquaintance, Sir Colton."

❧ 12 ❧

W I DIDN'T EXPECT MADDIE TO BE EXACTLY HAPPY WHEN WE ARRIVED back at the house two hours late, but I certainly wasn't prepared for the frigid reception she gave Taylor. We found the O'Neils in the kitchen, where Maddie was washing dishes. When Taylor moved to kiss her cheek, he caught a cold glare and the back of her head instead. He looked at me, lifted a brow, then sidled around the bench and sat at the table across from Mr. O'Neil. "Well," he said, talking to the back of Maddie's head, "I'm happy to say my library days are done for a while. I brought back enough books to keep me busy for a couple of weeks."

I leaned in the doorway and watched him attempt to make amends for our late arrival. I had the feeling that defrosting Maddie would be about as impossible as counting waves, but I knew I ought to try. "I'm sorry we were late," I said, stepping into the room. "It was my fault. I got caught up in daydreaming about Cahira, and the time just slipped away. Then we took the wrong road, and went about twenty miles before we realized we were heading in the wrong direction."

Taylor looked at Maddie with one eye closed in a cautious slit, as if viewing a bomb he expected to go off at any moment. She didn't explode, though; she just turned and frowned at him with cold fury.

I couldn't take anymore. I could endure feeling like an interloper, but Maddie would cut her own throat if she mistreated Taylor. In a brightly false voice I called out, "Maddie? Can we talk for a minute? Maybe outside?"

Her mother shot her a warning look, but Maddie wiped her wet hands on a dishtowel and sailed past Taylor, past me, and through the foyer. I smiled at Mrs. O'Neil, then looked at Taylor. "We'll be just a minute."

The air in the foyer seemed chillier than it had a moment before. Maddie had left the door open, and I could see her standing outside on the little stone porch, her arms wrapped around herself. I followed her outside and closed the door tightly, so no one inside could overhear.

I pasted on a nonchalant smile and met her gaze. "We could walk down to the creek, don't you think?"

She set off across the parking lot without a word. I followed, a little amazed that she would step outside with me at all. I knew she saw me as public enemy number one, but here she was, probably ready to lay down the terms of my surrender.

She moved over the gravel with long, purposeful strides, then stopped at the picnic table and benches beneath a sprawling beech tree. Maddie perched on the edge of the table and crossed her arms, her hot eyes fixed on the creek, her hands clenched tightly against her ribs.

Standing before her, I ran a hand through my hair and hoped I'd find the right words. "Maddie," I began, "first, don't be upset with Taylor because we were late. We are late partly because I lost track of time, and partly because we got lost. It's not Taylor's fault."

Maddie was apparently in an Old Testament mood, and unwilling to turn the other cheek or forgive. "Fine," she snapped, her blue eyes boring into mine. "Is that all you have to say?"

"No, it's not." I pressed my hand to the back of my neck and sent up a heartfelt prayer for wisdom. "I think I know what's wrong between us, and I want you to know you shouldn't be intimidated by my friendship with Taylor. He and I have been friends for a long time, but that's all we are: *friends*. He doesn't love me, and I don't love him." I barked a short laugh. "Sometimes I think he considers me just one of the guys. There's nothing between us—at least nothing that need concern you."

"Don't you think I know that?" Maddie answered in a choked voice. "I know you're just friends. I knew that the day I met you both."

I gaped at her in confusion. "Then why—"

"Why am I upset? Because . . . I'm not his *everything*. I don't know if you can understand this, Kathleen, but I want to be Taylor's friend, his lover, *and* his wife. I want to be his *best* friend, and it's right that I should be. It kills me to know he tells you things he wouldn't tell me. You two have secrets I'll never learn, and you've shared so many things I'll never be a part of."

Her pale blue eyes brimmed with threatening tears, and I felt helpless—and guilty—at the sight of them. "Maddie, you will become everything to Taylor in time. You're going to be his *wife*. You're going to share things with him I can't even fathom. You're going to lie in his arms, kiss him to sleep at night, and bear his children, for heaven's sake. I'll never do that—I don't *want* to do that. The past Taylor and I share is nothing compared to the future you have before you."

I bit my lip, finally realizing something myself. "While we're being honest with each other, I should probably come clean about something. Taylor and I will never again be as close as we once were, and perhaps that's why I've been resenting you. My friendship with him will diminish every day you two spend together. Maybe I've been jealous of that . . . I know I haven't wanted to lose him. I came on this trip hoping I'd find some way to convince him that marrying you is a mistake, but now I know it wouldn't be. You two are different, but Taylor loves the differences you bring to his life."

Sniffling, she wiped her cheek with her hand. "Really?"

I nodded. "Yeah. He told me so, just today. You're all he ever talks about."

Her tears were flowing freely now, wetting her cheeks, and her nose was running. She sniffed again, then hiccuped a sob. "I'm sorry, I know I've been a witch. But you haven't exactly been easy to live with."

Her remark may not have been designed to sting, but it did. I drew a deep breath, told myself I deserved that barb, then looked at her again. "I'm sorry, too. And while I can't stop being Taylor's friend, I could go home. I will, if you want me to."

Her gaze dropped like a stone, and for the longest moment she didn't say anything. I stepped toward the house, taking her silence for agreement. I was about to go upstairs and start packing when she shook her head. "You can't go. Taylor really wants you here for the wedding. It would kill him if you left now."

So. *She* wouldn't mind me going, but for Taylor's sake she wanted me to stay. Sacrificial love in action.

"I'll stay." I swiped my hand through my bangs and stared out at the horizon, where the sun was about to touch the tips of the hedgerows along the road. "And I'll try to be conscious of the times I might be treading on your toes, okay? I really want you and Taylor to work."

She nodded again, gave me a wobbly smile, then slipped off the picnic table and walked toward the house. I watched her go, then slipped my hands into my pockets and turned toward the road and the setting sun. Funny—I had come to Ireland fully intending to convince Taylor that this marriage would be a mistake. And just when I was ready to admit that Maddie and Taylor made a pretty good pair, I had accidentally caused more trouble than I ever had on purpose.

I heard the heavy wooden sound of the front door and knew that Maddie had gone inside. She'd find Taylor, murmur her apology and accept his, then they'd probably sit on the couch and whisper whatever lovers whispered to each other when they'd had one of those minor tiffs that felt like the end of the world.

Not wanting to intrude on their private moments, I began to walk down the long drive. The temperature had dropped in the last hour, and I shivered as I hunched inside my sweater. It felt good to be outside, and even better to be alone. I should have come to Ireland with Aunt Kizzie, even if I had to beg or borrow the money for our hotels and airfare. If I were traveling with her like a regular tourist, I'd be able to concentrate on Cahira O'Connor without being distracted by this soapy version of *As the Farm Turns*.

I lifted my head and listened to the cascading duet of birds in a nearby tree. Beneath the music, Maddie's words echoed in my brain. She wanted to be Taylor's *everything*. Was any woman ever everything to a man? No wife I knew could make that claim. My parents, who'd had a comfortable marriage until the day they died, weren't everything to each other. They were too different. My father was a hunter and a sports nut; my mother loved books, art, and music. Despite their differences, or perhaps because of them, they lived separate lives in the week—Dad stayed in New York, Mom in Connecticut. On the weekends, for my sake, they came together. On Saturday afternoons my father took my mother and I to a mild and entertaining movie—Mom didn't approve of violence or cursing. As predictable as the rising sun, my dad would march to the concession stand and order three small boxes of buttered popcorn, three small sodas, and one box of Raisinettes to share. On Sunday we attended the New Haven Baptist Church as a family, and afterwards Dad peeled out of the parking lot so we could beat the crowd to the local cafeteria. On Monday morning, without fail, my dad went back to the city, and mom retreated to her Monday through Friday world. When I went to college, they shifted their Saturday afternoon movie to Saturday night, probably feeling a little like youngsters out past curfew.

The accident happened on a Saturday night, as they returned from the movie theater. The drunk driver who hit them head on would never realize how completely his thoughtless actions had destroyed the order and stability of my world.

Somewhere in the distance a cow lowed. I had reached the end of the drive, where a wooden sign hung from an iron post and swayed in the wind. Though the paint had all but weathered out of the fading letters, I traced the indentations in the wood and read "Ballyshannon, Home of Graham Red."

Graham Red? Who was he, some fierce ancestor? I made a mental note to ask Maddie about the sign, then looked down the road that led north to Ballinderry and south to only-God-and-the-Irish-knew-where. Hesitating only a moment, I climbed up on the jutting stone wall that bordered the road. Though the wide gray stones were covered with a carpet of ivy, they seemed solid enough to walk upon. With neither a shoulder nor sidewalk by the road, I walked northward upon the fence, treading carefully over the towered stones as I sorted through my thoughts.

Maddie, I decided, had definitely read too many romance novels. She fancied herself a character in some Meghann McGreedy novel and was trying to shape Taylor into the typical romantic hero. She wanted him to fight for her and stick to her side like a cocklebur, but Taylor was a mature man living in the real world. If I were a man, she wouldn't care that Taylor and I were close. But I was his friend and a woman. No amount of wishing or wanting would change either of those facts, so she'd have to learn to deal with me as part of Taylor's life.

Teetering on the edge of an unstable rock, I turned to regain my balance and caught a glimpse of the stately farmhouse. The shadows of evening had begun to stretch across the ground, and a light gleamed from the front window. I knew I ought to turn back, but I wanted to give Taylor and Maddie time to sort out whatever needed to be sorted out. Besides, the quiet darkness seemed innocent and pleasant. The hills around me stretched and sighed with the moaning wind, rustling the ivy at my feet and lifting my hair in a cold rush.

Overcome by the magic of the moment, I slowly lifted my hands to the darkening sky, wondering if Cahira had ever stood outside on a night like this one, driven out of her home by the tensions inherent in being a king's daughter. I closed my eyes, straining to hear the sounds of ancient music on the wind, and something within me shriveled when I heard the clattering growl of a diesel engine instead. The vehicle, coming up unexpectedly from behind, startled me so that I dropped my arms and lost my balance on the unsteady wall. I may have even shrieked. All I can remember is hanging by my toes on the edge of a rock, my arms pinwheeling as I realized my position was violating every known law of gravity. This thought had no sooner crossed my mind than I fell into the path of the approaching car.

For an instant the fabric of time ripped, and my ears filled with the spine-chilling screech my parents must have heard when the car in front of them swerved and left them to confront Virgil Winters, fifty-one, recently divorced and fresh from a night of drowning his troubles at the Good Times Bar in Schenectady. My adrenal glands dumped such a dose of adrenaline into my bloodstream that my heart contracted like a squeezed fist. The squeal of brakes competed with my own frantic scream, and the car stopped six inches from my head.

Fear and anger knotted inside me as the driver's door flew open. I took a deep breath, realized I was alive and intact, then saw that a dark masculine form had appeared in the road. A deep voice roared in the silent night, filling my buzzing ears with words I had never heard or read in any book.

"'Tis raining bloomin' eejits!" The man, still bellowing, advanced toward me, and my cluttered brain began to make sense of his language. "Are you escaped from the loony bin or just takin' a stroll in the dark of night?"

"It's not dark yet," I snapped, lifting my head. Pain shot from my ankle all the way up to my knee, and I couldn't have cared less about this fellow's inconvenience.

The man slapped his forehead. "Ah, sure, and it's a Yankee tourist." He stepped back, as if the aforementioned class of persons carried a dire communicable disease. "Are you hurt, then? Stand up, and let's have a look at you."

I straightened myself with dignity, brushed the dirt off my jeans, and tried to summon the energy for a confident, regal glare. But when I eased my weight onto my throbbing ankle, I couldn't help but wince.

"Ah, so you are a little worse for wear. Is it the foot?" He stepped forward into the twin beams of his car, and I caught a glimpse of a trim waist, khaki trousers, and expensive leather loafers. "Can you walk?"

"Of course I can." I lifted my injured leg and hopped toward the stone fence, leaning on it with an air of independence. "I'm fine. Drive on, go ahead. I wouldn't want an American tourist to slow you down."

He stepped closer, and I could see his hands on his hips and the gleam of a smile through the darkness. "Look, I'm sorry you got a fright. Tell me where you're staying, and I'll drop you there."

I thought about refusing the offer, but my ankle had begun to throb. And the darkness had settled and thickened around me, so I'd be hobbling home in the dark. Streetlights weren't exactly common-place in rural Ireland.

"All right." I spoke in a clipped voice, determined to show him that *this* American tourist was no weakling. If he had murder or mayhem on his mind, he'd find me an unwilling victim, injured ankle or not. "I'm staying at the O'Neil farm. It's the B&B just ahead."

"I know the place." He rubbed a hand across his face, and I could hear the faint rasp of an evening stubble. "I spoke with Maddie earlier today, and she said they didn't have any guests."

Good grief, these rural folk had a gabby grapevine! "I'm not a guest," I answered, a little miffed at the intrusion into my privacy. "I'm, uh, a friend. Visiting for a while."

"Right so." He tipped his head back as understanding dawned, and I glimpsed a generous mouth, a straight nose, and a handsome profile dark against the rising moonlight. He slipped between me and the passenger side of the car, then opened the door. "Will you be able to make it this far?"

"Of course." I gritted my teeth and hobbled over, wincing as I placed my weight on my heel.

I thought I heard him laugh softly as he closed my door, but then he came around to the driver's side, slid into his seat, and put the car into gear. He drove slowly, watching for the drive and the break in the fence, then turned into the driveway with a confidence I envied. Taylor and I had driven past the overgrown entrance twice on our way back from Terryglass.

As the car moved slowly down the drive, I glanced around the car. A leather briefcase lay on the floor behind the driver's seat, and in the glow of the dashboard lights I could see the dim outline of a suitcase on the back seat.

I looked up at my rescuer. "Traveling yourself, are you?"

"A bit," he answered, swinging the car into the parking lot. He killed the engine and stepped out, and as he came around to open my door, yellow rectangles of light from the front windows illuminated my reluctant hero. I bit my thumbnail as I studied him. He was attractive in a just-rolled-out-of-bed sort of way, with a wealth of dark curly hair crowning his head and his tall, wide-shouldered frame. I lowered my thumb as he swung my door open, irritated by his dramatic display of graciousness and my own helplessness.

"Thanks," I muttered. I tried to rock myself out of the seat, but the car crouched close to the ground, and I didn't have enough leverage. Before I could pull myself up or even ask for help, his wide hands gripped my elbows and lifted me upward. In less time than it took to catch my breath I found myself practically in his arms. I stood there, breathless and stunned by his closeness, then automatically spat out the words I'd rehearsed a thousand times in case of a mugger's attack: "I know how to defend myself, so release me this instant, you creep."

His hands opened and he stepped back, his hands lifting in a "don't shoot" pose. His mask of concern shattered in humorous surprise. "You're all right, then? You don't need help?"

I struggled to catch my breath. "I'm fine. Thanks very much, but I don't need anything else. You can just get back in your car and be about your business—"

He wasn't listening. As I continued telling him what he could do, he turned and walked toward the front door, then twisted the knob and disappeared into the house.

I took a quick, sharp breath, then hopped after him on my good leg. "Shouldn't you knock?" I wasn't quite certain what sort of etiquette would apply in this case, but it seemed only polite to knock first, then enter, even if the house was a B&B. What nerve this man had! Either the farmers in this area were a lot friendlier with each other than I imagined, or this guy had used me as a way to get inside the house so he could rob the O'Neils and Taylor, too. Stranger things had happened—in New York, at least.

"Hey, you!" I bounced into the foyer, then hobbled through the hall, too far behind the fellow to stop him from moving through the swinging door that led to the kitchen. The guy had headed straight for the sounds of activity, and by the time I reached the kitchen he would either have the O'Neils lined up against the wall or he would be entertaining them with a story about a stupid Yank who nearly got herself run over.

Dreading either scenario, I pushed the swinging door open. Mr. and Mrs. O'Neil and Taylor were sitting at the table, as calm and contented as fat cats, while Maddie had her arms wrapped around the big lug, squeezing him so tightly that he was bound to pass out at any moment.

Taylor grinned up at me. "I hear you've met Patrick."

I pushed my hair off my damp forehead and stared at Taylor in dazed exasperation. "Who?"

Taylor shaded his mouth with his hand, then mouthed a message to me: "Maddie's brother."

Oh. Feeling relieved and foolish, I slid onto the bench at the kitchen table, then propped my swollen foot on the radiator against the wall. No one even noticed my discomfort. Every eye was fixed upon the tall man hugging Maddie in the center of the kitchen.

I heard Mr. O'Neil take a deep and insulted breath. "I thought you couldn't tear yourself away from your work," he said, sudden anger lighting his eyes.

Turning to face his father, Patrick lifted his clinging sister from the floor, then gently lowered her back to the ground. The play of body language looked almost as if he were using Maddie as a shield against his father's verbal darts.

The wariness in Patrick's eyes froze into a blue as cold as a glacier, though his mouth remained curved in a polite smile. "Maddie rang me up and convinced me to come."

I parked my chin in my hand and narrowed my eyes. So this was the O'Neil brother, the infamous black sheep of the family. I stared wordlessly as Maddie stepped out of his embrace and surrendered her place to Mrs. O'Neil, who clucked and daintily patted Patrick's shoulder while dabbing at her eyes with a lace handkerchief.

Black sheep indeed. The title fit, for out on the road he'd certainly impressed me as someone dark and dangerous. But here in the kitchen, where I could see him plainly, I couldn't think of a single reason why a family wouldn't be proud to claim such a son.

⚜

AN HOUR LATER WE WERE STILL SITTING IN THE KITCHEN, BUT A sense of order had been restored. Taylor had been thoughtful enough to find a bag of ice for my swollen ankle, and Mrs. O'Neil fluttered from Taylor to me to Patrick, refilling our dinner plates the moment a bit of china appeared beneath the delicious Irish stew. Maddie spent most of her time beaming at her brother, but her smile faded every time her eyes shifted in my direction. Our most recent conversation must have been weighing on her thoughts—perhaps she'd changed her mind and wanted me to leave.

But as I accepted a cup of tea from Mrs. O'Neil, I noticed that the elder woman's attitude toward me had definitely improved. Either Maddie had told her about our clear-the-air talk, or Patrick's arrival had lifted her spirits to the point where she could overlook even an American in her kitchen.

Mr. O'Neil, however, seemed strangely quiet—but maybe he was feeling a little sick. He didn't respond to Patrick's comments or clever jokes, but merely sat at the end of the table, his pipe jutting out one side of his mouth, the smoke streaming across his face.

And as for Patrick—well, it was easy to see why the women were thrilled to have him home. Not only was he a downright pleasure to look at, but a few moments into the conversation I realized that wit, intelligence, and an encyclopedic mind lurked beneath that handsome facade. When Maddie asked about his latest project for Intel, he described it with an offhanded fluidity that made the work seem simple, but I couldn't follow a word of it. When Mrs. O'Neil asked about some man down at Dugan's Pub, he smiled and told her that yes, he had stopped in before coming home, and everyone there had asked about her health.

As I listened, I grew conscious of a small stirring of jealousy in my breast—why couldn't I have had a big brother? Maddie O'Neil was the luckiest girl I knew. Patrick held himself with the graceful air of an individual who is at home in many worlds, yet he was humble enough to listen attentively to every word that proceeded from Maddie's and his mother's lips.

Why was he wasting his time in computers? The guy should have been running the country.

"So, Maddie, tell me what you're thinking of doing with yourself after you marry this man." Patrick crossed his arms on the table and nodded in Taylor's direction. "You've got a degree now—so what will you do with it?"

The tip of Maddie's nose went pink, and she looked somewhat abashed. "I don't rightly know yet, Paddy. Taylor wants to earn his doctorate, so I'll probably take some kind of job to help ends meet while he's teaching half-days and going to school."

Patrick cast Taylor a glance of well-mannered disapproval, then turned again to his sister. "Listen, love, you don't want to be wasting your education. I'm sure this Yank is a lovely fella, but you're more than a sidekick, haven't I said so? You ought to be making plans of your own and thinking further ahead than next year."

"She has a mind of her own, Paddy." Mrs. O'Neil smiled in exasperation. "And she'll be wanting to make Taylor happy before she finds a job. Don't you worry about her—tend to your own business."

Gently rebuked, Patrick lifted his mug to his lips while I looked down at the table and hid a smile. Patrick O'Neil sounded like a bona fide pioneer for women's rights, but I doubted that such liberal notions would be welcomed here in the country. Ireland, after all, was staunchly conservative, one of the few nations in the world where divorce and abortion remained illegal.

"I've been encouraging Maddie to consider social work," Taylor said, looking at Patrick with something like an apology in his eyes. "She'll have to get her master's degree, of course, but I think she has a natural temperament for counseling."

"Aye, she's a great one to listen to other people's troubles," Patrick agreed, one shoulder lifting in a shrug. "She's heard enough of mine over the years."

No one responded to that cryptic comment, and the house seemed to fall silent around us, as if it were listening. The wind blew past the kitchen window with soft moans. Then the back door creaked, and Erin Kelly blew into the kitchen, her face flushed, her eyes bright, and her sweater most decidedly low-cut. She pulled her long hair forward over one shoulder, then stepped inside and stared at Patrick like one dazed. "Hello," she said, her voice a breathy whisper in the room.

Every O'Neil greeted her, but Erin had eyes only for Patrick. He lowered his coffee cup and gave her a twinkling smile. "Hello, wee one. Shouldn't you be home and safely tucked in at this hour?"

"Patrick, that's no way to welcome Erin," Maddie scolded. "Go give the girl a proper hug."

Sighing heavily in mock reluctance, Patrick slid his long frame off the bench and stood, opening his arms to the girl. Erin stepped into his embrace and rested her bright cheek on his chest, her eyes closed.

I shaded my eyes, then glanced at Taylor and shared a smile. I'd never seen such an extreme case of puppy love. I'd had a bad case myself when I fancied myself in love with my tenth-grade science teacher, but never would I have dared to touch him, much less advertise my interest with a daring sweater and sparkling eyes.

I leaned toward Maddie and lowered my voice. "How'd she know he was home? You can't see this farm from the road, and you certainly can't see it from the Kelly house."

A secretive little smile softened Maddie's lips. "I called Erin and told her Patrick was coming home." Almost as an afterthought, she added, "She's very fond of him. Like a little sister."

Little sister, my big toe. No little sister I knew would dress like *that* to greet a brother.

Mr. O'Neil tasted his pipe, then twinkled up at Erin. "Will you sit and have some tea with us, then? And have you had your dinner? We've plenty to share."

"I've eaten, thank you." With obvious reluctance, Erin pulled herself from Patrick's embrace and slid onto the kitchen bench in the space that had existed between me and Patrick. I looked from Mr. O'Neil to his wife and saw them exchange a knowing smile.

I clicked my nails against the handle of my teacup. Wasn't this cozy? Tea and coffee for two couples—three, counting the O'Neils. Patrick and Erin on this side of the table, Taylor and Maddie on the opposite, Mr. and Mrs. at each end.

I was suddenly overcome by an urge to flee the room.

I gave Maddie a twisted smile. "I'm sorry to leave this little party, but my ankle is throbbing. I think I'll excuse myself for a bit of reading." I slid to the end of the bench and balanced on my good ankle. "Thanks for the dinner, Mrs. O'Neil." My eyes moved into Patrick's, and I stiffened when I saw him squint with amusement. "And thanks for your help, Patrick. Good-night, everyone."

As I hobbled from the room, I noticed that no one protested my departure.

❧ 13 ❧

Taking care to favor my ankle, I limped upstairs to my room and sat on the edge of the bed, wondering if I could sleep. Though the sky outside my window was black and icy with a wash of brilliant stars, the afternoon was only just beginning to wane in New York. My biological clock, still set on Eastern Standard Time, wasn't ready to wind down.

A heaviness centered in my chest as laughter from downstairs seeped through the floorboards. Defying my own melancholy, I picked up a library book on Irish history, then decided to hobble back down to the sitting room. My room, bare as it was, seemed unsuitable for anything but sleeping and dressing; the sitting room would be infinitely more comfortable. This afternoon I had noticed logs stacked in the fireplace, so perhaps the O'Neils wouldn't mind if I lit a fire and settled into one of the easy chairs. From the look of that cozy tableau in the kitchen, I suspected they might sit around the table and talk for hours.

I found the sitting room deserted, so I dropped my book on the sofa and shuffled to the fireplace. A log and a pile of kindling lay ready for lighting, and it only took a moment to find the box of matches on the mantle. I knelt by the fireplace, lit a match, and held it to the pile of kindling . . . then watched the flame disappear.

"You'll be needing a bit of paper."

The deep voice startled me, and my hand shook as I dropped the dead match and glanced up. I expected to see Mr. O'Neil, but Patrick himself stood behind me, a bemused expression on his face.

My nervousness shifted to irritation. "Well—do you have a scrap of paper?

"Right so." He bent and took a section of newspaper from a stack near the easy chair, then crumpled the top sheet and leaned forward to place it between the log and the kindling. Uncomfortably conscious of the fact that our shoulders were practically touching, my fingers trembled in earnest when I took another match from the box and struck it. Fortunately, the paper caught instantly and flamed to life, and within a moment I heard the snap and crackle of burning kindling.

Patrick rose and dropped his tall frame into the easy chair, then extended his arm toward the sofa, wordlessly inviting me to take a seat. I picked up my book, displaying it rather obviously as I sank into a corner of the sofa. I didn't want him to think I wanted company or that I was alone and feeling sorry for myself, though both were truer than I wanted to admit.

"The light is much better here than in my room." I reached out and switched on a lamp, just to prove the point. "And I have so much reading to do."

Patrick didn't speak, but fastened his gaze to the fire. So—maybe *he* was the one feeling melancholy, though I couldn't think of a single reason he should feel anything but content. I opened my book and began to read, but couldn't concentrate on the text before my eyes. My rebellious thoughts kept circling around the man sitting across the room.

I shifted my position, propped my book on a pillow, and studied him above the book's edge. His blue eyes were wide and blank as windowpanes, as though the soul they mirrored had long since ceased to care.

Where were his thoughts? They weren't with me, and I doubted they were with the joyfully noisy group in the kitchen. The expression in his eyes seemed as remote as the ocean depths.

"Did Erin go home?" I asked, daring to break the silence.

He lifted his gaze from the fire and turned to me. "What?"

"Erin. Did she go home?"

"I expect she's still in the kitchen."

He stared at me, probably wondering what had prompted such a comment, and I lifted one shoulder in a shrug. "Then I would guess she's wondering where you went. She seems quite fond of you."

One corner of his mouth pulled into a slight smile. "She's like a little sister."

I laughed, amazed that such an intelligent man could be so blind when it came to understanding the feminine heart. "I'd say she's in love with you. And she's plenty old enough to know how she feels."

His thick brows nearly shot up to his hairline. "Love? She fancies me, perhaps, but that's all. She's not old enough to know her own mind on the matter."

I remained silent, turning his words over in my mind. *She fancies me.* I liked the word *fancy*. It implied a feeling stronger than *like*, but not as strong as *love*. We Americans needed an intermediate word because I knew too many people who married because they more than liked a person, then bailed out when it became clear their feelings had nothing to do with love.

"My sister thinks you fancy Taylor, you know."

This time he caught me by surprise. Shock caused words to wedge in my throat, and I had to force a light cough before I could speak. "Me, fancy Taylor? I might have once, but I don't now. We're friends, that's all."

"'Tis a bit extraordinary, a man having a woman for his best friend."

I shrugged. "Taylor's not an ordinary guy, and we're a lot alike. But that's it. We're just friends."

"So tell me," he leaned back into the chair cushions and folded his hands across his chest, "are you happy about the marriage? I know my sister, but I don't know this Yank. I want to be sure Maddie's marrying a good man."

"This Yank, as you call him, is as Irish as you are—genetically, at least. He can trace his ancestors all the way back to Rory O'Connor, Ireland's last high king."

Images of the firelight smoldered in his gold-flecked eyes. "Lass, half the people in Ireland can trace their lineage back to the O'Connors. I was more concerned about his character than his roots."

"Taylor is a good man." My voice softened. "I know him and Maddie, and I believe it will be a good marriage. I didn't think so at first, but I do now."

Patrick's glance sharpened. "Whom did you doubt? Taylor or Maddie?"

"Neither. I just thought they were too different. But now I see that differences can be good. They will complement each other."

He sat there for a moment, just smiling at me, then he said: "True enough. Maddie is stubborn, like Dad. So I'm really surprised she invited you here, especially if she knows how you once felt about Taylor."

I felt an unwelcome blush creep onto my cheeks. "I offered to go home, but Maddie wants me to stay. For Taylor's sake." I laughed softly. "But I can't help but feel a bit in the way here. Maddie and Taylor are trying to prepare for a wedding and plan their lives together, and here I am, stuck in the middle of everything like a useless fifth wheel."

"I don't think you could ever be useless. You've already made it clear you might be useful if—how did you say it? If a 'creep' comes calling."

Patrick's eyes twinkled at me, and something warmed in the depths of my spirit. Why, when this man wasn't shouting about American tourists, he could be quite charming! And he might be willing—if I made it clear I merely wanted to stay out of Maddie's way—to take me around to some of the Connacht sites I wanted to incorporate in my Cahira story. I had seen a good-sized suitcase in the back of his car, so perhaps he intended to stay a while.

"How long will you be home?" I began, trying not to seem too obvious or desperate. "Are you visiting just through the weekend? Or for longer?"

A spark of some indefinable emotion filled his eyes, then he looked toward the fire and rubbed his stubbled jaw.

"If all goes well, I expect I'll be here until the wedding." His voice flattened out. "Maddie wants me around, and Dad needs the help, though he won't admit it."

"If it's not too much trouble," I looked away as another blush burned my cheek, "perhaps you could tell me about some places I ought to visit for my project on the O'Connors. I don't know how much Maddie told you about my work, but I'd like to explore some of the old castles and ruins in County Roscommon."

"So you're looking for a tour guide?"

I glanced toward him, expecting to encounter a hostile glare, but his eyes were dark and smiling. I felt myself relax. "I don't want to put you to any trouble, but I have a feeling Maddie wouldn't mind me making myself a little scarce. She'd like to have Taylor's full attention as they plan the wedding."

"As luck would have it—" he placed his hands on the arm of his chair and began to push himself up—"Dad wouldn't mind me becoming invisible, either. Sure, I'd be glad to take you around after I see to the milking. I promised Mum I'd do that much for her as long as I'm home."

"And how many times a week do you milk the cows?" I leaned forward as he stood and moved toward the doorway. "Is tomorrow a milking day?"

"Every day is a milking day." He turned and smiled at me as if I were a small child. "The cows are milked every morning and every night without fail. So we'll do a bit of sightseeing, but the tourin' will have to work around the cows."

He left me then, and I sank back into the sofa cushions, amazed that I had effortlessly acquired a handsome escort and a little perplexed that I would play second fiddle to a cow.

◌⳹◌

Not wanting to push myself on Patrick, offend Maddie, or embarrass Taylor, I walked on eggshells for the next week. Mrs. O'Neil treated me with the practiced deference I suppose she extended to all her B&B guests, but she did invite me to eat my meals in the kitchen with Maddie and Taylor. A few B&B guests came and went, leaving a pile of laundry and dirty dishes in their wake.

I moved my laptop, library books, and note cards into the little building outside the main house and gradually overcome my embarrassment at reading and writing in the room Patrick slept in every night. Taylor told me the entire story of this arrangement one morning when Mrs. O'Neil stepped outside. That first night after Patrick's return, he had gone into the family quarters and sought out his old room, only to find that Mrs. O'Neil had given it to Taylor. Patrick didn't make a scene, Taylor told me, but Maddie seemed to realize that Patrick might feel that he'd been forced out of his own family by a Yankee husband-to-be. Though he could have taken one of the guest bedrooms at the front of the house, Maddie thought that arrangement might make me uncomfortable.

"Yes, I'm sure she was worried about me," I remarked at this point in Taylor's retelling. Maddie was not a particularly bright girl, but she was intuitive, and I wondered if she had any sense that something had begun to develop between me and Patrick. *I* wasn't certain that something had, but Maddie knew her brother better than I did.

"Anyway," Taylor continued, "Fiona suggested that Patrick sleep out in the little house, as long as you don't mind. So it's yours to use during the day, and Patrick's to sleep in at night. And he's an early riser, so you don't have to worry about waking him up in the morning."

So Patrick and I were now co-tenants of the little house. I discovered that no matter how early I rapped on the wooden door, I never caught him asleep. Though the bed was usually strewn with his sweaters and socks and jeans, he never touched my computer, my papers, or my books. After a day or two, I saw that he had set up his own laptop at the end of the long desk, and though his living quarters looked as though a hurricane had blown through it, he kept his work area as neat as a GI's footlocker.

Now that Patrick was helping with the farm work, Mr. O'Neil spent most of his time in his room or the kitchen. For the first time, I recognized signs of the illness that was sapping his strength. I often saw him wince as he lowered himself into a chair, and I realized he must have been an incredibly strong man if he had been able to maintain his schedule for months without help. I was certain his wife and daughter noticed the difference in the man he had become compared to the man he used to be, but I saw only a quiet man who enjoyed crossword puzzles, his pipe, and Irish pub songs.

Erin Kelly usually managed to pop by every day at lunchtime when Patrick came in from the fields, and no matter what the weather or what she'd been doing, she always looked eager and freshly scrubbed. Her clothing—whether a sweater and skirt or jeans—always emphasized a body so curvaceous a teenaged boy might have sketched it, and I couldn't help wondering how Patrick remained unaware of her silent entreaties. She was woman enough to advertise her availability, and girl enough not to give a fig about her pride. But each time Patrick saw her, he simply gave her a friendly smile or rumpled her hair, then asked for the potato salad or bread or whatever his mother had set out for lunch. Patrick O'Neil, it seemed, kept his mind on food when he came to the table.

On Thursday, however, just before Patrick headed back out to the barn, I caught his sleeve. "Patrick," I lowered my voice so none of the others would hear, "Maddie is planning a luncheon for her bridesmaids tomorrow. If I'm around, they'll be forced to invite me, but if I have plans. . . ."

His eyes narrowed as they looked into mine. "So you'd like to do a bit of sightseeing, then?"

I nodded. "If that'd be okay with you."

He lifted a brow. "Sure. In the morning, then. We'll be out before you have a chance to get under Maddie's feet." He gave me a devilish grin. "I've seen her all of a dither, and 'tis best to stay out of her way. We'll be off right after the milkin'."

I wasn't sure what time the milking was usually done, but I rose early and dressed, then went down to breakfast. The clock on the wall said 7:30, and Mrs. O'Neil seemed quiet and tired as she sipped her tea. A big bowl sat in the middle of the table, covered with a plate to keep its contents warm.

I lifted the edge of the plate and saw a mound of scrambled eggs and several strips of bacon in the bowl. "Shall I serve myself?" I asked, quietly.

"Aye." Mrs. O'Neil lifted her hands and rubbed her temples. "Please do. I'm not much in the mood for cooking this morning. Thank the Lord there are no guests coming today."

I took a plate from the cupboard and spooned out a helping of the eggs, then took a single strip of bacon, leaving lots for the others. There was no sign of Patrick, Maddie, or Taylor, and I knew they'd be hungry.

I slipped into my usual place on the bench, said a silent prayer, and lifted my gaze to find Mrs. O'Neil watching me.

One of her auburn brows lifted slightly. "Are you a religious person, then?"

"I'm a Christian, yes." I lifted the piece of bacon and took a small bite, then nodded toward the statue of the Virgin Mary atop the microwave. "I see you and your family are Catholic."

"Sure." Mrs. O'Neil nodded, then took a sip of her tea. "And Taylor's going to see the priest today. He'll have to be confirmed in the Church before the wedding."

I stared at the statue of Mary and said nothing. Taylor and I had never talked much about his religious beliefs, and I hadn't even considered the possibility that he'd be asked to join the Catholic Church. Would it make a difference to him? I honestly didn't know. If he even had a personal relationship with God, it was covered by so many activities and studies and concerns and relationships that I'd never seen it.

I smiled at Mrs. O'Neil and mentally chalked up a potential obstacle in this marriage. If I'd known about this church situation in June, I certainly would have brought it up, but I couldn't say anything now. I had promised to keep my mouth shut and to wish the happy couple well. If Taylor had qualms about Maddie's church, he'd have to raise his own objections.

I scooped up my eggs and ate quickly. Mr. O'Neil must have been restless with pain in the night, for deep lines of strain bracketed Mrs. O'Neil's mouth and blue half-moons of exhaustion lay beneath her eyes.

"Is Mr. O'Neil feeling okay?" I asked, knowing the question sounded inane.

"He's asleep, finally."

After placing my knife and fork across my plate, I stood. "I hope he rests well today. Having Patrick home to help with the work must be a tremendous comfort to him."

Mrs. O'Neil snorted, and the unladylike sound was so unlike her I nearly dropped my plate. "A help? A thorn in the flesh is more like it. Paddy and James don't get along, and 'tis only because of the sickness that James accepts him home at all. I've been praying for years that Paddy would come home, and here he is. But if the Lord's to work a miracle, he'd better start soon."

She rose suddenly, her chair scraping across the linoleum, and dashed a tear from her eye. I hesitated for a moment, giving her time to calm her emotions, then carried my plate to the sink. I didn't know how to comfort her, but I thought I should try.

Finding an obscure comfort in the ordinary act of cleaning up, I began to rinse my plate. "Sometimes God answers in ways we don't expect," I said, running the hot water over my dish. "When my parents died, I prayed for lots of things—revenge, mostly. The drunk driver who killed them got five years in jail, but I wanted him to rot in prison. I was so upset I couldn't go back to school for two years. I couldn't do anything but work and pray and call the courthouse to see if that guy had been put away yet. Finally he was, and then something happened."

Mrs. O'Neil didn't speak, but she lifted a brow as she put out her hand for my plate.

I handed her the dripping dish. "The guy wrote me a letter. A man had visited him in prison and shared the story of Jesus Christ. He became a Christian and is now planning to become a chaplain when he's released. He's already led twenty of his fellow inmates to Christ." Something bubbled up from deep within me, a raw emotion I thought I'd buried long ago. My voice bobbled when I added, "He asked me to forgive him."

Mrs. O'Neil bent to slide the plate into the bottom rack of the dishwasher, then straightened and met my gaze. "Did you?"

I felt my flesh color. "I know it should have been easy. I should have been delighted. I should have understood that this was the good thing God was going to bring out of my parents' deaths. But it took me a long time before I could see things that way. Sometimes I have a hard time tracing the rainbow in the rain."

"I will pray for you." The words were spoken so softly I nearly missed them, but then I felt the light touch of her damp hands on my shoulders as she squeezed me from behind in a light embrace. The thought that *she*, burdened with so much, would offer to pray for me—well, the rising tide of emotion within me threatened to overflow. I lowered my hands back into the sink and looked for something else to rinse.

"I've been praying for Patrick and his father for a very long time," she said, her voice soft as she moved to the table and began to gather the other breakfast dishes. "And I'm worried about Paddy. I don't think he's been going to church in Limerick, and it breaks my heart to think he could abandon his faith."

When I could speak with a steady voice I asked, "Did he ever really have it? Faith, I mean."

"I don't know." She brought two empty plates, both clean, and stacked them on the counter. "He loved learning about God when he was a little boy, but then he seemed to lose interest. I don't think he's ever come to the place . . . of surrender." Her eyes clouded with sadness. "Neither has James. Oh, he's a good church-going man who fears God, but he's terrible set on doing things his own way."

A moment of companionable silence fell between us, then I noticed the empty plates. Obviously, Patrick and James had not eaten breakfast.

"Is Patrick awake yet?" I had not yet been downstairs this early, and thought he might still be asleep. "He promised to take me for a drive today. We thought we might do a bit of exploring."

"Paddy's been up since sunrise—you'll find him out in the barn."

"Thanks, Mrs. O'Neil." I shut off the water and wiped my hands on the dishtowel, resolutely turning my thoughts from past problems to future possibilities.

I FOUND THE METAL GATE THAT LED TO THE ENCLOSED AREA devoted to the real work of Ballyshannon, then lifted the latch, and slipped through the opening. No one had ever told me guests weren't allowed into the barn area, but the arrangement of the house made it clear that certain areas belonged to guests while others were reserved for family. Guests could take their ease in the sitting room and dining room, the front lawn and the garden. The kitchen seemed to be a neutral territory into which a brave guest *might* venture. But the back wing bedrooms and the barnyard were definitely private property, so I felt a little like a trespasser as I walked toward the long rectangular building.

Three buildings occupied this area, four if you counted the roofed structure without walls. Under that aluminum roof I saw a tractor and other kinds of farm equipment I didn't recognize, as well as dozens of bales of hay stacked at least ten feet high. Next to this shed stood a smaller building with padlocked double doors. Immediately behind the hay shed I could see another long and rectangular roofed structure.

The O'Neils' little terrier, Shout, came running toward me, then stopped in my path, his hyperactive paws beating the ground in a canine dance of delight. "You want someone to notice you?" I bent and scratched behind the dog's ears. "Believe me, I know the feeling."

Shout accepted my affection with delicate pleasure, then his ears pricked to attention as his eyes saw something in the distance. Without a warning, he was off and running again, leaving me alone. Just like every other man in my life.

Shoving my hands into my pockets, I walked toward a separate building at the edge of the pasture. Through a pair of yawning double doors the sound of contemporary music spilled out into the silent barnyard.

"Patrick?" I stood on the threshold and called his name, but saw neither man nor cow in the small room beyond. A rectangular silver tank took up most of the available space, and a series of white plastic tubes ran along the ceiling and disappeared into a hole in the concrete wall. The lid to the container stood open, and as I walked forward, I saw an ocean of creamy milk stirring in the refrigerated tank.

I looked up at the tubing again and saw the pulse of liquid beneath the plastic. They weren't white tubes, but clear, and filled with milk.

A cinderblock wall separated this refrigeration room from another, and the music poured through another doorway. I crossed the spotless cement floor, then stepped into the milking room.

I don't know what I expected to see, but the actual sight was delightfully interesting, especially to a city girl. A dozen black-and-white cows stood in front of me—six on each side—with their tails to the center of the room. Their heads hovered above round cement feeding troughs, which they sniffed and snuffled and licked, as if completely oblivious to the activity taking place, well, down south. In the center of the room three automatic milking machines hung from the ceiling above a concrete well, and from each milking machine four tubes extended outward and locked onto the udder of an apparently contented cow. I crept forward, amazed to see that each milking tube divided into four vacuum-type cylinders, each one slipping—comfortably, I hoped—around each teat of an udder.

I leaned against the wall and smiled as I watched the milk flow into the milking machines. The loud hum of the machines nearly drowned out the radio, but as Patrick moved from cow to cow, checking the apparatus, I could see his lips moving to the words of a song—Donna Summer's "She Works Hard for the Money."

"I guess you do work hard," I told one cow who turned to stare at me. "You do this twice a day?"

As the first milk machine filled and quieted, Patrick stepped up to the first cow. I watched, fascinated, as he disconnected the vacuum mechanism, squirted the cow's udder with something from a spray bottle, and then wiped the area with a clean towel. He did this with all six cows on one side, occasionally giving the animals an affectionate pat on the flank. Then turned and saw me. For a moment his eyes narrowed and his face brightened in a flush, then he cracked a smile.

"Morning," he said, climbing out of the long well where he'd been working. He moved toward a bar that kept the cattle penned in their places, then jerked his head toward the wall on my right. "You might want to step aside, lass. These girls are going out to play."

I hurried out of the way and watched in amazement as he swung the bar wide. With only a slight prod to the first cow's bony rear end, the line of cows ambled forth. Patrick seemed to have a word or touch for each, even knowing them by name, though the only difference between them I could see was the little numbered tag each cow wore in her ear.

"You know them?" I yelled as he swung the bar back into place. I followed him as he stepped back into the well and walked to the far end of the shed. "You talk to them like you know them."

"You'd know them, too, if you stared at them every day." He stepped up out of the well again and opened another gate, beyond which a larger group of cattle stirred restlessly in an enclosed pen. Patrick lifted the bar, then urged the nearest cow forward. Within moments, six more cows had filed into position, ready to be milked.

"Are they dangerous?" I crossed my arms, a little frightened of the huge beasts. "They're so big."

"They're mostly placid," Patrick answered, slapping one cow on the flank in good-natured humor. "But single-minded, for certain. They're not bright, but they can be determined. I've heard of people being trampled in a herd for attempting to separate a calf from its mother."

Milking was like a ballet, I thought, stepping aside as he moved to the head of the line. He squirted each cow's udder with spray antiseptic, wiped the udder clean, and then attached the milking apparatus. When each cow on the left side was contentedly chilling out on the good vibrations, he turned to the opposite line of six cows and began the unhooking ritual again.

"How many cows do you have?" I yelled as he moved to send another group out to pasture.

"Thirty-three," he answered, but in the peculiar Irish manner of ignoring *th* sounds, his answer came out "tirty-tree." I was charmed.

I leaned against the metal railing that separated the cows from the milking well and shook my head, amazed at the ritual. How many times had I drunk milk without giving a thought to where it came from? Of course I knew milk came from cows, but I'd never let my imagination even *attempt* to picture how the milk moved from the cow to my glass.

As Patrick moved back down the three steps that led into the milking well, he tugged on my sleeve and gestured for me to follow. I did, and when six new cows had come down the chute, he grabbed my shoulders and positioned me right behind the first cow's rear end. The sight of a pillow-sized udder, full and white, met my startled eyes.

Patrick squirted the cow, wiped the milking area clean, then picked up the milking gizmo and pressed it into my hand. When I gaped at him, he propped an elbow on the metal railing and gave me a smile that set my pulses racing. "Give it a try, then."

"Me? Milk a cow?" I stared at the four rubber attachments and the tubing. The machinery wasn't intimidating, but before me, just behind the metal railing, stood two tree-trunk legs, a pair of sharp hooves, and a vastly engorged udder with four elongated teats.

"I don't think I can." I pressed the milking gizmo back into Patrick's hand, but he wouldn't take no for an answer.

"Here." Moving to my side, he pressed the vacuum thing into my right hand, then took my wrist and extended my arm. Quavering in every muscle, I gritted my teeth and positioned one of the little vacuum cups beneath a teat, then gasped in surprise when it jumped into place with almost no effort on my part.

"It's easy, you see?" Patrick guided my hand and expertly fitted another into place. "'Tis foolproof; anyone could do it. I think I could do this in my sleep."

When all four nozzles were in place, I withdrew my hand and watched in amazement as the machine went to work. Within seconds, a stream of white liquid began to move along the tubing and into the holding tank behind me.

Patrick left me standing there and moved to the next cow, which had begun to stamp her foot in impatience. Altogether pleased with myself, I stood back and watched him work, admiring the confident manner he exhibited with the animals. He climbed up the railing and peered closely at her head, then yelled that she had an infection in her right eye, so we'd have to call the vet before we could leave the farm.

I noticed something else about Patrick, and as the hour wore on I began to suspect I'd found the reason he blushed when I entered the barn. As he worked the milk machines and studied the cattle, his shoulders broadened, his eyes brightened with pleasure, he whistled and sang and smiled at the beasts. He may have preferred to hide the truth, but I saw clearly that Patrick O'Neil, computer wunderkind, loved his cows. He loved dairy farming. He probably loved this farm too, for I hadn't heard one word of complaint in the entire week he had been home.

So why had he stayed away so long?

I pondered the question until the milking was done. Patrick herded the last cow into the pasture, then fastened the gate, and hosed out the entire building. After closing the lid on the refrigerated tank, the last bit of business, he pointed to four buckets of milk standing along the wall.

He lifted a brow and flashed a killer smile. "Can you carry two of those for me? I wouldn't be asking a guest to pitch in, but Maddie assures me you're not afraid of hard work."

"I'm not." To prove my point, I lifted a bucket, then wondered if this raw milk was what I'd been pouring over my breakfast cereal. "Um —do these go to the kitchen?"

Patrick laughed. "No, to the stable. The milk is for my calves."

He picked up the other two buckets, then I followed him to the other long building. Patrick opened a small door, allowing me to enter first, and I grinned in delight when I saw four little black-and-white calves waiting in a straw-filled pen. The animals were no taller than ponies, and their brown eyes gleamed faintly blue in the shadowed light of the barn.

"How adorable!" I gently lowered the buckets of milk to the floor, then leaned forward to stroke the soft nose of a curious little fellow who'd come running to get his breakfast. His ears flickered at my touch, then he turned his head toward the trough Patrick was already filling with raw milk.

"How many calves do you have?"

"Just the four now, but we'll have them all year long." He tossed the empty bucket away and reached for another as the calves greedily pressed forward.

"Excuse the city girl's ignorance, but why don't the cows feed the calves?"

It may have been a stupid question, but Patrick didn't laugh at me. "We keep the cows with the calves for only four or five days, until the cow's milk is suitable for human use," he said, shrugging a little. "The udders fill with colostrum, you know, when the calves are first born. After that, we bring the calves in here so they don't form too great an attachment to their mothers. 'Tis hard to separate them if you keep them together much longer than a few days."

"Oh." I searched my brain for information about cattle and found very little. "I suppose you don't keep a bull on the premises," I began, feeling confident of at least one bit of information. "Aren't most calves today the result of artificial insemination?"

Patrick dropped the second bucket with a clang. "Most farms use AI, but we don't," he said, his tone coolly disapproving. "My father insists upon using Graham Red."

A dim ripple ran across my mind, and I snapped my fingers as I identified the source. "The sign at the beginning of your drive! Doesn't it say something about Ballyshannon being the home of Graham Red?"

Patrick's answering smile seemed more a mechanical civility than a genuine expression of pleasure. "Yes. He was a good bull in his day; some of the best cows in the county are descended from him. But his time has come and gone, and Dad can't seem to accept that."

At the mention of the word bull, I looked toward the back of the barn. A much larger pen stood there, and in it stood a large brown hump—above the biggest head I'd ever seen.

I pointed toward the beast. "Is that—?"

Patrick nodded and picked up another bucket of milk. "'Tis Graham."

"Well," I lightened my tone, "If he's still producing babies, he can't be that worn out."

"He's producing only through AI." Patrick's smile flattened. "He's blind and too old to venture far out of his pen, but my father won't even think about using another bull to enlarge our herd. He's stuck on Graham, and he's stuck in the old system."

Sensing that I'd hit upon a sore subject, I let the matter drop and reached out to a little calf that had looked up at me. "How old is this little guy?"

"That lovely little fella is about five weeks." Patrick reached out and scratched the ears of another curious calf. "We wean them when they're six weeks old and turn them out with the herd."

"What kind of cows are they?" The guy I'd been scratching suddenly darted away.

"Dutch Friesian," Patrick answered. "I've been after Dad to get some Scottish Angus into the herd, but he won't hear of it. The Angus are the best beef cows, but they're smaller. We can't mate an Angus cow to Graham because the calf would be too large to fit through the birth canal. We'd have quality calves and safe delivery if we used AI to mate our Friesian cows to an Angus bull, but Dad thinks 'twould be disloyal to old Graham, or some such thing."

"You seem to know a lot about cattle," I watched his eyes, "for someone who works with computers."

"How could I not know," he drawled with distinct mockery, "when I've lived here all my life? My father inherited this farm from *his* father, and my grandfather from his father. Five generations of O'Neils have lived at Ballyshannon and worked this farm."

"You're kidding." I couldn't imagine any American family living in the same city for five generations, much less choosing the same occupation. "And does your father expect you to run the farm when he—" Too late, I realized that retirement was the furthest thing from Mr. O'Neil's mind. He was struggling to survive his cancer long enough to see Maddie married and happily settled.

Patrick lowered his gaze, probably sensing my embarrassment, so I ended my comment with an abrupt question: "Does he want you to run the farm?"

"I don't know what my father wants," Patrick answered, his mouth set in annoyance. He bent to pick up the empty buckets and gathered the handles of all four in his hands. "Now—if we're to be off soon, why don't you go collect your things? I'll be along shortly."

I nodded and left the barn, but my cheeks burned as I walked back to the house. I'd been politely dismissed in that last moment, probably because I led Patrick to the brink of a painful topic he didn't want to discuss. But how could he help it? With his father within months of dying and a family business in the balance, how could he ignore the fact that his family needed him?

❧ 14 ❧

An hour later, when Patrick emerged from the family quarters freshly scrubbed and dressed in a warm sweater, he suggested that we not go far on our first day of sightseeing. He made some excuse about expecting an urgent e-mail from a friend in Limerick, but I suspected his father's sleepless night might have had something to do with his desire to remain close to home. James O'Neil was suffering through a painful day, and Patrick didn't want to be gone too long.

We drove first to the library at Terryglass, where I greeted Mrs. Sullivan and returned an armload of borrowed books about Irish history and the Norman invasion. Mindful of Patrick's concern for his father, I didn't linger or visit the rare books room, but hurried back out to the car. We drove northward for about forty minutes on a twisting country road, and I couldn't help but remark on the beauty of the river looming against the western horizon.

"The Shannon," Patrick explained, "is truly a remarkable river. It passes right through the center of Limerick, and I never tire of looking at it."

Finally we reached Clonmacnois, ruins of a sixth-century monastic city. A sign near the entrance to the ruins told us that over the centuries Clonmacnois was plundered and burned dozens of times by the Vikings, Normans, and English. In spite of those disasters, the monastery flourished and became one of medieval Ireland's foremost capitals of scholarship and artistic production.

I stepped forward and scanned the gray relics of eight churches, two round towers, and over 200 gravestones, some so ancient no trace of the engraving remained. A cold wind blew, and I felt the wings of tragedy brush lightly past me, stirring the air and lifting the hair on my forearm. Cahira O'Connor had surely visited Clonmacnois. Colton might have, too, in the company of Richard de Burgo, the man who would ultimately destroy one of my ancestors.

Patrick slipped his arm around my shoulders to guide me through a knot of Japanese tourists who had stopped to listen to a small girl singing for pennies. "There's something over here you should see," he said, leading me toward one particular stone. "'Tis located near the high altar where Toirdelbach Mór was buried in 1156."

I went with him willingly, but stopped in mid-stride when I saw the spot and the sign that lay directly in front of us. He had led me to Rory O'Connor's grave, a place more ancient than Cahira herself.

With a quick intake of breath, like someone about to plunge into freezing water, I stepped forward and read the poem on a nearby sign:

> There they laid to rest the Seven Kings of Tara,
> There the sons of Cairbrè sleep—
> Battle-banners of the Gael, that in Kiernan's plain of crosses
> Now their final hosting keep.

"The verse was written by Angus O'Gillian to honor our last great high king." I heard a note of nostalgia and regret in Patrick's voice, as though he missed Ireland's colorful past.

A hard wind swept over the lonesome graveyard, scattering leaves and tourists, and I shivered beneath the thin material of my long sleeves. "Had enough?" Patrick asked, seeing me shiver. "We could head back now if you'd like."

I wondered for an instant if he was already bored with my company, then I remembered the situation at Ballyshannon. Taylor was studying, and Maddie was busy with her bridesmaids' luncheon, which meant Mrs. O'Neil was taking care of her husband alone. No wonder Patrick wanted to get back.

"I've seen enough. Perhaps we can do Athlone later in the week?"

"I don't think I'll be wanting to go that far any time soon." He didn't offer any reason for his refusal, and I didn't ask.

The house was quiet when we returned. Leaving me in the kitchen, Patrick slipped through the door that led to the family's bedrooms, then I heard the murmur of voices. A moment later another door slammed, and when I glanced out the window I saw him moving toward the little house, his shoulders hunched forward, his hands deep in his pockets.

Not knowing what else to do, I went upstairs to read.

WEARING AN ARTIFICIALLY BRIGHT SMILE AT DINNER, MADDIE TOLD us all about her hen party. "It's tradition," she told me, "that all the bride's female friends gather small items for the kitchen such as frying pans, egg beaters, mixing bowls, wooden spoons, and such. Since we all know the way to a man's heart is through his stomach—" she winked at Taylor—"my friends were quite generous with their gifts. I expect I'll be baking brown bread and apple tarts for Taylor very soon."

Considering that her mother would undoubtedly welcome her help, I was about to ask why she hadn't started baking already, but Mrs. O'Neil looked much more rested than she had this morning. She had prepared a wonderful dish of beef tips on noodles (I couldn't help but wonder what kind of cow I was eating), and Mr. O'Neil took his place at the table as if nothing in the world were amiss. There were no B&B guests, and the mood seemed lighter and more relaxed than it had in days.

Maddie went on at great length about her party, the gifts, and the many laughs she had shared with old friends. "We got a darling little toaster from Constance O'Hara, and a wonderful fry pan from the Kellys," she said, her eyes snapping with excitement. "And Erin dropped by, no doubt looking for you, Paddy." She winked at her brother, but Patrick only snorted and helped himself to another serving of noodles.

Mr. O'Neil's eyes seemed glazed, as if he couldn't quite enjoy a conversation about toasters and blenders, so I leaned toward him. "I saw your calves this morning," I whispered conspiratorially. "And the famous Graham Red. Though I didn't get too close, I thought him a handsome fellow."

A smile nudged itself into a corner of Mr. O'Neil's mouth, then pushed across his lips and over his lined cheeks. "Aye, he is a handsome dote, isn't he? The pride of four counties, he is. I've had offers to sell, but I would never part wit' old Graham."

"Old Graham will be the death of your herd," Patrick said, each word a splinter of ice.

Maddie's smile froze on her face, and Mrs. O'Neil seemed to wither in her chair. Taylor, however, seemed oblivious to the change in mood. "Why would a bull make such a difference in the herd?" he asked, pausing to take a sip of water. "I thought all dairy farmers were pretty much using artificial insemination these days." He looked from Patrick to Mr. O'Neil, then caught my warning glance. "Sorry—are we not supposed to talk about such things at the table?"

"We talk about such things all the time," Patrick answered, watching his father with a keenly observant eye. "But no one listens."

"It has to do with health issues." Maddie jumped into the conversation, her hand on Taylor's arm. "Remember when Britain went bonkers about mad cow disease? Well, the price of beef dropped drastically when people stopped buying it, and the market shifted. Now people don't want great *quantities* of beef; they want quality beef instead."

"But our father insists that nothing has changed." The tensing of Patrick's jaw betrayed his deep frustration. "We ought to be raising Scottish Angus, but he insists upon using Graham for our cows. We're producing nothing but Dutch Friesians—great milkers, big beasts—but no one wants gigantic steers anymore."

I fumbled with my knife and began to slice a generous hunk of beef, regretting that I had brought the subject up. I was on the verge of making a harmless remark about the weather when the continual drone of the kitchen television suddenly ceased. The silence roared for an instant, then an invisible clock began to chime the hour. A picture of the Virgin Mary appeared on the small screen and, as one, the O'Neil family lowered their forks and bowed their heads as a bell chimed for a full sixty seconds.

I stopped eating, too, and caught Taylor's eye across the table. We didn't move until the six o'clock moment of reverence had finished, then we watched silently as the O'Neils—except Patrick—blessed themselves with a great waving of hands. Then they picked up their forks, and Maddie began to babble about her party again.

I gripped my fork, speared a particularly succulent piece of beef, and idly wondered if I was nibbling on an Angus or Friesian steer. Learning about cattle had piqued my curiosity, but I wouldn't have brought up the matter again for a million dollars.

Instead, I said something about the televised moment of silence. "I wish we had something like that in America," I said, pointing toward the television with my fork. "You rarely see such visible signs of piety in our culture. Most people seem pretty intent upon keeping God out of everyday life."

Mr. O'Neil's face went blank with surprise. "You don't have the Angelus?"

Unfamiliar with the term, I shrugged. "Apparently not. We have lots of television preachers and evangelists like Billy Graham, but we don't have six o'clock prayers." I frowned into my salad bowl. "We've got some really good preachers and some really strange ones. I once met this backward preacher who told me women were placed on earth only to help men. He said he wouldn't even let women hang curtains in his church."

"That sort of foolish notion could only come from a Yank," Mrs. O'Neil muttered, apparently forgetting that two of that nationality were sitting at her table. "How I hated to see Maddie go to New York! I was so glad when she came home."

Chewing on my beef, I looked at Taylor and lifted a brow. Had Mrs. O'Neil forgotten that her darling Maddie would be returning to New York after the wedding?

"Apparently we have an evangelist like Billy Graham, too," Maddie said, stabbing at her salad. "He's a Protestant, naturally, and I don't think many people will go see him. I hear he's preaching tomorrow afternoon in Birr. There's to be a big open-air rally, like the ones Billy Graham used to hold in Chicago and New York."

Mrs. O'Neil gazed at her daughter with an incredulous expression. "Why would he want to say Mass out of doors?"

"'Tis not exactly Mass," Maddie explained, basking in her store of American knowledge. "'Tis a sermon, most likely. There'll be music and preaching, and they're sure to take up a collection."

"Of course." Mr. O'Neil spoke up, his eyes snapping. "I hear those preacher types are big on robbing people of their hard-earned pounds. Just as the Yanks will rob us of our culture."

I hesitated with my fork in mid-air, then rose to the bait. "What do you mean? How are Americans robbing you?"

"Through that nasty thing." James turned in his chair and used his fork to point to the television. "Our language, our music, and our customs are being threatened by it. Everything's homogenized now, don't you see? Our young people are leaving the farms—" he flicked a gimlet glance at Patrick, who simply went on eating—"and heading to the cities for an American lifestyle. The Ireland of my youth is fast disappearing."

I tried to think of a defense, but couldn't, and sheer politeness kept me from pointing out the irony in his words. Though he might have resented the power of television, it buzzed in the kitchen for at least ten hours a day.

We ate in silence for a moment, then Patrick nudged me with his elbow. "Are you still wanting to go into County Roscommon? I could find some time tomorrow, if that suits you."

I nearly choked as I hurried to swallow my beef. "Sure. I'd love it. I'm anxious to see more of the Shannon."

Mrs. O'Neil made a small sound of exasperation. "Walk toward the setting sun from anywhere around here, and you'll see the Shannon," she grumbled. "Why you'd want to drive all the way up there is beyond my ken."

"I'm taking her all the same." Patrick looked around as if he would dare anyone to deny him.

I felt strangely relieved when no one did.

❧

After dinner, I made it my business to discover why Patrick had changed his mind about taking me to County Roscommon. Yesterday he had seemed intent upon remaining close to home, but now he wanted to drive several hours north. True, he and his father had gotten into a bit of a spat at dinner, but that didn't seem severe enough to cause a man to leave an ailing father to his pain.

Then again, Mr. O'Neil seemed much stronger tonight. Perhaps Patrick had merely decided to seize the opportunity to explore while his father was feeling better. Still, I wanted to know why.

I checked the little house and the public rooms but saw no sign of Patrick. From the window of my room I scanned the barnyard, but nothing moved in the vast empty space outside, and the barns were dark. I went down to the empty kitchen, then paused at the door that sealed off the family bedrooms from the rest of the house. Taylor's room lay off this hall, so I could have gone looking for him, but in Maddie's current state of mind such trespassing would not be easily forgiven.

I caught a lucky break when Mr. O'Neil opened the door and caught me standing on the threshold like a nosy eavesdropper. He drew back, as startled as I was. "Can I help you?"

"I-I was looking for Patrick," I stammered, backing away. "Thought I'd ask what time he wants to leave in the morning."

"Ah," Mr. O'Neil waved his hand in dismissal as he shuffled past me. "'Tis Friday night, so Paddy's gone to the public house. All the men go there. Maddie and Taylor are likely there, too."

I digested this news in silence. So, everyone decided to traipse off

167

and leave me alone? I could understand Taylor and Maddie wanting some time alone, but I knew a pub was a very public place—pun intended. They wouldn't have surrendered any amount of privacy by inviting me to join them.

"Um, where is the pub?" I slipped my hands into my jeans pockets and tried to look casually interested. "Is it far?"

"Not at all." Mr. O'Neil turned toward the front of the house and drew an imaginary map in the air. "You go to the end of the drive, turn right, and walk about ten minutes till you reach town. You can't miss Dugan's Pub—'twill be the only building with lights on and noise blasting out the door. There's great music on Friday nights."

I glanced up at the clock. "It's already nine o'clock. If they'll be coming back soon—"

"Och, girl, the boys don't even start to play until half past. Go on down, be wit' the young folks. Have a good time, and lift a pint in my stead, will you?"

Mr. O'Neil grinned at me then, and for a moment I saw a flicker of the man beneath the pain.

"All right." I lifted my chin and took a step toward the stairs. "Will I be safe walking in the dark?"

"As safe as a babe in his mother's arms." Mr. O'Neil hesitated by the sink, then turned and gave me a smile. "Are you going, then? Down to the pub?"

I hesitated, wondering what he meant. "I thought I might."

He scratched his chin, looked around the kitchen counter as if he had misplaced something, then tilted his head and gave me a sly smile. "Wait for me, will you, lass? Let me get my coat, and I'll walk you down. I couldn't let a young woman walk alone at night, no matter how safe 'tis."

The corner of my mouth twisted in a half-smile. "Mr. O'Neil, you're not well. And your wife—where is she? She wouldn't want you going out in the dark, not after the day you've had."

"Herself is sleepin', God love her, and what she doesn't know won't hurt her." He shuffled to the back door and pulled a blue jacket from a hook on the wall. When he turned again, his brows lifted in surprise.

"Still there? Get your sweater, lass, and let's get moving. I want to enjoy the music before my wits are too addled to recognize what I'm hearing."

Uncertain and unsure, but grateful for the company, I raced up the stairs, pulled my sweater from the bed, and hurried down to meet my unlikely escort.

❦

IT TOOK US HALF AN HOUR TO WALK A DISTANCE I COULD HAVE covered alone in fifteen minutes, but I didn't regret aiding the escapee when I saw how joyously the crowd at Dugan's Pub welcomed James O'Neil. The moment we walked through the door, a horde of Irishmen surrounded him. He winked at me and let himself be patted on the back, embraced, and led to the counter, where a bartender poured him a glass of dark murky stuff.

"Sure, and don't I owe thanks to the lass who sneaked me out," he shouted, turning to smile at me. He lifted his glass in my honor, then gestured to the man behind the bar. "Tell him what you'll be havin', Kathy."

My smile jelled into an expression of shock as the question hammered at me. I was standing in an Irish pub, which appeared to be a shade more bar than restaurant, and this probably wasn't the time or place to explain that I didn't drink—not alcohol, anyway. I took a deep breath and adjusted my smile. "I'll have a diet soda."

As the men around the bar exploded in raucous laughter, the bartender's brows lifted in surprise. "No Guinness?"

"Not for me." I smiled and shook my head. No sense in going into detail here about my religious convictions, for the Irish certainly wouldn't understand. As in most European countries, alcohol flowed here like water. Drunkenness was frowned upon, but strong black beer —Guinness, in particular—was considered the elixir of life. Later, if Mr. O'Neil asked, I might explain my teetotaling by telling him about the drunken driver who killed my parents. But at that moment I didn't feel like offering explanations, especially depressing ones.

The bartender slid a diet soda across the counter to me, so I picked it up, thanked him, and left Mr. O'Neil in the company of his friends. Feeling awkward but desperate not to show it, I saw an empty chair against the wall and slipped into it. A small band had set up a keyboard, drums, and a guitar in the corner of the pub, and the musicians were still tuning their instruments. To my surprise, I saw Maddie and Taylor standing behind the keyboard. She whispered something to one of the musicians, then he smiled and pulled a sheet of paper from a folder. With a smile of satisfaction, she handed the paper to Taylor, who blushed and shook his head.

"Ladies and gents, attention please." The guitar player thumped on his microphone until the crowd quieted. "Tonight we're celebrating Maddie O'Neil's hen party and her coming marriage to this nice young American. So if you'll give Maddie your attention, she is going to lead us in 'Paper and Pins.'"

The music began, and Maddie stepped forward and clapped, encouraging the audience to join her. After a few seconds of musical introduction, she leaned into the microphone and sang,

> "I'll give to you my paper and pins,
> For that's the way that love begins,
> If you'll marry, marry marry marry,
> If you'll marry me."

THE CROWD LAUGHED AS SHE PULLED TAYLOR FORWARD, THE SHEET of paper in his hand. "Your turn," she said in a stage whisper, and the crowd laughed as Taylor went crimson.

"No, I don't want your paper and pins," he sang, stumbling over the words and the rhythm, "and I won't marry, marry marry marry, I won't marry you."

The pub crowd seemed to enjoy the catchy, lighthearted song—at least they enjoyed Maddie's verses. Taylor and I seemed to be the only two people who thought it a bit embarrassing.

I glanced around the smoky pub, searching for Patrick, and wondered if he'd be angry with me for bringing his father along. It didn't take a brain surgeon to realize that this father and son didn't agree on most things, but surely Patrick wouldn't mind his dad getting out for a little fun.

I finally found him in a dark corner, talking to two other young men who seemed as sober and serious as Patrick. Like him, they all wore what I now considered the uniform of an Irish farmer—a hand-knit sweater, long trousers, and knee-high Wellingtons. I took another sip of my soda and rested my chin in my hand, wondering what Patrick wore when he worked on computers in Limerick. A short-sleeved shirt with a pocket protector? A sport coat with a Palm Pilot in the pocket? Somehow none of those images fit him as well as the sweater and jeans he wore now.

"So you're the American staying with the O'Neils." The older woman at the next table acknowledged my presence with a nod. "Working on a book, are you?"

"Yes." I crossed my legs and shifted slightly, grateful that someone had spoken to me. "My book is about the O'Connors of Connacht. It's very interesting work."

The woman nodded again, her bright eyes beaming beneath a mass of small curls that twisted and crinkled across her forehead. "Ballyshannon's a lovely place. And James and Fiona and lovely people."

"Yes." We shared a smile, and I had to admit that while the conversation wasn't terribly exciting, it was . . . lovely.

"Terrible pity about Fiona's only having the two children, and then having one go bad." A weight of sadness fell upon my new friend's face. "But I suppose you've heard the story by now."

I sipped my soda, stalling for time while my thoughts raced. This woman had just led me to the brink of a fascinating topic, but if I said I didn't know the story, she might clam up. Yet if I pretended to know what she was talking about, she'd continue without a word of explanation, and I needed explanations—or at least I *wanted* them. Curiosity, my mother always said, may have killed the cat, but it continually tortured me.

"I know about Patrick and his father," I ventured, stepping out onto safe ground. "But I don't know much about the family's past."

My friend's face lit up with the jaunty superiority of a woman who knows a secret. "Well," she said, leaning closer to me, "Fiona and James were overjoyed with the births of their lovely son and daughter, but the third baby nearly killed her. She woke up in hospital, with the doctors telling her they had to do a hysterectomy, don't you see, to save her life. And the third baby, a lovely little fella, died at three days old. James was pure mad about that little one, and Fiona stayed in a desperate bad humor for months about losing the child and not being able to have any others. 'Tis a terrible fate for a woman to suffer, I've always said so. And then Patrick and his sister grew up, with Patrick being so odd in his way—"

"Odd?" I uncrossed my legs and leaned closer. "What do you mean?"

She stared at me, complete surprise on her face. "Sure, and you don't think anybody that smart is odd? I taught him myself when he was but a wee lad, and I'll never forget the day I marched up to Fiona and told her the boy had a photographic memory. I had set twenty little objects out on a table then took them away, and asked the children to list how many they remembered. Patrick got every one without even straining to recall! Fiona thought my opinions were a load of rubbish, of course, but soon enough she realized the truth. There's never been a child like Paddy O'Neil in these parts. 'Tis no wonder his family doesn't know what to do with him."

On and on she rambled about the O'Neils' consternation, and I pretended to listen while my heart broke for the little boy Patrick had once been. How sad that his brilliance had been discovered by people who considered him strange. At least he had found his way out of Ballinderry and into a profession that valued and rewarded gifts like his.

"Excuse me, ma'am." I placed my hand on my talkative friend's arm and gave her a smile. "But I see Patrick over there, and I need to ask him a question. But it's been lovely talking to you."

"Do come again," she answered, her bright smile practically jumping through her lips. "I'd like to hear all about life in New York. I've never been there."

Gathering my courage, I slipped out of my chair and made my way to the corner where Patrick stood with his friends. He fell silent as I approached, then nodded in my direction. "Gents, this is Kathleen O'Connor, a guest of my mother's. She's staying at Ballyshannon until Maddie's wedding."

The two fellows nodded and grinned, and I returned their smiles before addressing Patrick. "I hope you don't mind that I brought your father out," I began, aware that Patrick's two companions were drifting away, "but I wanted to find you, and he insisted upon coming along."

Cold dignity created a stony mask of his face, but still something stirred in his eyes. "I washed my hands of my father's business long ago."

"I was wondering—I wanted to ask—"

"What?"

I took a deep breath and plunged ahead. "You said you couldn't take me to County Roscommon, but at dinner you changed your mind. Why?"

He studied me thoughtfully for a moment, then his gaze lifted and moved into the center of the pub where Maddie and Taylor and James were laughing and singing. "Did you change your mind?" he asked, not looking at me. "Do you not want to go?"

"No, I still want to go—" the words poured out of me like water— "but I like to know what my friends are thinking. If you're feeling pressured, I don't want you to be. I know these are trying times with your father's illness and Maddie's wedding, and the last thing you need is an American woman telling you to take her here and there—"

"Then it's settled. We'll go tomorrow." After giving me a quick smile, he moved away. I sighed in relief, and it wasn't until much later that I realized he had never answered my question.

❧ 15 ❧

The next morning when I woke, I moved to the window and listened, immediately identifying the low, mechanical rumble of the milking machines. Patrick must have risen early to bring in the cows, which could only mean he intended to make an early start of things.

I pulled underwear and socks from a dresser drawer, pulled a clean sweater and slacks from the wardrobe, then tiptoed into the bathroom. After showering and dressing, I arranged my notebooks, pens, and camera in my book bag, then hurried downstairs.

There were no B&B guests, so the usual bowl of eggs, bacon, and sausage sat in the center of the kitchen table. I lifted the lid, inhaled the heavy scents of fried foods, and found myself inexplicably longing for a Pop-Tart.

Taylor and Maddie had risen early, too. They sat across from each other at the table, but neither was eating. Maddie had a pen in her hand and a legal pad before her; Taylor's nose was buried in a book. I tilted my head to check the spine: *A Modern Criticism of Kipling's Kim and Other English Novels*.

I smothered a smile as I sat down and buttered a piece of soda bread. If I had married Taylor, we'd probably both read at the breakfast table, so neither of us would make it out the door on time. Maddie might be flighty, but she possessed a drive Taylor sorely needed.

Determined to atone for all the gloom I'd caused, I gave Maddie a sunshiny smile. "What are you two doing today?"

Maddie's lower lip edged forward in a pout. "Nothing very exciting, I'm afraid. Taylor's reading for his thesis, and I'm working on the guest list. But I'm nearly done, which means I'll soon have nothing to do but watch Taylor read."

She frowned and parked her chin on her fingertips, but suddenly her eyes brightened. "Hey! You and Paddy are driving up to Roscommon, right? I could go with you! It's been ages since I've been up that way."

The heavy bread seemed to cling to the roof of my mouth, and I stopped chewing. Maddie wanted to come with us? A dozen objections rose in my brain like a flock of suddenly startled birds. If she came along, she'd want to sit beside Patrick in the front seat, so I'd be stuck in the back, once again feeling like an outsider. She would occupy Patrick's attention the entire time. They'd laugh at stories and people they had known for years, while I would hover on the fringe of every conversation, if they included me at all. It wasn't fair that she should push me away from Taylor and keep me from the closest thing to a friend I'd made in Ireland. She was Patrick's sister, after all, and had enjoyed his company most of her life. Why couldn't she let me enjoy him for one day?

The weed of jealousy stung like the nettles I had brushed against on one of my walks through the pasture. The pain caught me by surprise, and surprise brought me back to reality.

Not one of my objections was legitimate. Of course Maddie could come. She was Patrick's sister. They hadn't spent much time together since his homecoming, and soon she'd be marrying an American and moving back to the United States. Patrick and I had no relationship to speak of, so there was nothing for her to intrude upon.

Grateful that I hadn't said anything to reveal my foolish feelings, I lowered my head and hoped she wouldn't notice my flushed cheeks.

My thoughts were interrupted by Patrick himself, who entered the kitchen and stomped his feet on the rug inside the kitchen door. "Morning," he told me, then smiled at his sister. "Glad to see you're up early, Maddie. After singing half the night away, I didn't expect to see you before noon."

"Paddy, I have the most wonderful idea." Maddie clapped and jauntily cocked her head to one side. "Taylor's going to spend all day in his books, and that's no need for me to waste a day. Why don't I come with you to County Roscommon? We had hardly a minute to talk since you came home."

Patrick moved slowly to the sink, then washed his hands under running water. "Sorry, but you can't be going with me today," he answered, intent upon his scrubbing. "I need you to stay behind in case we're delayed. We should be back by six, but I want to know someone's here to take care of the milking if Dad's not feeling up to it."

Maddie stared at him, astounded. "Me, milk the cows? Why, I haven't been out to that milking shed in years! I wouldn't know how to do it. Mum and Dad are the only ones who tend to the cattle these days."

"Perhaps it's time, then, that you are learning about the family business." Patrick shut off the water and picked up a towel to dry his hands, then leaned back against the counter and fixed his sister in a stern glance. "Taylor can help you, and Mum can remind you of anything you've forgotten. But she's exhausted with caring for Dad, and Dad's not as well as he thinks. So stay here like a good lass and keep an eye on things, will you?"

Maddie stared at her brother, her face a mask of incredulity, then she turned and fixed her gaze on me.

For some reason I felt slightly guilty, but I brushed off the feeling and stood. "Let me get my things," I told Patrick, eager to be away from the kitchen. "I'll be down directly."

Patrick was fairly quiet as we left Ballinderry and drove north, and I couldn't help but wonder if he was suffering pangs of guilt for leaving his sister at home. After a few minutes he switched on the radio, and we laughed together as a perky radio disc jockey regaled her listeners with delightful stories from her childhood.

I studied the scenery as we drove, thinking that the emerald hills of Ireland had to be one of the most beautiful spots on God's earth. In places where the road climbed a hill and the hedgerows had been clipped, I could see an immense patchwork of gold and green fields stretching toward the horizon. Cattle and sheep dotted the pastures, and huge rolls of mown hay adorned others. Once we had to stop the car and wait for a farmer to herd his cattle across the street, and I smiled as I recalled a postcard I had seen in the airport. The postcard scene was much like this—a farmer stopping traffic to herd sheep, while the caption below proclaimed, "Irish traffic jam."

I decided I far preferred the Irish version to the New York variety.

"Tell me what you see," Patrick said, gesturing toward the window when we began to drive again.

I craned my neck to study his face. Surely he was joking. "What do you mean?"

His dark blue eyes twinkled with merriment. "It's not a difficult question. Just tell me what you see outside the car."

"Grass and fields. Fences. Cows and sheep."

"All right. Now tell me how many shades of green you see."

I stared out the window, stumped by the question. How many shades? There had to be at least half a dozen. There was the deep emerald of the soft grass, the slight golden green of the sun-lit hayfields, the darker green of the trailing ivy. . . .

"You make me wish I had my thesaurus handy," I grumbled, still staring out the window. "But I'll take a wild guess. I think I see six different shades, give or take one or two."

The glint of humor returned to his eyes. "Very good, for a Yank. Most tourists see four or five, but you're ahead of the game."

"How many do *you* see?"

His gaze shifted to the rearview mirror as he pulled around a slow-moving tractor. "A true Irishman can count at least forty. I think I've identified forty-five."

I grimaced in good humor. "You're joking, aren't you?"

"Not at all."

We drove through Terryglass and Lorrha, sizable towns by Irish standards, but still quaint and provincial to my way of thinking. My stomach had begun to growl by the time we approached Birr, and I hoped Patrick would think about stopping for lunch. To my delight, he slowed the car as we approached the city limits, then glanced at the clock on the dashboard. "Ready for a bit of a stop?"

"I was hoping you'd think so. I'm getting hungry."

He gave me an apologetic glance. "I'm not sure what we'll find in the way of food, but there should be something. I was thinking of stopping at the town center—the American evangelist is here, you know."

I stared out at the street as bits and pieces of information flew together in my brain. Maddie had mentioned the preacher last night at dinner, and while her family ridiculed the idea, Patrick remained silent. A far-fetched idea occurred to me, but still I had to wonder: Had he wanted to drive out with me today just to hear an American evangelist?

The town of Birr was a beautiful community with broad streets lined with the unruffled design of Georgian homes. A spacious square stood at the center of the town, and Patrick resolutely steered the car toward the town's center.

I said nothing as Patrick maneuvered the car into a parking spot. Then we got out and studied the town square. Several shops stood on the main street, including a sandwich shop. Patrick noted it, then his gaze drifted toward a wooden sign pointing toward a park. Even from the street I could see that an amphitheater had been carved into a gently sloping hill.

"Will you come?" He looked at me then, and I was surprised to see naked entreaty in his eyes. "I've been wanting to hear this man, and—" he shrugged as his voice faded away. "Well, there's no time like the present, right?"

"Of course I'll come." I stepped up onto the sidewalk, then waited for him to join me. He seemed so nervous and ill-at-ease that I instinctively reached out and took his hand. His palm was clammy, but his hand tightened around mine as we fell into a stream of pedestrians and made our way into the amphitheater.

There weren't more than a hundred people seated on the benches, I thought, looking around as we found seats in the warm sunlight. What had appeared to be a decent crowd on the sidewalk turned out to be a horde of shopkeepers and bankers going to the square to eat lunch outdoors; few of them had actually come hear the American Protestant preacher. But from where they sat on the grass they couldn't help but hear his message, and as a woman stood in the center of the stage and sang a song about grace, I noticed that several of the picnickers turned to watch.

I leaned sideways and nudged Patrick with my shoulder. "Is this why you asked Maddie to stay home today? Are you embarrassed by your curiosity?"

I was about to add that he shouldn't be, for without curiosity one never learned anything, but Patrick looked at me with a touch of sadness in his faint smile. "I'm not embarrassed. . . but Maddie wouldn't understand this. Neither would my parents. They are content in the Church."

"And you're not?"

Something that looked almost like bitterness entered his face. "I'm not content in anything."

I would have pressed him further, but the singer sat down, then a man stood and walked to the center of the stage. His name was Thomas Smithson, he told us, and God had called him to be a witness to Ireland and her people. He had not come to bring strife or division or trouble, but to teach the Word of God to those who wanted to hear it.

I've been going to church all my life, but this guy's approach was different from anything I'd ever heard. For one thing, he didn't tell stories about people burning in hell or read pages and pages of Scripture. He read only one verse, John 3:16, then he explained that God loved the world so much that he provided a perfect sacrifice—his only Son—in order to reach out to every man and woman who would accept his gift.

"God created you perfect and complete," Smithson said, his unamplified voice rising clearly from the stage, "but sin destroyed the fellowship we were meant to have with God. Now we suffer from an emptiness where we should enjoy communion with the One who created us in his image. If you feel empty and incomplete, God longs to fill you. This is the mystery of love, that the God who created you for a unique purpose desires to have you know him so much that he sacrificed his Son. Accept his provision today, trust his plan for your life, and you will never know emptiness again."

Some observer from the grass called out a rude remark, but Smithson only lifted his hand and bowed his head. "My blessed Father and God," he prayed, apparently oblivious to the catcalls from the picnickers, "I thank you that we do not need a priest or sacrament or indulgence to approach your holy throne. Your Son is the bridge between man and God, and through Jesus alone we can know peace with you. Let your Spirit touch the hearts that are ready to be filled; give courage to those who are ready to make this decision. I lift this prayer in the blessed and holy name of Jesus, my Savior."

I felt a slight shiver when he mentioned the name of Jesus. Not many American ministers dared to be so bold in a public arena. Most were eager to talk about God and faith and the spiritual life, but few these days actually spoke Jesus' name. Fewer still would acknowledge him as "my Savior."

My thoughts filtered back to my last dinner with Aunt Kizzie, and her words rippled through my brain: *I'm not worrying about you, love, but thinking of the people you'll meet. Will you tell them about Jesus, or will you spend your time prattling about this Marcy Anne Wilkerson?* I didn't need Kizzie to tell me that Marcy Anne Wilkerson wouldn't be talking about Jesus if she was here.

As the prayer ended, I opened my eyes and glanced around at the circle of benches. An organist was playing soft strains of "Just as I

Am," but Thomas Smithson was no Billy Graham. The aisles remained clear; there were no hordes rushing down to speak to counselors and receive booklets about how to become a Christian. There was, in fact, no movement at all. Thomas Smithson had apparently misinterpreted his call to come to Birr.

"Ready to go?" I reached down to pick up my purse. "I hope you weren't too disappointed. These rallies are a much bigger deal in America. The Irish probably aren't accustomed to an evangelical altar call."

Patrick didn't answer, and for the first time I looked up. He was still standing there with his eyes closed and tears glistening on his face.

Suddenly my shuttered mind blew open. God had sent Thomas Smithson to Birr for Patrick O'Neil.

೧ೞ

PATRICK WAS QUIET AS WE WALKED BACK TO THE CAR, AND I FELT SO burdened by guilt I didn't know how to speak to him. I had blithely imagined that he was a Christian. Hadn't he gone to church all his life? Didn't he and his family drop everything and say prayers every evening at Angelus? There was scarcely a room in the house without a picture of Mary or Jesus or both, and Mrs. O'Neil was obviously a devout believer. Yet Patrick had desperately wanted to hear this preacher, wanted to badly enough to leave his ailing father, alienate his sister, and use me for an excuse to get away.

But he kept his word. After we grabbed sandwiches at the shop we'd seen near our parking spot, we drove into County Roscommon and visited all the places I wanted to see. On the road to Boyle we found the impressive ruin of Roscommon Abbey, a priory founded in 1253. Though the building was erected long after Cahira O'Connor's death, Felim O'Connor's tomb was located in the remains of the church. My heart began to beat almost painfully in my chest as I stood and looked down at Cahira's father's grave. His refusal to bargain for terms with Richard de Burgo had cost him dearly, but now that I was looking upon the fair land of ancient Connacht with my own eyes, I could understand his reluctance to surrender.

After leaving Roscommon Abbey, Patrick drove me to Clonalis House, ancestral home of the O'Connor clan, but that mansion had been built in the nineteenth century, more than six hundred years after Cahira's death. I thanked Patrick politely for taking the time to point out the place, but refused to go in. Nothing inside would help with my research, and Patrick did not seem particularly eager to see a fancy house filled with artifacts.

I thought he would shrug and turn the car around for the drive back to Ballyshannon, but at the stop sign he pointed the car north. "There's one other place you must see while we're here," he said, pulling out onto the road. "The source of the Shannon itself."

Just when I had begun to fear we would ride for hours in silence, Patrick asked about my work. As we drove past meadows of purple, white, and yellow wildflowers, I told him about meeting Professor Howard in the library and my first research on Cahira. I talked about Anika of the knighthood as we passed mountains splashed with golden light spilling through towering clouds. As I told him about Aidan the artist and Flanna the Civil War heroine, I watched the River Shannon wind through the fields, bright as a spill of molten metal from a furnace.

Finally, as we pulled off a busy road and drove onto another shaded with towering trees, I told Patrick that Professor Howard had been convinced some incredible fate awaited me because I bore the same mark of Cahira's other extraordinary heirs—the streak of white in my red hair. He took his gaze from the road long enough to give me a quizzical look, then he smiled.

"Of course, I don't think I'm the type to pick up a sword, hop a ship, or go to war," I said, looking out the window as we drove. "I'm not sure what I'm supposed to do with my life."

Lines of concentration deepened along Patrick's brows and under his eyes. "The seventeenth-century satirist Jean de la Bruyere said man has but three events in his life—to be born, to live, and to die. We are not conscious of our birth, we suffer at our deaths, and we forget to live." His gaze shifted to me again. "Don't forget to live, Kathleen."

"Are *you* living, Patrick?" My impulsive question brought a hushed and awkward silence to the car. Patrick kept driving, his eyes on the road, and when he spoke again, his voice seemed tighter than usual.

"I am now." He swung out into the right lane to pass a tractor on the road. "But five or six years ago I wasn't. My father and I were at each other's throats constantly, so I left. Washed my hands of him and the farm, said farewell to Mum and Maddie."

He eased the car back into the left lane as another car rushed directly toward us, and I exhaled, releasing the tension in my shoulders and back. "So—you're happy now?"

"As happy as a man can be, I suppose." He expertly eased the car around a sharp bend. "I went into the computer business and made a place for myself in Limerick. 'Tis a different life altogether, but I like it well enough."

We drove in silence while I considered his answer. For all I knew, he had a girl in Limerick and a full circle of friends who couldn't wait for him to come back.

"If you don't mind me asking, what was the problem between you and your dad?"

He shot me a penetrating look. "What *wasn't* the problem? He's as stubborn as a stone and about as agreeable. He does things the old way, or he doesn't do them at all. I'd suggest an improvement with the cows or bring up the idea of importing new stock, and he'd look at me as if the devil himself had suggested the idea. And then there was the thing about the girl—"

I smiled, though the words sent a sharp pain through my heart. "The girl?"

Patrick made a soft sound of exasperation. "Five years ago, Dad wanted me to marry Erin Kelly's older sister Mary. Most men around here marry local girls, they always have, so our families got together and arranged everything. Mary herself was a fine girl and willing, but I just couldn't wrap my mind around it. Mary's dad has four daughters, you see, and no son to inherit the farm, so they decided that Mary and

I would unite the two farms as one." He shifted uncomfortably in the seat. "Anyhow, I couldn't see marrying for business and not love, and so I broke the engagement. Mary was heartbroken, and Mr. Kelly righteously furious. And so that night, before they could bend me to their will, I packed my bags and walked to town. I caught the bus to Limerick and never looked back."

Till now. Those two words hung between us, unvoiced. I turned them over in my mind, knowing that Patrick was just as obstinate as James. The son was eerily like the father, and their intractability might be the undoing of them both.

Patrick finally turned onto a narrow dirt road and stopped the car. Without explaining where we were, he stepped out onto the grass. I joined him and stared at what appeared to be a lake a few meters away. A simple sign told me we were looking at the Shannon Pot.

I put my hands on my hips and stared at him, not understanding. "The pot?"

"*Log na Sionna* in Gaelic, the source of the River," Patrick answered, striding through the long grass. I followed, wishing I'd worn my hiking boots instead of tennis shoes, and soon found myself standing at the edge of an unremarkable tarn about twenty-five feet wide. The water was as black as India ink and fringed by hawthorn and stunted willow trees.

"The Shannon Pot is supposed to be bottomless, but they've discovered it's really about twenty-five feet deep," Patrick said, his blue eyes sweeping the surface of the lake. "The old folks used to swear 'tis impossible to drown here. The miracle, of course, is that the pot is always full, though no one has ever found the water's source. Yet from it the Shannon flows 214 miles, filling an entire chain of lakes before spilling into the Atlantic."

I stared at the water, appreciating its natural beauty, yet unable to understand Patrick's fascination with it. The landscape was pretty enough, and the river lovely, particularly from the higher elevations where it appeared as a blue ribbon draped over a mottled green carpet. But we had mysterious springs and supposedly bottomless lakes in New York.

"Does this place have something to do with the O'Connors?" I asked, thinking perhaps Cahira had visited this site. "Is that why you brought me here?"

He shook his head. "I brought you here because it reminded me of something the preacher said today. The emptiness—like a bottomless tarn. Have you ever felt empty, Kathleen?"

The question caught me unprepared, and I had to take a moment and gather my thoughts before answering. In the last few weeks I had felt lonely and useless, but something told me Patrick wasn't talking about mere human emotions. He was referring to something far deeper, a *spiritual* condition.

"At various times," I chose my words carefully, "I have felt lonely and hurt. But no matter how I feel, I know God loves me."

He lifted his chin. "What I did today—have you ever prayed those words?"

"Yes, of course."

"Then it's a Protestant thing."

"It's a *holy* thing, Patrick. The words you say really aren't important. What God honors is a sincere and contrite heart. If you surrendered your life to him today, he accepted it."

He kept his gaze on the horizon, his brow wrinkling with deep thoughts. "I just want to be like *Log na Sionna*, never empty. But now I don't know what to do. I don't know what comes next. I feel like I should go to confession or say a prayer, that I have to do something to keep this full feeling in my heart."

I reached out and put my hands on his arms, turning him to face me. "I'm not a preacher, Patrick, but I do know that *doing* is the least of it. Today you trusted in what God did for you. You can serve him out of love and gratitude, but the spiritual things you do won't improve your relationship with God. He has made you his child, and nothing you can do—good or bad—will ever change that."

A furious blush glowed on his cheekbones. "So you're saying that I belong to Jesus—always and forever."

"Yes." I smiled. "Even though it sounds simplistic and a little quaint to put it that way."

He regarded me with a speculative gaze. "Why does it sound quaint?"

I drew in a deep breath and exhaled slowly. How could I explain the idiosyncrasies of American culture to a new Irish Christian? "In America, especially in New York," I began, "people don't usually say Jesus' name unless they're cursing. And it's politically incorrect to talk about personal faith in public. If you do, people are apt to become offended or think you're loony."

Patrick gave me a quick glance of utter disbelief. "I know about your American loonies. Half the tourists who stay at Ballyshannon are American, and they're always complaining because Ireland's not like America. Where's the sense in that? And we get Jerry Springer on the television, so if your New York friends are anything like those eejits—"

"Not all Americans are like the people you see on Jerry Springer." I squeezed his arm. "Look, Patrick, it's not right that people are embarrassed to talk about Jesus. But sometimes you have to be careful. We don't want to cast our pearls before swine, so most Christians tend to stay quiet about the things that matter most to us. It's impossible to be on the wrong side of a public argument if you don't take any side."

He lifted a brow at this. "'Twould be impossible to be on the *right* side, either. Or haven't you considered that?"

I sighed, wondering if the Lord had tapped the right person for the job of introducing Patrick to the joys of the Christian life. I had been a believer for a long time, long enough to understand that a walk of faith isn't necessarily going to lead through a rose garden. Even if it did, as long as we were in the world, the roses always had thorns . . .

We had a long drive ahead of us, and the sun was already coming down the sky. "Come on," I gently tugged on his arm, "let's get back to the car. You probably need some time to think."

"In a moment," he said, resisting me. "I don't get up here often, and I'd like to watch the pot for a little while."

And so I turned to watch the pot with him, and felt my heart turn over when he placed his hands on my shoulders and sheltered me from the bawling wind. Though my eyes scanned the lake, my thoughts wandered in a hundred different directions. I had a feeling my answers had only brushed the surface of his questions, for Patrick O'Neil was nearly as deep as the source of the Shannon itself.

A faint wind breathed through the trees, bringing with it the distant sounds of ancient merrymaking, sending memories ruffling through my mind like wind on the Shannon's water. . . .

❧ 16 ❧

S aturday, September 23, 1234
   Athlone, The Kingdom of Connacht, Éireann

AFTER THE TOURNAMENT, CAHIRA WILLINGLY AGREED TO DRESS IN
her women's clothes for the feasting to follow. Philip's wife led her and
Sorcha into a private chamber, then the lady closed the door and
leaned against it with her arms crossed. Cahira did not know the
woman well, but as she looked at her hostess she thought the lady's
face seemed marked by anxiety, her eyes shadowed with doubt.

"Your father must be thinking terrible things of my Philip," the
woman said, her face abruptly crumpling with unhappiness as Cahira
began to change her clothes. "But you must tell him the truth—Philip
has not promised this Richard anything but friendship. He has always
made it clear that he is loyal to your father, the king."

The corner of Cahira's mouth twisted with exasperation. "I know
my father values your husband," she said, twisting the fabric of her
gown until it fell smoothly over her hips, "because he would consider
Philip his friend whether he was king or not."

A blush ran like a shadow over the woman's cheeks. "Of course. I didn't mean to imply otherwise. It's just that people have to wonder what Philip intend by allowing the Normans to camp here at Athlone."

"My father knows it would be hard to refuse Richard." Cahira sat on a low stool and dutifully lifted her chin so Sorcha could wrap the face-framing wimple around her head. "Fear not, dear lady. My father understands how difficult your situation is."

A smile trembled over the woman's lips. "'Tis a relief to be hearing it, Cahira. You will never know—" She flushed again. "Your example today inspired us all, even the men. 'Tis a good thing Richard says he has come in peace. For a moment, when our folk were cheering on the field, I thought we might almost be able to take the Normans if they should come against us."

Cahira helped Sorcha position the veil that draped over her hat and wimple. "I didn't do much." She turned slightly and caught her hostess's eye. "You'd have done the same thing if the idea had occurred to you. So don't be faulting yourself for a lack of boldness."

The lady nodded slightly, then sniffled as Cahira stood and smoothed the wrinkles out of her skirt. When she was certain every garment was in its proper place, she followed her hostess back out to the great hall. The feasting had already begun, but a group of Gaels immediately cleared a space for her at their table. She slid happily onto the rough-hewn bench, nodding and smiling as the jubilant warriors passed food and drink her way.

As she nibbled from the serving bowls and made small talk with a circle of Gaelic admirers, she couldn't help but notice that the Normans kept to themselves, occupying tables in the far corner of Philip's hall. Richard de Burgo sat at a goodly sized table at the head of the room, with only one woman to share it. For a moment Cahira stared at the unusual pair, confused, then realized that the elegantly dressed porcelain creature who sat with him had to be his wife. She wore an exquisite gown of shimmering scarlet silk, with laced-in sleeves of bright amethyst. A high, wide hat with a veil, barbette, and wimple completely covered the lady's hair, revealing only a pale face with bony cheekbones, like tent poles under canvas. Her lips, uncurving gray lines, seemed never to have known a smile.

The man sitting next to Cahira followed her gaze and laughed. "Aye, and if that's what they call a lovely lass in England, I'll be glad to stay home in Éireann." He leaned closer and gave Cahira a sly wink. "Be a good lass, will you, and help the lady out into the light? A few rays o' sunshine would do her a world of good."

Cahira rolled her eyes and reached for a bit of bread, then chewed slowly as she continued to scan the hall for interesting faces. She finally spied Sir Colton sitting beside Oswald at a far table. Though Colton seemed to be in good spirits, Oswald sat slumped forward, his head resting on his hands, his face drawn and morose.

Cahira shivered when she felt the pressure of Colton's dark eyes upon her. He smiled when she met his glance, but she looked quickly away, confused by the tingling in the pit of her stomach. The Normans were dangerous, everyone said so, and yet she saw no peril in Colton's eyes—only interest and an almost eager affection.

What did it mean?

Music and merriment followed the feasting as the festivities moved outside to the courtyard. Philip's skilled musicians—players of the fiddle, flute, and harp—gathered outside the hall. The music began with the steady beating of the *bodhrán*, and honest laughter spilled upon the late afternoon air as the Normans attempted the tricky patterns of Gaelic dances. But though the Normans seemed clumsy in their armor and heavy boots, all of them had great stamina. Though they were awkward dancers, they did not tire easily, nor did they give up.

Cahira danced with everyone who asked her to join the circle, and she was not surprised when she turned, hands on her hips, and found Colton shuffling in the line in front of her. His eyes gleamed black and dangerous in the sunlight, and he seemed not to care that his feet hopped and kicked in a completely different rhythm than everyone else's. She threw him a deliberately flirtatious smile, then laughed, and followed the advancing line of women, grateful that the exuberant dance would account for the blush that seared her cheek.

When a brilliant sunset blazoned the western sky, cloaking the hills and hedges of Athlone in a dreamy haze, Murchadh and Sorcha brought the horses up from the pasture. Cahira looked around the courtyard, half-hoping she would have another chance to speak to Colton, but he was nowhere to be seen. Reluctantly, she placed her foot in Murchadh's hand and let him hoist her onto the horse's back.

You are a fierce fool. She turned her horse toward the road to Rathcroghan and gathered the reins in her right hand. Why did she suddenly feel such melancholy? She had accomplished all she set out to do: She had uplifted Gaelic honor and pride before a pack of overconfident Normans. Why, then, did her heart feel strangely bereft?

"We'd best hurry," Murchadh said, swinging his thick leg over his gelding's back. "I wouldn't want your father to be worrying about us out in the dark. Though 'tis unlikely that Richard would attempt to delay us, surrounded by friends as we are, I do not trust the sly scoundrel."

"Father won't worry about us." Cahira uttered the words while she glanced over her shoulder. Was there anyone in the hall or the courtyard who *might* worry about her? Anyone who even cared?

Why should there be? Colton might have liked her—she thought she had seen at least some small trace of favor in his eyes—but perhaps his comrades had spent the afternoon chiding him for his part in setting up their humiliation. Oswald certainly despised her. Colton might soon learn to dislike her, too, out of loyalty for his friend.

She swallowed hard and pulled her cloak more tightly around her shoulders, for the wind had turned fresh and cold. Behind her, Murchadh's mount snorted and leapt to the head of the little pack, so she gave her horse a little ripple of the reins and urged him to follow. The animal obeyed instantly and lifted his feet in a steady trot, a bone-jarring pace that just might shake some sense into her by the time they reached Rathcroghan.

Darkness rose like an underwater spring, filling first the hollows, then flooding the hills, rising up tree trunks and hedges as darkness engulfed the ground. Murchadh and Sorcha rode side by side in front of Cahira, seeming to sense that she wanted to be alone with her thoughts. Their velvet tones filled the cool air, the voices of two people who had grown infinitesimally closer over the space of an afternoon.

Cahira closed her mind to their conversation and gazed wistfully at the purple sky, wishing that someone rode beside *her*.

A wind blew past her with a faint moan, bringing with it the faint but frantic sound of galloping hoofbeats. Cahira turned in the saddle, the muscles of her throat moving in a convulsive swallow as she waited to see what sort of madman had followed them. Without looking, she knew that Murchadh had turned, too, with his dagger in his hand and ready to fly.

Would Richard dare attempt to capture her? Such folly was unthinkable, with her father's best man standing guard and her kinsman's warriors assembled at the rath, but perhaps he was more scheming than she realized.

"Cahira." Murchadh's voice was still and serious; to disobey was unthinkable. "Get behind me, lass."

Fear blew down the back of her neck as she leaned forward and nudged her horse with her heel. The animal had just begun to move when she looked over her shoulder and saw the solitary rider—a man in mail armor and a blue and white surcoat. The knight reigned in his horse and slowed to a walk, then lifted his hand in greeting. "Hallo! I seek Cahira of the O'Connors."

Cahira felt her heart pound when she recognized the voice, but Murchadh was not disposed to look kindly upon any late-approaching intruder.

"Why, Sir Knight, do you hail us?" Murchadh's tone suited the twilight; he spoke in a dark, liquid voice brimming with restrained power.

"Pardon me, *s'il vous plaît*." The knight removed his helmet and held it close to his chest. "But I only wished to speak with the lady."

"The lady is a king's daughter." Murchadh showed his teeth in an expression that was not a smile. "She cannot be approached so casually."

"I will hear him." Cahira turned her horse to face the knight, then took a deep breath. No matter what his reason for this unusual encounter, the answer to her next question would either warm or break her heart. She might as well ask and hear the truth straightaway.

She looked directly at him, and felt pleased when he didn't pull his eyes away in a grimace of embarrassment. "What brings you away from Athlone, Sir Colton?"

The knight leaned forward in his saddle and softened his smile. "Only the pleasure of your company, my lady. I knew you had an able escort, of course—" he nodded in Murchadh's direction—"but such a rare treasure should not be entrusted to one man alone. If it please you, I would like to offer my company until you reach your home. Then I shall return to Athlone."

Cahira thought she might burst from a sudden swell of happiness. He wanted to be with her! After all she had done on this day, still he fancied her.

A flurry of soft curses and warnings poisoned the air in Murchadh's vicinity, but Cahira ignored his strangled noises and smiled at her bodyguard. "Murchadh, this knight will ride beside me until we reach Rathcroghan. You and Sorcha shall lead, and we will follow."

"'Tis most irregular," Murchadh growled.

Cahira gave him a glare fit to sear his eyebrows. "'Tis what I desire."

Murchadh lifted his gaze to heaven as if appealing to a higher authority, then turned his horse and snorted in contempt. Sorcha gave Cahira a clear warning look, then urged her mount to follow Murchadh. Thankfully, Cahira noticed, Murchadh and Sorcha set a walking pace. Murchadh might have been in a hurry to return home, but he knew it was hard to talk to a companion while the beasts were trotting, and well nigh impossible at a canter. And it was most important that she talk to this knight.

"Aren't you doing your horse a great disservice?" she asked when he pulled his huge mount alongside her smaller gelding. She glanced pointedly at his animal's lathered chest. "If you would remove that heavy seat from his back and leave off that clanking tunic you knights seem so fond of—"

"This heavy seat enables me to remain on his back while I am jousting," Colton interrupted, with no trace of irritation in his voice.

"And this clanking tunic, as you call it, has saved me from many a glancing blow."

"Truly?" Cahira gave him a look of disbelief. "It hardly seems substantial enough to withstand a battleax."

His eyes lit with mischief. "I've not been tested with an ax, and I've no great desire to be. And 'tis certainly not impenetrable. I've seen a spear pierce a suit of mail like a knife through butter, and a direct hit with an arrow can part the links." He glanced down at the mail sleeve covering his arm, then grinned at her. "But it sheds glancing blows as easily as a duck sheds the rain. I'm surprised you don't have such a suit in your own wardrobe, Princess Cahira."

Cahira felt herself blushing and looked away, rattled. Though her name sounded lovely on his lips, it did not fit at all with that peculiar English title.

"Please, call me Cahira," she said, finding her tongue. "My father is the king of Connacht, but who knows which of my kinsmen will be king after him? We have a saying: *Is ferr fer a chiniud*—a man is better than his birth. You are whatever you make of yourself."

He smiled at her, his eyes twinkling with gallantry. "'Tis a lovely saying, and far lovelier when you say it. There is much I'd like to learn about the Irish . . . about your people. I have been in this province for only a few weeks, and I am well aware of my ignorance."

"If you would be knowing the Gaels—" Cahira raised her chin— "you might begin by knowing the land itself. Look around you." She lifted her hand, indicating the dusky green hills, the darkening sky, and the verdant hedgerows that bordered the trail. "We have a saying—if you don't like the weather, don't worry, it'll change soon enough. Our people are just as changeable, in their way. They are friendly, like the land; stubborn, like the cliffs; and sweet, like the warm wind. 'Tis not a bad thing to be Irish."

He listened with a smile that lingered on her, more warming than the fading autumn sun. A gleam of interest filled his dark eyes. "I like the people I have met here. And I would like to learn as much as you will share with me, Cahira."

Again, that delightful shiver when he said her name. Cahira stiffened upon her mount's bare back, well aware that Colton's gaze had wandered from her face and slid down to the soles of her shoes. Her cheeks flushed hotly against the cool air. "And who says I will be sharing anything with you?"

He gave her a friendly, confident smile that sent the blood rushing through her veins. "The Almighty himself says a man who follows God will find the desire of his heart."

"And what would your heart be desiring, Sir Knight? Connacht's hills? Her farms?" Cahira's mind burned with the memory of Richard, saucy and bold, offering her father's own servant as an archery target. She couldn't keep a thread of bitterness from her voice. "Or perhaps you're just wanting to help your Lord Richard enslave my father's people. Are you a mindless slave to your master, or will you be thinking for yourself?"

His jaw clenched, his eyes narrowed slightly. "I took an oath of loyalty to Lord Richard, and I intend to keep it. But I am no mindless servant. I obey him because he is an honorable man."

"Honorable?" She shot him a cold look. "Is using an old man for target practice an honorable tradition in—well, wherever you come from?"

"Normandy—and no, 'tis not exactly fair. But if the man was a thief—"

"Old Brian's no thief. A drunk, perhaps, but he has no need to steal. I'm sure the charge was false."

Colton frowned, but said nothing for a long moment. They rode without speaking, letting the silence stretch between them, and finally he spoke again. "Hear me, Cahira. I'm a knight, not a baron. I don't want land, and I wouldn't know what to do with Ireland's hills if the Almighty himself stepped out of heaven and offered them to me. But if God would deign to give me one of Ireland's fair daughters," his voice dropped to a lower, huskier tone, "I would certainly do my best to please her, now and forever."

Caught off guard by the sudden vibrancy of his voice, Cahira stared at the tips of her horse's ears and struggled to frame a reply. Were his words a declaration of wooing or mere flattery? Did he truly fancy her, or did he intend to use her? If she allowed this knight to call on her at Rathcroghan, her father would be forced to reach some sort of peace with Richard de Burgo. All who knew of Colton's courtship would believe that her father had accepted the Normans' presence in the land. But Cahira knew he could not, he *would* not, do so.

And yet, how could she turn this knight away? She had never met a man like him.

"If you would be wondering about how to please a Gaelic lass," she whispered, her voice trembling with tension, "let her know you value her for herself alone, not for who her father is. For many an Irish woman's temper is as bright as her hair, and she'll not be trifled with, no matter how smooth-tongued the suitor."

"Cahira," he whispered. Just that. And he lifted a brow and pulled back on his reins. She followed suit, and together they waited, breathless and silent, until Sorcha and Murchadh had progressed several paces farther down the trail.

"I do beg and pray you will give me leave to call upon you." Colton was looking directly at her now, examining her face with considerable absorption.

Cahira shook her head. "My father distrusts Normans, especially your master. You would not be welcomed at Rathcroghan, no matter what the reason."

"I didn't ask to call upon your father. Give me leave to call upon *you.*" His voice deepened as he studied her with a curious intensity. "Is there some private place we can meet?"

Her thoughts jackrabbited through her mind, scampering in all directions. "Unescorted?"

"Of course not. You bring your maid, and I'll bring my friend. But I must see you again."

"Why?" The word fell from her lips before she could guard the thought, and his lips curled at the question.

"Why? Cahira O'Connor, have you no idea what a treasure you are? I am a man of sense and sensibility, and I know a rare beauty when I see one. Please, lady. Say you'll meet me on the morrow. Name the time and place."

"But your master—"

"Lord Richard has not forbidden us to follow our hearts. Indeed, I cannot help but believe he would welcome an alliance between any of us and the people here. His intentions are honorable. He longs for peace."

Biting her lip, Cahira looked out into the gathering darkness and prayed for a guiding light. Her father wanted peace. And Richard, no matter how misguided he might be about the value of human life, had not said anything to her today about pressuring her father.

"There's a place where the banks of the River Shannon meet with the cattle trail leading to Rathcroghan," she answered quickly, her eyes upon Murchadh's shadowy back. "Meet me there tomorrow, in the first hour after midday. You know the spot—you stopped to water your horse there yesterday."

Surprise blossomed on his face. "*You* were the girl in the water? By heaven, I should have known!"

"Please, I must join the others." She gestured toward Murchadh and Sorcha, who were very nearly out of sight. If she delayed much longer, Murchadh would turn around and ride back to discover why she lingered in the deepening twilight. "Return to your master now and meet me tomorrow, if you will."

"I will be there, Cahira of the O'Connors." Colton lifted his hand in salute, then flashed an irresistibly devastating grin. "Until tomorrow."

Cahira nodded, then waited until he turned his horse and turned the animal toward Athlone. "Until then," she whispered, watching him ride out of sight.

❧

CAHIRA WALKED OUTSIDE UNDER A THICK BLACK SKY WHILE Murchadh went in and reported the day's adventures to her father. In a most unflattering display of cowardice, Sorcha fled to the kitchens, preferring to give Mags the good news about Brian's rescue rather than be scorched by reflected heat of Felim O'Connor's wrath.

Cahira shivered within her cloak, then paced slowly before the wide oak doors. She felt like a coward herself, waiting out here instead of standing with Murchadh, but he had insisted that he tell the story. "Me father was a *filid,* a natural storyteller," he told her as they stabled their horses, "and when I'm done with telling your father, he'll be thinking you're the most brave, most lovely daughter a man could have."

Somehow, he had convinced her. And while Cahira didn't quite believe him, she had to admit the hall seemed quiet within. She'd heard no bellowing, no shouting, thundering, or weeping. But, then again, Murchadh would only tell the heroic parts of the story.

Her teeth had begun to chatter by the time the door opened. Murchadh stood there, his face a study in gold and shadow in the torches' flickering light. "Why, it's the wee imp," he exclaimed, his eyes wide with false surprise. "Why are you hiding out here? Come in at once. Your father is ready for prayers."

Cahira gave Murchadh a grateful smile as she stepped into the hall. "He's not raving mad?"

"He's furious."

She saw the smile hidden in the corner of his mouth, and sighed in relief. "Thank you, Murchadh, for explaining things. Now, if you will only promise not to mention the knight who pursued us on the road—"

Murchadh held up his hand to silence her. "Felim would never admit it, but he's frightfully proud of what you did for old Brian. He's only worried that you'll never find a husband who can outshoot you. And as for that knight—" He scratched at his beard. "Did I see a knight? Faith, my memory slips more with every passing day. If you're wanting to tell your father about such things, you'll have to do it yourself."

Cahira pressed her fingers to her lips, quelling the sudden urge to laugh. Murchadh slipped his arm around her shoulder and gave her a squeeze, then he slipped out into the darkness, leaving Cahira to face her family alone.

She dropped her cloak on a bench in the entry, then walked to the small chapel off the great hall. Her father stood before the altar, an open prayer book in his hand. Her mother knelt on a cushion, her eyes already closed in prayer. Without a word, Cahira knelt by the railing and allowed herself to fall under the spell of her father's voice as he recited the canticle. His melodic voice usually echoed with humility as he approached the throne of Grace, but Cahira couldn't help but notice that a hint of boastfulness lined his voice tonight.

"The Lord is my light, my salvation," her father prayed, his hands lifting with the eloquence of his words. "Whom shall I fear?"

He's thinking of Murchadh's story. He believes I humiliated the Normans. But my wee contest may not quench Richard de Burgo's greed.

"The Lord is the refuge of my life; of whom shall I be afraid?"

Father God, what does he think I have done? I only wanted to make a point. I did not want to keep our people forever at odds. Connacht needs peace, and we must find some way to establish peace with Richard. Until we do, I will never be able to acknowledge my feelings for Sir Colton.

"I believe I shall see the goodness of the Lord in the land of the living. O wait for the Lord!"

Cahira and her mother joined in the refrain: "Have courage and wait, I say, for the Lord."

Turning from the wooden cross over the altar, Felim rested his right hand upon Cahira's head, his left hand upon her mother's. "See that ye be at peace among yourselves, my children, and love one another. Follow the example of good men of old, and God will comfort you and help you, both in this world and in the world which is to come."

"Amen."

With prayers thus concluded, Felim O'Connor folded his hands, cast his wife a meaningful glance, then nodded at Cahira before leaving the chamber. Cahira sank to the cushion where she had been kneeling. Her mother had obviously been charged to dispense either a rebuke or a compliment, and there was nothing to do but wait for it.

Cahira watched, mystified, as her mother continued kneeling at the prayer rail for another moment, then she lifted her chin and cast a weary smile toward the cross. "Come Cahira," she said, standing. As she gracefully made her way to the hall and a chair near the fireplace, Cahira felt herself being drawn toward her mother's kind smile in the same way moths are drawn to flame on a summer night.

After seating herself, Cahira's mother plucked a bit of lacework from a basket and began to work her needle, quietly humming under her breath.

Will she not speak?

Cahira dropped in a most ungraceful heap at her mother's knee and stared at her open hands. "If I have done anything to displease you, please forgive me." She dared not lift her gaze to her mother's face. The sight of a single tear upon that pale cheek would be enough to break her heart, and a glint of disapproval in those gentle eyes would snap her spirit like a dried twig.

"You could never displease me, Cahira." Her mother's voice echoed with love. "And though I would not have approved your actions had I known of them beforehand, 'tis not my right to say what you ought to do. You are a woman grown, and as a woman, you will answer to your father or your husband. In this case, your father takes pride in your courage and your skill. Most important, you saved Brian's life. Any man in the house—or woman, too—would be proud to claim that honor."

Cahira relaxed, resting her temple against the arm of her mother's chair as a warm glow flowed through her. The sight of a woman on the contest field might have affronted the Normans, but the Gaels were not offended. 'Twas not so long ago that Gaelic women had gone into battle beside their men, babies hanging from one shoulder and thirty-foot long battle pikes resting upon the other. They had fought, wounded, killed, and died upon the green fields and in the woods, beside their husbands, brothers, and fathers. They were not weak, nor were they cowards.

Let the Normans prefer their pale women in extravagant clothes and castles. She was descended from the warrior Gaels and proud of it, unless—

Cahira bit her lip as a terrifying thought struck her. Did the Normans really prefer delicate, porcelain women? Lord Richard apparently did, and probably Oswald and the rest of them. But the light of genuine interest had flickered in Colton's eyes. Hadn't he followed her from Athlone and begged to meet her again? Would he have done so if he liked helpless, simpering women?

"Mother," Cahira lifted her gaze to her mother's smooth face, "how will I know when a man begins to love me?"

Her mother's eyes tenderly melted into Cahira's. "How will you know?" Slowly, she lowered her lacework into her lap, and her eyes took on a dreamy expression. "First comes liking—you can't have anything without that. Then you begin to fancy one another more than any other man or maid. And then, after marriage and the sacred vows, love moves into your heart and binds you together as one soul." The silence of the chamber flowed back into the space their conversation had made, until the room was as still as if neither of them had ever spoken.

Shifting in the silence, Cahira rested her back against her mother's chair. She certainly *liked* Colton far better than any of the other Normans, and he must like her as well, for there had been no sign of revulsion in his eyes even when she announced her true name and gender. He had been surprised, certainly, but not offended.

And she fancied him—oh yes she did. His appearance pleased her tremendously, far better than any man in all of Connacht, and she could find nothing objectionable in his manners, his speech, or his character. He seemed gentle, compassionate, and courageous, and he had dared leave his master long enough to ride after her today . . . so perhaps he fancied her as well. Would he have come if he did not?

Her mother's soft voice spun into Cahira's tumbling thoughts. "Did you see your kinsman Rian today? Your father thought he might have chosen to go to Athlone."

"Rian?" Cahira frowned, unable to recall. Her kinsman may have been at the tournament, but she had paid little attention to the Irishmen. She had spent the greater part of the afternoon searching the crowd for glimpses of a tall, dark-haired Norman with sparkling eyes.

"Rian is a good man, Cahira."

Cahira nodded absently. "Of course he is."

"You know your father has decided to promote him as his successor. He has begun to speak to the other chiefs about Rian's strength and abilities."

Cahira resisted the urge to shrug. This was no surprise; everyone in the *tuath* assumed that Rian would one day take her father's place as king of Connacht. Her father was young, with many years left to rule, and Rian would be mature and capable when his turn came. None of the other chieftains seemed inclined to challenge his position.

"Rian will make a fine king," she said softly, hugging her knees to her chest. She rested her head on her crossed arms and sighed deeply. Colton would make a fine king, too, but a Norman would never be entitled to rule an Irish kingdom. The chieftains decided such things, and the man best fitted to rule over the ancestral line had to be accepted and inaugurated by the members of his own clan. No stranger could ever hope to govern an Irish province.

"Cahira," her mother's voice floated down, "you should not be afraid to follow your heart. It is easy to love a good and godly man."

"In truth, I know you are right." Cahira breathed the words in a heavy sigh as she stood to prepare for bed. "I never realized how easy until today."

⊗⅗⊗

SNUGLY WRAPPED IN A WARM WOOLEN BLANKET, CAHIRA TWISTED in the wooden chair and studied the star-thick darkness beyond her window. The noises of the house faded as she focused her attention on the trail outside and sharpened her thoughts toward Athlone.

Somewhere beyond that field, behind those trees and over the trail, Colton lay wrapped in his cloak beneath the same sky. She held her breath, straining to hear some sound on the wind that might have blown past Athlone, but the dense silence was like the hush after a storm when the leaves hang limp and nature seems to catch her breath.

A whisper of wind lifted the hair over her ears, and she brought her hand to her cheek. Perhaps the same wind that touched her face had just caressed his! She smiled at the fanciful notion. Sorcha would roll her eyes at such drivel, but Sorcha had never felt like this . . . nor had she felt the power in Colton's eyes when he smiled.

Cahira shivered and pulled the blanket more closely around her. The night was cool and clear, but the gusting wind hooted over the outbuildings and fluttered the garments the laundress had hung on a rope outside the kitchen.

What sights were meeting Colton's eyes at this moment? What thoughts filled his head? Was he thinking of her?

"Cahira! Where are you?"

Sorcha's frenzied whisper shattered the stillness of the dark chamber, and Cahira closed her eyes in resignation. She had hoped to pass an hour in rare solitude, but if she didn't answer, Sorcha would light a torch and wake the others.

Cahira reached out from behind the covering tapestry and waved her hand toward the dancing light of Sorcha's candle. "I'm here, by the window."

The candle lifted, lighting Sorcha's worried face. "Come away from the window, lass, or you'll catch your death of the cold. And then what would your mother say?"

"She wouldn't say anything." Sighing, Cahira slipped from the chair and let the blanket fall like a mantle to the floor, then she shuffled toward the bed she shared with her maid. Compared to the bright, clear coolness of her curtained window seat, the chamber felt uncomfortably warm and stuffy.

"Come to bed, lass, and that's the end of it. What, can't you sleep?"

"Not really." Cahira obediently crawled onto the large bed in the corner of the room, then scooted to the far side. Sorcha blew out the candle, then settled in with a loud sigh, pulling the blankets to her chin and tucking her arms neatly out of sight. Across the room, in two other beds, six of the other female servants tossed, turned, and snored in various stages of exhaustion and sleep.

How could Sorcha lie down to sleep so calmly? Cahira rose on one elbow and propped herself up, staring at the dark spot where Sorcha's face should be. For some time the maid had fancied Murchadh, so perhaps she *had* experienced feelings like these. Though it was hard to envision Sorcha sighing for Murchadh's rough touch, stranger things had been known to happen.

Cahira reached through the darkness and poked the mound of blankets. "How can you sleep?"

Sorcha drew a ragged breath. "What? Is something amiss?"

Cahira leaned forward, her voice controlled and tight. "How can you just lay there after the day we've had? Are you dreaming of him, then? Or are you making fanciful thoughts inside your head?"

Cahira heard the creak of straw as Sorcha twisted on the mattress. "Cahira, go to sleep. 'Tis not the time to be playing games."

"I'm not playing games. I want to know if you're thinking of *him*."

"And who would *him* be?" Annoyance struggled with embarrassment in Sorcha's voice as she snapped at Cahira in the gloom. "Just who would I be thinking of at this hour?"

Cahira lowered herself back to her pillow and eased into a smile. "You're thinking of Murchadh. Just like I'm thinking of Colton."

"*Och,* you little eejit, mind what you're saying!" In a fit of embarrassment, Sorcha flung the blankets up over her head, retreating to that private place where the girls had whispered and giggled in confidence for years. Cahira immediately followed, then listened in the warm darkness for the steady sound of Sorcha's breathing. Though maturity had taught her that things whispered under the blanket were easily overheard, the dark cavern of the bedcovers seemed a place of magic and secrets.

"Did you note the knight, then?" Cahira whispered. "Isn't he terrible handsome?"

"He's a Norman, and not one you should be thinkin' about."

"But you have to admit he's gallant. He didn't have to take old Brian's place at the post, but he did."

"You suggested the idea first. Until that moment, he was quite willing to shoot at Brian's fool head."

"But he saw reason, so he's not thick-headed like so many of the others." Cahira brought her knees to her chest, curling into a ball. "And he *is* devilish handsome. His hair is as black as Mag's cat, and his eyes as dark as the night."

"And you, lass, are as foolish as a lass who judges a horse by its harness. Can you be forgetting how your father feels about the Normans? He bears them no love."

"He bears them no hate, either. And if indifference can turn to love—"

"He does not trust them, nor will he trust one with black cat hair and night-colored eyes. Though I'll admit the knight is right fair and noble-looking," Sorcha sighed, her voice resigned, "your father has Rian in mind for you, and everyone knows it. Your kinsman is a good man, full of life and humor."

Cahira laughed to cover her annoyance. "I like Rian well enough, but mother says I should fancy the man I will marry. I can't say that I'll ever fancy Rian. I'm right fond of him, sure, and he's a lovely gentleman, but he is not Colton." She hesitated, unable to clothe her thoughts in words. How could she explain the feeling that leapt into her heart whenever Colton so much as glanced her way? Her spirits had ebbed as they rode from Athlone, yet when Colton came thundering into view, her heart had well nigh burst with happiness. And the feeling was mutual and reciprocated, she knew that well. Even after all the unwomanly things she had done, he still fancied her and wanted to see her again.

And on the morrow he would come. She would meet him by the river and hear his proposition. By this time tomorrow night she would know if he meant her heart good or ill.

"Sorcha," Cahira lowered her voice to the barest whisper, "tomorrow I must take you into my confidence and keep you there until this thing be resolved. Do you agree to take my part in this, or shall you run to betray my secret? Even Murchadh must not know."

For a long moment there was no answer, then Cahira heard the rush of Sorcha's resigned sigh. "I will keep your secret," she answered, "but have you considered the risk? Your father will be furious."

"He is not angry with me. He is proud."

"Only because he thinks you made the Normans look like eejits. And what of Richard de Burgo? If he learns one of his knights is courting a daughter of Felim O'Connor, will he not try to take a hand in it?"

Cahira frowned at the hint of censure in Sorcha's tone. "I do not know. But God will watch over us. If Colton's intentions are noble, all will work for the best."

"So you say," Sorcha answered, her voice heavy with sarcasm. The straw mattress creaked as she thrust her head out of the covers and rolled over. "I will keep your secret, Cahira. But do not make me sorry for doing so."

⊗

"FELIM." ALONE IN THEIR TORCHLIT CHAMBER AT RATHCROGHAN, Una reached out and touched her husband's arm. "Have you noticed that our daughter seems in a strange state of late?"

Felim's left eyebrow rose a fraction as he lowered the book he'd been reading. "Hasn't she been in a strange state since her twelfth year?"

She gave him a sympathetic smile. "A wee bit perhaps, but no more than any other woman." Taking pains to smooth her voice and her facial features, Una dropped her needlework and shifted to face him. "Husband, I believe our daughter has begun to warm to the idea of marriage. She is behaving as if love has befuddled her senses."

"Love?" Felim's smile vanished, wiped away by astonishment. "Our daughter? When has she had time to find love? She's been so busy shearing her hair and out-shooting the Normans—"

"She asked me about love tonight, after prayers." Tilting her head to one side, Una stole a slanted look at her husband. "Trying to be discreet, I mentioned Rian, of course. Cahira led me to believe she has finally begun to fancy her kinsman as a husband."

"'Tis about time." Felim pulled back his shoulders and lifted his granite jaw, then sniffed with satisfaction. "Good. The boy shall have the kingdom and my daughter. All is as it should be."

Una blinked back tears of nostalgia as she recalled memories of the carrot-topped youngster who had terrorized the household. "Murchadh will be lost without her."

"I shall miss the girl." Felim's gaze shifted and thawed slightly when his eyes met his wife's. "Things will be quiet without her."

"She won't be far away." Una reached out again, squeezed his arm, and sighed in contentment when Felim's hand slipped over her own. "Lasses grow into women, and women into mothers. And fathers give them away to other men—"

"Who aren't nearly good enough for them." Felim's voice was gruff, but Una heard a strong note of affection in it. "Well, I've always liked Rian. The lad has many fine qualities. He will be a good husband for our Cahira."

Una said nothing, but turned her hand and laced her fingers with her husband's. They sat still for a long moment, taking pleasure in the simple warmth of togetherness. Finally Felim cleared his throat. "I should send for Lorcan at once. It may be difficult to find him."

"It is only right that he be here," Una agreed, squeezing his hand. "A brehon should certainly be present at a future king's wedding."

❧ 17 ❧

The next morning Cahira rose and dressed under the hot light of Sorcha's disapproving eyes. From the wardrobe trunk she pulled a simple long-sleeved gown of blue, then slipped into a sleeveless white overgown. The colors, she remembered, were those the knights had worn in honor of their lord. Perhaps today Colton would notice her effort to please him.

When she had finished dressing, she sat at the little stool and picked up a mirror, momentarily startled by the odd reflection that met her gaze. So little of her hair remained it seemed pointless to even attempt to dress it, but Sorcha insisted on brushing the ruddy tresses until they shone and fell smoothly to Cahira's shoulders. The maid also produced a pair of scissors and evened up the untidy ends, then disguised the absence of hair with a wimple, hat, and veil—far more headgear than Cahira usually wore at home. When Sorcha placed the mirror in Cahira's hand again, she had to admit the result was pleasing. Different, definitely, but far from repulsive.

When all matters of toilette had been completed, Cahira and Sorcha slipped down to the hall where her father and his men were breakfasting. Rian sat at her father's right hand, as usual, and as Cahira entered he lifted his head and gave her a warm smile. "How lovely you look today, Cahira," he said, the warmth of his smile echoing in his voice. "That hat suits you. I have never seen you wear that one before."

From lowered lids, Cahira shot a commanding look at him. "I doubt you've ever seen me wear *any* hats, Rian, but I thank you for noticing." Cahira sat down at her father's left side and motioned for Sorcha to take the seat next to her. Frowning, Sorcha shook her head, and when Cahira looked up, she understood why the girl had balked. Murchadh, tall and towering, stood opposite the king, his face a study in fierce displeasure.

"My king," he bowed his head slightly in Felim's direction, "the horses are saddled, and all is ready."

"Very well."

Cahira glanced up in surprise as her father and the rest of his men stood. "Going out so soon, Father? Is something amiss?"

"Nothing that can't be handled." Her father bent for a moment to kiss her cheek, then he straightened and gestured toward her kinsman. "Rian will remain here to look after you and your mother. Murchadh and I are out to do a little hunting."

Frowning, Cahira turned her attention back to her bowl. Her father did not lie well. If he truly intended to hunt, the hunting party would include nearly every man in the castle, including Rian. If he intended to hold a meeting with the other chieftains of Connacht, Rian would attend as well. So where was he going?

She glanced toward her mother for some clue, but Una kept her head down as if she found her porridge utterly fascinating. The king and his men stalked out of the hall with a great clattering and gathering of weapons, then the wooden door closed with a sound like thunder.

Cahira saw her mother flinch at the sound. She lifted her gaze from her bowl, stared at the door for a moment, then turned to Cahira and forced a smile. "Rian will say prayers with you today," she said, standing. "I will make my morning prayers in solitude. I feel the need for a special time of . . . supplication."

Cahira lifted a brow in Sorcha's direction, but her maid only sank to the bench and propped her head on her hand, blocking Cahira's view.

Was this a conspiracy? Cahira dropped her spoon and pressed her hands together, glancing around the nearly empty table. Her father's men had all vanished; only Rian and a handful of serving women remained. Her father was not likely to purposely exclude Rian from any venture, so the fact that he had been left alone with Cahira must signify—

She stiffened, abashed, when the truth hit her. This was matchmaking, pure and simple. Hadn't Sorcha plainly said that her father had Rian in mind for her? Apparently her parents had decided that nineteen was a ripe age for marriage, and today a propitious day for proposing.

She pressed her hand to her forehead as her thoughts flitted back to the previous evening. "Rian is a good man," her mother had whispered, and Cahira naturally agreed. Her agreement, apparently, was tantamount to assent.

Sure, and hadn't she gotten herself into a fine mess? Cahira rubbed her temple and took a wincing little breath. She had no desire to hurt her parents or her dear kinsman, but she could not marry Rian, not as long as a man named Colton lived. She would just have to explain the situation to her parents. Sorcha and Murchadh had met the knight, and they would understand, even if they would not approve.

A knot formed in her stomach at the thought of Murchadh. Even now he rode with her father, and at this very moment her father might be asking for more details about the tournament at Athlone. Would he speak of Colton? Would he reveal her secret?

"Rian, I will meet you in the chapel when you are finished breaking your fast," Cahira whispered, her voice sounding weak and tremulous in her own ears. "I will engage in private prayer until you are able to join me."

"But I am ready now, Cahira." Rian nearly toppled the bench in his eagerness to stand. "I lingered at the table only to keep company with you."

"Then let us begin our prayers." Cahira stood and moved away from the table, then fairly sprinted into the chapel. She collapsed on the kneeling bench before Rian even entered the room, but her apparent panic did not dissuade him from joining her. He knelt at her side only a moment later, the manly scents of peat and horses filling her nostrils as he leaned toward her.

"Is something troubling you, Cahira?" His voice broke in an awkward gurgle, and she realized he was as nervous as she.

Cahira shook her head and gripped the railing. "Nothing that need concern you, friend. I'm just feeling a sudden need for God's grace."

"You call me friend now," Rian's warm, damp hand fell upon hers, "but surely you know I would have you soon call me husband."

Cahira felt as though she had swallowed a large, cold rock that pressed uncomfortably against her breastbone. This painfully sincere man was her kinsman. She would not willingly hurt him for the world, but she would not marry him either. Before yesterday she might have eventually accepted his proposal. But in the bright light of Colton's glory, Rian seemed completely ordinary.

She took a deep breath to quell the leaping pulse beneath her ribs. "We must pray for wisdom, Rian," she finally managed to whisper, "so God would clearly reveal his will to us."

She sighed in relief when Rian lifted his hand and turned toward the prayer book on the altar.

As soon as morning prayer ended, Cahira slapped one hand atop her hat and veil, then sprinted out of the room. Rian would probably think she had lost her wits, but as the morning office dragged on and on, Cahira had convinced herself that Murchadh's overbearing sense of loyalty would overrule his promise to keep silent about Colton's approach last night. The warrior seemed ill at ease this morning, his face more troubled than it should have been if he were only concerned about Rian's ill-fated proposal of marriage. Perhaps his conscience had kept him awake during the night; perhaps even now he had resolved to tell her father about Colton's bold pursuit on the road from Athlone.

"Cahira!" Rian's voice echoed in the hall behind her, but Cahira flew through the doorway and into the courtyard, desperate to know the truth before anyone had a chance to soften or convolute it. Lifting her skirts, she forfeited her hat and veil to the wind, then hurried across the courtyard toward the main gate. A guard from atop the rampart saw her and called out a warning, but Cahira ran on, too desperate to heed his call. Let them chase her. By the time they caught up, she might have learned what she needed to know.

She had no trouble discerning the path her father and Murchadh had taken, for fresh hoofprints led only in one direction from the gate. Her head down, Cahira walked swiftly over the trampled trail, her nerves strung as tight as a fiddle string. Her heart had congealed into a small lump of dread, yet her mind was cold and sharp, focused to an awl's point. If her father would not allow a Norman to court her, she would defy him and marry Colton anyway—unless Colton had no desire to marry. If such were the case, she would enter the convent at Clonmacnoise and devote herself to prayer and good works. But never, *ever* could she marry Rian. With one look in those faded blue eyes this morning, she had known that her red-haired kinsman could never be her husband.

The wind caught the hair at her neck, blowing it forward toward her face. Her fingers absently flew upward to catch her hat, then she remembered that she had lost it somewhere between the door and the gate. All that remained was her wimple, which doubtless looked silly without a hat and veil. She had intended to meet Colton dressed as a proper lady, but the wind and her own impetuosity had ruined all chance of that. In a wave of irritation, she yanked the long wimple free and sacrificed it to the wind, too, her steps growing unsteady as her vision clouded with tears of frustration.

Oh, how unjust, to discover the love of her heart and then learn her parents intended her to wed another! Her parents would not be so cruel as to make her marry a man she did not fancy, but only last night her mother had insisted that love *followed* marriage. *As long as you like Rian*, she would insist, *happiness and love will grow.*

Not with Rian it wouldn't. Cahira knew that as surely as she knew the sun would rise on the morrow. Yesterday she met the man God designed to fit her temperament and taste, and it was no matter that he was a Norman . . .

The sound of voices caught her ear, and she froze on the trail, then ducked behind the hedgerow bordering the road. Behind the closest hedge she saw a blur of movement in the pasture. Normans?

She moved closer and parted the greenery, peering through branches and leaves until she saw a pair of horses snuffling the earth, searching for some overlooked bit of grass. She could not see the men, for the horses blocked her view, but her stomach clenched when she recognized her father's robust voice. At one point the horse turned his head, and she caught a glimpse of her father's flushed face. By heaven, what had Murchadh told him?

Cahira parted the branches of the hedge further, insinuating herself into the bush. One of the horses heard the rustling of the evergreens and lifted his head in curiosity, then whickered softly and went back to his search for greenery.

"'Twas the Normans," she heard her father shout, his voice rolling with thunder and indignation. "Who else would take advantage in this way? When I find the guilty party, I will have his head, no matter who defends him!"

Cahira clung to the branches of the hedge, her heart pounding in her chest. What had Murchadh said to rouse her father to such a state? Colton had done little but *speak* to her, and in all things he had behaved with honor and great civility. He had not taken advantage in any way.

Her father's horse stepped to the side, moving on to a more profitable bit of pasture, and Cahira gasped. Her father and Murchadh were standing in a field of carnage unlike anything Cahira had ever seen. At least ten of their prized longhaired cattle lay dead on the ground, their bloody entrails coloring the faded winter grass with congealed crimson blood. Someone—or something—had descended in the night to wreak this bloody havoc, for the herd and been alive and well when she and Murchadh passed at dusk the night before.

Her father was pointing now at a slaughtered animal whose great head had been split. "Only a Norman and his broadsword would do this," she heard him say. "Look, no one has taken the carcasses; not a single skin has been carried away. This deed was committed for sport. 'Twas born out of sheer evil and recklessness. I shall demand that Lord Richard de Burgo pay for every animal."

"You'll have a time persuading him one of his men did it," Murchadh answered, turning toward the hedge. "He'll blame everyone from a rival tuath to your own people."

Cahira ducked as her father turned as well.

"My own people wouldn't kill the cattle they need to see them through the winter, would they now?" A thunderous scowl darkened her father's brow. "I've tried to hold my tongue and keep my distance from Lord Richard, but this will not be borne!"

Murchadh's square jaw tensed visibly. "Have you considered that someone may be trying to provoke you? Whether this is Richard's doing or not, perhaps 'twould be wise to wait until your temper has cooled."

In a silent fury that spoke louder than words, Felim of the O'Connors turned toward the south, where Richard de Burgo and his knights were camped, then lifted his fist and shook it.

Cahira shrank back in dismay, remembering that Colton would soon be coming from that same direction.

Ꚗꚗ

SHE DID NOT RETURN TO THE RATH, BUT WALKED STEADILY northward, past the gates of Rathcroghan and on toward the river. Her feet felt leaden, her heart completely lifeless. Her father was furious with good reason, for no Gael would kill cattle in such a meaningless way. The idea was inconceivable. Any man who would do such a thing cared nothing for property or the future. And the only men in these parts who fit that description were the Norman knights who fed from Lord Richard's table.

But why would knights do such a thing, and why would they do it *now?* For over six weeks they had been guests in the land, partaking of Philip's hospitality, denied nothing but an audience with her father. Yesterday they had seemed quite content with their sojourn, eagerly joining in the dances and merriment.

That memory brought another in its wake, with a chill that struck deep in the pit of her stomach. They had not *all* seemed eager to join in the dance, nor had they all been merry. Colton's friend Oswald had not danced, nor had he once smiled at her. In fact, she could not recall seeing him at all after dinner. Perhaps he had remained in the hall, sulking over his bowl.

Could he have committed this bloodshed? And could his anger have sprung from her performance at the tournament?

Walking on, she stared at the sun-dappled ground where shifting silvery patterns danced as the wind blew through the trees. Colton's affections might prove to be as changeable as these shadows. She had known him only two days; had spoken with him only thrice. In the hours they had been apart, Oswald might have poisoned his heart, turning his kind thoughts into disdain. He might have even been among the mysterious marauders who slaughtered her father's cattle last night.

Colton might not keep his appointment with her. And if he did not, at least she would know why.

She reached the river before midday, then moved to the bank and looked north and south, half-hoping Colton would have already arrived. But the riverbank stood silent and empty as the muddy, dimpled waters slid by on the way to Athlone and Clonmacnoise and Clonfert.

Disappointed, Cahira moved to a wide, flat rock, then sat and drew her knees to her chest, her skirts spilling around her. Beyond caring about her appearance, she pasted a blank expression on her face and tried to corral her troubled thoughts. Last night she had slept in a soft cocoon of happiness and joy, but the morning's complications had ripped her from that safe and contented place.

Was love itself so fragile and ephemeral? If so, was it a thing worth having? Worth fighting for?

"You may be the biggest fool Connacht has ever seen," she told her reflection, idly running her fingers through the chin-length tresses framing her face. "You sit here, alone and unescorted, waiting upon a man your father counts as his enemy. If his intentions are dishonorable, you will discover it within the hour. But if they are—"

She had no time to finish the thought, for the sound of hoofbeats reached her ear. She raised her head, too tense to call out, but something in her heavy heart lightened when two mounted knights appeared on the trail. The foremost knight spurred his mount when he saw her, then swung himself from the saddle in one easy movement.

"Cahira." Colton smiled when he said her name, and the sight of that smile dispelled her fears. "You came."

"Of course I came." She wrapped her arms around her bent knees as he approached. "Were you thinking I would not?" She studied his face, searching for some flicker of disloyalty or shame, but she saw nothing in his eyes but honor and truth.

"You came alone?" The question came from his companion, Oswald, who remained on his mount. Cahira barely glanced at him, then nodded. "My father was occupied with troubling matters, so I left on my own."

Colton was staring at her as if he hadn't heard a word. "Will you walk with me?" he asked, his eyes brimming with a curious deep longing.

Cahira didn't hesitate. "Yes."

He took her hand, helped her from the rock, and for a few moments they walked along the riverbank without speaking. Cahira was beginning to wonder if he regretted asking her to meet him, but then he stopped and abruptly turned to face her.

"If we were in my country," he said, watching her intently, "I would speak to my lord, who would send a representative to your father to arrange a marriage. If your father was agreeable, we might be wed without spending another hour in each other's company. We would meet again outside the doors of the church and then spend the rest of our lives together."

Though a delightful shiver ran through her, Cahira strove to keep her voice light. "In my country," she countered, "I would speak to my father, who would send a representative to your master. He would ask about many things before a marriage could ever be arranged."

"What sort of things would he want to know?"

Cahira shrugged and allowed her eyes to drift over the silent river, which moved without a ripple in the windless calm. "He'd want to know if you have bad habits. Are you profane? Do you honor God and seek to serve him? Are you kind to orphans and old men?"

"No, yes, and I think so." He turned to survey the river, too, and thrust his hands behind his back. "Anything else, Lady?"

"Of course." Cahira pressed her hands together, delighted for an opportunity to learn more about him. "Have you a family?"

"No. I am an orphan and belong only to Lord Richard."

"No brothers or sisters?"

"None."

"Are you overfond of ale? Are you *underfond* of bathing?"

A deep chuckle rose from his throat, but he quickly cloaked it in a mantle of dignity. "No and no. I am only one step shy of sainthood in this life and assured of it in the next. I am kind to animals, I give alms in the church basket, and I confess my sins every night."

"You're not a very agile dancer." She tossed the accusation at him from beneath half-closed lids. "I saw you stomping about with the other knights. Though you may liberally dispense grace in your words, that elegance does not extend to your feet."

"But you, Lady, have refinement enough to cover my lack."

Cahira felt one corner of her mouth lift in a wry smile. Murchadh would certainly not agree with that assessment, neither would her mother. They had too often seen her mud-spattered, bedraggled, and soaked through with rain and river water.

"I think," her voice softened, "I would be pleased with those answers when I heard them."

"You are not fair." Colton lifted a brow in accusation. "I might send my representative out with a list of questions, too."

Turning to face him, Cahira crossed her arms. "What sort of questions?"

"Do you gossip?" He bent toward her, his eyes bright with merriment. "Do you cook? And most important, Lady, do you snore?"

Cahira's eyes widened. "No, no, and no!"

His grin flashed briefly, dazzling against his tanned skin. "How do you know you don't snore?"

"I know! My maid would have told me!"

"And you don't cook?"

Cahira's indignation cooled as if he had thrown water upon it. The snoring question was a joke; the cooking was another matter. Every woman was supposed to know how to cook and clean and keep a house, but she had never taken the time to learn.

She debated telling a lie, then decided to give him the truth. "I don't cook or clean or keep house very well," she answered in a rush of words. "But I can shoot an arrow and wield a sword and throw a dagger with the best of my father's men. I can trim a hoof and milk a cow and —when no one is looking, vault a fence. And I can dance!"

"My lady," he said, his extraordinary eyes blazing, "your accomplishments far outweigh what I have any right to expect."

The eager affection coming from him confused and warmed her at the same time. She looked away, trying to think of a snappy repartee, but for once in her life words failed her.

"I have never met a woman like you," he said simply, his gaze as soft as a caress. "And I have decided to observe the honorable rites in my land and yours in order to win your hand. If you will have me, Cahira of the O'Connors, I will pledge my heart to your service this very day."

Cahira took a quick breath of utter astonishment. She had expected polite words, perhaps a bit more idle flattery and foolish flirtation, but never had she expected him to come so directly to the point. "Are you saying," she swallowed, "that you would like to marry me?"

"I would wed you this very day if my lord and your father would approve." In a burst of earnestness, he took her hand and pressed her palm to his chest. She caught her breath—even beneath the fabric of his surcoat and mail, she could feel his heart pounding. Indeed, his entire body felt as taut as a bowstring.

What to do? Her emotions were bobbing and spinning like a piece of flotsam caught in the rushing river, and her mind, usually so logical and certain, wavered between extremes. She fancied him—aye, she might even love him, for in the space of hours he had unlocked her heart and soul. But he was a Norman, and such brutal men had not been seen in Éireann since the Norsemen invaded so long ago. Not even the Vikings would kill good cattle for sport.

"We are in my country," she whispered, her voice breaking as she looked up at him, "and my father would never approve of my marriage to a Norman. This morning he found evidence of cruel mischief in our pasture. More than a dozen of our cattle are dead, and he believes Norman swords slaughtered the beasts."

Colton's face went blank with shock. "Has he proof of this?"

"He needs none. No Irishman, particularly one of Connacht, would harm his cattle, for we all profit and suffer according to the fate of the king. My father lends cattle to others of his family; they repay him over time. 'Twould make no sense for any of our people to kill the cattle."

Colton's empty look slowly filled into a bewildered expression of hurt. "You can't believe I had anything to do with it."

The question hung in the air between them, shimmering like the reflection from the river. Cahira searched her heart, then searched Colton's face and found no trace of deception there. "From what I am knowing of you, sir," she answered, hoping that the yearning in his face was not quite so apparent in her own, "you could not do such a thing. But my father does not know you, and at the moment he is not disposed to meet any Normans, be they friend or foe."

His eyes shone moist, and his voice went suddenly husky. "Does this mean you no longer wish to see me?"

Cahira bit her lip. She had come to one of those places, like a fork in the trail, where she must choose to follow her heart or her mind.

Following her mind meant the approval of her parents, a loveless marriage with Rian, the steady suffocation of her heart under the heavy mantle of royal leadership. She had been the unwilling daughter of a king; soon she would be the unwilling wife of another one. If she did what she was expected to do.

But if she followed her heart—Colton would walk with her. Though he was a Norman, and overconfident in his own way, such things could be forgiven in so exceptional a man. The road ahead would be uncertain, possibly hard, but what was life, if not a series of difficult choices? "Be happy while you're living, for you're a long time dead," she murmured.

"What?"

"Something Murchadh once told me." She took a step toward him, compelled by her own eagerness. "I could never wish to be rid of you. My father the king will do as kings must, but I am a free woman. Last night my mother told me to follow my heart. That is what I intend to do."

His hands closed around hers in a warm and comforting grip. "Tell me what you require, Lady, and I shall do it. I cannot disavow my oath of service to my master, but my heart is unfettered and free. I would gladly surrender it to you."

Cahira smiled as a wave of peace and satisfaction washed over her. "Meet me here every day for a week, so I may know your love is constant. If you keep this part of our bargain, and if in seven days we still feel the blessing of God upon this union, then on the seventh day I'll go with you to find a priest, where we shall vow our lives to one another forever." She lifted her gaze and found her mirror in his eyes. "Then you shall possess my hand and heart, Sir Colton, for as long as we both shall live."

The lines of heartsickness and worry immediately lifted from his face. He clasped her hand tighter, then pulled her to him, his kiss sending the pit of her stomach into a wild swirl.

"Fear nothing," he whispered as he held her, trembling, in his arms. "I'll see to everything. If I have to find the guilty butchers and drag them before your father with an apology and bags of gold, I'll do it.

But our people will remain at peace, and we will be married seven days hence."

Cahira closed her eyes and nodded, secure in his arms and in his promise.

⊗⋇⊗

THE DRIED GRASS MADE A CRISP SLICKING SOUND AGAINST THE horses' legs as Colton and Oswald rode back to Athlone. Though Oswald had done nothing but grumble about his empty stomach ever since leaving the river, Colton could not keep a grin from his face. By heaven, the woman was remarkable! Fearing her father's retribution, she had insisted that Colton ride around Rathcroghan rather than return her to her father's gates. "I would rather walk than see you struck down," she had whispered as they parted. "Do what you can to find the men who slaughtered the cattle. When guilt is assigned, my father's anger will be assuaged. He is a fair man, and he cannot deny your suit if you have done him a service."

After one final embrace, Colton mounted and spurred his horse with renewed purpose. Though he hadn't wanted to implicate his own comrades in the crime Cahira described, he knew any one of Lord Richard's knights might have been guilty of the cattle slaughter. His men had grown restless in days past, and the tournament had done little to slake their thirst for activity. Pastoral, verdant Ireland did not have much to offer knights of tempestuous blood, and Lord Richard had warned his men not to trifle with Connacht's womenfolk. . . .

But the wasteful slaughter of another man's meat could not be excused. He himself would find the guilty parties and bring their misdeeds to Richard's attention. Once Lord Richard had paid restitution to the king of Connacht, the breach would be healed—and Colton would be free to call upon the king of the O'Connors.

"I don't understand." Oswald's reproachful words spurred Colton out of his reverie. "There are women a plenty in Philip's settlement, maids just as comely as that firebrand. Why must we ride for an hour to seek out a single red-haired vixen?"

"There are none like her anywhere." Colton smiled in the calm strength of knowledge. "I am not surprised she is a king's daughter. Each time I meet her, I am more surprised by the strength of her will and character. She fears nothing, Oswald! Can you name a single maiden in England or Normandy with such fierce courage?"

Oswald frowned, a shadow of mockery in his expression. "You should think twice, my friend. Doesn't the Holy Book teach us that a man cannot take fire to his bosom without being burned? If ambition is your motive, you'd be far better off courting one of de Burgo's daughters. He is more likely to win control of this land than the O'Connors are likely to keep it. You must look to the future, Colton, and pay no heed to the pretty green eyes fluttering before you."

"I'm not interested in ambition."

Oswald snorted. "You are a fool, then. Marriage should be made for gain, not love. If you love the wench, keep her as your mistress. But give your hand and your worldly goods—which aren't yet considerable, I should remind you—to a woman who will bring a dowry of her own. This Irish wench, princess though she may be, will soon be bereft of all her lands and titles. Lord Richard is only waiting for the right moment to assert his claim."

"My marriage will have nothing to do with Lord Richard's affairs."

"But your lord's affairs are yours as well." Oswald's dark eyes flashed a warning. "He is your sworn master, so you are beholden to him in all things. Have you considered whether he will give his permission for this marriage?"

Colton considered the question. He had always felt secure in Richard's favor. In fact, he was fairly certain his lord valued him above all other knights. And he need not worry about offending Richard by not courting one of his two daughters, for Richard was ambitious and would want his daughters to marry noblemen, not mere knights.

Colton smiled as another thought came to him. His lord might even rejoice in the thought of an unequal marriage of Irish princess and Norman knight. The situation might seem unnatural to him, but its very existence would imply that the daughter of an Irish king deserved no better than marriage to a mere knight.

The idea did not do justice to Cahira or her position, but Richard de Burgo would approve it.

"His lordship will of certain give me his permission to marry Cahira," Colton answered, his voice grim. "He would love to see Felim O'Connor's daughter living in a little house behind his castle."

"Aye? Do you think, then, that your lady's father will give his blessing?" Oswald snapped the question like a whip. "Think, man! What if our lord decides to hold your bride hostage to win her father's capitulation? You say you are not interested in our lord's ambitions, but you'd be a fool to ignore them. Our lord Richard would be overjoyed for you to take this Irish king's daughter, for your love will condemn her people."

Struck by the harsh truth in Oswald's observation, Colton fell silent and remained so for the duration of the journey to Athlone.

❦ 18 ❦

Cahira had always thought time was like a waterfall, flowing constantly, steadily, and easily from an abundant source. After meeting Colton, however, time flowed in fits and spurts. Rare moments spent with Colton left her thirsting for more, while the hours she spent working and worrying at Rathcroghan seemed a flood of emptiness.

True to his word, Colton came to the river every day, always accompanied by Oswald. In order to avoid impropriety, Cahira bade Sorcha accompany her, but first swore the maid to secrecy. While Cahira and Colton walked along the river's edge, the Norman knight and the nervous maid sat silently in a forced and uneasy peace, bound to this conspiracy by duty, friendship, and mutual distrust.

Cahira's heart had nearly pounded its way out of her chest on the second day when Colton shared his uneasy thoughts about their marriage, and only his quick assurance of his commitment to it slowed her racing pulse. "I will marry you no matter what the cost," he vowed, "but I fear this wedding not be easily accomplished. If an English priest marries us at Athlone, your father will be disadvantaged. But if by some miracle we are married at Rathcroghan with your father's permission and blessing, Lord Richard will feel I have conspired with the enemy. He would be well within his rights to order my execution, for I would have violated my oath of allegiance to him."

He spoke with only slight hesitation, and only the tightening of the muscles in his throat betrayed his deep emotion. Cahira listened and understood the full implication of his words, but took comfort in his presence at the river. If he had doubts, he had only to remain at Athlone, and she would know he had counted the cost . . . and found the price too great.

⊗⋇⊚

On the third day, Colton arrived at the river even before Cahira. She saw his and Oswald's horses by the river and urged her own horse to hurry, then pulled up beside her startled knight and flashed him a smile. "Feel like a ride?" she asked, leaning forward on her horse's broad back. "There's a place I'd like to show you."

Though Oswald's smile drooped into hanging jowls of displeasure, Colton caught his horse's reins and mounted without a word of protest. Nudging her gelding's ribs with her soft leather slippers, Cahira led the way northward along the riverbank, pulling her horse to the side of the trail so Colton could ride abreast.

The September sun was high and proud in a cloud-scribbled sky, turning the smooth river the color of tarnished silver. The horses seemed to anticipate the joy of the journey. They danced beside the glassy river, their heads held high and tails whipping through the air.

Colton sent her a congratulatory smile. "May I compliment you, Lady, on your skill with a horse. I don't know many men who could sit a beast without a saddle, yet you ride as if you have been born to it."

"In a way, I have," Cahira answered, grinning at him. "'Tis not our way to encumber a beast with all that nonsense." She jerked her chin toward the wooden saddle on Colton's destrier. "If you would sit on him without that heavy boat, I'm thinking the horse would have a better sense of what you want him to do."

Colton's gaze slid rapidly over her form, taking in the sight of her exposed ankles, then he smiled again, beaming approval. "I know no other way to ride, Lady, but I'd be a fool to suggest that you ride in any other way. So lead on, and take me to this place. Is it far?"

"A good distance," Cahira answered, glancing back just long enough to see that Oswald and Sorcha still followed behind them. Both rode with absent, distracted expressions, as if mentally fleeing to another place and time. Cahira closed her eyes, wishing that Sorcha would make the effort to be a little more pleasant. Though the maid seemed to appreciate Colton's qualities, she cared very little for his comrade.

"Then we shall have time to talk." Colton tugged his mount to the left, bringing him closer to Cahira's side.

"That was my thought."

They rode in silence for a few moments, each content to be with the other. To their left lay the forest filled with gray and blue-green shadows and the quiet murmur of the wind through the trees. To their right lay the river embroidered by tufts of wildflowers and skirted by thick shrubs.

Sighing in perfect happiness, Cahira breathed in the tangy scents of plants, fresh water, and warm mud. She loved this land and wanted desperately for Colton to love it, too. Though she would be willing to follow him anywhere, she could not imagine leaving her home.

"'Tis beautiful here," he said, shifting in the saddle to look toward the low horizon where the land began on the other side of the river. "A truly marvelous island. No wonder Lord Richard loves it so."

"He may love it till the end of time, but loving will not give him the right to claim it." She gripped her reins more tightly. "We have to talk about this, Colton. If we marry, peace will not automatically come to our people. My father will be furious, and your Lord will still covet this land for himself."

"I know." He pulled back on his reins, slowing his horse to a walking pace more suitable for conversation. "I have been thinking, and I feel I should go to your father. I have no reason to fear him; I have done nothing to earn his ire. I am a man of honor, as is he. Let me go to him and ask for your hand."

"No." Cahira shook her head in dismay. "If he were just any father, there would be no problem, but he is a king. And so he will not speak as my father, but as my king. And his answer would be no."

"It is precisely because he *is* a king that I should go." Colton turned in the saddle to face her. "His position requires that I humble myself before him. You are not just any woman; you are a daughter of the king."

"No!" Trying to disguise her annoyance, Cahira pasted on a thin smile. "My father inherited his position after I was born. I was not born into a king's house, nor do I wish to marry in one."

Colton looked at her, his eyes bright with speculation, his smile half sly with understanding. "One would almost think you were ashamed of your position."

"I'm not ashamed." Heat rose from her neckline and flooded her face, giving lie to her words. "I would have to care before I could be ashamed. Truth to tell, I care nothing for this business of being a king —or the daughter of one."

"'Tis a great honor to be the daughter of a king."

"'Tis stuff and nonsense. People expect you to be special, but I am an ordinary woman. I want only to be like everyone else."

"Come now." His words were heavy with rebuke. "You can't expect me to believe that. Would an ordinary woman dress like a man to best Lord Richard's archers? Would an ordinary woman offer herself to stand as a human target? Would an ordinary woman slip away from her father's fortress to go riding with one of the enemy?"

"That's quite enough," she retorted, a heavy dose of sarcasm in her own voice. "All right, so I'm different. But I would be different even if I were the daughter of Felim the *man*, not Felim the king. It's—" she flung out her hand, as if trying to pull the right word out of the air— "it's the *position* I despise. I love my father, but I don't want to be known as a king's daughter. I don't want to be set apart from other people, don't you see? If you're thinking I want to be fussed over, then you're not knowing me at all, Sir Colton."

"I know you well enough." He looked at her with lazy laughter in his eyes. "And I know enough of the world to realize that if you don't have the confidence to live your position publicly, you don't really have a position at all. You see, before I took my test of knighthood, I was a lowly squire. I worked in the garrison and served the other knights. But even as a squire I could tell knights from ordinary men even when they were dressed alike in simple tunics. How? By their attitudes. Sworn knights are confident of their position, for they've earned it and fought for it. Another man might pretend, but he would wilt in a time of trouble."

She threw him a quick frown, then looked away to consider his statement. Why were the Normans so conscious of *position?* In their world everyone had a place on the social ladder, and a man could not be judged until he had learned his place and studied how to keep to it. And what position did she have? None, really. She hadn't fought for anything. Everything had been handed to her.

"This is not Normandy," she answered, lifting her gaze to meet his again. "I haven't had to fight for what you call 'my position.' Perhaps that's why I don't want it."

"Position," Colton went on, his eyes fixed on the horizon as if he hadn't heard her, "is obtained through commitment, and obedience must follow. Obedience, however, requires inconvenient and unpleasant sacrifices. No doubt your father has discovered this, . . . as have you."

She stared at the trail, thinking of her father's haggard face. Since inheriting the mantle of leadership, worry stole his sleep and sapped his strength. He had not worn a smile since Richard came to Connacht.

"Cahira, like it or not, you are a king's daughter. Out of respect for him, I want to ask for your hand. He will respect me if I go—"

"He will kill you!" She stared at him, her heart pounding. "This position you hold in such high regard will require him to sacrifice my happiness!"

"Perhaps not." His voice was low and soothing; apparently he had given his argument a great deal of thought. "I have faith in God and in your father. My love toward you is honorable—"

"Colton, my father does not trust any Norman, especially none affiliated with Richard de Burgo. I have faith in God, too, faith that he will bless us if we follow our hearts. After we are married, time will soften my father's heart. I cannot speak for your master, but I know my people will accept us . . . in time."

He looked at her, his eyes dark and remote, as if he had pulled away to consider her words. He did not leave her comfortless, however, for he reached out and pressed his hand over hers, squeezed it tight, then pulled away and urged his horse forward.

She followed, knowing that he wanted time to think.

THE SLANTING RAYS OF THE SUN HAD STREAKED THE WATER CRIMSON by the time Cahira pointed toward a curving path that cut through the sweeping willows and thick hawthorn that edged the river. Colton pulled back on his reins, allowing Cahira to lead the way to a clearing on the riverbank. She dismounted in a flurry of skirts, then stepped forward and lifted her face to the lowering sun, allowing its rays to gild her skin with radiant beauty.

Colton dismounted as well, then gestured for Oswald and Sorcha to do the same. Before dismounting, Oswald pointed to Colton and lifted a brow. "You will pay for this, my friend. I had not planned on a full day in the saddle."

"Be a man—and be quiet," Colton retorted, waving his friend away.

Leaving Oswald to help the maid, Colton jogged after Cahira, who had wandered down a path along the water's edge. He followed her to the shoreline, then gazed in amazement at the shining surface of the water. The river seemed to end here, for the shoreline curved away toward the east and then southward again, forming a nearly perfect circle. Yet there were no waterfalls, no mountains, no obvious source of such a great river.

He ran his hand through his hair. "Is this the source?"

Cahira nodded. "'Tis *Log na Sionna*, the heart of the river. A sacred place."

Colton stared at the watery landscape, understanding how such a beautiful spot could well be considered holy. A pair of dragonflies hung over the water near the shore, shining like emeralds. In unison, they dipped toward the still water like a pair of lovers curious about their reflection, then rose and vanished into the mist.

"It is beautiful here." He reached out and took Cahira's hand, and something in him melted in relief when she did not pull away. Their disagreement on the trail could not tear them apart. There had to be a way for them to be together, and he would find it.

"There's a log over here where we can sit." Cahira tugged on his hand and beckoned him with a shy smile. "And if you're careful, you won't get a bit wet."

He saw what she meant in the next moment. An ancient tree, as thick as a man's shoulders, had toppled into the water so that it rested half in, half out of the tarn. It was not so much a tree now as a skeleton of one, leafless and scoured stone gray by the wind. But its surface was smooth and inviting.

He went first, stepping into the shallows as he swung one leg over the tree trunk. Straddling the trunk like a horse, he scooted toward the far end, then heard Cahira laughing softly as she lifted her skirts and followed. The skirt of her gown was full, he noticed ruefully, so he'd get no more than another glimpse of ankle as she inched her way toward him.

"Don't be looking at me, and mind where you're going," she scolded, catching his eye as she sidled toward him. "You'll be falling in the lake before you know it, and with all that metal on you're likely to sink like a rock."

"I've been wearing this armor for years," Colton retorted, grinning back at her. "It's like a second skin. Besides, the water's not deep."

"'Tis a bottomless pit."

"Impossible."

"Are you not believing me? I'd not think it possible that you, a knight, could doubt a woman of my *position*—"

He looked back and saw wicked glee dancing in her green eyes. The sight was so irresistible that he reached back, intending to pull her toward him for a kiss. His hand caught nothing but empty air, however, and the sudden change in position threw him dangerously off balance. He grappled for something to cling to, but the tree trunk was as smooth as polished glass. There was nothing to keep him from slipping into empty space.

"Cahira!" No sooner had her name slipped from his lips than he fell, head and shoulders first, into the lake. The cold water slapped at his face, then flooded his heavy mail tunic, pulling him down into darkness.

Staring upward, he saw Cahira's startled eyes through the sun-streaked water, then her image receded and blended into a slivery brightness broken only by the submerged branches of the dark tree. These reached out to him like twisted arms, but all too quickly he slipped past their grasp. A cloud of silvery bubbles shot out of his mail armor and rushed past his face, while his feet, weighted by his heavy boots, carried him ever downward into a black abyss.

He struggled, moving his arms in sluggish movements that sounded muffled in his ears. The bright surface moved away at an increasing speed, the light growing dimmer as the waters around him thickened and pressed upon his ears and chest. In a moment of mindless panic he felt a scream rise at the back of his throat then choked it off, pressing his lips together to imprison his last breath. His chest burned with hot pinpricks from beneath his skin, and his ears pounded and roared. Then something cold pushed at him from the darkness and sent him hurtling back toward the light.

For an instant he thought he had met death. He wondered if the approaching light was a heavenly beacon, then the sound of watery movement filled his throbbing ears. His eyes widened as he rode a cold current upward toward the tree branches, then he bobbed up in the water only inches from the spot where he had fallen in.

Cahira was leaning toward him, one hand extended, her eyes large with concern. "Are you all right?" she asked, grasping his hand as he reached for her. "In faith, I should have warned you."

Colton took a deep, shuddering breath, then hooked his other arm over one of the tree branches. The steady pressure beneath him eased like a sigh of the river's breath, and again he felt the tug of gravity at his boots. But he had a strong grip on the tree, and he wouldn't let go.

With his blood still pounding thickly in his ears, he rested his cheek on the log's smooth surface and turned to Cahira. "Forgive me for not believing you. You did say the water was deep."

"Aye. But I should have added that no one ever drowns in *Log na Sionna*. Even the cattle rise back up to the surface."

"A sacred place," he repeated, panting. She straightened her posture and nodded primly, and Colton noticed that she had been certain enough of his ascent that she hadn't even bothered to call for help. Though Sorcha stood on the shore, wide-eyed and pale, Oswald had remained on the trail with the horses. The lazy lout was probably fast asleep.

Taking another breath, he summoned strength from some place that hadn't been paralyzed by fear and began to pull himself onto the log.

"Now you see," Cahira said, and though her mouth smiled, her eyes did not, "that I would not lie to you, Colton. I know this land, and I know its people. And though I love you for wanting to speak to my father, I know 'twould be foolish. Believe me, love, and take my advice to heart."

Looking up at her through a tumble of his drenched, dripping hair, Colton could only nod his agreement.

❦

ON THE FOURTH DAY CAHIRA BROUGHT HER OWN DIRE NEWS TO their meeting place at the river. "I've just learned that my father sent for Lorcan, the brehon," she explained breathlessly as Colton dismounted. "I'm not certain, for no one has spoken directly to me, but I'm thinking he intends me to marry my kinsman Rian once the brehon arrives. Lorcan must be present to record important events, so I'm thinking 'tis marriage my father has in mind."

Colton blinked in bafflement, then took her arm and drew her away from Oswald and Sorcha. "Did you assent to this marriage? Does a vow exist between you and this Rian?"

"Of course not!" Cahira cried, hurt that Colton could even think such a thing. "But Rian is in line for my father's position, and 'tis only natural that he should marry me in order to confirm his claim. We are friends, so I am fond of him, but I never promised him my love!"

"Then you shall not be required to give it." Colton fell silent for a moment, then his brow wrinkled with an idea. "This brehon—has he the authority to perform a marriage as well as to record it?"

Cahira nodded absently. "Sure. The brehons are the keepers of Irish law. If he adjudicates a matter, the matter will stand."

"Then let him judge us to be truly married. And we will let the matter stand."

Her heart singing with delight, Cahira reached out and touched his surcoat.

"So tell me." Colton's dark eyes held more than a hint of flirtation. "Where might we find this brehon?"

Cahira shook her head. "I don't know, but I think he will be already on his way. My father sent a messenger to find him, and the rider returned last night with news that Lorcan would arrive in two days. He and his student walk from rath to rath."

Colton lifted his chin and called to the other knight. "Oswald! Care to go hunting for a brehon?"

"A what?" The dour knight quirked his eyebrow. "Is it something good to eat?"

"It's a man, very much like a priest." Colton glanced down at Cahira, then slipped his arm about her waist. "'Twill be the man who marries us, if we can find him."

Oswald's lips twisted into a cynical smile. "I've yet to meet a man I couldn't capture. I could bring Lord Richard himself if you want a witness."

"That won't be necessary." Cahira spoke softly, thrilled by the knowledge that her dreams were about to become reality. "Sorcha will be with me, and you will have Oswald. If you can find Lorcan, bring him to the stone lodge at Carnfree. Sorcha and I will meet you there tomorrow."

Colton shot her a twisted smile. "Carnfree?"

"'Tis our ancient place, where the kings of Connacht are crowned." Cahira smiled. "Lorcan will know the way. Find him, tell him what we propose, and meet me there on the morrow. I will be waiting."

"I shall do nothing, then, until I find this brehon," Colton answered, sealing his promise with a quick kiss.

"One more thing." Cahira pulled out of his embrace, then tipped her head back to look him in the eye. "Have you any news of my father's dead cattle? I had hoped to be able to tell him something that might ease his mind about you."

A muscle flicked at his jaw, but he kept a gallant smile on his face. "I'm sorry, Cahira. Oswald and I have asked every man in the garrison, but all plead innocent or ignorant. No one seems to know anything about it."

She dropped her lashes quickly to hide her disappointment. "Sure, and perhaps my father was wrong," she whispered, placing her hands on his chest. "'Tis just as well. Think no more of it. We'll be wanting to dwell on more important things now."

His gaze traveled over her face and searched her eyes. "Until tomorrow."

"Aye. Until then."

◈◈◈

THINKING OF THE DAY TO COME, CAHIRA BARELY SLEPT AT ALL THAT night. At sunrise she rose, washed her face and hair, and donned one of her best gowns. After dressing, she picked up a book and pretended to read until the other maids woke and slipped from the chamber. Then she dropped the book and lightly swatted the only sleeping lump still abed. She had just awakened Sorcha and asked her to pack a bundle with a few personal possessions when her mother strode into the chamber, a pair of village women trailing in her wake.

"I hope you have made no plans today," her mother said, gesturing for one of the women to lower her basket. "I was thinking 'tis time we began to sew your wedding dress. Though I know you hate frills and veils, you will want something special when you marry."

Cahira stared across the chamber, her heart going into sudden shock. For a moment she feared she had talked in her sleep or Sorcha had babbled Cahira's secret through the kitchen, then her mind cleared. These women weren't here to make a dress for *today*—they were preparing a dress for the wedding to come. The wedding to Rian.

She straightened, her eyes meeting Sorcha's horrified gaze. *Say nothing*, she silently warned her maid with a glance, *do nothing unusual*.

"Cahira?" Her mother's voice echoed with concern. "Are you well? You look pale."

"I am fine, Mother." Her voice was low and controlled, but even she could hear the undertone of desolation in it. Somewhere outside, beyond Rathcroghan, Colton and Oswald sat in the early morning sun and waited for Lorcan. Before the day was half gone they would take Lorcan and his student to Carnfree, where the four men would loiter in a stone hut and wait for Cahira . . . while she stood here and prepared for marriage to another man.

She pressed her hands together and tried on a smile that felt a size too small. "Mother, I do not want a special wedding dress. I have so many lovely gowns, I will wear one of those—even this one suits me well."

"Nonsense. Rian has seen you in everything else, and he so rarely sees you properly dressed." Her mother gestured toward the woman with a roll of fabric in her arms. "See this lovely silk from Waterford? The color would be quite nice against your fair skin."

Cahira gritted her teeth and resisted the urge to scream. Her mother did not often impose her ideas, but when she spoke, she expected her voice to be obeyed. And unless Cahira thought of something quickly, she would be held in this chamber for the better part of the afternoon while women draped her with fabric and set about their stitching.

She couldn't do it. She couldn't bear to wait here while the walls closed in upon her, nor could she continue this charade. Her mother was no king; a woman's heart still beat in that slender frame.

"Mother!" Risking everything, Cahira rushed forward and reached for her mother's hands. "Please, I beg you, don't make me do this. I've been wanting to tell you for so long. Truth be told, Mother, I can't marry Rian."

Her mother sank to a stool, her face a mask of disbelief. "Not marry Rian? But I thought—you said—you asked me about love."

Cahira released her mother's hands and sank to the floor. "I know, 'tis true. But I wasn't thinking of Rian when I asked. I was thinking of someone else."

Her mother's face crumpled as the words took hold. Cahira held her breath, but then her mother's expression cleared and she shook her head. "Sure, and you're talking nothing but nonsense. Perhaps you *fancy* someone else, but love, as I've told you, follows marriage. You can't put the cart before the pony, lass, and you can't love a man until after you've married him."

"It's not mere fancy, mother." Cahira glanced back at Sorcha for help, but the maid's face had gone blank with fear.

"It has to be mere fancy, my dear." Her mother's voice trembled slightly as she turned and looked at the two workwomen. "'Twould break my heart to think I had misread you. I was so sure you had begun to fancy Rian. Your father and I would not have chosen him for you if he weren't a fierce good man."

Cahira hid a thick swallow in her throat and lowered herself to the floor in the posture of a penitent. If her mother would not even *consider* the fact that Cahira might love someone else, she certainly would not be pleased to hear Cahira loved a Norman. And while she might be able to stall this marriage with Rian by raising a fuss, 'twould only mean days of storming and ranting and bearing up under her father's fierce temper. . . . When she could be with Colton, and safe in his embrace.

Cahira pushed herself up from the floor, then turned toward the window and studied the slanting rays of the morning sun. The hour was early, time just beginning to flood the day. She would have to keep her chin up and bear this foolishness quietly. Perhaps, if she were attentive and good, the gown could be fitted upon Cahira, then draped over a serving maid for the finer points of alteration.

Feeling like one of the martyrs of the Church, Cahira turned and walked to the center of the room, then lifted one arm as the seamstress unrolled a measure of shining silk.

❧ 19 ❧

From his hiding place behind a large gray rock overlooking the trail to Rathcroghan, Colton tossed another pebble into a standing puddle and stared at the blooming circle of rings. In the past six hours, at least twenty men had passed over the worn and rutted boreen, yet not a single pair of them had fitted the description of the brehon and his student. Cahira had described the elderly brehon as a thin, balding man with an air of dignity and pride. Several elderly men had passed, yet none of them had been precisely thin, and none had been traveling in the company of a younger companion.

"You're wasting your time, you know," Oswald called from the grass beyond. He lay on his back in the sun, his cloak shielding his face from the sun's bright rays. He had slept through most of the afternoon, blissfully slumbering amid the weeds and wildflowers while Colton's heart quickened at the sound of every footfall, then slowed when the men on the trail proved to be insignificant.

Colton glared back over his shoulder. "I'm not wasting my time. This is the road to Rathcroghan, and this is the trail he will take."

"I was speaking of the marriage. 'Twill come to nothing. Her father will have it annulled, for certain. If she returns tonight to her house, her father can rightly say that no marriage took place." Oswald lifted the edge of the cloak and rose up on one elbow, then plucked a sprig of ragwort and paused as if hesitant about saying his next thought. "You haven't thought this through, friend. You'll have to hide for a time, mayhap a full week. Only when you can return her good and married will her father give the wedding any credence."

Colton tossed another pebble, his uneasiness spiced with irritation. Oswald was brazen, but he did have a point. Colton couldn't very well keep Cahira out under the stars all night, but if he returned her to Rathcroghan with the marriage only a few hours old, her father would laugh in Colton's face. But neither could he take her to Athlone, for Richard would doubtless see Colton's Irish bride as little more than a political prisoner.

"Cahira will know what to do," he muttered, half-ashamed he had no answers himself. "Or God will reveal a way for us to be together. What matters is that we vow ourselves to one another before this man of the law. He may have the answer."

"You'd best pray he does." Oswald dropped his head back to the earth and laced his fingers together upon his chest. "Or all of this will have been for naught."

Colton closed his eyes and resisted the tide of guilt that washed up from his bones. Though his duties of late had been few, he felt he had been bereft in them. In an effort to use the tools of diplomacy instead of warfare, Lord Richard had been content to give his knights lax schedules and tasks, but they were supposed to intimidate the popu-lace by openly training in the knightly arts of sword fighting, archery, and horsemanship. Though Colton was as skilled as any man in Richard's service, of late his riding had consisted only of clandestine journeys to and from the River Shannon. He had spent more time honing his skills in the art of love than his swordsmanship, and regarding archery—well, even his intended bride had proven herself his equal in that field.

He tossed another pebble, then the sound of voices sent a thund-erbolt jagging through him. Rising, Colton peered around the edge of the rock and saw two men approaching on the path—one elderly, bald, and stooped, and the other younger and with a full head of auburn hair.

Colton flattened himself against the rock and drew a deep breath, then bent and pitched a pebble so that it landed squarely in the center of Oswald's forehead. Oswald scowled, then tossed off his cloak and sat up, one brow lifted in a silent question.

Colton nodded, held up two fingers, then pointed toward the trail. Without a word, Oswald stood and pulled his sword from its scabbard.

Colton stepped out into the path and planted both feet firmly in the soft earth. The travelers halted, the younger man's face flushing to a crimson shade. The older man merely looked at Colton, his mouth twisting in what looked like bitter amusement.

With his hands at his belt, Colton looked the brehon directly in the eye. "Greetings, sir. Are you Lorcan, the brehon of Connacht?"

The old man gave Colton a bright-eyed glance, full of shrewdness. "Who asks—you or the sword?"

Puzzled, Colton glanced behind him. Oswald stood there, his sword drawn and ready, its blade shimmering in the sun.

Colton gestured for Oswald to put the weapon away. "If you are Lorcan, we have no need of a sword. I have heard that you are a man of good sense, generous spirit, and unexcelled wisdom."

The old man snorted with the half-choked mirth of a man who seldom laughs. "Faith, can this be a Norman spewing such golden words?" He tilted his brow and looked at Colton uncertainly. "Perhaps you should tell me why you have need of a man with wisdom. I was under the impression you Normans were the sole possessors of that quality."

"I need a wise man acquainted with Gaelic law," Colton continued, his words pouring forth in a rush. "Cahira O'Connor asked me to find you. She waits at a place called Carnfree—I am to take you there so you may unite us in the rites of holy marriage."

Colton saw a tiny flicker of shock widen the brehon's eyes. "I know Carnfree, and I know Cahira." He smiled with a distracted, inward look, as though he was listening to some voice only he could hear. He remained in that odd posture for a moment, then his brows flickered as his eyes focused and came to rest upon Colton's face. "It seems the Almighty approves. So I suppose I can get to know *you* as we journey to that ancient place." He turned, then extended his hand in the direction from which he had come. "Shall we go?"

Colton scrubbed his head in confusion. Was it to be this simple? He had feared a protest, he had half-expected he'd have to bodily carry the man to Carnfree. The brehon, however, seemed completely at ease with this unexpected development.

"You would unite the daughter of an Irish king and a Norman?" he asked, his thoughts spinning. "You find no fault in this union?"

"I'm not the one to be answering that question." The brehon dropped his arm and looked at Colton with warm and gentle eyes. "That question is for you and the lass to decide. But I cannot help but believe this union may work for God's greater good."

Colton's mind whirled at the brehon's dry response, then he whistled for his horse and joined Oswald in following the brehon away from Rathcroghan.

⚜

As the afternoon progressed, Cahira almost believed her mother was actually encouraging the seamstresses to work slowly. Though her words and manner were gentle, she criticized every idea, every seam, every stitch. Idle gossip, fairy stories, and soft feminine giggles overflowed the tedious hours until Cahira was ready to drown in a flood of frustration. Not until sunset stretched glowing fingers across the western sky did the women finish their work and quit her chamber.

Biting back a scream of rage, Cahira slipped from the room and hurried through the twilight to the stables. In the golden light of a torch, she found a bridle and expertly slipped it into her favorite gelding's mouth, then pulled the leather straps up and over his ears. When the bridle was in place, she climbed the fence and climbed upon the animal's knife-edged spine, ignoring the idle piping of the stable boy in the next stall. He paid her no attention, probably thinking she had come out to give the horse a treat before bedtime.

"Whist, little one," she warned the horse, ducking as he whickered and made his way out of the stall and through the doorway of the barn. "Quiet now, through the courtyard. No calling to the others, there's a good lad. Be silent, be swift, and get me to Carnfree!"

Unsettled by the unusual routine and the urgency in her voice, the gelding snorted and danced his way through the fortress gate, then responded eagerly to the prodding of her heels. Cahira let him set a pace of his own choosing on the main trail, knowing that freedom would work the restlessness out of him.

While her mount flew over the path in a relaxed canter, Cahira's heart raced ahead, praying that Colton had not given up and departed for Athlone. How she had tried to get away! She pretended to have a headache—a pretense that quickly proved true when it became clear her mother would not let her leave. She complained of weariness, she fidgeted and fretted. Even now she wore the silk wedding gown, a simple creation truly fit for a queen, but one which would never be worn in marriage to Rian of the O'Connors.

A score of questions niggled at her brain. What if Colton had not found the brehon? The old man had not yet appeared at Rathcroghan, which was a good sign, but he could have been detained on the road by any sort of emergency. But what if Colton had found him and the brehon refused to grant Colton's request? Or what if Lorcan's student resisted, and in the scuffle someone had been injured . . . or killed?

Oh, what a risk they were taking! Though she thought Lorcan a fair-minded man, she might have been foolish to think he would condone a marriage between two people of opposite races. He might have been offended by the very idea, and, if so, would certainly tell her father. Perhaps he would speak to Rian, too, who would be so affronted by the thought that Cahira preferred a foreigner's love to his own that he would turn his back even on their friendship.

The dark sky hovered over the horizon, and streamers of night were already falling by the time she caught sight of the elevated mound at Carnfree. The ancient holy place had been used for crowning O'Connor kings since time immemorial, and the ring of beehive-shaped huts, used only during the festive times of coronation, looked like dark burial mounds in the gathering gloom.

Please, God, let him be there.

Tugging on the reins, she turned the gelding up the pebbled trail, then leaned forward in anticipation. A light glowed before one of the huts, and a man walked there—no, two! Four men! He had waited!

When the horse trotted into the circle, she slipped from his back and ran to Colton. A thrill shivered through her senses as he wrapped his arms around her and asked no questions.

She babbled the answers anyway. "My mother detained me! I had to sneak away!"

Colton wore an expression as relieved as her own, but his arms were strong and sure. "I knew you'd come."

"Cahira?" She turned at the sound of Lorcan's voice. The brehon stood beside the small crackling fire, his lined face lifting in a smile. "You truly wish to marry this Norman, and not the man of your father's choosing?"

"I do, Lorcan. I wish it with all my heart."

"You know this will cause strife in your family?"

"We are hoping," Colton answered, "that in time our marriage will bring peace to our people. We need time, sir, to calm hearts and cool passions. Then, perhaps, peace will come."

Lorcan's lined, narrow face showed no more than mild interest, but his eyes were alert in their deep caves of bone. His questioning gaze shifted from Cahira's face to Colton's, then he seemed to reach a decision. "The highest provinces of peace are bought with sacrificial blood, dear ones. Something in me wonders if you have blood enough to pay."

Cahira swallowed against the unfamiliar constriction in her throat and forced a confident note into her voice. "No one will die here today, Lorcan, nor tomorrow. Our people are at peace now—we just want to insure it."

She saw the Adam's apple bob in the brehon's throat as he swallowed. "Then it is time to fulfill what God has ordained."

Suddenly shy, Cahira looked at Colton. He took her hand and followed the brehon, who entered the circle of standing stones and moved toward the stone altar. When he turned and extended his hands, they knelt before him, side by side.

"Do you, Norman knight, promise to love the woman God has given to you? Will you honor her above all others, keep you only unto her, comfort and cherish her for as long as God grants you the gift of life?"

"I will."

Lorcan turned to Cahira. "Do you, Cahira of the O'Connors, promise to love the man God has given to you? Will you obey him, honor him as your lord and husband, and keep only unto him for as long as God grants you the gift of life?"

"I will."

"Do you bring a gift, sir, to seal this vow?"

Cahira turned in surprise as Colton fumbled with the leather bag hanging from a strap around his waist. After a moment, he pulled out a wide silver band that shone in the moonlight. She gasped in delight as he turned the ring and allowed her to read the inscription. "*Gaol, Dilseachd, Cairdeas*," she read, then looked up at him. "Gaelic for love, loyalty, friendship."

"I asked one of Philip's servants for the words," he confessed, a flush of pleasure rising to his cheeks as he slipped the ring onto her finger. "Because I pray our love will lead to loyalty between our houses and friendship between our people."

With a sigh louder than the rising wind, Lorcan clapped. "Then I hereby ordain what God decreed before the earth was born. Go you into the world, my children, and live according to God's holy laws. Be you kind to one another, honest in your dealings, true in your expectations, and faithful in your friendship. And may love grow between you from this day forward, until we meet him who is the Author of love."

The brehon stepped forward and pressed the flat of his thumb against Cahira's forehead. She closed her eyes while he made the sign of the cross, then looked up to see him make the same sign above Colton's brow.

This done, Lorcan stepped back and clasped his hands again. "It is done; you are one." He glanced at his student. "Peadar and I should now be on our way to Rathcroghan."

Sudden fear seized Cahira's heart. "You won't—tell my father?"

"I shall have to tell him something," Lorcan answered, drawing his cloak closer about his lined throat. "I shall certainly tell him I married you. But I don't think I shall tell him where you are."

The old man's eyes moved into Colton's. "What you do now is important, lad. Felim O'Connor is a man of great personal restraint, but no one has ever taken his daughter before. I'm thinking he will want Cahira returned, and no number of counselors will be able to reason with him."

Colton's hand flew automatically to his sword, but the brehon shook his head. "You must not even think of violence. Felim will *want* his daughter, but he will not know where to find her. If I were in your situation, I would send my companion back to Athlone and charge him to say nothing for the space of three days. By the time Richard learns one of his men has married Felim's daughter, I will have had time to help Felim see reason. Both our peoples can find a way to dwell peaceably in this province."

A faint light twinkled in the depths of his dark eyes. "You can remain here tonight—the huts are dry and warm. But on the morrow, move across the river and into the province of Meath, away from your Lord Richard *and* Cahira's father. I will arrive at Rathcroghan tomorrow and will not divulge your whereabouts until Felim is able to see the wisdom in uniting two powerful peoples . . . and two young lovers. Perhaps then he will be willing to parlay with Richard and put an end to this impasse." His eyes glinted with merriment as he looked at Cahira. "Don't you be worrying about your father, lass. I'll tell him I've talked to your knight and found him a good man."

Cahira shyly wrapped her hands around Colton's arm and pressed her cheek to his shoulder. "Thank you, Lorcan. I trust you."

The brehon turned to Oswald, who watched with Lorcan's student from the periphery of the stone circle. "I think perhaps you should return to Athlone, Sir Knight. Do you think you could cover your comrade's absence for a few days?"

Oswald's mouth twitched with wry amusement. "On my word of honor, no one will miss him."

Nodding in satisfaction, the brehon gestured to his student, then began to move over the rocky trail in small, careful steps. "Spend time together, my children, so none can say you were not rightfully and legally married," he called, his voice echoing over the barren hilltop. "And may God's peace go with you."

Cahira and Colton stood in the stone circle until the brehon, the student, and the knight had moved away, then Cahira closed her eyes, listening for the last footfall and clomp of hooves. When all was silent save for the snapping fire outside the huts, she opened her eyes and found Colton watching her, his eyes watering in the wind.

Her husband. Her love.

He opened his arms, and she stepped into them, then he raised her head and cupped her face between his hands, love glowing strong in his dark eyes. And when they kissed and he lifted her into his arms, Cahira rested in the knowledge that she had finally found a place to belong.

✺ 20 ✺

Only two days from full, the moon lit the soft hills of the western horizon with a cold radiance and threw black shadows on the south-winding trail. Oswald kept his horse at a slow walk, willing himself to give the brehon time to become fully at ease beneath the vast plain of evening. Lorcan and the student were walking in the opposite direction, toward Rathcroghan, but they would never arrive.

Oswald reined in his horse and sat in the silence, thinking. The old man and his companion would not walk far, for they had to be tired. He could not tarry too long, for if they bedded down in a pile of brush, Oswald might never find them in the shadows of the dark. And it was important that he find them quickly—and without attracting attention.

The horse whickered and shook his head, setting the bit to jangling in his mouth. "Patience," Oswald murmured, slowly turning the beast, "easy now."

He made a clucking sound with his tongue and started the horse off again at a quick pace. With a flick of his hand he guided the animal to the soft earth beside the hardened trail, effectively muffling the sound of the stallion's hooves. The animal broke into a canter, eating up the distance as smoothly as a shadow. Within a few moments the mound of Carnfree passed at Oswald's right hand; within a few moments more he spied the white robes of the men he sought. He immediately pulled his mount to a halt, leaning forward to pat the skittish stallion on the neck as the animal pranced forward.

The brehon and his student were walking in silence, but the younger man seemed to be searching the open fields, presumably seeking shelter for the night. The brehon's head did not move, but remained forward, not stirring even when Oswald's horse blew gustily and nodded its great head in impatience.

The student turned, however, and tugged on his master's sleeve. Recognizing danger, Oswald slipped from his mount and drew his sword.

"So," the brehon called, his voice juicy with contempt as he turned slowly, "this is how you plan to begin the story? Do you not know, Sir Knight, that a tale which begins with blood must end with blood, too."

"Master, do you think he intends—?" The student's voice braked to a halt as his features filled with a sudden shock of sick realization.

"His intent is obvious, Peadar. If I were you, I would leave immediately."

"No!" Oswald lunged for the younger man, his sword singing as it rent the empty air, but the student turned and dove into a hedge, then scrambled out the other side and sprinted toward the dark horizon.

The brehon's hand closed like an iron vise around Oswald's arm. "Let him go. He cannot hurt your plan. He might even help you."

Oswald's lips thinned with irritation as he watched the retreating figure. "What do you know about anything, old man?"

Shadows rippled over the brehon like water over a sunken rock. "I know you and your lord want to instigate war with Felim O'Connor. I know you are thinking that if I do not persuade Felim to approve his daughter's marriage, the king of Connacht will ride to Athlone and impulsively attack the Normans there. But they will be ready for him, aye?"

Oswald gave the brehon a hostile glare. "Sometimes a man can be too wise for his own good."

A flicker of a smile rose at the edges of the old man's mouth, then died out. "Aye. Sometimes he can."

They stared at each other across a sudden ringing silence. Oswald felt his hand grow clammy, and he gripped his sword more tightly. It would be easier to do this if he were angry or on the receiving end of some insult.

"I'm not afraid," the brehon said, a bright mockery invading his stare. "I have lived a full life and am ready to meet my Savior. But I feel I must ask you, Sir Knight, to reconsider this act. Not for my own soul's sake, but for your own. Will you be ready to stand before God with an innocent man's blood on your conscience?"

Oswald stepped back, torn by conflicting emotions.

"If the love you bear your friend Colton is real, think yet again. You think you know him, but a man in love is not as predictable as you might believe. He will fight to defend Cahira. He may even turn against you."

There was a blank instant when Oswald's head had swarmed with words, then a burst of anger tore through him at the sound of Colton's name. "You talk too much!" In a surge of killing anger, he lifted his sword and brought it down, the blade slicing through shoulder and neck and chest until it caught somewhere in the vicinity of the brehon's rib cage. The old man said nothing, but his eyes widened slightly at the first bite of the blade, then he swayed on his feet and put out a hand as Oswald wrenched the blade free in a desperate tug.

Oswald swallowed, forcing down the sudden lurch of his stomach. The brehon took one unsteady step forward, then fell to his knees, gouts of blood pumping from his throat and flowing over his white robe. The man opened his mouth as if he would speak again, then fell forward onto the earth, his pale hand reaching over the dirt toward Oswald.

Oswald stepped back and sheathed his sword, shuddering as the murderous passion left him. Fury had its own intoxication, but the black and dizzy vortex of aftershock was overpowering.

He walked to his horse, placed his foot in the long stirrup, and struggled to swing himself into the saddle. The brehon's body lay in

the road like a discarded toy, blood shining wet and black in the moonlight. Gathering his reins, Oswald stared down at the road. Should he
hide the corpse? He hadn't hidden the carcasses of the slaughtered
cattle, intending them for a warning. Well, this would be a warning,
too.

Turning his horse toward Carnfree, he pursed his lips and forced
himself to whistle one of the Gaelic dance tunes the harpers played
every night at Athlone.

❦ 21 ❦

Adrift in a sea of fragmented dreams, Colton swam toward wakefulness, keenly aware that his God-ordained place in the universe had changed. Before last night he had been born and bred to battle, a man of the sword, of chivalry, and of loyalty to a sworn master. But after taking his vows to Cahira, he had added a more pressing duty. He could no more cast off his heritage or his loyalty to Richard than he could rid himself of his shadow, but he could be true to his bride no matter what the cost. He had loved her spirit from the moment he saw her lift her chin in defiance of Richard's order to shoot toward the old man. He had come to love her intellect and her womanhood as she opened herself like a gently unfolding blossom. And last night, when he held her in his arms and loved her as a husband, his blood had soared with the conviction that he would kill to defend her, would die to preserve her honor. From the beginning of time, God had made her for him, and Colton rejoiced to find the piece of himself that had been missing for far too long.

Safe and snug inside one of the stone huts, he opened his eyes as his ears filled with birdsong. Cahira lay stretched out on his mantle, silky strands of red hair draped across her dreaming face, the pale white streak glowed in the slanted sunlight from the narrow window.

Propping his head on his arm, he lifted himself and studied her. By heaven, she was a treasure! As elemental and primitive as this green and pungent land, imbued with a stunning, vibrant beauty that could not be found in the pale-faced damsels of English and French courts.

A gust of wind blew through the chinks in the stones, lifting the hair on Colton's arm. When he reached out and tugged on Cahira's cloak to cover her bare shoulder, a smile flickered over her face.

Was she awake? Her eyes did not open, but surely women did not smile when they slept . . . unless they dreamed of pleasant things. He had not been in a room with a sleeping woman since leaving his childhood, for he had spent his youth and manhood amongst men. Perhaps women were a race apart.

He lowered his head, wondering if he should be so bold as to kiss his new bride to wakefulness, then froze at the sound of a footstep on the gravel outside. Oswald had promised to return at an early hour to see if Colton wanted to send any message to Athlone. Eventually Lord Richard would have to be told about this hastily arranged marriage, but the disclosure would have to be made with great discretion and tact. Richard had been mightily offended by the Irish king's refusal to meet with him, but perhaps he would be encouraged by the news that Felim's daughter, at least, had proved herself open to the idea of accepting Normans . . . and loving one.

Reluctantly tearing himself away from his bride, Colton thrust his head and arms through the woven tunic he wore under his mail, then walked to the door and opened it. Wearing an indulgent smile, Oswald leaned against another of the stone huts. "How fares the groom?"

"Well enough." Colton couldn't keep a smile from his own face. Though for years he had written love songs as part of his chivalric training, the concept was but a moon-cast shadow compared to the reality of resting in his beloved's arms. "Did you pass a good night? I thought you might ride back to Athlone."

"I didn't want to arouse suspicion by passing the night guards without you," Oswald answered, his brows drawing downward in a frown. "And my night was tolerable, though nowhere near as pleasant as yours."

"Ah—well." Colton felt almost embarrassed at the tingle of happiness running through him. Oswald must think him a sentimental fool. "I've thought about it, and the brehon's plan is a good one. Cahira and I will go into Meath while Lorcan counsels her father. 'Twill be very helpful if you can disguise my absence for a few days. But if Lord Richard notices that I am missing, give him the truth, but gently." Colton forced his lips to curve in a still, calm smile. "Assure him that all is well, and that Felim of the O'Connors will soon have a new reason to consider establishing a peace. We will place our faith in God and the brehon."

Oswald's eyes gleamed like glassy volcanic rock beneath his helmet. "I can cover for you as long as a week. There's no need for you to rush away—after all, you are traveling with a woman."

"I appreciate your consideration, but Cahira is no fragile flower." Colton reached for his friend's hand and clasped it warmly. "Thank you. Someday I will return the favor."

Oswald jerked his head in a brief nod. "I doubt it will be the same favor. I can't see myself marrying an Irish wench."

"Neither could I, until last week." Colton released Oswald's hand, then smiled. "'Tis passing strange, how God can change our plans."

❧

CAHIRA WOKE TO THE SOUND OF BIRDS AND THE CLATTER OF HOOVES upon gravel. Opening her eyes, she saw that she was alone in the hut. She rose, slipped quickly into her gown and mantle, and stepped out into the sunshine.

A few feet away, Oswald sat upon his horse and Colton stood by his side, speaking to him in a quiet voice. A moment later Oswald picked up the reins, and Colton swatted the big stallion's flank. Away went the horse and rider.

Cahira felt her heart turn over when Colton turned and smiled at her. Her husband! She would have preferred waking in his arms, but it was also nice to awaken and find him waiting for her.

She flew over the stones and flung herself into his arms, her mouth hungrily seeking his.

"Well," Colton whispered when they finally parted, "if that is the greeting I shall receive every morning, I shall take pains to keep you with me always."

"I would go with you always," Cahira answered, meaning every word. "If you must travel with Lord Richard to England, or Normandy, or France, I will go with you. I will sleep in the rain with you, and make my home among the cliffs—"

"How you talk." Colton slipped down to sit on a rock, then pulled her firmly onto his lap. "I know you would travel with me, and moreover, I know you could. But I want to protect you, Cahira, to set you in a safe place where we shall be free to make a home and a family. Lord Richard must be consulted, for he is my master, but I am confident he will allow me to settle on his estate in Limerick. And if all goes well with our plan to unite my master and your father, mayhap we can one day settle on an *Irish* estate." His eyes brimmed with tenderness. "I would not separate a princess from her people."

"I have told you," Cahira lowered her forehead until it gently grazed his, "I care nothing about being a king's daughter. I care only for you, Colton. If our marriage can help bring people to your people and mine, then I am happy, but if we must live in Meath, or in Limerick, or even in Normandy, I am content as long as I am with you."

"You are a wonder," he murmured, nestling against her. Cahira shivered at the heady sensation of his lips against her neck. "But as sweet as this place is, now we must think of the future." He lifted his head and gazed into her eyes. "Oswald will disguise my absence at Athlone, and Lorcan will speak peaceably to your father, but we will not have many days without interference. We must make our way to Meath."

Cahira nodded, sobered by the thought of discovery, while Colton turned toward the east, his face shining in the light of the rising sun. "Walter de Lacy rules that province. While he and Lord Richard are civil to one another, they are not close. If we beg de Lacy for sanctuary until our people come to terms, I see no reason for him to refuse our petition."

"Across the river, in Meath," Cahira gestured toward the east, "stand several of the ancient towers. They are nearly impregnable; we could hide there for many days, even if this de Lacy is not disposed to aid us."

"I might be locked in a tower with you for days?" Colton pasted on an expression of mock horror as his hands tightened around Cahira's waist. "Heaven help me, how I am to stand the torture?"

"Withstand the temptation, you mean." Cahira brushed a gentle kiss across his lips. "And as much as I'd love to pass the morning sitting here on your lap, I'm thinking we should begin to move. My father might send out patrols, and if they find us at Carnfree, all will be lost."

"I won't let them take you from me." Colton kissed the pulsing hollow at the base of her throat, then lifted his gaze into hers. "Before we go, there is one thing I must know. Are you sorry, Cahira O'Connor, for having wed me? I have taken you from a life of comfort and thrust you into danger and exile. I do not even know where we shall eat our next meal."

With careful deliberateness she placed her hands against the side of his head and bent until their faces were but a breath apart. "I am not sorry for one moment I have spent with you, Colton. And if, God forbid, we should die before dark, I would know that I have found more love in the space of one glorious day than some folks discover in a lifetime."

❧ 22 ❧

Murchadh's heart was squeezed so tight he could barely draw breath to speak, but he forced the dreaded words out: "Sorcha, we know Cahira has left the rath. Tell us where she is."

The maid stood in the center of the women's chamber, her arms wrapped about herself. An aura of melancholy radiated from the girl's pale features, and her soft brown eyes flickered with pain and despair. Yet she did not speak.

"Sorcha!" Felim's voice held a note halfway between disbelief and pleading. "You are her maid—you are entrusted with her safety. Tell me why my daughter did not sleep in her bed last night!"

The maid flinched at the question, yet she only lowered her eyes in response, seeming to study the wooden floor. Una extended her hand toward her husband, warning him against pushing the girl too hard, then she stood from her chair and took a step toward Sorcha.

"We know you are loyal to our Cahira," she whispered, her own voice emerging as a despair-crusted croak, rusty with swallowed frustration. "And I am not forgetting she is a stubborn lass. She has gone somewhere and told you not to tell us, I know it as surely as I know the sun will set tonight."

The girl's thin shoulders began to tremble; her head dipped in a barely perceptible nod.

"But Cahira does not know the depth of her risk, dear Sorcha. Her head is too full of daydreams and fancy to know about the dangers of matters between lords and kings. And if she is caught up in some mischief where she might be ill-used by the Normans, I fear for her."

The girl's jaw trembled in a dry, choked spasm, but she neither wept nor spoke.

"Damnation!" His patience at an end, Felim slammed his fist against the wall, then nodded at Murchadh, who stood at his side. "Fetch a whip from the stable. If the girl will not speak, I'll beat the truth from her."

Murchadh's thoughts roiled with disbelief. "Felim, you cannot mean to do this. The girl is only obeying her mistress."

"The girl forgets she must obey her king!"

"But you cannot be thinking of beating her like a common animal! She's a faithful servant, trusted by your own daughter—"

"By heaven, Murchadh, if you persist in this folly you shall administer the whipping yourself!"

"No!" Sorcha's eyes welled with hurt, her tears spilling over cheeks as pale as parchment. "Don't force him to hurt me. I couldn't bear it."

"Then tell us where Cahira is." Una walked forward and drew the sobbing girl into her arms, pulling the maid's heavy hair from her eyes as she soothed her. "Speak, Sorcha, and no harm will come to you."

Sorcha wept aloud, rocking back and forth in Una's arms, then she lifted her head and peered woefully at Murchadh through tear-clogged lashes. He gazed at her, despairing, until she began to speak. "She has gone to marry the Norman knight. She is in love with him and cannot be dissuaded."

"Impossible!" Felim roared. "No Irish priest would marry her without my consent."

The maid shook her head, her eyes large and fierce with pain. "The knight . . . was going to abduct Lorcan. Cahira was certain the brehon would agree to marry them."

Utter stillness reigned in the chamber; even the hooting of the wind seemed to hush in a conspiracy of silence. Murchadh closed his eyes, feeling as though the room swirled around him as he absorbed the terrible news.

"Murchadh! Felim!" The sound of pounding footsteps and Rian's voice broke the tension, then the young man stalked into the chamber, his face contorted in a fearful grimace.

Felim waved the young man away. "This is not a good time for bad news, Rian. We have just heard more than we can bear."

Rian lifted his chin, boldly met his king's gaze, and spoke in a trembling voice. "This cannot wait. Peadar stands in the courtyard with news—Lorcan has been most foully murdered by a Norman knight!"

A wave of grayness passed over Murchadh, a kind of dark premonition. Cahira had gone to marry a knight—a knight who was going to abduct the brehon—and Lorcan had been murdered? How could this be? The imp was not particularly known for good sense, but Murchadh would have sworn that Colton was a man of honor.

Felim's brows drew together in an agonized expression, then he fixed a grim look to his face. When he spoke, his voice simmered with barely-checked fury. "Murchadh, call for my men. Prepare the horses. We will ride at once."

Murchadh stiffened at something he heard in the king's voice, something sharp and cold, like words torn by the blade of a dagger.

Una heard it, too. "Felim, remember! She is our daughter!"

"I shall not be forgetting that, woman!"

Sorcha broke into fresh sobs as Felim stormed out of the chamber, and Una automatically drew the girl into her arms again. "Whist, now, stop your crying," she murmured, stroking the maid's back. She lifted her gaze and met Murchadh's. "How could I have so misread my own daughter? Is it possible that the light in her eye of late sprang from love for a cursed *Norman?*"

"She begged me not to tell—she made me swear I wouldn't tell," Sorcha babbled, wailing in the reckless abandon of the newly confessed. "But she loves this man, and she said she would marry him no matter what anyone said or did to stop her."

"God, grant me wisdom," Murchadh prayed, moving out the door-way. "Help us bring Cahira home."

⚜

OSWALD SWUNG OUT OF HIS SADDLE, THEN STUMPED TOWARD THE thatched-roof building that Philip dared to call "the great hall." Compared to the magnificent stone castles of Normandy and England, the building was neither great nor a proper hall, but Richard seemed content to headquarter there. Oswald could not wait until they could leave this mud hut and take possession of the land. Then they'd show these backward Irish what a proper castle should look like.

The guards at the door, a pair of Irish lads who looked pitifully underdressed in their short tunics, sandals, and cloaks, nodded grimly as Oswald approached. The Gaels had observed the knights for nearly two months, yet they did little to imitate them. The guards still kept watch with simple spears and axes at hand; the horsemen still rode bareback on steeds as slender and delicate as porcelain china.

Simpletons. They don't even have the sense to recognize superior warriors when they see them.

The girl was to blame for the guards' indifference, of course. Ever since that blasted tournament when the brazen hussy had shorn her hair and pulled on men's clothing, the Irish warriors had regarded the Normans with bored apathy. But she would soon learn to respect Norman strength.

"I am looking for my master, Lord Richard de Burgo." Oswald directed his comments to the tallest man on guard. "Is he within?"

"Aye." The word slipped from a mouth that curled as if on the edge of laughter.

"Then let me pass." Oswald did not wait to hear the reply, but stepped between the two men and entered the gloomy chamber beyond. A pair of chickens clucked in the corner; a pair of serving women bent and cackled over the wide fireplace that filled the room with heat. But there, in the far corner, Oswald saw his lord sitting before a board and game pieces. His master was teaching the Irish barbarian how to play chess.

Oswald crossed the room in long strides, then fell to one knee before Richard. His master looked up, distracted, then smiled when he recognized the face. "Oswald. How fares the land of Connacht?"

Oswald took a deep breath, flashed a glance at his Irish host, then bowed his head before his master. "Truth to tell, my lord, I have important news. I have just ridden in from Carnfree."

Philip's brow wrinkled, and something moved in his eyes. "I know Carnfree. 'Tis a most holy place to my people, the altar where kings are consecrated and crowned."

"Indeed?" Richard's brows rose, graceful wings of scorn. He dropped a pawn onto the chessboard, then folded his hands, and gave Oswald his full attention. Drawing a deep breath, Richard lowered his voice and spoke in carefully modulated French: "Perhaps you should explain what drew you to this holy place. Unless you're planning on declaring yourself king of Connacht, I cannot fathom what you were doing there."

Answering in French as well, Oswald dropped his gaze in a show of humility, "I would never think of myself as king, but I cannot speak for another of your men, my lord. Colton has proceeded with his plan. Felim's daughter is with him now. Time is of the essence, for I believe they are planning to escape to Walter de Lacy's province of Meath."

Richard cocked his head to one side, as far as his multiple chins allowed. A faint glint of humor filled his eyes. "Let me understand you. Felim's daughter has run away and married my captain?"

"I witnessed the ceremony myself." Oswald drew a deep, exasperated breath. "The brehon who performed the ceremony vowed he would convince the Irish king to accept the marriage."

The amused look suddenly left Richard's eyes. "Does this brehon still live?"

"No, my lord. He lies somewhere on the road between Carnfree and Rathcroghan. Felim's warriors will find him soon enough."

"Finally," Richard whispered, his hand gripping a marble chess piece so tightly that his knuckles whitened, "the cursed Irish king will venture out of his fortress! He will ride out on a reckless tide of anger, and we shall be waiting for him."

Oswald remained silent for a moment, allowing his master to enjoy his thought, then he lifted a hand. "Sir, what of Colton and the girl?"

Richard frowned. "What do you mean? The girl will mean nothing once Felim is destroyed." He lifted his head and idly rubbed the fur at his collar. "We should probably lay a trap for him at that ridge of hills just outside Athlone. . . ."

Oswald lifted a brow. "Forgive my intrusion, but I think I should point out something about your captain. Though he appears to be one of your most loyal men, apparently he has been asking questions of the Irish—wanting to know about their way of electing kings, their approach to marriage, and so on. He has learned, for instance, that anyone can become king with the consent of those he governs. If a man lays claim to the throne through marriage to a royal daughter, and if the marriage itself took place at the holy place of Carnfree . . ."

A deep red patch appeared over Richard's rounded cheekbones, as though someone had slapped him hard on both cheeks. As Oswald waited, his master drew a long, quivering breath, mastering the passion that made him tremble. Philip lifted a brow, but Richard did not look toward his host. He kept his eyes fixed sternly upon Oswald.

When he spoke, the words came out hoarse, as if forced through a straining throat. "You think Colton means to install *himself* as a king of Connacht? Before I can even press my claim? Can greed and ambition have such a grip upon his heart that he would forget his oath of allegiance to me?"

Oswald lifted one shoulder in a shrug, then lowered his head in an air of remorse. "I do not know everything in Colton's heart, but I know ambition resides there. Did he not rise to the highest position of leadership among your own knights?"

Oblivious to the curious gaze of his host, Richard stood, sliding his chair back with such force that it toppled and crashed onto the floor. Bracing his hands on the table, he leaned toward Oswald, the muscles of his face tightening into a white mask of rage. "I never dreamed I would find such brazen disloyalty among my own men."

"The matter is not without remedy," Oswald answered smoothly, "because the marriage was most irregular. Colton spirited his bride away in the dark, and the rite was performed by a kidnapped brehon, not a true priest."

"Then they are not married in the eyes of the Church." Richard straightened and reached for empty air, then closed his fist around it as if grasping a thought. "The marriage can be annulled. It *will* be annulled. I cannot have one of my own men laying claim to an Irish crown!"

Oswald said nothing, but pursed his lips together. His master saw the expression. "You disagree?"

Oswald shrugged and spread his hands wide. "I thought mayhap the girl might prove useful as a hostage. If, perchance, Felim escapes during the coming attack, you will have leverage if you hold the girl in your prison. From all accounts, the king is a doting father. And Colton has already managed the girl's capture and restraint."

"By heaven, Oswald, you have the devil's own genius!" Richard's eyes darkened and shone with no pleasant light. "We will take her. We'll keep her here, and when her father comes, we'll settle this stalemate without losing a single man. He'll give his life for hers, and he will forfeit his claims to Connacht as he forfeits his life—"

Oswald bit back an oath. Richard was far fonder of expounding upon his dreams than acting upon them, and time was slipping away. He pointedly cleared his throat. "Sir, by now Felim O'Connor has realized his daughter is missing. Before sunset, without a doubt, he'll be searching for her. If we're to take her, we must do so quickly or we'll meet Felim O'Connor in the countryside before we have secured our hostage."

Richard slammed his fist upon the table with such force that the chess pieces jumped. Philip sat back, his mouth agape, but Richard pressed on. "You are wise, Oswald. Order the men in the garrison to mount up. We'll ride at once for Meath and bring the girl back. Colton will stand trial for his treachery, and Felim O'Connor will find himself forced to meet with me—and to agree to my terms."

Richard transferred his gaze to Philip, and spoke in English. "I beg your pardon, sir, but duty calls me away from our game. We shall have to conclude the match when I return from Meath."

"Meath?" Philip asked, his gaze curious and questioning.

"De Lacy's kingdom." Richard tapped Oswald on the shoulder, his eyes glowing with a sheen of purpose. "And if I find that my dearest enemy Walter de Lacy is harboring one of my own men, I shall take the matter to the Crown." He laughed, the sound muffled by his broad hand as he rubbed his jaw. "This bit of trouble may pay off handsomely for both of us, Oswald."

"I certainly hope it benefits your lordship." Oswald stood and bowed as his master moved away from the table. "As for me, I am happy only to serve you."

❧ 23 ❧

Taking pleasure in the simple fact of Colton's nearness, Cahira tied the reins of her horse to his saddle, then climbed up into the wooden saddle that was roomy enough for two. They set out at a relaxed trot and followed the river as the sun rose to its zenith. Finally they found a place where the river narrowed sufficiently for them to cross to the other side—the province of Meath.

Cahira's stomach had just begun to growl when they approached a small farmhouse where a woman stood in the yard scattering grain for a clutch of chickens. Noisily calling "Chook-chook" to her hens, the woman watched Cahira and Colton advance with a wary eye.

Cahira nudged Colton into silence as he pulled the horse to a halt. "Good morning to you," she called out in Gaelic. "I wonder if we might find a bite to eat in your house?"

The woman didn't answer, but her eyes narrowed as she studied the trappings that encased Colton and his mount. Understanding the woman's wariness, Cahira slipped from the saddle and walked toward the woman with her hands open. "Welcome, and good morning to you," she began again, softening her tone, "but the stranger and I have had nothing to eat. Might you have a bit of something to spare?"

The question seemed to amuse the woman. "Should I be feeding a Norman," she asked in Gaelic, her eyes almost disappearing in her taut, bony cheeks, "when they are doing their best to starve us? Our new lord de Lacy already demands more of us than the land can give."

"Please." Cahira dropped her hands. "I am Cahira of the O'Connors, from Connacht. I know not what evils your Norman lord has heaped upon you, but you may trust in this—the man you see on yonder horse is not like the others. Like me, he dreams of peace."

The woman remained silent for a moment, her eyes shifting from Cahira to Colton and back again, then she nodded brusquely. "I've a bit of bread and cheese to spare, but that's all. Come into the house— just you, lass—and I'll give it and send you on your way."

"I thank you." Cahira followed the woman toward the house, waving to Colton behind the woman's back. A cat darted out as the woman pushed the door open, and within a moment Cahira found herself in a small dark house loaded with the scents of animals and hay. The woman pressed a half-loaf of bread and a hunk of cheese into her hands.

"You don't look like you have the strength to do much about this peace you're dreaming of," the woman remarked as Cahira turned to leave. "But they say a raggedy colt often makes a powerful horse. I'll be praying that God will yet make you strong."

Cahira hesitated in the doorway, half-tempted to tell the woman that she had strength aplenty, thank you. She was a king's daughter, educated and skilled, with courage enough to marry a man whose will matched her own . . . but a thought clicked in her mind. She *had* been a king's daughter, but she walked away from that position and privilege, forfeiting all for Colton and freedom. She lifted a brow, intrigued by the unsettling thought. She had disdained her position for so long, but she felt curiously bereft without it.

She thanked the woman, walked outside, and let Colton pull her up behind him. She smiled when he bowed his head in deference to their reluctant hostess.

"She didn't seem to think much of me," Colton remarked as they rode away. "She couldn't have looked more displeased if the devil himself had ridden up to her house."

"She didn't think much of me, either," Cahira remarked dryly, recalling the woman's comment about a raggedy colt. "But at least she was kind. I don't think she had much to share; she said her Norman master demands too much."

"De Lacy is no more beloved than any other baron." Colton lifted his arm and pointed to a stone tower near the river's edge. The waters ran quiet and slow at the narrow spot, and a nearby copse of trees would provide a small measure of camouflage for the horses. "Shall we stop there and break our fast? I can water the horses at the stream, then climb into the tower and scout the trail ahead."

"A wonderful idea."

Within a few moments Cahira stood in the river, the cold water lapping around her ankles. Colton was fitting hobbles around the horses' legs, leaving them free to graze while he and Cahira ate their meager meal.

Cahira shivered as a cool wind blew, then retreated from the river-bank. It was a cold day, but a bright one, the sun gilding the ancient tower and the surrounding fields. She closed her eyes, enjoying the warmth of the sun on her face, and banished all bittersweet thoughts of Sorcha, Murchadh, and the other loved ones she had abandoned. All that mattered was that Colton stood only a short distance away, so her heart and her future were in safe reach.

The distant sound of thunder echoed from the horizon. Cahira looked up, tucking a stray strand of hair behind her ear as she looked up and searched the emerald vista. The sky was a faultless wide curve of blue, so what had caused the thunder?

Leaving her shoes on the grass, she climbed to the highest point of the riverbank and turned toward the sound. A cold hand passed down her spine when she saw a shadow on the earth, a dark cloud of horses and dust, of warriors set upon a quest.

Not thunder—hoofbeats. A steady drumming sound, signaling at least a dozen riders, coming from the northwest. From Connacht.

"Colton!" Gathering up her skirts, Cahira turned and sprinted toward the stone tower. He would not have time to free the hobbled horses; they would have to hide and hope the warriors rode by without stopping. If her father caught them in the heat of his anger, he would be more likely to kill Colton than forgive him.

What happened to Lorcan's plan?

She flew up the grassy hill beneath the tower, slipping in her bare feet, grasping at grass and rocks and weeds. "Colton!" she screamed again, but her voice sounded strangled and rasping in her own ears.

And then she stood outside the tower, her hands twisting until she found a half-rotten ladder someone had left in the underbrush. Calling upon all her strength, she pulled it free of dying foliage and vines, then propped it against the tower, all the while calling Colton's name.

❦

AFTER HOBBLING THE HORSES NEAR THE RIVER'S EDGE, COLTON BENT to wash his hands in the river, then wiped them dry upon his surcoat. The cleared land on the other side of the river rose in a gradual incline toward the south, and against the horizon he saw dust rising in a peculiar straight pattern, almost as though an invisible scythe were stirring up the ground beneath it. He swiped his hand through his hair, recognizing the wide V formation the knights used when scouting for any sign of an enemy. They were advancing from the southwest, from Athlone.

He felt a bead of perspiration trace a cold path from his armpit to his rib. Richard was coming for him, then. Oswald had failed, and his master's wrath had been kindled too soon.

"Cahira!" he turned and yelled. His frantic eyes found her at the base of the tower, struggling to hold a ladder upright. Leaving the horses, he sprinted away from the river.

"'Tis the only way," she panted, already climbing the ladder's rungs when he reached her. "We can pull the ladder up after us."

"Go," he urged, glancing over his shoulder.

The tall, cylindrical towers dotted the Irish countryside, as ancient as they were out of place. Though Colton could not imagine what enemies could drive the ancient Gaels to seek shelter in such towers, suddenly he felt a profound gratitude for them.

The thunder of hoofbeats grew louder, coming from two directions now, and he urged Cahira to move faster on the yielding ladder. "Hurry," he challenged, looking down as the earth receded beneath him. Cahira moved upward, then fell into the tower's rectangular opening, and Colton followed. With one quick glance he saw that the rotting floor had broken through in several places. "Stay near the edge of the tower," he called, gripping the ladder. "Don't walk into the center of the chamber."

"Let me help." Kneeling by his side, Cahira thrust her arms through the opening and pulled, too. They had just managed to pull the ladder into their chamber when the first group of riders appeared on the riverbank. The warriors, Irishmen all, thundered across the river, sending a froth of white ripples to the shore. They might have ridden by, but one of the riders yelled and pointed toward the two hobbled horses. Within two minutes, the Gaels had dismounted, and a tall man with an air of authority was studying the tower.

"Murchadh," Cahira whispered, her voice breaking. She sat with her back pressed to the wall, her face a picture of misery. "He's seen the horses, and he knows we're here. In a moment my father will demand that I come down."

"We will have to come down eventually," Colton answered, taking pains to keep his face in shadow as he peered out the doorway. "But we will do so on our own terms, Cahira. Though we didn't think to make peace in quite this way, the opportunity is about to present itself. Look to the south."

CAHIRA OBEYED, AND THE SIGHT OF MOUNTED NORMANS ON THE riverbank sent a chill through her blood. She might have been able to persuade her father to forgive her, to be merciful to Colton, and to give the marriage a chance, but what could she do with a pack of Normans listening to her every word? While her father might have been moved by an appeal to his compassion or fatherly love, he would not allow his heart to soften while his enemy watched from a few feet away.

And yet cold sweat prickled on her forehead as she thought of

Colton's predicament. She was responsible to her father, but how much more responsible was Colton to Lord Richard! He had taken a vow of loyalty and obedience to that Norman baron, and Cahira knew he did not hold that vow lightly. Though she had spent her entire life rebelling against her parents and keepers, she did not think Colton had ever disobeyed his sworn lord.

Her parents loved her and forgave every insubordination, but Lord Richard de Burgo would not feel similarly inclined to forgive Colton. He was a proud man, and a cruel one. She couldn't allow Colton to face that overbearing Norman.

Biting her lip, she watched as the company of knights slowed to a trot and warily approached. Finally, the leader—surely it was Lord Richard under all that mail and silk—lifted his hand and signaled for the others to halt. With the River Shannon meandering between them, the leaders of the Normans and the Gaels sat upon their horses and regarded each other in silence.

Who would be the first to speak?

She glanced at Colton, who reached across the open doorway and took her hand. "Do not be afraid," he said, speaking in an odd, gentle tone. "If 'twas God who led us this far, he will not desert us now."

She nodded in response, then turned her gaze toward the spectacle on the riverbank.

"Normans!" She heard her father's voice, steel-edged and strong. "I know not what brings you here, but I have come to rescue a daughter from a murdering devil. Lorcan, our brehon, lies dead in my courtyard even now, cut down by a Norman knight's blade."

Cahira shivered as an icy finger touched the base of her spine. Lorcan dead? It couldn't be true. Her father had to be lying, making up a story to paint Colton in evil colors.

Colton must have had the same thought. "It can't be true, Cahira. Lorcan must have failed in his attempt to speak reason, and your father's anger has turned against him."

Lord Richard nudged his mount and rode forward a few paces, while something like a smile flitted across his broad face. "Greetings, Felim O'Connor. Indeed, I am sorry to hear that the brehon is dead, but I can assure you I knew nothing of it. I have, however, heard of your daughter's dilemma and am more than happy to grant her to you. I have come to reclaim a wayward knight, and if his sword be found with blood upon it, I can promise you he will pay for the deed with his life."

"It *was* a knight!" A new voice rang out, and Cahira searched through the crowd of Gaels to place the speaker. A cold knot formed in her stomach when she saw the brehon's student, auburn-haired Peadar, sitting astride one of her father's horses. His hands were wound in his horse's mane, his legs pale against the bay's dark flank.

Grief struck her like a sudden blow to the stomach, and she had to swallow several times to choke back the bile that rose in her throat. Peadar would not leave his teacher unless something had happened, so her friend Lorcan *was* dead, and evil stalked the land.

"He came upon us in the darkness!" Peadar threw back his head, shouting to anyone who would listen. "My master thought only of me and sent me away, but in the moonlight I saw the murderer clearly. He wore blue and white, mail and helmet, and spoke like a Norman. He murdered my master for no reason!"

"The reason is obvious," Richard answered, his voice crisp and dry. "The knight killed the brehon in order to keep him silent. And all my knights are accounted for, save one. The knight we both seek, therefore, must be the renegade."

Cahira groaned, her heart aching, as Colton uttered a gasp. Lorcan's words, spoken only hours before, came back to her on a terrible wave of memory: *The highest provinces of peace are bought with sacrificial blood, dear ones.* Why had Lorcan been the one to sacrifice his life?

Through a haze of confusion and sorrow, she realized they had been utterly betrayed. Lord Richard should not know Colton was absent, and yet here he was, accusing Colton of murder and mayhem. Yet Colton had not wandered from her side last night, so only *one* knight could have killed Lorcan. He, Sir Oswald the Arrogant, rode now at Lord Richard's side with his jaw thrust forward and a shadowy sneer hovering about his narrow mouth.

Her gaze drifted over to the Gaels. Her people had been betrayed as well. Lorcan represented more than the law; he was the embodiment of their culture, their history, their ancient laws and religion. His young student, Peadar, had not yet even begun to learn all a brehon must know.

"It appears," she whispered, sorrowfully squeezing Colton's hand, "that we have misplaced our trust. We have been discovered before time could work on my father's heart."

"But how deeply are we discovered?" Colton stared out at the confrontation on the riverbank. "Do they know we are married?"

The question was answered in the next moment, when Cahira heard her father's voice, thick and unsteady. "This knight of yours has taken my daughter from her intended husband. It appears he may have deprived her of her maidenhood as well."

His caustic tone made Cahira flush in shame, but she and Colton had done nothing shameful. She let her gaze rove over the men with her father, then winced when she recognized Rian. What must he think of her at this moment?

"'Tis my understanding they were lawfully married, though not in the eyes of the church," Richard called, shifting in his saddle. "If you want to have the marriage annulled, the Church would certainly support you." He lifted his hand and made a dismissive gesture. "I know little about your Irish laws. Mayhap the marriage can be set aside on legal grounds as well."

"In a year and a day." Cahira whispered the words in the instant her father proclaimed them. According to ancient brehon law, either partner could leave a marriage after a year and a day had passed. *This* marriage, sealed by vows made before a brehon, could not be set aside until the allotted time had expired.

"I can do nothing at present," her father answered, turning for the first time toward the tower. "But I will take my daughter home. For that reason alone have I come here."

Richard called out his agreement. "I, too, have come only for my man. We should maintain this peace between us, and each take our own."

"'Tis another lie!" Colton hissed, his fingers tightening around Cahira's. "If your father had not first appeared with a company outnumbering Richard's, I am certain we would have seen a battle waged before our eyes. And before 'twas done, you would be Richard's hostage, and I his prisoner."

"And if Richard had not come," Cahira's voice broke as she captured his eyes with her own, "I fear my father would have killed you. He is a reasonable man, but he would not have gathered thirty warriors just to bring me home. He means to avenge Lorcan's death—I know it. Despite my love for you, he sees you as an enemy."

Colton looked at her with a shade of sadness in his eyes, then his gaze drifted toward the confrontation outside. "I must let you go with your father." His hand tightened around hers. "I cannot take you with me."

"But we are married! And you promised to keep me with you!"

"Look outside, love." Against her will, Cahira's gaze fell upon the waiting warriors. The Normans had spread themselves in an organized line on one riverbank; the Irishmen faced them on the other, battle-axes and spears at the ready. If the signal to fight were given, the Gaels would have the upper hand in numbers, but the Normans were better armored and far more experienced. Any battle, however brief, would end in horrific bloodshed on both sides.

"If I tried to take you from your father," Colton went on, his voice patient, "his men would attack. They are thirsty for blood."

Cahira said nothing, but clung to Colton's arm with both hands. She wanted to scream, "Come with *me*, then!" but if her father tried to take Colton, the Normans would charge across the river, their swords and lances ready to strike.

Grief welled in her, black and cold.

On the riverbank, her father had turned to face the tower. "Cahira! Come down at once! Your father and king comes to reclaim you."

Colton sighed heavily, his voice filling with anguish. "You must go with him. Just for now, have faith and go."

Cahira glanced around, about to suggest that they could remain in the tower indefinitely, but this was not a safe place. The flooring was unstable, and they lacked both food and water. If they chose to be stubborn love's sake, for love's sake they'd die within three or four days. She loved Colton with all her heart and soul, but she was no fool.

Her heart sinking, she turned to face him. "So be it. I'll return with my father, and I will convince him you had nothing to do with Lorcan's death. In time, he will learn to welcome you as my husband—and his son. I will not give up, Colton. For a year and a day and forever, you are my husband." She stopped and looked out at the Normans, her heart beating hard enough to be heard a yard away. "But what of your safety? Lord Richard is not a father to you. Will he welcome you back or punish you? By heaven above, Colton, if you think he means harm to you, 'tis better than you come with me. I would throw my body across yours to save your life—"

"Hush, wife." His dark eyes filled with humor and tenderness. "You are spouting lovely nonsense."

Even as he spoke, she knew he was right. Even if by some miracle the Normans did not attack if the Irish kept Colton, her father would merely send her away with Murchadh while one of the others dispatched Colton to heaven with a single stroke of the battle-ax. Her father's conscience would not even be troubled, for he was a king involved in a state of war, and Colton was an enemy.

Lord Richard's voice lifted to the tower. "Sir Colton! We know you are there, and we know what you have done. Descend at once, and bring the woman with you. Let us restore her to her father, while you return to your lord and master. Be courageous, be noble and true, and do not dishonor the vows of fealty you have taken."

Cahira's hand trembled as she reached across the opening to touch Colton's face. "Go with God and be careful, husband. If possible, try to come to me again. I will walk every day near the river, near the rock where we met. I will search for some sign of you until we meet again."

His strong voice dissolved into a thready whisper. "If God wills, I will come to you soon. And if I do not, know this—I have loved you with my life, and I do not regret a single moment. We had a dream for peace, and if God wills that my life should be the price of it, I am willing to pay."

A flash of wild grief ripped through Cahira's heart. Rising to her knees, she threw herself into his arms. As he held her, she inhaled deeply of his scent, relishing the texture of his skin, his hair, his strength. "I believe God will bring us back together," she whispered, the words forming a logjam in her throat. "Can it be his will to birth this love between us and then let it die?"

Colton did not answer, but pressed her to himself more tightly. They knelt in each other's arms for a moment woven of eternity, then Cahira heard her father's voice again.

"Daughter! My men stand ready to fire their arrows! Come down at once, before we force you down!"

Colton lifted his head and gave her a half-hearted smile. "Before you go, I want you to have this." With difficulty he pulled his sword from its sheath, then held it across his open palms and presented it to her like a peasant offering a precious gift to a king. "I've had it since I was knighted, years ago. They'll take it from me if I wear it now, and I want you to keep it—until we are together again."

Touched beyond words, she accepted the sword, then palmed fresh tears from her cheeks. Colton reached out and smoothed the last touch of wetness from her eyes with his thumb. "I'll have to give you the belt, too, or you'll never make it down the ladder."

She nodded, grateful for a practical consideration to divert her thoughts. She stood silent while Colton's arms slipped around her waist and buckled the sword belt, then she caught her breath as he took the blade and sheathed it. The weapon hung heavily from her waist and banged against her thigh. Every step would remind her of Colton and his promise to reclaim it.

He placed his hands on her shoulders. "It is time."

"I know." Conscious of the scrutiny of more than two dozen warriors who watched the tower doorway, she bent and placed a firm hand on the bottom rung of the ladder. "Help me with this, Colton, and never let them know that I wept here today. I am not afraid of Lord Richard. I place my trust in God . . . and in you."

"I have never met anyone less afraid." His hand fell on the ladder next to hers, and when she looked up, his eyes glowed with a steadfast and serene peace.

❦

COLTON WENT FIRST DOWN THE LADDER, THEN STOOD AND HELD IT steady for Cahira, resisting the surge of fury that murmured in his ear and banged in his blood. He had never been vanquished in a tournament, had never surrendered a fight. And yet here he stood, as meek as a kitten, and with no choice in the matter! But for Cahira he would bear it . . . for as long as he could.

She eased her way down the ladder, then turned to face the two groups who waited for them, her eyes blazing. Colton reached for her hand, then led her around the silent company of Irishmen. They walked to the riverbank and took their stand on the shore at a point equidistant between Felim O'Connor and Lord Richard.

"Lord Richard," Colton pitched his voice to reach across the river, addressing his master first. "I must beg your forgiveness, sir, for undertaking this endeavor without your permission. But I am prepared to give a defense of myself in the matter of the brehon. As God is my witness, I did not kill him. My marriage to this lady is sanctioned by God, if not the Church, and is appropriate under Irish law. We have vowed our love and our lives together, and did so with the purest of motives and unblemished honor."

"We will discuss this matter later," Richard answered, his eyes resting upon Colton only for the barest fraction of an instant. His face was as blank as stone, unreadable. "I suggest you unhobble your horse and prepare to ride back with us at once."

"Lord Richard."

Colton watched with acute and loving anxiety as Cahira stepped forward. The nobleman leaned forward in his saddle, his eyes flickering with interest. "My lady?"

Cahira looked at him, her face dazzling with strength and determination. "This man is my lawful husband, and son-in-law to the king of

Connacht. I will expect you to treat him with the respect and deference his position requires."

For a moment Colton feared Richard would laugh in her face. His small blue eyes grew somewhat smaller and brighter, then he lifted a brow and shifted his gaze to Colton.

"I will give him all he deserves," he answered, his lips pursing as if he wanted to spit. "You can be sure of that, my lady."

Cahira gave his master a curt nod of farewell, then she turned to him and rested her fingertips lightly upon his uplifted hands.

"I thought you didn't care anything about your positions and titles," he teased, lowering his head to look into her downcast eyes. "Yet here you are, bragging that your husband is son-in-law to a king."

"I spoke only of what Richard understands." She lifted her gaze, and the look in her eyes set the drops of Colton's blood to chasing each other through his veins. "You are worth far more than a king to me."

And then, without another word, she lifted her hands from his and walked with stiff dignity not toward her father, but toward the warrior Murchadh.

Colton would have stood and watched as she mounted her horse, but Oswald splashed through the shallows and abruptly caught him by the elbow. Colton obeyed the summons, taking only a moment to retrieve his horse. He mounted and directed the animal across the river shallows, then stared in surprise when Oswald stepped forward. The knight moved with a newfound assurance, a conviction of importance he wore like an invisible mantle. "You will not be needing a blade now, my friend," he said. He reached up to pull Colton's sword from its scabbard, then frowned when he found nothing. "Your sword?"

"I gave it to my wife," Colton snapped, gathering his reins. He wheeled his mount so that he faced the opposite riverbank. "And I will not leave until I am certain they will not harm Cahira."

Oswald lifted a brow, but said nothing. From the height of his horse, Colton watched silently as the glaring Irishmen turned and spurred their mounts. Cahira rode alone, one slender and colorful figure amid a sea of heavily armed warriors. Not one of the Irishmen looked back.

Oswald looked up as the last man disappeared from view. "You are fortunate that the O'Connors arrived first," he said, pitching his voice so that only Colton could hear it. "Lord Richard was planning to take the girl hostage in order to defeat her father the king."

Colton gritted his teeth as fury rose within him. "Tell me, Oswald —why was it necessary to kill the brehon? He was an old man who never could have harmed you."

Colton saw the small twitch of Oswald's shoulders. "The Irish would have listened to him." He lowered his gaze. "And Richard wants war. If you hadn't been so blinded by that Irish wench, you would have understood our master's wishes."

Colton gripped his reins as Lord Richard turned his stallion and pulled up within arm's distance of Colton's saddle. "I will deal with you when we return to Athlone," Richard said, bridled anger in his voice as he shifted to hold his spirited mount in check. "But do not expect to see that wench again, Sir Colton. Not in this lifetime."

With a touch of his spur and an oath, the nobleman charged ahead, leaving Colton behind.

❧ 24 ❧

Oswald watched as one of Philip's servants threw another bough on the fire, its impact sending a volcano of sparks across the floor. The December wind outside had turned wicked and cold, and even now bitter gusts blew through chinks in the log dwelling, numbing Oswald's fingers as it shivered his skin.

Silently cursing the day Richard had ever decided to ride for Connacht, Oswald reached for another hunk of bread, took a bite, and chewed it thoughtfully as he studied the head table where his master sat. Philip, who grew more taciturn and inhospitable every day, made no secret of his eagerness for Richard's departure. Though Richard kept talking about his return to Castleconnell, he had made no definite plans for departing to the province of Limerick. His attempts to bully Felim O'Connor into surrender had utterly failed, and the incident with the Irish king's daughter had only increased the tension and hostility between the two factions.

Most important, none of the other barons had answered Richard's pleas for support. Though he had sent letters to every other Norman who held feudal power in Ireland—Maurice Fitzgerald, Lord of Offaly; Hugh de Lacy, Earl of Ulster; the Berminghams, lords of Athenry; and a host of others—not one had offered to support Richard's current campaign against Felim of the O'Connors. Richard had lately confided to Oswald that the barons insisted the timing was wrong. Winter was upon them, a bad time for travel and provisioning an army. Perhaps later, in the summer, they might be persuaded to send a few archers or swordsmen.

If Connacht were to be won, Richard had decided, it would not be by diplomacy, but by the sword. But though they had a sizable company in Athlone, twenty knights would not be enough to sweep Felim O'Connor from his home. That king had warriors aplenty, and those men were as broad as tree trunks and nearly as thickheaded.

Ignoring the rough voices of the knights around him, Oswald leaned back and studied his master's face. Anxiety had etched lines of weariness upon Richard's wide forehead, faint marks that had not been there three months ago when they returned from the tower at the River Shannon. Colton's supposed defection had injured Richard's pride. If his own captain's loyalty could be shaken by the smile of a lovely Irish wench, what would happen to the other men if Richard lingered in this fair land? With crystal clarity, Oswald saw that his master's overweening self-assurance had at last been shaken. He would be leaving for Limerick and Castleconnell soon unless something or someone convinced him victory could be won.

Oswald picked up his mug, knocked the last drop of ale into his mouth, then dropped it back to the table, and wiped his chin. It was now or never. The opportunity would never be more ripe.

He stood, smoothed his surcoat, and approached the master's table. Falling upon one knee, he waited in silence until Lord Richard's gaze fell upon him.

In a voice cracking with exhaustion and despair, Richard spoke: "What is it, Sir Oswald?"

Oswald lifted his gaze to his master's. "If I might beg leave to speak with you for an instant."

Richard waved his hand in an absent gesture. "Speak, then. *Mais en Français, s'il vous plaît.*"

Oswald switched immediately to his native tongue. "If I might ask, my lord—what do you intend to do with Sir Colton?"

Richard's eyes flew up at him like a pair of bluebirds startled out of hiding. "What concern it is of yours?"

"If it please you, sir, the man was a friend. I am concerned about his welfare."

Richard's brows lowered. "If you must know, I have decided to kill him. We are accomplishing nothing here, and I'm thinking we should return to Castleconnell within a fortnight. 'Twould be wiser to rid myself of a disloyal knight than risk traveling with him to a province he no longer cares to defend."

Oswald winced with false remorse. "I beg you to spare him until we leave. I have an idea you might want to consider before sending his soul to heaven."

A faint line appeared between Richard's heavy brows. "Go on."

Oswald rubbed his hand over his face. "It has occurred to me that Colton might yet be of use to us. After all, if the fish nibbled once, perhaps it will strike at the bait again."

Richard's mouth spread into a thin-lipped smile. "Speak plainly, Oswald, before I lose my patience. I've had my fill of riddles and poets —this place is altogether lousy with them."

Giving his master a bland half-smile, Oswald spoke in his most direct tone. "Felim O'Connor's daughter loves your treacherous knight. If she could be persuaded to meet him, perhaps we could entice her to slip into our hands. A quirk of fate prevented you from taking her as hostage at the tower, but perhaps she might prove a hostage yet. You may still leave in a fortnight, sir, but wouldn't it be better to leave as the acknowledged Lord of Connacht?"

Richard sat in silence, considering the idea, then a blush of pleasure showed on his face, as if the idea had caused younger blood to fill his veins. "The idea has merit, but how will we convince the girl to venture away from her father's rath? Felim O'Connor is no fool; he is not likely to allow the woman to wander freely about the countryside."

"Cahira O'Connor is no ordinary young woman, my lord. You cannot have forgotten the spectacle she made of herself at the tournament. She is not afraid to defy her father. With one word in her ear, I am certain she would agree to meet Colton in some secluded place— where, of course, your lord and his men could take her into custody."

Offering the curious Philip a distracted nod, Richard drummed on the table and lifted his eyes to the fire shadows dancing on the ceiling. Oswald watched the Irishman, realizing that poor, ambitious Philip, who had probably hoped the Normans would increase his prosperity and standing, had received nothing for his hospitality but trouble and aggravation and the ill-use of his serving maids.

"I suppose," Richard said, still speaking in soft French, "you could draw her out? I've discovered you are nothing if not inventive, Oswald."

"I believe I could, sir." Oswald smiled. "If you will give me leave, I will don a plain tunic and ride to Rathcroghan without a saddle, in the manner of the Irish. The girl's maid knows me, and so does the captain of O'Connor's men. I know I could get a word to her."

Richard nodded slowly. "So be it. Ride tomorrow and arrange the meeting."

"There is one more consideration," Oswald ventured, taking a calculated risk. Richard had neither spoken of nor laid eyes on Colton since they returned to Athlone. After being beaten for his insubordination, the former captain had been locked in a cattle shed, deprived of all but the barest of food and water.

Oswald lifted a brow and met his master's gaze. "The girl, as I said, is no ordinary young woman. She may want proof that Colton still lives."

Richard scratched his beard for a moment, then nodded. "Then visit the prisoner and have him write her a message. But make certain he writes nothing of his confinement . . . or of anything else unpleasant."

"I will do it, my lord."

Bowing his head in submission, Oswald stood, crossed the stuffy chamber, and stepped gratefully out into the cool, crisp night.

CAHIRA WALKED SLOWLY ON LEADEN LEGS, HER THOUGHTS AS HEAVY as the air that surrounded her. The morning's gray promise had been fulfilled with a weeping drizzle that seemed appropriate for a joyless December afternoon. The rain fell in soft spatters that caught in her hair and lashes, blurring her sight like tears. The mown fields to her right and left, heavy now with wild ragwort, trembled in the wind, while somewhere in the distance a hawk screeched and wheeled for cover beneath the trees. She ought to be seeking cover, too, but what did it matter if she took a chill and caught a fever? Colton was gone, and not a single word had come from Athlone regarding his welfare. Did he still live?

Her father certainly behaved as if he did not. Though Cahira had spent an entire night after her return begging her father for under-standing and mercy, the king of Connacht stared past her in stony silence. In a fit of grief, Cahira dropped to her knees, then fell to the floor and gripped his ankles, crying that she would not release him until he acted on her beloved's behalf. With an effort, Felim of the O'Connors pulled himself free and proclaimed he had a funeral to arrange. Instead of sending warriors to Athlone, he dispatched runners throughout the province to summon free men and *filid* to mourn the brehon.

Two days later, a band of hired mourners sat outside the gates of Rathcroghan, splitting the air with their keening. Silent and defeated, Cahira watched them through the window of her upstairs chamber and felt as if she were mourning the death of her marriage, her love, and her hope.

Even after the great man had been buried and the guests sent away, Cahira's father refused to hear her pleas. Bound by brehon law, he could do nothing to void her marriage, for unless she was proved a widow it must last at least a year and a day. As the days melted into weeks and weeks into months, Cahira began to believe her father planned to ignore her until the requisite interval ended. His silence and indifference built a wall between them not even Murchadh's entreaties could breach.

When her father refused to listen, Cahira turned to her mother, who had retreated from the family discord by delving into religious practice. She spent nearly every free minute in the chapel, her lips moving soundlessly as she recited the seven offices of the day in an endless liturgy. Limited as she was by her husband's wishes, she could not offer her daughter comfort. "I have no answers for you, lass," she whispered one afternoon when Cahira wept before her. "But I'm certain God does. Pray, Daughter, and let the peace of heaven lift this heaviness from your heart."

Feeling lost and alone, Cahira turned to Sorcha, but her maid seemed as intent on avoiding all mentions of Colton as the rest of the family. There remained only Murchadh, and Cahira went often out to the courtyard to seek her uncle's company. He did not speak of Colton or of the Normans, but he often placed a bow in her hand and wordlessly guided her aim. In the discipline of archery she found a way to occupy her time, and Murchadh seemed to understand that she felt closer to Colton when she worked with the weapons that had brought them together. The sewing room and the great hall were not for her. She would never see herself as a *princess*, but a warrior's bride.

When she was not practicing with Murchadh, she walked or rode down to the river. Her father had commanded Murchadh and Sorcha to accompany Cahira each time she left the rath, but they were wise enough not to intrude upon her grief. Her two guardians usually rode several paces ahead, leaving Cahira alone with her thoughts as she followed.

Though her heart remained steadfast in hope, she began to wonder if Colton would ever keep his word and meet her at the rock on the riverbank. Day after day she searched for a note slipped beneath a stone or a message scrawled upon the broad face of the rock itself. Her heart sank each day she looked for a sign and found none. Then she would sit and pray and encourage herself with the thought that every day she passed was one less she would have to wait. Colton would come for her. It was only a matter of time.

But a shadow lay across her heart today, a deep and dark cloud of grief. This morning a messenger had come to Rathcroghan and asked for her father, and within moments of his arrival the sounds of shouting and merriment poured from the hall. As the king's men danced to the sounds of the *bodhrán,* flute, and fiddle, Murchadh found

Cahira and pulled her into the deserted stairwell. "There's news from Philip's rath at Athlone," he said, his expression withdrawn and worried. "They're saying Richard is planning to leave for Castleconnell soon. 'Tis said he'll be taking all his knights with him."

Despite the lively music coming from her father's hall, Cahira choked on air suddenly thick with the heaviness of despair. "Do you think," she touched Murchadh's sleeve, "that my father will ask for Colton's release before they go? If Richard holds him prisoner, my father could ransom him—"

"I'm thinking you'd be more likely to ask for the moon and get it." Pity and understanding mingled in Murchadh's eyes. "Your father is set in his ways, and he's set on marrying you to Rian when your time is up. I'm sorry, imp, but that's the lay of it."

Cahira had gazed at Murchadh in despair, then picked up her cloak and moved slowly through the door. Oh, that she could speak with her love! She had tried to send messages to Athlone, but since Sorcha trembled at the very thought of the king's disapproval, Cahira gave her letters to Murchadh, who had to send them with unreliable travelers occasionally spotted on the road outside Rathcroghan. Cahira doubted if any of her letters had been delivered to Colton.

Now, as Cahira walked toward the river behind her guards, she felt as though there were invisible hands on her heart, slowly twisting the life from it. Three months ago she had been a happy bride; nothing of that happiness remained now but the raw sores of an aching heart. She knew Colton would not willingly leave Connacht without her, so he either had to be in chains or dead.

Ceaseless inward questions badgered her brain as she tried to imagine Colton's situation. If he were free, he would have come to see her. Neither duty nor fear of his master had stopped him from coming before, so his absence could only mean that Richard had physically prevented him. And if Richard considered Colton's disloyalty grounds for imprisonment, what prevented him from ordering Colton's death? Cahira had already seen how little respect Richard held for life. He saw himself as lord and master of everyone under his authority, and he could have instigated Colton's death with little more than a nod.

If Colton was dead— Cahira tried to swallow the lump that lingered in her throat. For weeks she had been telling herself that Colton was strong and clever enough to prove his worth to his master. His tongue was quick; he would convince Richard to let him live. His arm was strong; he would fight and be victorious if allowed to duel for his life. His love was deathless; he would come to her as soon as he found a way to escape his master.

But he would not die. God would not let him die, for her baby would need a father.

Cahira's hand moved automatically to her stomach, where the seed of life fluttered like a wee butterfly against the smooth underskin. She had suspected that she carried a child a few weeks after her return home, and now she was certain. She had not shared her secret with anyone. Upon hearing the news, her mother would only retreat deeper into her prayer life, and Sorcha would go pale and sway on her feet. And her father—her father did not deserve to have an heir as extraordinary as this child. This child would have Colton's heart and strength, his sterling good looks and noble qualities. And if by God's grace he possessed a wee bit of her Irish nature and her father's leadership, one day he would make a king who might just be gifted enough to establish a true and lasting peace between the Gaels and Normans.

She broke into a smile and lifted her chin at the thought. Though it would pain her father to admit it, the Gaels would benefit from a touch of Norman blood. The outsiders were a ruthless and stiff people, to be sure, but in many things they seemed years ahead of the people of Connacht.

Cahira tilted her head, studying Sorcha and Murchadh. Those two rode together ahead of her, their horses covering the forest trail with slow, stately steps, their own thoughts probably a thousand miles away. If not for Cahira's trouble, Murchadh might have found the courage to ask her father for permission to wed the maid, but of late no one had dared risk the king's dark and dangerous mood to ask for anything.

Cahira felt her spirit stir as she crossed the invisible boundary between her father's fields and the primeval forest. Murchadh's gruff voice faded in the stillness, and she lifted her eyes to the tall, straight trunks surrounding her like masts of ships long-sunk in the sea. Once, when she was younger, her father had taken her to the coast of Connacht, where the tides roared in at the base of steep rocky cliffs and seagulls pinwheeled overhead. Awed by the power and frightening force of the sea, she had clung to her father's arm as the wind sprayed her with seawater. In time, when she learned that the crashing turquoise ocean would not hurt her, the scene filled her with a profound sense of understanding. It was as if God carved out this special place just to remind man how great the Creator was.

The forest spoke to her of the same truth. Cahira slowed her pace, allowing Murchadh and Sorcha to move farther ahead. A cathedral-like stillness pervaded the woods here, and by closing her eyes she could almost imagine that she had entered the throne room of God himself. If he would only look down and see her, an earnest petitioner ready to make intercession on behalf of another soul.

A rustling sound made Cahira's heart leap in her chest. A colossal horse with legs like tree trunks stomped through the ferns alongside the trail. Though the man astride the beast wore a common tunic and cloak, Cahira knew instantly that the rider was no Gael.

The stranger sat unsteadily on the animal, his eyes dark beneath his hood as he maneuvered the animal onto the trail. Cahira automatically hooked her thumb in her belt, where a small dagger lay hidden among the folds of her tunic, and her eyes darted toward the place where Sorcha and Murchadh rode, unconcerned and unaware.

"Do not call out, Cahira."

The low voice seemed familiar, and she frowned as she placed the voice with a name. "Oswald?"

He reached up and slipped the hood from his head, then gave her a dry, one-sided smile. "I thought I'd find you here. The river was your trysting place, was it not?"

Was? His use of the past tense startled her. A thousand emotions rose in her breast—hope, fear, and anger, for the man before her was a traitor and murder. And yet he would have news of Colton. He had obviously come from Athlone, and in disguise.

After a long pause, during which she fought for self-control, she demanded an answer: "Why are you here?"

A wry smile flashed in the thicket of his beard as he pulled a parchment from his tunic. "I have a message from your beloved. Colton is well and sends you his greetings."

Mindless of all else, she rushed forward and sprang for the letter; she would have torn it from his hand had he not relaxed his grip. Breaking the seal, she unfolded the parchment and turned away to read the inked lines. She would not let Oswald study her face while she read her husband's words. Since they had been so cruelly wrested apart, this was the first private moment she could share with him.

My darling wife—

Oswald has come and said I might write you. Though I do not understand his motives, I am happy to be able to tell you I am well. My heart longs for your voice, my eyes grow weary with waiting for some glimpse of your lovely face, and my arms ache to hold you. Most of all, I most earnestly desire to tell you all I have been thinking about the future, and I have not grown weary of praying for the peace you and I both earnestly desire.

Oswald urges me to hurry. He must be away before the guards resume their patrols. Dearest Cahira, know that I adore you and think of you constantly. Rest in our blessed Lord, and in my prayer for peace.

I remain your loving husband forever,

Colton

CAHIRA CLUTCHED THE LETTER TO HER BREAST AS HER EYES FILLED with tears. He was alive and well! He did not say if he was imprisoned or in want, but he seemed in good spirits.

"Is he truly well?" she asked, not turning around. "Has he suffered on my account?"

"No more than you have suffered on his." Oswald's voice softened. "Turn, lady, and let me tell you what he did not dare write in a letter."

Cahira whirled, hope setting her suspicions and fears to flight.

"My friend Colton," Oswald said, nearly disarming her with his smile, "wishes to see you. He is watched most carefully, of course, but of late his guards have begun to relax. He does not dare leave Athlone in daylight hours, but wants to slip away after dark and meet you at some convenient place."

Cahira's heart raced. "We have heard that Richard is leaving soon."

Oswald tilted his head, acknowledging her statement. "'Tis true. So if you want to claim your husband, you must agree to meet him in a private place. The riverbank is not safe, for it lies too close to your father's fortress. Carnfree would be better. The landscape on that hilltop is bare, so once the sun rises, any intruders would be visible as they approached."

Cahira let her eyes drift from the knight's face as she considered his news. Colton had promised to meet her by the river if he escaped. This perilous plan did not sound like anything Colton would suggest.

She looked at the disguised knight, her joy deteriorating into suspicion. This Oswald had betrayed Colton and murdered Lorcan. Though he came bearing an honest letter from Colton, he had already shown himself fonder of treachery than friendship. It was likely that he wanted to snare her in a trap, for Colton himself had warned her that Richard would like nothing better than to have the king's daughter for a hostage. Carnfree was secluded and convenient to Athlone, so if she went there alone, no one would hear her screams or see her abduction. And any number of men might be hiding in the little huts when she arrived.

She closed her eyes and bit back a scream of frustration. She wanted to go. She would have gone in a heartbeat if Colton had truly asked, but she could not risk herself because doing so meant risking her father and his men! Oh, that her father were not a king!

She returned her gaze to the knight's face. "When shall I meet Colton at Carnfree?"

"On the morrow, after sunset." His brows lifted. "I'm sure I don't need to remind you to come alone. Bring your maid if you must, but no guards."

Cahira folded the parchment and slipped it beneath the sleeveless tunic she wore over her gown, daring to hope that Oswald spoke truly. How Colton would rejoice when she told him her secret! News of the coming child would seal their marriage and signal God's blessing.

"I will come." Determined to test his story, she tucked one hand into her belt and studied Oswald's dark face. "But tomorrow will not be possible—and I must bring a guard. My father does not allow me to venture away from Rathcroghan without Murchadh."

"Impossible! Colton will not remain if he sees a warrior approaching."

"Colton has nothing to fear from Murchadh."

The knight's expression clouded in anger. "Your men were ready enough to kill him three months ago."

"Those were my father's men. Murchadh would not dare harm the father of the king's grandson."

Oswald's expression didn't change for a moment, then her words fell into place. "Colton sired a son in one night?" He slipped from his horse, his face twisting in an expression of remarkable malignity. "Or can it be that you are lying?"

She met his accusing eyes without flinching. "I'm not lying."

"Then perhaps," he came closer, "the child you carry is not Colton's at all. Perhaps you married him only to disguise your dalliance with some Irish peasant. Did you wed Colton only to cover the birth of your—what is the Gaelic word?—your fatherless *diolain?*"

Cahira stood her ground, unwilling to cower before the arrogant lout who came steadily closer. "My child was conceived in love and in honor," she said, fury almost choking her. "Though I am not surprised that you are familiar with the Gaelic word for a fatherless child. How many poor girls have you ruined during your stay in Athlone?"

His hand caught her arm and held it tightly. "Enough," he whispered in her ear, his stench filling her nostrils. "Enough to know there's not an Irish wench alive worth dying for. And Colton will die, my fair Cahira. Whether you come with me now or surrender at Carnfree on the morrow, Colton will die unless you present yourself to Lord

Richard. Your husband is disgraced, useless in the eyes of our lord. His only worth is as bait to lure a king's daughter."

Struggling in his grasp, Cahira found the knight stronger than she had supposed. She drew a deep breath to scream, but his free hand clapped over her mouth, holding her tight against his chest. "Your hairy giant is too far away to hear," he hissed. "How clever of you to walk so far behind! Cahira, my little rebellious princess, your obstinacy will get you into trouble if you do not yield!"

Urgency set Cahira's blood afire. Her hand flew to her belt, where she pulled out the little dagger and held it in the folds of her tunic. It was a small blade, more useful for whittling or cutting string than for defense, but Murchadh had taught her how to use it to maximum effect.

"Be still!" Oswald murmured, dragging her toward his horse. "'Twould have been easier if you had agreed to meet me, but I shall take you to Athlone nonetheless. If you truly are with child, for your own sake, be still!"

She relaxed for a moment, hoping he would believe she had acquiesced. In the instant she went limp in his arms, he turned his head and glanced over the horse's back. As he turned, Cahira tightened her grip around the little blade, then swung it in an upward arc, aiming directly for the fiend's eye.

The blade struck home. Oswald bellowed in a roar of pain and released her. Cahira stumbled from his grasp as blood poured over his cheek and hands, painting his face in a crimson devil's mask. For a long moment he stood there, his hands pressed to his eye, his fingers curling in a paroxysm of pain, then he staggered toward her, hate burning like a torch in his remaining eye.

"I'll kill you, witch!"

She turned to run, but hadn't gone more than five feet when his bloody hands gripped her shoulders. Before she had time to think, he turned her and swung his fist, the blow slamming a shaft of pure white pain through her head. The air smelled of male sweat and fury, the road vibrated with his inhuman roar, then she folded gently at the knees and crumpled, her eyes wide and unfocused.

❦ 25 ❦

When the world cleared again, Cahira lay with her head in Sorcha's soft lap. Murchadh stood before her, his eyes shiny with concern and kindness.

"He's dead, lass," he said, shrugging. "He'll not be bothering you again. But we'll have to take his body to your father and explain all this."

"He brought me news of Colton," she whispered weakly, her head throbbing where his fist had connected with her temple. "But I am certain 'twas only a trap. Colton is not so crazy in love that he would risk our lives."

"And you're a clever girl, haven't I always said so?" Murchadh stood, exposing the sight of Oswald's body draped across his own gigantic horse, the ground dark and damp where his blood had spilled.

At the sight of the dead knight, Cahira's tears began to flow again.

"You're not crying for that foul brute, are you now?" Sorcha frowned, her eyes dark. "The world's better off without the likes of him in it."

Cahira shook her head, unable to explain that she wept not for the loss of an enemy, but for the loss of hope. She would never see Colton again. And if Oswald meant it when he said Colton was useless except as bait for her, her husband was doomed.

FIERY LIGHT LICKED AT THE PLASTERED WALLS AS CAHIRA STOOD IN the midst of her father's councilors. Murchadh and Sorcha had already given their reports of what happened on the trail, but the king of Connacht had not yet called for his daughter's testimony. Finally, he looked at her, his handsome face reserved, his eyes wary.

Cahira stood, her legs feeling as insubstantial as air, then slowly began to tell her story. She started from the beginning, on the day she decided to enter the tournament at Athlone in order to show the Normans that the Gaels would not be easily conquered. She restrained her pride when she spoke of Colton's honor and courage. "This vile knight," she pointed to Oswald's body, which lay stretched out in the center of the hall, "killed Lorcan the brehon. Colton was with me the entire night, for we had just been wed. Ask Peadar, and he'll confirm the truth of it. My husband is a noble and virtuous man, and though for him I *would* have slipped away to meet the Normans at Carnfree, yet I could not. I will be loyal to Connacht's king, though Connacht's king would disown me if he could."

A silence settled upon the room, an absence of sound that filled the room like smoke from green wood. Cahira walked through that silence, pushing her way through the strangely thickened air, and sank to her chair as her father stood.

"Daughter." Her father looked at her with unguarded tenderness in his eyes. "You would have broken my heart had you gone to Carnfree—and you would have doomed our kingdom. I am that you have come to your senses about this Norman."

Cahira shook her head. "'Twas not only regard for your kingdom that kept me from agreeing to go to Carnfree. I refused because I knew Colton himself would not have approved. If my husband wanted me to be Richard's pawn, he would have taken me to Athlone as soon as we were bound in matrimony. But Colton knew his master's plans, so we went instead to Meath. We did all, Father, in the hope that our two peoples could dwell together in peace, safety, and affection." She held up her hand and lowered her gaze to the silver band that encircled her finger. "Love, loyalty, and friendship—that was our dream for Connacht."

Her father looked down, his long lashes hiding his eyes, and hesitated for a moment. "Perhaps I have misjudged your husband," he said, his voice dull and troubled. "There is honor in him, but still he is a Norman, and his master is set on returning to Limerick. When the required year and a day have passed, you will be well rid of him."

"No." Cahira's gaze shifted from her father to her mother. "I will not be rid of my husband, for I carry his child within me. In six months, Colton's child will be born in this house, and if the child is a boy, he will be part of our *rigdamnae* and eligible to be king. I will not leave my son fatherless."

The councilors gasped in surprised horror; even Murchadh blinked in amazement. The thin line of the king's mouth clamped tight for a moment, and his thick throat bobbled as he swallowed. Without speaking, he turned to his wife and reached for her hand.

Cahira's mother stepped forward, her free hand at her pale throat. "Daughter," a sudden spasm of grief knit her brows, "are you quite certain? It has been a stressful time—"

"I am certain." Cahira's hand flattened across her belly as her lips curved in a smile. "A child will be born in summer, and Colton will be his father."

Her father sighed heavily, sank back into his seat, and gripped the armrest of his chair. "Cahira," he commanded, his eyes meeting hers, "take your mother and your maid, and wait upstairs while I speak to my men. We will decide what we must do."

Cahira nodded and rose from her chair, then joined Sorcha and her mother at the doorway. *Perhaps*, she thought as she stepped into the chilly air of the entry, *Colton and I can accomplish through separation what we could not accomplish through unity.*

An hour later, Murchadh entered the chamber, ready to convey her father's decision. "The king has decided to ride to Athlone with the villain's body," he said, swiping his hand through his tangled hair. "When confronted with the proof of the incident, we pray Richard will stop his plotting and return to Limerick. We will do all we can to prove ourselves honorable, calm, and willing to work with the agents of his majesty King Henry. 'Tis the only way we can remain faithful allies and keep our land of Connacht."

"And Colton?"

A broad smile lifted the warrior's lined cheeks. "Your father the king is marshaling the largest force we can gather so that his request for your Colton will carry a reasonable amount of weight. He's not certain what he'll do with a knight, providing Richard is willing to part with him, but perhaps he can teach us a thing or two about Normans."

A cry of relief broke from Cahira's lips. Weeping with gratitude and joy, she fell into Murchadh's awkward embrace and scarcely heard his embarrassed words of comfort.

THE NEXT MORNING, MESSENGERS LEFT RATHCROGHAN JUST AFTER sunrise, and a return message set the time and place for the meeting: on the morrow, Monday, at midday of the first day of the new year, Lord Richard de Burgo would meet Felim, King of the O'Connors on the road between Athlone and Rathcroghan. "My intentions," Richard had scrawled at the bottom of the page, "are entirely honorable. We will not come to fight, but to parlay a peace."

"I'll believe Richard is sincerely interested in peace when I see him coming with a bigger army than ours *and* a flag of truce," Murchadh grumbled.

When the assigned day came, Murchadh met Cahira at the barn and helped her mount her horse. Though her father objected, she insisted upon riding with the king's party. She didn't know if Colton would be riding with Richard's men, but if he was, she had to look on his face. Richard might object to releasing Colton, but she could wait patiently for the issue to be settled as long as she knew Colton was well.

A cold, drizzling rain began to fall as they left Rathcroghan, and Cahira drew her cloak closer about her and rode in silence. The gray rain seemed to deepen the colors of the land around her—washing the green fields, darkening the muddy path, brightening the crimson berries on the roadside shrubs. They rode in silence for the space of half an hour, then Murchadh reined in his horse and pointed toward a rise on the path ahead. "There they are—in position for battle." A bitter edge of cynicism steeled his voice. "Lined up and ready for the charge."

"They won't charge." Cahira scanned the line ahead for any knight who looked like Colton, but from this distance one armored man looked just like another. Though none wore visors over their faces, mail hoods covered their hair, and nearly every man wore a beard.

"Bring the villain's body forward," Felim called, lifting his hand. As the Gaels spread out in another line, Murchadh rode toward the king, leading Oswald's horse. The knight's body, bound now in burlap, draped over the saddle like a sack of gourds.

Cahira turned her head as the malodorous burden passed. The traitor had been dead three days.

Urging his horse forward in a slow walk, her father stiffened and took on a regal air. "Hear me, Richard de Burgo," he called. "I have arranged this meeting on a mission of peace and to discuss a trade— one man for another. The man I offer you is dead, but since he is one of yours, I am returning the scoundrel's body instead of exacting vengeance for his assault upon a king's daughter."

Richard straightened in the saddle as the horse and its loathsome burden approached. Murchadh stopped just beyond the line of Gaelic warriors, then turned and flicked a whip at the dead man's mount. The animal jolted forward, then slowed and whinnied in the empty space between the two lines.

Richard jerked his hand toward a pair of knights, who rode forward and caught the beast. While one man held its bridle, the other dismounted and cut the strings around the shroud. He peered for an instant at the dead man, then turned away, his face contorted in a grimace of revulsion.

"My Lord," he called in a strangled voice, "'tis Oswald, and no doubt. His eyeball is pierced, and his throat's been cut."

Richard received this news in silence, then gestured for the men to bring the horse forward. When the animal and its dread baggage had passed behind the line and below the slope of the hillside, the nobleman rested both hands on the broad curve of his saddle.

"How do I know you did not murder this man without cause?" Richard called, his voice courteous but patronizing. "I can think of no reason Oswald would assault your daughter. I have only your word to account for the matter."

"You have my daughter's word as well," Felim answered in a rough voice. Cahira's heart stirred with pride as she stole a sidelong look at her father. His long face and glaring eyes, which could intimidate most men even from a good distance, filled now with beaten sadness. "I trust my daughter, Richard, above any man in Connacht. She would not lie to me. And she would not put her dagger into a man's eye without good cause."

An audible murmur rose from the long line of knights, and Cahira felt grim satisfaction in the sound of it. Did Norman women not know how to defend themselves? She'd strike the same way, and more forcefully, if any conniving traitor ever attacked her again.

◈

FROM BENEATH THE HILLSIDE, TUCKED OUT OF SIGHT, COLTON heard Felim's defense and the murmur that followed. He wasn't certain why Richard decided to bring him along for this meeting with the king of Connacht, but he was glad to be free of the miserable hut where he had been confined. And though his arms were still bound, signifying that Richard did not yet fully trust him, his heart rejoiced to know Cahira's father had finally proved willing to meet with Richard. God had certainly worked in an unexpected way, and the peace he and Cahira had dreamed of might be within reach today. Both leaders had spoken of peace, and both seemed willing to avoid conflict.

Despite these auspicious signs, the voice of uncertainty still nagged at him. He had not heard from Cahira in more than three months, and he suspected Oswald had not delivered his hasty letter of three days before. Most troubling was Felim's assertion that Cahira had wounded Oswald.

Richard's thoughts seemed to wander in the same direction. "Before I can accept the word of an Irishwoman," the baron was saying now, his voice crisp and clear in the chilly air, "I must know why your daughter struck my man. Was she seized in a fit of temper? Did she toss the blade and accidentally stick Sir Oswald? If this were Normandy or England, we would convene a court to hear this case and come to a clear understanding of the matter."

"This is Éireann and Connacht," Felim O'Connor answered, tossing the words across the void like stones. "And my daughter has told the story in my council, where she was completely cleared of any wrong. Your man, as you describe him, lunged for her, assaulted her, and would have abducted her—and this after learning she carries a child!"

The surge of sudden rage took Colton unaware, like a white-hot bolt of lightning through his chest and belly. Oswald had attacked Cahira? *Struck* her? And she was . . . with child?

His child. His wife, wherever she was, was carrying his son or daughter.

Biting back an oath, he pulled against the ropes binding his wrists. By heaven, he would stand idly by no longer! He had written the note that convinced her to listen to Oswald, half-hoping that Richard would succeed in bringing Cahira to Athlone, for at least they would then be together. With crystal clarity he now saw that those hopes sprang from selfishness and pride; God had been right to deny them. But if God was merciful and just, he would hear Colton's prayer now and grant him strength.

"I am sorry to hear that Oswald behaved in such an unchivalrous manner," Richard said, his voice smooth as the wind carried it over the hills. "And, of course, we will accept his body and take care of the burial. And peace shall continue to overspread this land."

"Hold, I am not finished with the matter of the dead man," O'Connor called back. "I must know why this murderous scoundrel was outside Rathcroghan. Did he come purposely to work mischief upon my daughter? Or perhaps he sought to injure our cattle and crops again."

Richard tilted his head and, watching from the base of the hill, Colton saw the gesture and recognized it. Richard adopted that posture when he was searching for words.

"I know nothing about cattle or crops, though a devil may work mischief wherever he chooses," Richard finally answered. "But I suspect Oswald was in your vicinity because your daughter enticed him to come. She has done nothing but flaunt herself before my men since we arrived in Connacht."

Colton gasped at his master's bald lie. Sputtering with rage and indignation, he lifted one foot over his saddle and slid from his horse, his hands still tied. Until that moment, he had imagined that Richard still possessed some honor, but if he was willing to accuse Cahira of immodesty in order to disguise his own ambitious plot, there was not a speck of genuine honor in him.

Bracing himself, he quickened his pace and panted up the hill, then pushed his way through the line of mounted knights.

"Lord Richard!" he roared, aware of startled expressions all around him. "I beg you, my lord! Hear me!"

A Sabbath stillness reigned on the field, with only a snatch of bird-song to disturb it. Though the warriors on the northern side of the field were an indistinct blur, his worried eyes caught a glimpse of a bright blue garment—a lady's gown. Cahira was there, after all. Nothing else mattered.

Richard turned slowly, the once handsome and compassionate veneer on his face peeled back to reveal the violence underneath. He regarded Colton with an expression he might have used to consider an especially repulsive insect.

"Get back!" he ordered, his low voice brimming with hate.

"No, sir." With a quick snap of his shoulders, Colton turned to face the Irish, lifting his bound hands into the air. Let them see him and know the truth. He had not deserted Cahira, nor had he sent Oswald to harm her. They might be thinking anything, but he would tell them the truth.

"Lord Richard!" Felim came forward on his horse, close enough for Colton to see the blue in the king's eyes. "I mentioned a trade—we have returned the scoundrel's body to you, and in return we would ask for this knight." He glanced at Colton for any sign of objection, then returned his gaze to Richard. "I see from the man's bonds that you have no longer have any use for him. If he is dead to you, let him live with us. Under Irish law, he *is* my daughter's husband."

Richard scowled, his brows knitting together. "You would exchange a dead man for a living one? Both men are mine, sir. This is no exchange at all. 'Tis robbery and murder, pure and plain."

Energized by anger, Colton stepped toward his master. "I must beg you, sir, to heed the king of Connacht and relieve me of my vows of fealty. In exchange for my bed and board I once swore my service to you, but the time has come for us to part. 'Tis obvious from your ill treatment of me that you no longer consider me of service."

"This is how you would repay me?" Richard's voice dripped with contempt as he stretched his arm toward the huddle of Irishmen. "You would prefer life with a band of barbarians to service in my garrison?"

"I once fought for you," Colton answered, his determination like a steady rock inside him. "Many times I have picked up my sword and struck men for no reason than your pleasure. But your pleasure of late has been to keep me chained like a dog, so today I swear I will fight for you no more! Kill me or release me, but I will not return in your company."

The veins in Richard's throat stood out like ropes. "You would disavow your allegiance to the king?"

"I bear King Henry no ill will. But if he and his Crown stand for deception, ruthlessness, and ambition, yes, I disavow my promise."

Silence lay upon the line of knights like a dense and heavy fog. Colton sensed the shock and horror of his comrades, but he dared not tear his gaze from his master's face. For an instant Richard's eyes showed white all around, like a panicked horse, then his jaws wobbled and he gestured to Gilbert, the knight who rode at his right hand.

He shifted slightly in his saddle. "Gilbert, bring your sword."

Colton stared, perplexed, as Gilbert slipped from his horse and unsheathed his sword. The barrel-chested knight advanced slowly and hesitated a few feet from Colton.

"Our friend knight has said we must kill him or release him," Richard continued, looking at Colton with a smile hidden in his eyes. "And the Irish across the way have given us a corpse to take his place. So I suppose we agree to the exchange."

"No!" A keening wail rose from the Irish crowd, lifting on the wind like the howling of an animal in pain. Colton closed his eyes at the sound, knowing Cahira had heard enough to guess Richard's intention. The nobleman's pride would not allow Colton to walk away; the knightly vow had been made for life. Colton's life was what Richard would take today.

"Hold there!" A swift shadow of anger swept across the Irish king's face, and the strength of this voice overpowered even Richard's. "That man is my son-in-law. Do not take his life, or this peace you speak of will die today as well."

Richard turned to face Felim, his eyes wide with pretend innocence. "Surely you do not expect me to let him depart with his hands still bound."

Richard looked down at Gilbert, who stood in front of Colton with a melancholy frown upon his face. "Nor can I," Richard pitched his voice to reach the two knights, and not a hair beyond, "allow you to join the Irish and lift your sword against us. Free him, Sir Gilbert, but do it by cutting off his right hand."

Terror lodged in Colton's throat, making it impossible for him to speak. He saw his master smile as he maneuvered his horse to stand between Colton and the Irish king, effectively blocking Felim's view.

"You will lose your arm, and quite possibly your life," Richard said, meeting Colton's gaze, "unless you beg my forgiveness and forswear this foolish marriage. The choice is yours."

Colton closed his eyes and thought of Cahira, then offered his arm to Gilbert's blade.

❧ 26 ❧

S unday, August 29, 1999
Ballyshannon

SOMEWHERE A ROOSTER CROWED, CALLING ME AWAKE. I DRIFTED
out of a deep sleep in which memories of the previous day mingled
with inchoate fragments of dreams. Sitting up, I ran my fingers
through my tousled hair, puzzled by images of Patrick at the Shannon
Pot, Cahira and Colton at Carnfree, of Lorcan the brehon's thoughtful
face as he warned the newly married couple that their path was fraught
with risk.

The risks had not lessened with the passing of time. By choosing a
different path than his family and most of the people in his village,
twenty-first-century Patrick would face hazards, too.

What had happened yesterday? Last night I had been certain
Patrick made a sincere commitment to Christ, yet I couldn't be certain
his decision would stand in the trials of the coming day. The parable of
the four seeds drifted into my thoughts. Jesus told a story of a farmer
scattering seeds along a path. Some seeds fell on the path itself and
were gobbled up by birds; other seeds fell upon rock and couldn't grow

because they couldn't put down roots. Other seeds fell among thorns, which choked the plants, but other seeds fell upon good soil, where they grew and yielded fruit.

To which group did Patrick belong? Thomas Smithson had planted a seed in the fertile soil of Patrick's heart, and I had witnessed an immediate growth, but I honestly couldn't say whether his response was based in emotion, intellect, or will. In the next few days I'd probably see whether the seed had landed on the dry rock of his considerable intellect or in the soil of his emotions. I'd pray that the seed of the gospel had taken root in a genuine commitment to Christ.

I swung my legs out of bed, stretched, and padded softly to the window. A chilly breeze had blown last night, but I lifted the window and leaned out on the windowsill, breathing in the pungent scents of morning, heather, and manure.

I grinned as I heard the rumbling sound of the milking machines and the loud blare of the radio. Patrick was up early, but as I leaned out the window and looked toward the barn, I was surprised to see him in the doorway of the milking shed. He stood there, propped against the doorframe, his head bent over a book.

Bemused, I leaned back into my room. What book could be so engaging that he snatched moments from the milking to read?

I showered and dressed, then went downstairs for breakfast. "Good morning," I told Mrs. O'Neil, who stood at the sink. She glanced at me over her shoulder, flashed a quick smile, and went back to rinsing a stack of dishes.

I sat on the bench and helped myself to toast and eggs from the serving platter. "Are Taylor and Maddie up already?"

"They're going to Dublin to look at flower designs," she answered, lifting one shoulder in a shrug. "'Tis stuff and nonsense, if you ask me. Simple is better when it comes to decoration. But Maddie picked up some peculiar ideas in New York. She wants the front of the church to be totally covered in flowers."

I ran my knife along the mound of butter and kept my mouth shut. If I defended the New York notion of a properly decorated church, I might alienate Mrs. O'Neil. But if I agreed with her, she might mention it to Maddie, who'd think I was complaining about her taste in wedding decoration. The less I said, the better off we'd all be.

My heart lifted at the sound of thumping on the back porch. I tried to appear indifferent and calm when Patrick entered the kitchen, but I couldn't help feeling happy that he'd come in.

"Morning, Kathleen."

I tingled as he said my name. Good grief, I'd have to be careful, or soon I'd be hanging on his every word like young Erin Kelly.

"Good morning yourself," I answered lightly, transferring my gaze to my toast. "You're up early."

"I couldn't sleep." He came forward with a book in his hand and dropped it on the table. As he sat across from me, I glanced at the leather-bound volume and widened my eyes: *The Holy Bible.*

He grinned at my reaction. "I've been reading half the night and in every minute I could find this morning." He folded his hands, ignoring the empty plate and the tray of food in front of him. "I thought I'd start reading at the beginning and make my way forward—but I didn't get far. Already I have questions."

"About Genesis?" I frowned, trying to figure out what might have given him trouble—creation versus evolution, the creation of man, or Adam's incredibly long lifespan. I tended to think of Genesis as fairly straightforward, but Patrick wasn't a typical reader. He possessed a questioning intellect, and there were a number of tough questions in the first chapter of Genesis alone.

He opened the Bible and turned a few pages. "I understand about Creation. We learned about that in Catechism class. But the thing that gives me pause is here, in Genesis chapter two."

"What's that you're reading?" Unable to control her curiosity any longer, Mrs. O'Neil peered over at us. "The *Bible?* What's got into you, Paddy?"

"Curiosity, Mum." He kept his eyes fixed upon me as he answered. "And reality. Consider this—in the Bible God said, 'It is not good that the man should be alone; I will make him a help meet for him.' So God caused a deep sleep to fall upon Adam, and while he slept, God took one of his ribs and closed up the flesh. And from the rib, which God took from Adam, God made a woman and brought her to the man." He looked at me expectantly.

"So?" I lifted a brow. "If you can accept the creation of the world from nothing, why can't you accept woman's creation from Adam's rib?"

"'Tis not the creation that gives me pause—'tis the *reason* she was created. Was woman meant only to be a helper for the man?"

Mrs. O'Neil laughed. "And what else would you have us be?" Vigorously wiping a wet dish, she turned to face her son. "'Tis what we are, helpers. I've been helping your father since the day we married, and I expect I'll be helping him—" She turned the catch in her voice into a cough, then shook her head. "Well, 'tis a woman's lot in life, the helping. If God decreed it, it must be so." Her face closed in a forbidding expression. "And you'd better not let your father hear you questioning God's holy Word. Accept it for what it is, and don't ask questions."

Patrick gave his mother a quick, denying glance. "I don't think God is afraid of my questions, Mum."

"That's right," I added, hoping she would understand that for Patrick, this was no small step. "The Bible says we can come boldly before the throne of grace. And the Lord promises to give wisdom to anyone who asks."

"Right so." Patrick leaned over the table, his eyes burning into mine. "Keeping that in mind, yesterday you told me about women who left the traditional roles of womanhood, and God blessed their efforts. Anika took up a sword, and Aidan a paintbrush, and Flanna entered war itself. They were far more than mere helpers, Kathleen. I just can't believe God would create something so lovely and competent—" his eyes clung to mine, analyzing my reaction—"and intend women only for helping."

His gaze was so compelling I didn't think I'd be able to answer. "I'm not sure I know what you mean," I managed to whisper, "but I was thinking about going back to the library at Terryglass soon. I could ask Mrs. Sullivan to help me look for a Hebrew dictionary and a copy of the Pentateuch. We may be able to find the answers there."

Patrick slapped the table in satisfaction. "Marvelous idea. I'll go with you. The library will be closed today, being a Sunday, but we'll go tomorrow."

The corner of my mouth twisted in a half-smile as I stood. Obviously, Patrick wasn't one of the seeds gobbled up by wild birds. He had already begun to put down some serious roots. The trouble was, God seemed to expect me to be the gardener. I didn't see myself as mentor material.

"You're not going to make it easy for me, are you?" I asked.

"I just want to understand. Curiosity, you know." Patrick grinned at me, then sniffed appreciatively at the sausage and rashers on the breakfast tray. "Smells great, Mum. I'm starving."

I left them alone in the kitchen and went outside to work on a less taxing project.

THE HOUSE WAS QUIET THE NEXT MORNING WHEN I CAME downstairs to meet Patrick. I knew he was waiting outside in the yard; I'd seen him from my bedroom window. Maddie and Taylor had stayed overnight in Dublin with one of Maddie's old school chums, so the house would be nice and peaceful today so Mr. O'Neil could rest.

I tiptoed through the foyer, drawn by the memory of a pretty bowl of fruit on the kitchen counter. Mrs. O'Neil kept the bowl well stocked, so I thought I might grab a couple of apples in case Patrick and I got hungry on the drive to Terryglass. I paused at the swinging door, though, when I heard the sound of hushed voices in the kitchen.

"Maddie is the key, you mark my words." The words were low and intense, but there was no mistaking Mrs. O'Neil's voice. "She'll convince him to stay. If he truly loves her, he will."

I backed away, mortified by the realization that I'd been eavesdropping. Apparently Patrick and I were not supposed to hear this conversation, but what did it mean? Maddie was the key to what? And who were they wanting to stay? Taylor or Patrick?

I reached the stairs, then turned and opened the front door, calling a loud and cheerful good-bye before I stepped out into the yard. Patrick looked up, and if I were a vain woman, I'd say his face lit up as I approached. Maybe the morning sun was playing tricks on me. Or—I was *trying* to be realistic—maybe he was just grateful I was finally ready to go.

We enjoyed the drive to Terryglass, and I was glad to see that Patrick seemed to genuinely relax in my company. Whatever pressures he felt at home did not follow him today, and he passed the time telling me funny stories about his flatmates in Limerick. I was pleased to note none of the flatmates had feminine names, so the rumors of Patrick's availability appeared to be true.

Mrs. Sullivan looked up from the reference desk and smiled when Patrick and I entered the library. "So you're back," she said, her smile broadening when she saw that I was returning several of the books she had loaned to me. "Were they at all helpful?"

"They were wonderful, thank you." I slid the books over the desk, then nodded at Patrick. "Mrs. Sullivan, I'd like you to meet Patrick O'Neil. He has a question about a Scripture verse in Genesis, and we thought we might check the original Hebrew to clear up any confusion about the translation."

"A Hebrew scholar?" Mrs. Sullivan's eyes flashed with admiration as she studied Patrick. "Well, we don't get calls for the Pentateuch every day, but I'll see what I can do for the young man."

As Mrs. Sullivan stepped away from the desk, Patrick looked at me. "Will you come?"

"I'm going to nose around in the Irish history collection for a bit," I said, pointing toward the rare book room. "But I'll come out later and see what you've found."

I had intended to spend only an hour in the back room, but I ran across an account of Felim O'Connor's latter days, so nearly two hours passed before I popped out of my cave and searched for Patrick. I found him hunched over a carrel, one finger pressed to the thick pages of a book.

I let my hand fall on his shoulder. "Finding anything interesting?"

"Kathleen, look at this."

Not lifting his eyes from the page, he shifted in the wide wooden chair as if inviting me to share the seat. Hesitantly, I lowered myself into the empty space and braced myself against the edge of the desk. "What did you find?"

He tapped the page with his fingertip. "Well, almost every translation says God created the woman to be a helper fitting, or suitable, for him, but the actual Hebrew word means something altogether different."

"Really?" I leaned closer, eager to see what he meant. Unless I was mistaken, Patrick was about to tell me something that might contradict everything I'd ever been taught about the biblical role of women. And, being a woman, I couldn't help being interested.

Patrick nodded. "The phrase we translate 'helper fitting him' is *ezer kenegdo*, but the Hebrew word *ezer* is a combination of two roots, one meaning 'to rescue or save' and the other meaning 'to be strong.'" His finger slid over the column of thickly-printed material. "There's more here, but I'm trying to abbreviate the information. In summation, the phrase *ezer kenegdo* should be translated as 'I will make a power or strength corresponding to man.' There is absolutely no sense of subservience in the word at all."

Patrick sat back in the chair, his face alight with excitement as his gaze met mine. "Don't you see? It makes perfect sense. God looked around at his creation and saw that he had created nothing to equal man. So he said, 'I will make a being equal to him.'"

"Hold on a minute, Patrick." I smiled, thinking of the brouhaha that would result if this doctrine were preached in Aunt Kizzie's conservative church. "For years women have been taught that we are lesser than men, and that's why we are to submit to them."

"That's what bothered me when I read Genesis yesterday morning." Patrick rested one arm on the back of the chair so we fit together more comfortably on the seat. "From all I know of God, I know he is just, and it didn't seem just for him to create one human gender lesser than the other. Besides—" he leaned forward and flipped to another page in the commentary—"submission does not mean one being is worth less than the other. Don't we believe that members of the holy

Trinity are equal in power and authority? Yet Jesus the Son and the Holy Spirit submit to the Father."

I ran my hand through my hair, urging my brain to greater effort. I'd been warned that Patrick was brilliant, but this was the first time I had brushed up against his incisive intellect.

"There are other verses," I began, feeling my way. "There's a place in the New Testament where Paul tells women to keep silent in the church."

"I read about that, and I also read another verse where he instructed men to keep silent, too, if someone else was speaking. Paul wanted to eliminate confusion and instill a sense of peace and order in the church. And it's very clear from other passages that he encouraged women to pray, prophesy, and teach."

I made a face. "Okay. Well, what about that other passage in Genesis? There's something in the curse God pronounced after Adam and Eve sinned. It says women will bring forth children in sorrow, and desire their husbands, and men will rule over them."

"I read that, too." Patrick grinned and flipped back a few pages. "Eve's curse—here it is, in Genesis 3:16. You have to remember, Kathleen, that God is not cursing Eve—indeed, he seems to be laying the groundwork for her ultimate redemption. God is telling Eve that since she chose to submit to sin, she virtually chose to give the devil a hand in her life. Hebrew scholars have declared that the phrase about childbirth would be rendered better as, 'A snare has increased your sorrow and sighing.' God did not intend children to be a curse, but the evil one lies in wait to turn blessed children into occasions for sorrow and sighing."

I fell silent as Patrick's words echoed in my mind. Had he begun to consider the implications of those words in his own life? His parents undoubtedly loved him, but the house fairly sizzled with tension whenever Patrick and his father gathered in one room. I knew Mrs. O'Neil mourned over their broken relationship. If ever a blessed child had become an occasion for sorrow and sighing, Patrick had.

"The bit about desiring a husband," his voice flattened as he continued, "has more to do with the potential action of 'turning' than 'desire.' The Hebrew actually reads, 'that you might turn to your husband, and that he might rule over you.' The word 'rule,' however, has the sense of 'protect.' This statement strengthens the institution of marriage, but there is no command for the husband to place his wife in a subjective position or consider her anything less than his equal."

Leaning my head on my hand, I watched the play of emotions on Patrick's face. He looked like a man who had just inherited a treasure chest and was delighted to discover that it contained gold and priceless jewels. His excitement and joy put me to shame.

"What has come over you?" I asked, thinking aloud.

He stared at me, surprised, and then a rich blush stained his cheeks. "Well, after Saturday—" He glanced down at the books on the table, then looked at me with determination in his eyes. "You seemed almost embarrassed to be a Christian, Kathleen. I lay awake all that night wondering what could make you feel that way. I thought perhaps there was something bad or socially unacceptable in the Bible, so I thought I'd have a look and see what I could find. I hadn't read more than two pages when I saw the bit about God creating the woman as a helper." He shrugged. "I thought maybe that was part of your problem."

I looked away in a shudder of humiliation. I couldn't have been more mortified if the Lord himself had appeared in the center of the library and announced that Kathleen O'Connor had been too embarrassed to acknowledge him even before her closest friends. Suddenly I understood how the apostle Peter felt when the cock crowed.

"There's nothing in the Bible that embarrasses me," I told him, my cheeks burning. "And I'm sorry if I gave you that impression. Sometimes, I'll admit, I'm embarrassed by people who call themselves Christians. The American media seems to zero in on fanatics who bomb abortion clinics and murder doctors and hold rallies to spew their hatred of homosexuals. I'm sorry, Patrick, but it's true. And most people don't go around talking about their faith in New York."

"Maybe they should." His eyes smoldered with fire. "Maybe things would change if more people talked about the things that are really important."

I had no answer for that, but I placed my hand over his and squeezed gently. A baby Christian was preaching to the veteran. Aunt Kizzie would get a kick out of this.

"The heirs of Cahira O'Connor," he said, nodding toward my notebook, "weren't such oddities after all. They broke out of certain molds society and the Church had forced upon them, but they followed the truer path God set them on." A mischievous look came into his eyes as he smiled. "They were strong women, equal in power and influence to the men around them. So don't run from your heritage, Kathleen. Seek it."

I pressed a fingertip to the cleft in his chin. "I'll fling that piece of advice right backatcha, Patrick. You are equal in power and influence to your father, so don't run from him. He's sick and he's lonely and he's afraid. He needs you now."

For an instant his blue eyes said, *watch yourself, take care,* then a thoughtful smile curved his mouth. He caught my hand, held it tightly, then pressed my fingers to his lips in a display of fervent gallantry. "Thank you," he said, his breath warm on my skin. "I'll consider what you've said."

৩✦৩

THE NEXT MORNING, I CAUGHT TAYLOR IN THE GRAVELED LOT AT the front of the house. Hunched into the car, he was filling a trash bag with assorted debris from his journey to Dublin.

Despite the warm sun, the wind was chilly, so I huddled into my sweater. "Did you and Maddie have a good time on your trip?" I asked, leaning against the car.

"A *divil* of a good time," he joked, aping the Irish brogue. His smile faded as he stood and straightened. "Honestly, Kathy, if I see another flower before the wedding, I think I'll do something desperate. I had no idea weddings could be so complicated—or so expensive."

"This is all good for you; it's teaching you patience." I looked up at the house and searched for signs of life at the windows, but all the public rooms were empty. The O'Neils had decided not to accept any

B&B guests until after the wedding. Privately, I wondered if she would ever take any more. When Mr. O'Neil passed away, she'd have to tend to the farm by herself, and she couldn't possibly run a B&B and oversee the dairy production without outside help.

"Taylor," I asked, thinking of the conversation I'd overheard yesterday, "would you and Maddie ever consider staying at Ballyshannon?"

He eyed me with a critical squint. "Whatever makes you think I would want to stay here? I like Ireland, but I'm not exactly a rural type. And I know nothing about dairy farming."

I crossed my arms and tucked my exposed hands into the warmth of my sweater. "I know, but have you thought about Maddie's family? Mr. O'Neil may not live another year, and then what will Mrs. O'Neil do?"

Taylor looked away, then shrugged. "Get someone to help her run it, I suppose. Or she could sell."

"She'll never sell. Ballyshannon has belonged to the O'Neils for at least two hundred years."

"Then she'll save it for Patrick. By rights, he'll inherit. And when James is gone, what's to stop Patrick from running this place the way he wants to?" Taylor bent to pick up another piece of trash, then straightened and gave me a suspicious look. "What made you ask about this, Kathy?"

"Something I heard." I bit my lip. "Mr. and Mrs. were in the kitchen, and Fiona said something about Maddie talking someone into staying here. I thought she meant you."

Taylor laughed. "I'm no farmer, and the O'Neils know it."

I left him alone and walked back toward the barn. The cows were out in the pasture and away from the milking shed, but Mrs. O'Neil had mentioned that Patrick planned to clean out the stalls today. I found him inside, dressed in his usual sweater, jeans, and boots, but he also wore a heavy rubber apron around his neck. He held a pressurized hose, and as I approached he was noisily blasting the dirt from every crack and crevice of the concrete stalls.

"Got a minute?" I yelled, raising my voice above the mechanical growl of the pressure cleaner.

Patrick kicked off the motor and grinned at me. "What's up?"

"Not much." I leaned over the railing around the milking well and looked down at him. He seemed so completely in his element, so relaxed and happy, it was hard to imagine him returning to a window-less computer office in Limerick. Maybe Taylor was right, and Patrick would inherit this place.

"I heard your parents talking," I said, hoping he wouldn't think I was as big a gossip as the woman I met in the pub, "and your mom said Maddie should encourage someone to remain here on the farm. I thought she meant Taylor, but he says he has no intention of staying in Ireland." I met Patrick's gaze and felt some of the buoyancy leave my voice. "He wants to finish his doctorate, you know. In New York."

Patrick lifted one wet hand and scratched at his brow. "So?"

"So—I was wondering if maybe you were planning on remaining here. It's your farm, and you might as well stay. Your father will be needing help soon; he's already weaker than when we first arrived."

Patrick shook his head and bent to adjust a knob on the pressure cleaner. "Sorry—I have to go back to Limerick. I've postponed two projects as it is, but I'll have to get busy after the wedding. My work is in Limerick."

"But this farm! It will be yours someday, so don't you care—"

He cut me off with a dry and cynical chuckle. "My father wouldn't leave this farm to me if his immortal soul depended on it. He'd rather see it go to the bank."

I opened my mouth to protest again, but Patrick kicked at a button on the pressure washer and sent water zipping out of his hose with a frantic rush. The growling machine more than adequately broadcast Patrick's mood.

I left him there, angry and alone.

IN THE LITTLE HOUSE, I STARED AT MY NOTE CARDS AND NOTEBOOKS and wondered why my thoughts wouldn't focus on Cahira's story. Every time I tried to summon up a mental picture of Colton, bleeding and wounded, my mind substituted the image of Patrick, his eyes flashing with hurt and anger and resolve. Though I wanted to help him, though I had gone out to the milking shed with every good intention, I didn't have the power to make a difference.

Who was I, after all? An outsider. A Yank. An unexpected and barely tolerated guest.

I leaned my elbow on the desk and parked my chin in my palm. No, that wasn't right. I wasn't being entirely fair to my hosts or to myself. Mrs. O'Neil had warmed considerably since my arrival, and I think Patrick honestly enjoyed my company. If not for the friction that surrounded us, our friendship might have deepened to something more. I certainly couldn't deny the way I felt when I was with him—alive and vibrant and downright happy. And, unless the man was blind, he'd have to know I admired him tremendously.

"I think I've begun to *fancy* him," I whispered, then snorted at my own foolishness. Patrick O'Neil and me, together? Might as well try to marry a lion with a lamb. He was too extraordinary for me, far outclassing anyone I'd ever considered as a future husband. Yet my heart broke for him every time I saw him exchange sharp words with his father, and every cell in my body yearned to comfort him even when he was being prickly. Maybe my maternal instinct was out of whack, or maybe I felt a bit responsible for him since he had decided to follow Christ.

I unparked my chin and forced myself to straighten a pile of scribbled note cards I'd assembled for the Cahira book. The name of a character adorned each colorful card—Felim O'Connor, Cahira, Una. Another pile featured the characters from the other books, and as I shuffled through them I saw the names of Aidan and Flanna and Anika. Patrick's own words came back to me: *The heirs weren't such oddities. They broke out of certain molds society and the Church had forced upon them, but they followed the truer path God set them on.*

Weren't they unusual women? Until now I had truly thought so, but now I was beginning to think otherwise. Perhaps they were ordinary women forced by circumstances to do extraordinary things. If Anika's father had not died, nothing on earth would have compelled her to pick up a knight's sword. If poverty had not trapped Aidan in a life of desperation, she would never have gone to sea. And if Fort Sumter had been fired upon the month *after* Flanna's final exams, she would have graduated from medical school, taken the train home, and lived out her life in pleasant obscurity.

I had always thought of Cahira's heirs as superwomen, but perhaps they were just like me, blighted by a freakish white streak of hair but perfectly content to follow life's road . . . until something unexpected happened. Until God led them in a different direction.

Please, God, not me. I lowered my head as the truth crashed into my thoughts like surf hurling against a jagged cliff. I didn't want adventure. I didn't want to love a difficult man, mend a fractured family, or make peace in a foreign community. I just wanted to tell a story, be with my friend at his wedding, and help where I could. I didn't want to be extraordinary.

Are you afraid?

A quiet voice inside me insisted upon an answer, and I curled my hands into fists, resisting the question. Of course I wasn't afraid. I was a New Yorker, at home in crowds, in subways, even in high-rise elevators where a suspicious-looking character could hop on at any floor. I could handle almost anything in New York. . . . But this was Ireland, and I was like a fish out of water here.

Still, I could get used to this beautiful place. Something in me had prickled with jealousy to think Taylor might actually be offered an opportunity to stay here. And while I could certainly see why he wouldn't be happy in Ireland, perhaps I could be. And with someone like Patrick by my side, I wouldn't be afraid of anything.

I stood and moved to the single window at the front of the house, then looked out across the lawn. Mrs. O'Neil was coming out of the garden, a woven basket on her arm. The bright heads of roses dipped over the edge of the basket and swayed with every step she took. Though the country was remarkably conservative, Ireland had always acknowledged the strength of its women, even electing a woman president. Ireland was filled with strong women who worked hard, supported their husbands, raised their children, patiently prayed in silence, . . . and loved without reservation or conditions.

How fitting, that the Emerald Isle had given birth to women like Cahira O'Connor. She, too, might have been an unremarkable woman if the Normans had not crossed her path. She might have married her kinsman, reared a castle full of kids, and died of old age, never to be mentioned in the history books.

I ran my hand through my hair, watching Mrs. O'Neil disappear into the house, then went back to my desk. I turned on my laptop, then clicked my nails against the case as the machine booted up.

It would be nice if people were as forthright today as they had been in the thirteenth century. I could go up to Patrick and say, "If you want to marry me, I'm open to the idea," and he could say the same. We'd go to the preacher and get married, then sort everything out later.

Of course, if Mr. and Mrs. O'Neil didn't approve, I suppose they could always banish us.

The computer beeped, and I frowned, looking around at the little house—my space by day and Patrick's by night. Maybe they already had.

❧

AN UNEASY PEACE RULED AT DINNER THAT NIGHT. MADDIE AND HER mother bobbed together at the end of the table over sketches of her bouquet and the church flowers. Staring straight ahead, Taylor ate with the enthusiasm of a robot, while at the end of the table Mr. O'Neil stirred his soup and didn't say much.

At my right hand, Patrick was equally silent. We ate quietly, pretending a polite interest in Maddie's babbling conversation though none of us, with the possible exception of her mother, cared a thing about orchids and white roses and baby's breath.

During a break in Maddie's conversation, Mrs. O'Neil looked up and threw her husband a pointed look. "Taylor," she said, her gaze still fastened to her husband's face, "James and I were wondering if you and

Maddie might give a thought to staying in Ireland for a bit after the wedding. You could live here, of course, and we could give you a helping hand while you manage to set a bit of money by for the future."

Surprise siphoned the blood from Taylor's face. "Live here?" he repeated dumbly, his gaze flying to meet mine. "But—"

"It'd be wonderful, Taylor," Maddie interrupted, squeezing his hand. A rush of pink stained her cheek as she leaned toward him. "You could go the university in Dublin or even take correspondence courses. You could still finish your doctorate, but you'd do it here, where we could live rent free." She lowered her eyes. "And I could be with my dad."

I looked down at my plate, aware that she had just struck the deathblow to Taylor's plans. He didn't want to stay in Ireland, but what could he say to a woman whose father was dying? He'd seem like an inconsiderate brute if he insisted they return to New York.

"Who knows?" Mr. O'Neil's deep voice croaked through the thick silence. "You might come to like farming, after all. We might make an Irishman of you yet!"

Taylor looked like a deer caught in the headlights of an oncoming car, but as Maddie kissed his cheek and Mr. O'Neil thumped his back, no one else seemed to notice his panic.

But Patrick, who had said nothing during the exchange, abruptly stood and slammed his way out of the kitchen.

❧ 27 ❧

Patrick wasn't hard to find. I knew the cows had already been milked and turned out to pasture, so I headed toward the barn where the calves were penned. An overhead light was burning when I opened the door, and in the dim light I could see Patrick's long and lanky form hunched over the railing of the bullpen at the back of the barn.

"He won't stay," I called, startling the calves as I passed their pen. "Taylor's not a farmer. He'd be lost here."

"Doesn't matter." Patrick pulled a piece of hay from a bale beside him and stuck it into his mouth, chewing the end like a nervous accountant worrying his pencil. "Dad's made his point. He'd rather give the place to a Yank who knows next to nothing than leave it to his only son." Raw hurt glittered in his eyes as he looked at me. "The point was well made, don't you think?"

"I don't know what your father is thinking." I came closer and stood beside him at the fence, then crossed my arms over the top rail and studied the old bull. Graham Red stood as still as a statue, his white head bowed low, and I was shocked to see that a milky white film covered both eyes. The famous O'Neil bull had gone blind with age.

"Tell me what first came between you." I stepped closer until my shoulder nudged Patrick's. "You told me about the girl you wouldn't marry, but you also said you and your father had been having trouble for a long time. So what is the root of the problem between you?"

"If I knew—" His voice trembled, as did the hand he lifted to his forehead. "If I understood him, I'd be happy to explain. But the old devil gets things into his head, and I'm not understanding a bit of it. He doesn't like the new ways. He doesn't want to part with his old bull; he wanted me to marry a girl I felt nothing for. We never got on too well when I was a lad, but we started having regular rows when I went away to university. Dad went all weird when I came home with new ideas. He fell into a desperate bad humor whenever I tried to suggest changing things 'round the place. And when I told him and Mr. Kelly that I wouldn't be marrying his daughter, that was the end of it. We had a terrible row, and he went into a dither, screaming about this and that. Then I said he could keep his farm and his name, too, for I'd be no son of his."

His head dropped on his folded arms. "And that was the last time I saw Dad, before I came home and found you and Taylor here. I wouldn't have come even then, but Maddie rang me up and insisted. She said she wouldn't be marrying without me, and she wanted me around to squire the American woman about."

The unexpected confession stung enough that I flinched. Suddenly his abrupt appearance made perfect sense. Maddie had felt threatened by my presence, so since she couldn't exactly ask me to leave, she did the next best thing. She called her handsome brother and insisted that he come home, knowing the brooding Irishman would turn the foolish American woman's head.

I took a deep breath and steeled myself for the truth. "So you've been spending time with me only because Maddie asked you to?"

Patrick didn't answer, but his answering sigh told me all I needed to know.

"Well," I pulled away from the fence, "thanks for baby-sitting me. I enjoyed our time together, but I know you probably want to get back to Limerick. Don't worry about Maddie; I have a feeling she's quite content. If you leave, though, Taylor won't have a choice. He'll have to stay at Ballyshannon and look after the farm."

"Kathleen—"

"No need to say anything else." I stepped back, my own feelings too raw to discuss or evaluate. "I'm tired, Patrick. I think I'll go in now."

"Wait." An urgent tone entered his voice, and the sound of it stopped me. Patrick lowered his head and stared at the bull, then leapt the fence in an easy movement.

"Patrick!" I called, alarmed. "Should you be in there without a tranquilizer gun?"

Patrick leaned forward, his hands on his knees, then he reached out and touched a dark spot on Graham Red's face. The bull snorted and shied away from this intrusive touch, and Patrick straightened, a grim look on his face as he studied his hand.

"Go into the house, will you, and tell Mum to call the vet. The bull is sick—I'd be surprised if he's not dying."

Fear spurred my feet to action.

I HAD JUST REACHED THE KITCHEN AND GASPED OUT MY NEWS WHEN Patrick's shadow loomed over mine. "We've got to call Dr. Murray," he said, moving past me toward the phone. "I think it's a virus. There's a discharge running from his eyes, and the hay is stained as well. At his age, he'll not be able to fight an infection unless we act quickly—"

"Put the phone down!" James O'Neil's dry voice cracked through the kitchen, startling even his son. "I still run things here."

Patrick halted in mid-step, and a light seemed to dim in his eyes as he turned to face his father. James leaned forward over the table and slowly pushed himself up, his hand trembling as he reached out to his wife. "Fiona, help me out to the barn. Let me look at the creature myself."

"Do you not think I know a sick beast when I see one?" Patrick's soft voice was filled with a quiet resentment, the more frightening for its control. "I tell you, Dad, we must call the vet."

"And for what?" The older man's nostrils flared with fury. "Do you think I want him strung up to some tube and kept alive by drugs and painkillers? Let him go in his own way, in his own stall, in God's own time. I'll not prolong his suffering."

Mrs. O'Neil lifted her hand. "James, Paddy's not saying we'd do that to the poor creature. But neither is it right to ignore his pain—"

Mr. O'Neil's blue eyes darkened like angry thunderclouds. "Graham has lived a full life, and I've not been blind to the fact that he's failing. But I'll not call the vet for him. He would only prolong the agony or kill the creature outright."

"Maybe you'd have me call the knackers, then." Patrick's hand gestured toward the phone on the wall. "Let them pick him up and toss him into a truck."

"Since when have you been so concerned about the bull?" Even in his weakness, Mr. O'Neil bristled with indignation. "You wanted me to sell him off. You've never cared about Graham, the glory of this farm! You'd see us raising a bunch of skittish Angus heifers with nary a bull on the place!"

Defiance poured hotly from Patrick's sparkling blue eyes. "I'd see us in the twentieth century, never mind that the rest of the world is moving into the twenty-first. You're living in a forgotten age, Dad, and people are laughing at you when your back is turned. 'Ah, look at James O'Neil,' they're saying, 'still in love with his blind old bull. The man's a wee bit touched in the head, for he's more faithful to that creature than he is to his own son.'"

Warm as it was in the toasty kitchen, I felt a sliver of ice slide down my spine. This argument wasn't about a bull—it was about a man and his son. And I was standing right in the center of it.

"Let me pass." Mr. O'Neil spoke the words slowly and deliberately. Patrick shifted before his father's hot gaze, giving him access to the door. He stalked forward, rocking on his hips in the way of very old men, then passed silently out into the night.

Mrs. O'Neil stared at her son, then looked at me. "This will be the death of him," she whispered, then she whirled and left through the door that led to her bedroom. I clenched my hands as a sudden shiver chilled me. I didn't know if she was referring to the man or the animal.

Without another word, Patrick stalked through the kitchen and blasted his way through the swinging door that led to the foyer. My heart filled with a horrible feeling as I watched him go—almost as if I was watching someone drown without doing anything to help. Trouble was, I had no idea how to help. We had become good friends in a short time, but the scene I'd just witnessed had touched him in deep places I couldn't fathom.

I stood for a moment in the empty silence, then turned, and walked through the foyer. Patrick was not in the sitting room, and as I moved into the dining room and looked out the window, I saw that the light had come on in the little house. He had retreated to his cave. If he had wanted to talk to me, if he had wanted any comfort at all, he might have remained in the sitting room where I could find him without feeling like an intruder. But he hadn't.

Moving with glacial slowness, I climbed the stairs and walked down the hall to my room. After undressing and tumbling into bed, I lay in the darkness and contemplated the shifting shadows on the plaster ceiling, my vision still gloomily colored with the memory of Patrick's defeated countenance and his father's bitter anger.

What was it with those two? Why couldn't they reach out to each other with understanding instead of mistrust? James should have been enjoying his son's compassion and care in the twilight of his life; Patrick should be growing through the experience of knowing that his father valued him as a man and a friend. But neither one of them were very good at reaching out. James had hobbled out to the barn alone, forsaking his wife's help, and Patrick had stalked back to the little house, physically reinforcing the impression the he couldn't stand to be under the same roof with his family . . . or me.

I heard the kitchen door open with a complaining screech, and knew that Maddie and Taylor had just come back from the pub or wherever they'd gone after dinner. Poor Taylor. Maddie had probably spent the entire night trying to convince him that living in Ireland would be great, convenient, and economical. If she knew what had happened in the kitchen while they were out, she'd have worked even harder to convince him. Apparently James *would* rather leave the farm to the taxman than to his own son, a son who would rather curl up and savor his anguish than share it with a caring friend.

I turned onto my side, hardening my heart to its own pain, then felt a small sprouting of hope when someone rapped on my door. "Yes?" I clutched the quilt to my chest as I sat up in the darkness. "Patrick?"

"It's me." The door opened, and Maddie's cloud of curls gleamed in the hall light. "Mum wanted me to see if you had enough clean towels for the morning. She didn't get the laundry done today."

I stared at her, perplexed by the odd question. Maddie hadn't knocked on my door once in the two weeks I'd been staying here. "I'm fine. The towels are fine."

"Good." She hesitated, then opened the door a little further. "Do you mind if I turn on the lamp?"

"Go ahead." I closed my eyes and waited for the bright light to slam against my retinas. I also dropped the covers; no need for modesty with Maddie. She was the last person on earth who'd care about seeing me in my silk pajamas. After she flicked the switch, I squinted up at her through a fluorescent haze. "Something on your mind?"

"You might say that." She came into the room and perched on the edge of my bed, her eyes dark and troubled. "Taylor and I had a long talk, and it looks like we're going to stay in Ireland for a while after the wedding."

I hugged my knees and looked up at her. "I figured as much."

Maddie pressed her lips together and tilted her head. "Trouble is, Taylor's not exactly thrilled with the idea. I have a feeling he might try to talk to you about it, and it'd be a great help to me if you'd tell him that things will be okay if he stays at Ballyshannon." She looked at me with wise little eyes, bright and calculating. "He values your opinion, and right now I could use every bit of influence I can get. If you will tell him to stay here—well, I think he'd be a lot happier."

Watching her, I couldn't stop myself from wondering what would happen if I advised Taylor *against* staying in Ireland. Would he come to believe that his engagement was a terrible mistake? Would he agree that I'd been right all along, that he and Maddie really were unsuited for one another?

Trouble was, I'd come to see just the opposite. They were opposites, but in areas where each could use a bit of balancing. In matters that counted they were remarkably similar. They were both committed to the ideals of home and family . . . and to each other.

I exhaled in a long sigh, then gave Maddie a tired smile. "I want to help, not because I believe Taylor would be happy in Ireland, but because I think he'll be happy with you, no matter where you live. But if you want to know my honest opinion, I think Taylor really needs to return to New York. It's his home. He'll be an outsider here, and he won't be happy."

"But we can't go back and—" she began, but I held up my hand and cut her off.

"It's Patrick that needs to stay here," I told her, realizing the truth as I spoke. "He's the one who loves this place. Can't you see it? He's happy when he's working in the barn; he's perfectly at home in the fields. He'd be miserable in a place like New York, and I expect he's not truly happy in Limerick."

"But Patrick and Dad don't get on well enough. Patrick would never come back here, and Dad wouldn't have him. He's only tolerating Paddy now because of me."

"I know." I gave her a conspiratorial smile, for I wasn't above a bit of bargaining myself. "Okay, if absolutely necessary I'll encourage Taylor to stay at Ballyshannon, but I think it'd be better if you'd help me influence Patrick."

Her face froze in an expression of absolute disbelief. "Whatever *are* you talking about?"

"I think you know. And I'm not asking for much, either—just a promise you won't oppose me. I'm trying to help Patrick sort through some things, and I know he values your opinion. Just promise me this:

If you see what I'm trying to do, consider adding a supportive word. That's all."

She lifted one eyebrow, suggesting in feminine shorthand that she was considering my proposal, then she nodded and slid off my bed. "Deal." She walked around the room for a moment, staring at the walls and dresser and wardrobe as if she had never seen them before, then she turned and gripped the footboard of my bed. She laughed softly. "Men! What would they do without us arranging their lives?"

"Live a lot more peacefully, I expect." I lay down, pulled the covers up to my shoulders, and closed my eyes. "Would you hit the light when you go out?"

She didn't answer, but the overhead light clicked off, then I heard her light footsteps retreating down the stairs.

SUSPECTING THAT PATRICK MIGHT WANT TO SPEND SOME TIME alone in his little apartment, the next day I gathered up my notes and laptop and moved to the picnic table out beneath the copper beech on the lawn. Though the morning was clear, crisp, and beautiful, it had rained during the night, and occasionally a raindrop plopped onto my notepad.

I was trying to work a bug out of my word processing program when Taylor came outside and sat down beside me at the picnic table.

"Hey," he said, rapping lightly on the weathered wood. "Got a minute for a bewildered friend?"

"That all depends," I answered lightly, tapping the command to scan the computer's hard drive. If only problems in real life could be analyzed and corrected this easily.

I left the computer to do its thing while I turned and gave Taylor a smile—he looked like he needed one. "Speak."

"I've been instructed to come out and talk to you." He nodded toward the house, where I knew Maddie was probably watching from a window. "She wants to stay in Ireland, but Ballyshannon isn't exactly where I wanted to be next year."

"She's worried about her father." I propped my elbow on the table and rested my head on my hand, letting my hair fall forward to block my face from anyone watching in the house. "Patrick is, too."

"Patrick." Taylor made a soft sound of dismissal. "He doesn't give a whit about this family. He's planning to leave after the wedding, right when Mr. O'Neil will need him most."

I struggled to maintain an even, rational tone. "Do you really think he has a choice? You weren't around last night when World War III broke out. Patrick tried to help the old bull, and James went ballistic. He doesn't want Patrick's help, and he's as stubborn as Felim O'Connor!"

Taylor's brow furrowed. "Who?"

"Never mind."

"Well, the bull's gone." Taylor's gaze lowered, as did his voice. "Maddie told me this morning. Her dad spent the night out in the barn, and this morning they found him asleep in the bullpen. The bull was stone cold dead."

I frowned at the distasteful image my mind conjured up. "Did they call the knackers?"

"The what?"

"The people who buy animal carcasses."

Taylor shook his head. "Fiona put James to bed, and Patrick went to work out in the pasture with a backhoe. I think he intends to bury the beast."

I lifted my eyes to the west pasture, where I could hear the chugging roar of machinery. The thought of Patrick taking the time to bury his father's beloved Graham Red touched me in a way I really didn't expect. Graham Red, the famous Friesian bull, would now belong to Ballyshannon forever.

Blinking the wetness out of my eyes, I turned to Taylor. "Did you know a native Irishman can identify forty different shades of green?"

His face screwed into a human question mark. "What are you talking about?"

I waved the thought away. "Nothing. So why were you sent out here to talk to me?"

"Maddie seems to think you want me to stay here," he mumbled, looking down at his hands. "And don't get me wrong, Kathy—I do like the place, it's beautiful. But it's not home. And I've got a position waiting at the college and coworkers who support me. Professor Howard was certain I could make full professor in just two more years, but all those plans will have to be postponed if I stay in Ireland indefinitely. The college will have to hire someone to replace me, so I might even lose my position."

"Don't worry. You'll go back to New York. . . eventually." I lifted my gaze again to the pasture, where I could see the bright yellow roof of the sporty little backhoe. "But don't you think you ought to at least consider staying, for Maddie's sake? Her father is dying. She just might want to spend time with him."

"I know he is, and I can't help it." The corners of his mouth went tight with distress. "I know that sounds heartless, but I can't sit here for months, possibly *years*, and wait for the man to die. I'll bring Maddie back if she wants to visit, but we can't put our lives on hold and wait for the man to die." He looked at me with eyes that were frankly pleading. "Surely you understand that, Kathy."

I softened my tone out of deference to his pain. "I think I understand more than you do, Taylor. I told Maddie I'd try to convince you to stay here, but you can't take Patrick's place. The farm is his by right, and by blood. Furthermore, he loves it."

Taylor stared at me for a moment, then burst out laughing. "Are we talking about the same man? Patrick O'Neil? The genius computer programmer?"

"We are."

"Seriously." He rubbed his hand over his jaw, as if to stop himself from laughing. "You really think Patrick will give up his cushy job and city apartment to come back *here?* I gotta say, Kathy, I think the country life has gotten to you. Patrick hates this farm and everything about it."

Not caring who watched, I reached out and patted his blue-jeaned knee. "You mark my words, Taylor Morgan. Paddy O'Neil was born to life at Ballyshannon, and he'll end up here. The bitterness you see in him isn't directed at the farm. It's James and Patrick who are at war, and I think it's nearly time to negotiate terms of surrender."

He tipped his head back, eyeing me with a calculating expression, and then understanding filled his eyes. "If you're thinking about a deathbed reconciliation, I'll admit, you may have a point. But the doctors say James will live at least another year. And the last year will be the hardest, which means he's going to need help, and lots of it. So that doesn't help my situation in the least."

I smiled. "I don't know what to tell you, Taylor, but I know God has begun to work in Patrick's life. I also know God wants Patrick and his father to be at peace."

One of Taylor's brows lifted. "I didn't know God had a particular interest in this situation."

"God is interested in *every* situation, and I'm sorry I don't point that out more often." I shrugged away my shame. "Last weekend Patrick and I went to hear that American evangelist, and I think Patrick made a decision for Christ. I'm not sure how his decision will change things, but I hope it means things will be different in this family. I think Patrick will want them to be different."

Taylor gave me a skeptical look. "Didn't Christ say something about coming not to bring peace, but a sword? If you meddle, you may only make the situation between Patrick and James worse."

I straightened, thinking of the terrible argument I'd witnessed the night before. "Honestly, Taylor, I don't think things could get much worse."

"I don't know about that." Taylor stood and eased himself out of the narrow space between the picnic table and the bench. "At least Patrick is still welcome here. If he forsakes the family church, James may forbid him to come home altogether."

For that I had no answer.

❦

TWO WEEKS PASSED, AND THOSE OF US LIVING AT BALLYSHANNON kept pretty much to our routines. I spent my time reading and writing about Cahira O'Connor, Taylor studied Kipling, and Maddie trooped into town for visits with her girlfriends, the parish priest, and the elderly woman who was sewing her wedding gown.

Patrick kept himself busy with the farm. Mornings and evenings he spent milking and examining the dairy herd, while afternoons he walked the pastures and inspected the fences. One evening he took his father's place at a dairy co-op meeting, and a few nights he spent by the fire with me. I devoured yet another volume about the Norman invasion while he argued aloud with a book about the pros and cons of cloning cattle. Sometimes he brought his Bible to the fire and draped it over his left knee while he flipped through the pages of a reference book resting on his right. Mrs. Sullivan, our favorite librarian, had sent him home with an armful of commentaries, Hebrew lexicons, and a concordance.

Patrick had definitely relegated his computer work to a lower priority, though I couldn't say whether he did this out of guilt or desire. When I asked him about the big project he had been working on when he first arrived at Ballyshannon, he simply replied that he had finished it. Apparently he had other projects, too, but none that required his undivided attention. A few afternoons when I worked in the little house he came in long enough to pick up his laptop, which he then carried to the picnic table on the lawn. Looking out the window, I usually saw him typing like a madman, but once or twice I saw him sitting with his chin parked in his palm, his eyes unfocused and staring out over the fields.

In such moments all my doubts and uncertainties vanished. I now knew with pulse-pounding certainty that Patrick O'Neil was a dairy farmer down to his socks. His computers, his life in Limerick, and his friendships with his bachelor flatmates were more his hobby than his life. Whether or not he wanted to admit it, his existence was rooted in Ballyshannon. Here, among the fields and in the milking shed, he seemed to shine.

I only wished that James O'Neil were able—and willing—to see what I saw in his son. Mr. O'Neil took to his bed the morning the bull died and had not yet found the strength to rise. He had no specific complaints, Mrs. O'Neil whispered over lunch one day, but the spirit seemed to have gone out of him when Graham Red died. "'Tis almost as if he knows the farm will be moving into new hands," she said, casting a wounded look at Maddie and Taylor. "Hands that won't care about the glory of Graham Red and his progeny."

At dinner a few days later, Patrick abruptly interrupted the conversation and announced that the dairy co-op would be holding a cattle show in Nenagh over the weekend. Speaking in a voice far too loud for casual conversation, he proclaimed that he'd like to drive over and take a look at the stock—particularly since he'd heard that several fine Angus bulls were being put up for auction. He'd also heard that at least one of Graham Red's get would be on display.

I drowned my smile in my teacup, fully understanding why Patrick shouted. Lowering my cup, I caught Mrs. O'Neil's eye and saw that she was smiling, too. Her eldest son wanted to be sure his proud, bedridden father heard the news.

Realizing, too, the concession he'd just made, I felt my heart flow toward Patrick, and the look in his eyes struck a vibrant chord when his gaze met mine. "I don't believe in the necessity of keeping a bull," he said, lowering his voice to reach my ear and barely a breath beyond, "and few fellows will go through the trouble of dealing with the dangerous beasts. But if buying a bull will give James O'Neil a reason to get out of bed . . ."

"And you're a lovely man, Paddy," his mother added, nodding in approval. She reached out and patted Patrick's hand, love and maternal pride shining in her eyes.

I smiled and strengthened my voice back to a normal level. "Shall we make plans, then?" Mr. O'Neil should know we were planning to go to the fair together. His miraculous healing would be less remarkable if we made the cattle show a major family affair.

"What fun!" Maddie clapped in glee, then squeezed Taylor's arm. "You'll adore the fair, love. 'Tis terribly interesting, and there will be music and dancing and all sorts of things to see."

Taylor gave me a wry half-smile. "I can't wait."

Maddie beamed at her brother. "Well, Paddy, what do you think—

should we invite Erin Kelly? She hasn't been out with us in ages, and she's bound to be wondering—"

"No," Patrick interrupted, his eyes flashing toward his sister. A hurt expression crossed Maddie's round face as she fell silent, and I lowered my gaze in hopes no one would remark upon the color that flared upon my cheeks.

❦ 28 ❦

Right on schedule, Mr. O'Neil's remarkable improvement occurred the morning of the fair. When I came downstairs, I found him sitting in his own place at the breakfast table, eating his way through an impressive plate of eggs, sausages, rashers, blood pudding, and the ever-present tomato. His jowls hung in flaps like the flews of a hound, but his eyes seemed more focused than when I had last seen him, as though a film of indifference or resignation had been peeled away. His wife hovered over him, refilling his teacup and buttering his bread with tender patience. Not even the steadily dripping rain outside seemed to dim his spirits.

After breakfast, we drove to Nenagh in two cars—Maddie, Taylor, Patrick, and I rode in Patrick's car, while Mrs. O'Neil drove her husband in the other. Despite the rain, Maddie was in high spirits. She was probably hoping to meet old friends before whom she hadn't yet had a chance to flaunt Taylor. Quietly acquiescent, Taylor scarcely said a dozen words on the drive. A cattle show was probably the last thing on earth he wanted to see, but at least the event would be a break from what had become a monotonous routine. He had actually visited the milking shed several times in the last few days, but he seemed about as enthusiastic about the prospect as a convict going to the electric chair.

Patrick and I rode together in the front seat. Though he had been careful to avoid his father at breakfast, I knew from the gleam in his eye that he was pleased his plan had worked. The older man was out of bed, energized, and, for the moment, observing a cease-fire in the war with his son.

I peered out at the long, wavering runnels on the car windows. "Will they have the fair if it's raining?"

Patrick laughed. "The weather changes here every five minutes, love. If the cows don't mind it, why should we?"

Fortunately, the rain faded to a mere misty drizzle by the time we reached Nenagh. On the outskirts of the city, we pulled off the road, drove down a muddy dirt path, then rattled and bounced our way through a pasture. Finally Patrick stopped the car—following the inexplicable Irish pattern of parking, which is no pattern at all—and shut off the ignition. "We're here," he said, looking at me as though I might challenge his statement.

I got out of the car, craned my neck in all directions and saw . . . cattle. I don't know what I expected to see—a Ferris wheel and hot dog vendors, I suppose. But when Patrick called it a cattle fair, he spoke the truth. Of course there were lots of people in the pasture and a few dogs, for a sheep herding trial was being held in the next field. A group of men stirred around a flatbed trailer from which a sign proclaimed that the Johnny Kelly Trio would be performing at noon, one, and two. But mostly I saw cows. Most were in makeshift iron pens; several wore bridles and followed their handlers with a morose, plodding steps. A few men in raincoats walked before the cattle and eyed them with an appraising glance.

I looked around to check on our party and saw Mrs. O'Neil helping Mister over a slice of earth wounded by a heavy truck. He seemed well, though, and wore a smile as wide as Texas.

Maddie pulled Taylor toward the tweed-coated dog people. "Oh, and look, there's Nattie O'Hara and her new husband! Won't they be pleased to meet you! Come, love." Taylor threw me a what-am-I-doing-here? look while his spirited bride-to-be led him away.

Patrick watched them go, then took my hand. "Wouldn't want you to slip out here," he said simply, leading me over the damp grass. We walked toward a huddle of farmers gathered around a fierce-looking black bull.

A cold wind blew over the field, but I didn't feel it, so wrapped was I in the invisible warmth emanating from Patrick. I moved closer to him, holding his elbow with my free hand, absorbing assurance from his confident posture. While we stood and stared at the huge black beast, one thought kept running through my mind: By persuading his father to come, Patrick had set a bit of a miracle in motion.

"Patrick O'Neil," I tipped my head back and looked up into his eyes. "You're a wonder, do you know? You've done a generous and compassionate thing here today."

He gave me an answering smile, then looked away to the crowd around the bull. "You see those men clapping eyes on that Angus? They're interested in him, but they're interested using him for AI. Not a one of them wants to actually own the beast; they'd rather pay for a vial of bull semen. My dad's the only fellow who'd be loony enough to make an offer for the creature."

I looked at the bull, my thoughts scampering vaguely around as I tried to follow Patrick's thoughts. "I thought your dad didn't like Angus cattle."

"I am hoping he'd bend a little." Patrick glanced over his shoulder for some sign of his father, then sighed and looked back at the bull. "I'm willing to keep silent about the keeping of a bull if he'll realize that Friesians aren't the kind of bull he needs to keep. If he'll get a fine Angus, we'll be able to produce good beef cows *and* good dairy cows. That will ensure Ballyshannon's productivity for years to come."

He leaned forward, his eyes narrowing as he studied the lines of the big black beast. "Years ago, you see, farmers wanted Dutch Friesians, for those huge cows give tons of milk. But milk's not as much in demand today, and we've had to form a co-op to keep prices from falling altogether. The government urges us to keep production at a reasonable level, so we're going to have to concentrate on beef cattle if Ballyshannon is to survive in this economy."

I nodded, not understanding completely, but realizing enough to see the sense in his words. I'd heard about the same thing in the United States—the government actually pays dairy farmers *not* to produce milk because a glutted market would drive prices down so far no one could make a profit.

"Paddy O'Neil? Can it be you?" A short gentleman pulled the pipe from his mouth and squinted at Patrick. "Saints above, 'tis! What brings you out here on such a wet day as this?"

Patrick stepped forward and shook the man's hand. "Well, old Graham Red passed last week," he said, sliding his hands into his pockets. "We thought Dad might like to get out and have a look at the new bulls. I'm hoping he'll bid on an Angus."

"Aye, and I just saw your father." The man nodded, then hesitated a moment, waiting for Patrick to introduce me. In an effort to avoid embarrassing Patrick, I thrust out my hand.

"Kathleen O'Connor," I said, managing a tentative smile. "I'm visiting Ballyshannon for a few weeks."

"Ah?" The old man's bushy brow shot up. "Ronan Murphy, miss, and pleased to meet you. Though your name's Irish, something tells me you're not from these parts."

"She's from America," Patrick inserted. "New York."

"Right so." The man shrugged as if that were all that needed to be said, then looked at Patrick with a probing gleam in his eye. "How is your dad these days, Paddy? I'll be wanting to know the truth, so speak plainly."

Patrick looked down, the fringe of his lashes casting shadows on his cheeks. "He's been better, and he's been worse, Ronan. Last week I was half-afraid he'd given up all together, but he rallied himself today. We're trying to keep his spirits up."

Mr. Murphy's eyes were gentle and contemplative as he puffed on his pipe. "The doctors have done all they can, then?"

Patrick swallowed hard and squared his shoulders. "Yes."

"Sorry to hear it." With an admirable economy of motion, Mr. Murphy turned and pointed across the field with the stem of his pipe. "Your dad's over there now, bidding on a fine black and white bull that's come out of your own Graham Red. I'd have bid on the creature meself, but he looks like a bit of trouble."

Patrick nodded and murmured his thanks, managing to quell his irritation until Mr. Murphy moved away. Then, taking me by the elbow, he practically pulled me across the field.

"Do you think he's really buying another bull?" I asked, amazed that a man in Mr. O'Neil's condition would buy anything.

"Likely he couldn't resist," Patrick growled as the wet grass swished around our ankles. "The bull is descended from Graham Red, so Dad will have to get him before someone else snatches him up. 'Tis the pride thing, don't you see? The old fool won't listen to reason."

A moment later I saw James O'Neil standing outside a bullpen, his thumbs hooked into his vest, a proud smile gathering up his sagging cheeks. The bull behind him was the spitting image of the animal I'd seen in the Ballyshannon barn, but this creature wasn't slow and shuffling. His beady eyes were alert and dark, his hooves pawing the dirt as the crowd churned around him.

"Will you pose for a picture, James?" a photographer called, balancing a Nikon atop his nose. "I don't expect you to climb in with the wee beast, but if you could get a little closer, I could get the animal in the shot. But hurry, the rain is coming again."

"I'm not eejit enough to climb in with a bull," Mr. O'Neil answered, "but a shot with an animal would be nice, wouldn't it now?" He turned and moved toward the gate of a pen in which a black-and-white cow stood with her calf. "Take your picture here, with the cow," he called to the photographer. "They're both out of me own Graham Red, and proud I am of having a part in such fine animals."

The cow blinked and turned her massive head toward the interloper, but Mr. O'Neil went through the gate and walked toward her, his hands confidently parked in his vest pockets. Outside the pen, Mrs. O'Neil held a sheet of damp newspaper over her hair and gave her husband an encouraging smile.

Hanging over the railing, the photographer leaned from left to right, striving for the best shot of James and the cow. "There now—just there. Och, can you back up a bit? If you could just take another wee step back, James, I'll be able to get the calf in the picture."

Mugging for the camera, Mr. O'Neil took another step back while I rose on tiptoe to whisper in Patrick's ear. "Your dad sure looks like he's enjoying himself."

"How's this?" Mr. O'Neil beamed for the camera, the crowd clapped in appreciation, and the startled calf mooed at the stranger who had invaded her space. The mother cow moved forward, butting Mr. O'Neil's back with her head, and he lost his footing in the mud and fell backward against the calf.

The events of the next few moments will be forever be imprinted in my brain. I froze, one hand lifted toward Patrick, as the calf bawled out its anxiety and leapt forward. The protective cow, displeased with the stranger molesting her baby, lunged toward Mr. O'Neil, her huge head flipping him onto his back in the mud. While he gazed up at her with wide, startled eyes, the cow pressed her head against his chest, then brought one hoof forward and stepped on his abdomen.

A scream ripped through the astounded crowd, but for all I know the sound could have come from anyone, including me. Through a haze of disbelief I saw Mr. O'Neil flailing at the cow with his fists, but that bony head didn't give way for an instant. She just kept pressing on him, and through the din I heard sharp cracking sounds of bones breaking.

Like a child, I lifted my hands to cover my eyes, but then Patrick made a hand-leap over the railing. As he rushed toward the determined cow, I experienced a moment of empty-bellied terror, the sort you get at the top of a roller coaster. I found myself praying out loud: "Help him, Jesus. Protect them both!"

The crowd around me seemed dumbstruck. The cows in the milking shed had impressed me as the most placid animals on earth, but this beast was a wrathful mother intent upon killing the man who'd dared touch her calf. Strangely enough, she seemed not to even notice Patrick, who grabbed her by the ears and braced his heels into the dirt to pull her away. The muscles in his back knotted and writhed beneath his jacket, his face darkened with exertion, but that cow didn't budge.

An idea struck me, and now I'd have to say simple ignorance probably saved the day. A more experienced farmer might have tried something else, but I did the only thing I could think of—I reached through the fence and grabbed the calf around the neck, then hugged him to me with every ounce of my strength. More frightened than ever, the calf bawled in earnest, and that jittery, bleating sound cut through the screams and shouts and curses long enough for the cow to lift her head and look for whomever was bothering her baby now.

She looked at me, blinked, and stumbled forward with a bellowing roar. I released the calf and scampered back so quickly that I fell hard on the ground, but the distraction worked. Once the cow's attention was diverted, a half dozen men leapt into the pen and formed a human fence, separating the animal from the O'Neils, while Patrick stood over his father and hoarsely called for help.

I sat on the ground, breathless and shaken. The cow, only inches away, eyed me through the fence and bumped her head against it. For a fleeting moment I wondered if the temporary pen would hold her if she charged it, but something about the calf's warm presence seemed to satisfy the cow's thirst for vengeance. Though breathing heavily, she stood and stared out at me, twin streamers of drool dripping from her velvety mouth.

An ambulance appeared as if from nowhere (I later learned it had been parked at the dog show), and Patrick dismantled a section of the pen so the paramedics could reach his father. The members of the human fence remained in place, several of them calling encouragement as the paramedics lifted James onto a stretcher.

"There now, girl, are you all right?" Mr. Murphy appeared from the crowd and helped me to my feet. "That was quick thinking, if I do say so myself."

He looked at me, obviously expecting an answer, but I couldn't speak. My mouth was as dry as sandpaper and the warm scent of damp cow seemed to choke my breathing.

"Ah, now, and I'm sorry you got a fright. 'Tis the way of the beasts; they're unpredictable at best and mostly temperamental with a calf. But the ambulance will have James in hospital before you know it."

I looked at Mr. Murphy through a haze of confusion. "In hospital?"

"Aye, he's pretty shaken up. But Paddy will ride with him, and Maddie and her young man will bring Fiona. Do you mind riding with me, then?"

Too upset to ponder travel arrangements, I brushed mud and grass from the back of my jeans. "I'm awfully dirty. I'd hate to mess up your car."

Mr. Murphy threw back his head and laughed, and I marveled at the Irishman's ability to chuckle in the face of calamity. "Listen to her," he slipped his arm around my shoulder, "worried about my car! Nothing beats a Yank for worrying about unimportant things."

Bewildered, I pushed my hair out of my face and followed him as the rain began to fall in earnest, sharp as needles against my skin.

༺༻

AN HOUR LATER, MADDIE AND TAYLOR JOINED ME IN THE WAITING room of the hospital. They had been inside the emergency ward with Mrs. O'Neil and Patrick, but after the doctor's initial examination, he suggested they wait outside. I thought it a little strange that Patrick did not come out, too, but perhaps he wanted to remain with his father.

Maddie wept openly, her pretty face all red and splotchy. Taylor sat beside her, cradling her head against his shoulder, and for a moment I longed for the strength of a masculine, comforting arm. Abruptly, like an afterthought, a realization struck me. Six months ago I would have wanted Taylor to comfort me, but now I didn't want him at all. I wanted Patrick.

The wide double doors opened, and Mrs. O'Neil stepped out, marks of grief etched into the lines beside her mouth and eyes. "He's going to be all right, thank God." Her voice trembled with suppressed emotion. "Or as well as he can be, in his condition." Her gaze moved across the room and met Maddie's. "Though he has a couple of broken ribs, we're not going to lose your dad yet, love. He said he still intends to walk you down the aisle."

Maddie broke into fresh tears at this, and I closed my eyes, relieved beyond words. James O'Neil was a dying man, but God had decided to leave him with his family for a few more months. That was a mercy.

I looked up and caught Mrs. O'Neil's eye. "Is Patrick all right?"

A small frown settled between her brows. "I haven't seen him, dearie. I thought he was with you."

I sat back, momentarily confused. Where could Patrick have gone? He had left his car at the cattle fair, so he couldn't have left the hospital. This was the emergency waiting room, so if he wasn't here or in the examination room, he had to be in another public place, perhaps the cafeteria or the gift shop, if there was one.

I stood, and squeezed Mrs. O'Neil's hand as I moved past her. "I'll go find him."

I asked a nurse for directions to the cafeteria, but Patrick wasn't among the visitors or white-coated doctors eating at the small tables. I asked for directions to the gift shop, and was directed to a closet-sized room filled with cards, crucifixes, and arrangements of silk flowers. No sign of Patrick.

Standing in the gift shop, I considered one other option. "Can you tell me," I asked the young girl behind the counter, "if there's a chapel here?"

That's where I found him. The small room was lit by candles and a single light burning over a huge wooden cross, but I immediately recognized the broad shoulders hunched over the railing before the kneeling bench. Entering silently, I walked forward and knelt at his side, then closed my eyes as I added an "amen" to Patrick's prayer.

When I lifted my head, Patrick was looking at me, an almost imperceptible note of pleading in his face.

I sank back to the kneeling bench, then reached out to touch his arm. "Your father is going to be fine. A couple of broken ribs, they say. But he'll be well enough to walk Maddie down the aisle next month."

For a brief instant Patrick's face seemed to open, so I could look inside and watch my words sink in. I saw surprise, a quick flicker of anxiety, then his tense expression melted in an outpouring of relief.

"Thank God. I thought I was going to lose him. I've been kneeling here, trying to pray, but I don't think I've ever felt so far away from God. Why *is* that, Kathy?"

"God is not far away, Patrick—he's right here, waiting for you. But you must set things right with your father because you can't be angry and in close fellowship with God. He will not allow anger to consume people, and he doesn't want you to remain separated from your father."

He stared mindlessly over the railing at the cross, with only a slight squint of his eye and a sideways movement of his jaw to indicate he had heard.

I took a deep breath and tried again to reach him. "You are going to lose your father, Patrick, for these physical bodies aren't designed to live forever. But you don't have to spend your father's remaining days in unhappiness. Go to him and make things right. There may never be a better time than now."

"I was afraid he would die without giving me the chance to ask what I've done to make him hate me so." He spoke the words without heat, but they fell with the weight of stones in still water, spreading ripples of pain and regret. "Now that he's going to live, I don't think I have the courage to speak to him."

Turning to face him, I took his hand and held it between both of my own. "Patrick, I can't imagine how your father has hurt you, but I do know this: Jesus understands. He was hurt, too. And still he taught that we must be open and honest with those who wound us. Just as we are to ask forgiveness from those we wrong, we must also go to those who wrong us."

"I've tried so many times." He spoke in a wavering, tremulous whisper. "Everything I did, I did for him and Ballyshannon, but he never appreciated anything." A dry, cynical laugh escaped him as he raked his hand through his hair. "Once, in school, I did a project on the results of inbreeding grade Holstein-Friesian cattle. The work took every spare minute of nine months, and I earned top marks for it. But was my father impressed? Not a bit! He just remarked that no bull would come near the quality of Graham Red, and only an eejit would waste his time studying such things."

His chin wavered, and beneath his strong countenance I saw traces of the boy who'd been crushed by his father's harsh and careless remark. Opening my arms, I drew him close, letting him spend the tears of a frustrated and anxious childhood. He clung to me like a drowning man clings to a buoy in the water, and something in me marveled at the strength in his shaking shoulders. My own childhood had been stable and happy, so I found it difficult to believe that mere words from a parent could so wound a child and haunt an intelligent adult.

But hadn't Felim O'Connor wounded his daughter with words and prejudices? In the same way, something had turned James O'Neil against his son, and Patrick still struggled beneath the weight of that rejection. Yet he had only exacerbated the problem by pulling away.

Cold, clear reality swept over me in a terrible wave. Patrick's anger and disappointment had burdened him long enough.

"It's time to end this, Patrick," I whispered. I pulled his head upright and gazed into his wet blue eyes. "Misery depends upon isolation, and you don't need to be miserable any more. Go upstairs and talk to your father. Don't put it off another hour."

He looked at me for a long moment, his eyes searching mine, then he nodded slowly and took my hand, lifting me with him.

❧

WE FOUND MR. O'NEIL IN A LARGE, RECTANGULAR WARD OF EIGHT beds. A nurse smiled at us as we came in, but her sober eyes flashed a silent warning: *Don't upset my patient.*

Mrs. O'Neil was sitting in a chair by the bedside, but she stood as we approached and came forward to slip her arms around Patrick's waist. "Maddie and Taylor were just here," she whispered, patting Patrick's back. "But they've gone now, and Taylor's going to bring your car from the fair ground. I thought you and Kathleen might want to head home soon."

"I do, Mum, but first I have to speak to Dad."

Mrs. O'Neil's bright eyes searched his face, then she nodded and stepped away. I watched her retreat, certain that she, too, knew the time had come to settle old scores. I crossed one arm over my chest and watched her, wondering if she understood the barrier that stood between this father and son.

Patrick moved to the edge of his father's bed and looked down. "Dad?"

James O'Neil's eyelids flickered, as if his eyes were moving behind the closed lids, then he opened his eyes and managed to give his son a tremulous smile. "Paddy." He spoke the name with quiet emphasis. "I hoped you'd come. I wanted to thank you . . . for saving me miserable neck."

"Somebody had to. Besides, you should be thanking our American guest. 'Twas Kathleen who got the terrible beast off your chest" Patrick's words and smile were playful, but his meaning was not, and James took the hint and turned toward me.

"'Tis true, I should thank you, lass. I'll never be forgetting what you did for me out there."

I gave him a smile that said *no big deal*, then looked at Patrick, silently urging him on. He met my gaze and seemed to take courage from something he saw in my eyes. Taking a seat in his mother's empty chair, he leaned forward and braced his elbows upon his knees.

"Dad, I want to talk to you. There's been something between us for years, and 'tis more than the fact that my ideas and your ideas don't mix. I don't think I've ever had an idea you liked, but let's forget about that now. Truth to tell, I don't want to be your enemy, Dad. I'd really like to be your son."

Overcome by raw emotion, I glanced away and saw Mrs. O'Neil standing in the ward doorway. Tears glistened in the wells of her eyes, and she held a handkerchief knotted in her hand.

I pressed my hand to my forehead, hoping to stifle the fountain rising inside me, then looked back to the man in the bed. His face had twisted at Patrick's words, his eyes screwing tight as if to trap the sudden rush of tears, but they streamed down his temples and into his dark hair while his shoulders shook in silent sobs.

"Dad, I don't want to upset you." Patrick reached out to smooth the sheet over his father's chest. "I've caused you enough pain over the years. I just wanted you to know I'm sorry for all that—just like I'm sorry 'twas little Mark that died instead of me. I know you doted on that baby something fierce."

I heard Mrs. O'Neil's quick intake of breath and realized that this revelation was as much a surprise to her as it was to me. James shook his head back and forth on the pillow, like a sick child refusing the medicine that would make him well.

"Ah, no, Paddy, you shouldn't blame yourself for that." Mr. O'Neil's voice scraped terribly, as if he labored to produce it, but the words began to come faster and flow. "The troubles between us had nothing to do with the baby, nothing at all. 'Twas just that I didn't know what to do wit' you." He paused, one hand rising to claw the air as a harsh keening sound rose in his throat, then he closed his eyes as a wall of resistance seemed to break inside him. He took a deep breath, pulled his mouth in at the corners, and brought his trembling hand to his lips. And then, though his face looked old and tired, a younger, more insecure man looked out from those blue eyes and stared at his son.

"Ah, Paddy, you should know the truth, I owe you that much. The teachers said you were bright, and you came home wit' all sorts of ideas that made no sense at all. At first I let you go your way, prattling about this and that. But when you began to look about the farm, you talked of ideas I couldn't follow, let alone put into practice. Sure, I wanted you to help me with Ballyshannon, but everything with you had to be more complicated, more economical, and more sensible. I could never see any sense in any of it." A note of wistfulness stole into his expression. "You were always so far ahead of me, Paddy. I had no idea how to keep up wit' you."

"I'm so sorry, Dad." Patrick gulped hard, tears slipping down his own cheeks. "I didn't mean to make you feel that way. You're a good farmer, and no one knows cattle like you."

"You wouldn't have known that today, would you now?" James barked a short laugh, then grimaced in pain and pressed his hands to his ribs. "Och, I can't be laughin' for a while yet, my ribs pain me something fierce." His gaze moved into his son's, and his hand rose from the blanket and reached for Patrick's. "But I want you to know that even though I didn't know what to do wit' you, I always knew you were special. Trouble was, I thought God gave you to the wrong man. You should have been the son of a doctor or a barrister."

A dim flush raced like a fever across Patrick's strong face. "I never wanted to be anything but your son, Dad. And, if it's all right, I'd like to stay on at the farm. I want you to rest and enjoy Maddie's wedding."

For a moment the older man's expression darkened with a host of unreadable emotions, then he stretched out his arms. Rising from the chair, Patrick gently lowered himself into his father's embrace. I stood at the foot of the bed, crying like a baby, and then felt Mrs. O'Neil's solid arm slide around my waist.

"I don't know what you've done to our Paddy," she whispered, tilting her head toward my shoulder, "but bless you for it, love. I've been praying years for this miracle."

❦

THE NEXT MONTH PASSED IN A FLURRY OF PRE-WEDDING ACTIVITY. The bed and breakfast officially closed, the "public" rooms becoming "family" rooms for all to enjoy. James came home and rested in a bed we moved to the sitting room so he could watch all the goings-on and enjoy the company that stopped by to deposit bridal gifts. Taylor wrapped up his Kipling studies and mailed a heavy manuscript to New York City College, along with a note to remind his department head that he'd be returning in time for the beginning of second semester.

A week after the cattle fair, a new bull, an ebony Scottish Angus, arrived to fill Graham Red's bullpen. A day after the bull's arrival, I sat outside on the picnic table and watched Patrick paint the weathered sign that had hung at the beginning of the drive. In bright red letter-ing, the sign now proclaimed, "Ballyshannon—Home of Graham Red II."

After seeing to the new bull, Patrick took a few days and drove to Limerick to settle his affairs and vacate his apartment. He asked me to go with him, but by that time I was knee deep in obligations to Maddie. She had recently changed her mind and decided that I should be maid of honor. Not a bad promotion—from unwanted houseguest to chief lady-in-waiting in a matter of days.

The night before the wedding, the other bridesmaids came to the house to escort Maddie to an impromptu hen party, this one at Dugan's pub, the center of Ballinderry social life. Thankfully, Maddie excused me from this little tradition.

Ordinarily the groom's friends would have taken him to the pub for a stag party, but since Taylor had no Irish friends (and, truth be told, no desire to make any), he was perfectly content to sit in the front room and read while James and Fiona watched American movies from the video rental. Taylor's mother was too involved with her new husband and his career to make the trip to Ireland, but if her absence bothered him, I couldn't tell. Patrick hadn't yet returned from Limerick, though his mother and sister had threatened him with certain bodily harm if he didn't return by morning on the big day.

After dinner, I went to my room and began organizing my clothes, mentally preparing myself for the task of packing for the trip home. Tomorrow I'd see Taylor and Maddie safely down the aisle and married, then I'd sincerely wish them well as they departed for their honeymoon. None of the O'Neils had mentioned my departure from Ballyshannon, and I had a feeling I would be welcome if I wanted to stay a few more days and finish my work on Cahira. Eventually, though, I'd have to sort through my feelings and discard a few things—and a few *feelings*—as I readied myself for the long trip back to New York.

Might as well begin.

I picked up a photograph Patrick had given me. The photo, snapped in the instant before James fell, showed a confident, smiling Irishman with his hands braced in his vest pockets. The cow that nearly killed him filled the background.

I stuck the photo between the pages of my Bible so I'd see it often in the months and years ahead. I'd see it and remember to pray for the O'Neils, and then I'd think of Patrick.

I couldn't deny that I had developed strong feelings for him. We had been through so much together—his acceptance of Christ, his struggle with his father, and that moving reconciliation scene in the hospital. My life had become entangled with his at several crisis points, so the sooner I got back to New York, the sooner I could *untangle* myself and pick up the strings of my blissfully ordinary life.

My life wouldn't be the same, though. Patrick probably didn't realize how his insistent questions had forced me to reevaluate many of the things I'd been taught since childhood. To this day I don't think I will ever again accept a preacher's opinion without wanting to hear supporting evidence. My faith, after all, isn't blind. It is based upon the Word of God, upon the testimony of ancient witnesses, upon the evidence of God's creation and the order I see every time I look across these rolling green hills.

The longer I stayed in Ireland, though, the more I realized that too far many people felt it was wrong to question established traditions. Patrick was an exception, but he was right—God couldn't be afraid of honest questions. As the creator of curiosity and human intellect, how could he ever fear us? And if he is the Truth, as I believe he is, our curious questions certainly can't upset him.

So I was going back to New York with a new outlook on my life. I had always thought I'd settle down and marry some academic type, but now I wasn't so sure I wanted to get married at all. Maybe I could pursue a career in historical research after I published the Cahira books—*if* I ever published the Cahira books. Or maybe I could take a job for the *Times* and win a Pulitzer. Anything was possible.

A knock sounded on my door, and I called "come in," without even bothering to look up.

"You shouldn't invite strangers into your room."

I whirled at the unexpected sound of Patrick's voice. "Patrick! When did you get in?"

"Just now," he said, his face smooth with secrets. He stepped into the room, a stalking, purposeful intent in his walk, and I gasped in surprise when he reached out and drew me into his arms. "Mum tells me you handled the milking tonight."

"Well—" I looked down to hide my self-satisfied smile—"Taylor helped me drive the cows in. But I did the actual milking, yes. And I'll confess—I borrowed your Wellies for the job. They were muddy, so you'll find them on the back porch."

He cocked a brow at me. "They fit?"

"I wore double socks and stuffed the toes with newspaper. But yes, you could say I managed to fill your shoes very well."

"You're amazing." His hand, sure and strong, caught my jaw and lifted my face to meet his. We stood together, breathing each other's breath, then he pulled me closer and gently pressed his lips to my forehead.

"Patrick," I whispered, my emotions rioting within me, "what are you doing?"

"Kissing you." His lips seared a path from my forehead to my temple, then swept to my cheek. "Do you mind?"

Mind? Why should I mind if you break my heart?

Pulling away, I looked into his eyes and saw that they were dark and blue and soft with emotion. In an effort to still the trembling that had begun somewhere at my center, I lifted my hands and clasped his upper arms. "What's come over you?"

"I've had a lot of time to think."

"And?"

"And I love you, Kathleen O'Connor. I want you to marry me and remain here at Ballyshannon. To paraphrase what Ruth said to Naomi, 'Your God will be my God, and my people will be your people.'"

Clinging to him, I looked away and tried to throttle the dizzying current racing through my veins. I had dreamed of being crushed in his embrace, my body had ached for his touch, but never had I imagined that he'd propose. This was crazy, unthinkable! His emotions were still raw from the encounter with his father, and perhaps the advent of Maddie's marriage had affected his thinking.

"Patrick." My eyes closed as his lips brushed my brow and trailed over my eyelid. "Patrick, you're not yourself."

"I know. I feel like a new man."

"No, I mean you haven't thought this through." I brought my hands to his chest and literally pushed him away. That abrupt movement startled him enough to break the spell.

"Think, Patrick." I glanced away, unable to bear the pain and disappointment in his eyes. "Your father believes Ireland is in danger of losing her uniqueness. Your people—everyone in this county—expects you to marry a local girl like Erin Kelly. The folks at the pub who complain about American television won't be happy if you take a Yank for a wife."

"I don't care." His teasing eyes caressed me again. "The world is shrinking, Kathleen, and the past is past. Ireland will never be what it once was. We're already part of the European Union, and Ireland will never again be an island unto itself. The world is changing, and I'm ready to change with it. But I want to face the future with you."

He pulled me to him again, but I kept my hands on his chest, keeping a careful distance between us. "I was thinking, Patrick, about going home. You taught me that a woman is more than just a helper, so I want to try life on my own for a while."

"Ah, Kathleen!" His eyes were blazing with an inner fire, brighter than the lamp on the bureau. "Take it from a man who's tried life on his own long enough—two can accomplish more together than either could alone. We would make a grand team, you and I."

My lips trembled with the urge to smile. "Really? Like horse and cart—where I'm the horse?"

His hands locked around my waist. "Och, nothing like that. More like the sea and the shore—one ends as the other begins, and both need each other."

"You're so poetic."

"Not really." His smile softened, and his eyes grew serious. "I don't want you to go, Kathleen. I want you to marry me."

I listened, I believed him, and in truth, I loved him, too. But things weren't as simple as he wanted them to be.

"Your family won't like this."

"My family loves you. You saved Dad's life, and Mum loves you like a daughter."

"Maddie won't like this."

"Maddie loves you. Aren't you her maid of honor?"

I grasped at a last desperate straw. "Young Erin *definitely* won't like this."

"Erin who?" He kissed me then, and the touch of his mouth was as tender and light as an autumn breeze over a field of Irish heather. His lips were more persuasive than words could ever be. By the time he lifted his head to look into my eyes again, my heart was ready to promise him anything . . . but my head still wasn't convinced.

"'Tis your destiny to be with me." His breath tickled my ear as he pressed his cheek to mine and held me close. "Deny it no longer, love. Say you'll marry me."

"But we're so different." I closed my eyes, shutting off the streaming sensations evoked by his touch. "I'm neat; you're sloppy. I'm American; you're Irish. I like words; you like numbers."

"Didn't you tell me opposites could complement one another? I seem to recall you saying that about Maddie and Taylor."

"But we can't get married! We haven't even dated."

"So? We've talked enough to know we believe the same basic things. You are strong, Kathleen, and bright and beautiful and everything I could ever want in a wife."

"I'm an outsider here."

"You've found your way into my heart. And I don't care about the others."

"I care. A lot."

I lowered my head, pulling my lips—and my brain—away from the powerful force field that seemed to surround him. "At least give me some time to think. It's a big decision. I can't answer that kind of proposal without praying about it. I have to be sure I'm doing the right thing."

Apparently an appeal to the Almighty worked where an entreaty to logic would not. Patrick released me and backed away, though his lips still wore a confident smile.

And as he left my room and closed the door behind him, I collapsed on the bed in a molten pool and wondered how in the world I had arrived at this place.

I hadn't come to Ireland to stay forever. In the hope that I might find some clue about why I bore the mark of all her descendants, I had come to finish my story about Cahira O'Connor.

In a barely comprehendible flash of insight, I realized where I could find my answer.

✻ 29 ✻

M onday, February 5, 1235
Rathcroghan

"DO YOU THINK YOU'RE READY TO GO OUT?" CAHIRA ASKED, A
shadow of concern in her eyes. "I don't want you to use up your
strength, not with you being so soon over your fever."

"I'm fine." Colton heard the sharp edge in his voice, and instantly
regretted his tone. Cahira had been a kind and devoted nurse in the
month of his convalescence, but he had married to protect and serve
her, not to be served and protected.

Sometimes, when night fell and she lay sleeping beside him, Colton
lifted his eyes to the thatched roof of their small hut and wished he
had died on the road. He nearly had, for blood spurted from the cut
limb with alarming force, but Murchadh rode forward like a madman
and tied a rope around the bloody stump. Just before Colton fainted
dead away, he saw his former friends and comrades turn their horses
toward Athlone, leaving him to bleed his life away in the grass.

Now he heard that Richard had left Athlone as well. And although
Colton had been utterly sincere in his disavowal of that lord and his

principles, some part of him still felt abandoned. He loved Cahira with all his heart, but even love could not change the fact that he was the only Norman in these hills, a stranger among people who did not speak his native tongue or understand his references to places and people a world away.

For weeks he lay in his sickbed and closed his ears to the melodic sound of Gaelic, a language he could not follow. Even when the men of Rathcroghan spoke English, they used phrases and terms he did not understand. And no matter how graciously Felim's family treated him, he did not enjoy feeling foolish or being patronized.

He found his only joy in Cahira. Sometimes, as they walked together in the winter sunshine or lay beside the window and looked out at the stars, he could almost forget the sorrows that shadowed his life. The gently rising mound of his wife's belly comforted him, but occasionally he would reach out to caress that living flesh and find nothing at the end of his arm.

Richard, that cruel lord, had taken more than Colton's hand. With it he had also taken Colton's strength, livelihood, and honor. His left hand, the weaker one, was all remained to caress his wife and hold the reins of a horse.

Would he even be able to hold his child? Feeling clumsy and awkward, he shuddered at the thought. He'd probably drop the babe on its head.

"What are you thinking there?" Cahira sank onto the bench beside him, her pretty brows creased with worry.

"Nothing."

"Something surely put that frown on your face, and I'll not have you hiding it from me. Speak, Colton, for we are man and wife. There should be no secrets between us."

He looked away, wondering if he should burden her young heart with the bitterness that tinged his own. How could a dream go so sour? He had hoped their marriage would eventually illustrate that two different races could come together. Instead it had wrecked his life and separated the two races even further. And they had not heard the last of Richard de Burgo. Richard did not like to lose, and he would not slink away in surrender. He would return to enforce his claim upon the land.

Colton took a deep breath and let it out in an audible sigh, then gave Cahira a weary smile. "I was just thinking that you would be better off if Richard had killed me. I wouldn't be a burden to you or your people."

"A burden?" She threw back her head and placed her hands on her hips. "I never thought to say so, but you're talking like an eejit, my love. How could you be thinking such a thing? You are no burden, none at all. You are my own joy, and I'm happy to help you always. Besides," she gentled her tone, "you won't be needing my help much longer."

"I can't even pull a bowstring." He met her gaze, finally willing to let her see the helplessness in his eyes. "I can't use a sword, or wield a dagger, or lift one of those battleaxes your father's men like so much. I'm useless to you and your family. 'Twas only pity convinced your father to count me as your husband."

"My father has never felt a day of pity in his life." Her smile vanished, and he could see no trace of amusement in her black-lashed eyes. "He shows mercy to those who deserve it, but he demands that each man pull his weight. And you shall, Colton, we all know it. So 'tis not pity that drives him to welcome you, 'tis respect. And if not love, 'tis at least liking. He was mightily impressed with the things you said to Richard."

"Richard will be back," Colton said dully. "He'll come back with an army, Cahira. I don't know where he'll get one, but I'd wager he's working on the problem right now. He'll go from baron to baron, promising land and money or support in exchange for archers and knights and foot soldiers. When he is certain his force will outnumber your father's, he'll come back to Connacht."

Her green eyes shimmered with light from the window. "Ah, Colton, don't you think we know it? My father paints a brave picture for the simple folk, but he knows the Normans. We have only to look at the treachery of those who have invaded the southern provinces to know Richard will not rest until our land is his."

"Then why isn't your father *doing* anything to resist?"

One corner of her mouth twisted upward. "What else would you have him do? He's prepared his warriors and sent his other men home to work in their fields. Our people have to eat, no matter what trouble looms on the horizon." She reached out and gently fingered a lock of his tangled hair. "Perhaps the best thing he's done is take a Norman knight into his home. You think like a Norman, love, though you love like a Gael. My father trusts that you will be able to help us when Richard comes again."

Colton felt himself shrivel at her confident expression. "Richard saw to it that I could never help your father. I cannot lift a sword; I cannot even manage a catapult."

"He cares nothing for those things." Turning his head, Cahira buried her hands in his thick hair and gazed up at him. "Don't you understand, you dote? 'Tis your spirit he values, and your knowledge. And you are strong, Colton, stronger than the men who come with Richard, because you will be fighting for the land and the people you love. You will stir our warriors to defend themselves. You will teach us the secrets of Norman warfare. And, if God is good, we shall defend ourselves honorably."

Colton closed his eyes, seeing a mental image of his life spread out in a line, its humble beginning in Normandy, and its end on a green field somewhere in Connacht. He would breathe his last with the men of Éireann, these brave, friendly, free souls who would rather die than work their own soil for a foreign master.

His mind kept turning to a song he'd heard Murchadh singing at dinner:

If all my days were happy, could I say
In Éireann fair God wipes all tears away?
My tears, my pain, my loneliness,
E'en my death may be God's way to bless.

He would die, as all men did, but his life might not be meaningless. He would leave behind a child, a blend of Ireland's bravery and Normandy's pride. He would leave a wealth of memories with Cahira, who would guard them with her life and her own considerable courage.

He lowered his head, then pressed his left hand to the burgeoning weight that swelled beneath the fabric of her gown. "Be sure the child survives," he said, knowing she understood completely. "No matter what happens, you and the child must be safely away from the trouble."

"Nothing will happen," she whispered, pulling his head down to her shoulder. She held him there like a mother comforting a child, and both of them knew she lied.

✦

THE BITTER COLD OF FEBRUARY SHARPENED IN THE WINDY DAYS OF March, then melted into April's rains and gilded sunsets. As Colton struggled to train the warriors of Rathcroghan in the techniques of war, he kept one eye on the southwestern horizon, watching for any sign of smoke or the dust of an approaching army. But his eye saw only emerald ribbons of foliage and the bright patchwork of ripening fields.

He wasn't sure which was more exasperating—waiting on Richard, waiting on the coming child, or waiting for his Irish warriors to settle down and get serious about the art of war. The men of Rathcroghan preferred the Irish battleax to the heavy broadsword, despite Colton's contention that a man could be run through with a sword while he stopped to lift and lower an ax. On the pretext of strengthening his left hand and arm, Colton engaged Murchadh and several of the others in mock duels, but the Irish had little interest in pretend fighting. Their natural talents, Colton decided, leaned more toward dreaming, talking, and arguing than fighting, training, or plotting. A single well-scored point in a duel was reason enough for breaking into riotous celebration, and the telling of a cook's interesting dream would find a more rapt audience than Colton's lesson on dueling techniques.

Rumors trickled down upon Rathcroghan like the gentle rains that watered the fields nearly every morning. Dozens of men were assembling at Richard's castle in Limerick, the traveling poets reported, some of whom spoke nothing but French. The soldiers were giants, armed with pikes and broadswords so heavy that a man needed two strong arms to lift them.

The Irish laughed at the rumors and kept an eye on their greening fields. When Colton insisted that the stories might be true, Felim asked, "So what would you have us do, lad? The cattle must be fed, and furrows plowed. Our men don't lack for bravery, but there isn't time enough to sit around and worry."

As the month of June waxed and waned, Colton felt his own wariness fade. Cahira's time was imminent, and her moods and twinges far more fascinating than the stories swirling about the countryside. Still, he couldn't keep himself from glancing at the southwestern sky every morning and night. If Richard were to attempt an invasion, it would be likely to come in temperate weather.

Cahira's time of travail began on the twenty-second day of June. Sorcha, breathless and red-faced, brought the news to the men in the king's hall, and Murchadh, Colton, and Felim instantly retreated to the chapel. The king and the burly warrior completed their heartfelt prayers and stood to depart, but Colton lingered by the altar, caught up in a desperate need to do something useful while his wife struggled in childbirth. She had borne so much for him. . . . Though it was probably unseemly for a man, Colton quietly told God he would gladly bear the pain of childbirth for her, if such a thing were allowed.

He was still kneeling in the chapel two hours later when Murchadh entered, his face ashen. "Colton, you are needed now." His voice wasn't much louder than a whisper, but the effect was as great as if he had shouted in Colton's ear.

Colton whirled. "Has something happened to Cahira?"

"No." Fear radiated from the older man, and the somber look on the warrior's face sent a thrill of alarm shooting through Colton's middle. "A scout has raised the alarm. An army is approaching from Athlone."

Colton closed his eyes as the hair on the back of his neck rose with premonition. *Richard.* Awkwardly, he cleared his throat. "How many?"

"More than we've ever seen. The scout says the hills are crawling with them."

Colton silently held up his hand, then turned again to the altar. *God, this is the time*, he prayed, lifting his eyes to the cross mounted on the wall. *You have brought me to this place and saved me for this day. You have given me a wife and a child and a people . . . and I return them all to you. Do with us—do with me—as you will.*

Rising, he silently followed Murchadh from the chapel.

༺✾༻

THROUGH A VEIL OF WEARINESS AND PAIN, CAHIRA SAW COLTON leaning over her bed. "What are you doing here?" Despite her exhaustion, a smile crept to her face. "Come to look at your son, have you now?"

"I've seen him. He's beautiful." Colton sank to the edge of the bed and reached for her hand, then gripped it tightly in his own. "We have to talk, my love."

Cahira grimaced as she turned and shifted her weight. Portions of her skin burned and her muscles ached, but the pain was nothing compared to the joy of enfolding her son in her arms.

Aedh. Named for another king of Connacht.

"Can we talk later?" Her lids slipped down over her eyes. "I'm tired. I don't know what you're knowing about childbirth, Colton, but 'tis no easy thing I've done here today."

"Cahira," Colton clung to her hand, "You must take the baby away at once."

His voice was a bolt of energy, conveying a force of will that demanded her response. She opened her eyes and stared at her husband, stunned . . . and yet not surprised. He had said all along that Richard would come again when the weather improved.

She lifted her head to give emphasis to her words. "I haven't the strength. The birth was more difficult than I expected."

"You can rest later, Cahira, after you're safely away. Swear to me that you'll take the baby and go, right now. Richard is coming."

Cahira leaned back and read her destiny in his somber eyes. The time had come to fight, just as Colton had predicted, and all of her dreams vanished in the light of the looming battle. What did her dreams matter when her people's fate hung in the balance?

The next few hours would decide the future of Connacht. Since Colton had been right about Richard's return, he would most likely be right about the outcome of the battle as well. Richard would not have returned without an invincible army.

"What will happen when he comes?" Her voice faded as she considered the inevitable. "Will he have my parents killed?"

For a moment Colton studied her intently, then his vivid brown eyes filled with a distant stillness. "He will doubtless burn this place and anyone in it, for it is the king's house and a symbol of the past," he said, his voice flat. "But after his victory, Richard will only destroy those who threaten him. If your father survives the battle, 'tis likely Richard will let him live, if only to curry favor with the people." His mouth curved in a mirthless smile. "Richard will need the people to till the land and care for his cattle."

Cahira nodded, digesting this answer, then forced another, more crucial question across her lips. "Will he see our son as a threat?"

Colton bent over her, his hand smoothing her hair. "If your father takes a vow of fealty, 'tis almost certain his heirs will swear allegiance to Richard as well." His voice was rough, torn by despair and longing. "The boy will be safe, Cahira—as long as he and your father survive this day."

"Then I swear the child will live." Cahira grasped his hand and gazed steadily into his eyes. "You have my oath on it."

He pressed his lips to her damp forehead, then rested his cheek against hers. "Good-bye, my love." His voice, like her nerves, was in shreds. "Remember this—as life is eternal, love is immortal. Death is only a horizon, and a horizon only the limit of our sight. I will see you again."

He squeezed her hand one final time, pressed another kiss to her lips, then turned to join the battle.

Staring at the space he had just occupied, Cahira reached out with trembling fingers and traced his image in the dust motes shifting in the slanting sun's rays. The Normans were coming, and her husband, armed only with a sword in his left hand, was determined to resist every step of their advance. They might strike him down with her father and many of her friends, but they would *not* harm her innocent baby.

"Sorcha!" Gathering all her strength, Cahira pushed herself up on one elbow and waited until the maid crept into the room, her eyes red-rimmed with weeping. "Take my child, swaddle him in warm blankets, and go. I want you to ride north toward the kingdom of Tir Conaill. Do not stop, and do not look back."

Sorcha crossed herself, nodded a scared-rabbit kind of assent, and bent to pick up the baby. "One more thing," Cahira murmured, reaching toward the child. "Take Murchadh with you. If my father objects, tell him it is for his grandson's benefit. The two of you should go at once, and guard my son with your life. In him flows the royal blood of the O'Connors. If you do not reach safety, he will be the last."

Sorcha scooped the baby into her arms, then lowered him to Cahira's side long enough for her to press her lips to the child's wrinkled brow. He was a beautiful boy, perfectly formed and pink, with swirls of dark hair that would one day be as thick and lustrous as Colton's.

Cahira bit her lip, her anguish nearly overcoming her control. Why had God allowed her and this innocent one to be caught up in this inescapable tragedy? If her body was not so weak and exhausted, she'd at least *feel* in charge of her destiny, but there was nothing she could do here but wait for the enemy.

She swallowed the lump that had risen in her throat and trailed her fingers over the baby's cheek. If she were a man, she'd be on the battlefield between her father and husband, fighting for Éireann and freedom. But because she was a woman, she lay here instead, weakened by pain and fatigue, bloodied by the honor of bringing a new life into the world. She reveled in the joy of it, but she could not dismiss her regrets.

"I pray God," she whispered, resting her cupped palm against the baby's round head, "that those who come after us will shine like the stars, yet have the courage to break free from their foreordained courses and restore right in this murderous world."

Sorcha said nothing, but trembled so violently Cahira feared she would drop the baby.

"Go." Cahira held her emotions in check until her maid left the room, then she fell back onto the bed and dug her fingers into her pillow, watering it with hot tears.

᠖᠅᠍᠍᠊᠊

Two hours later, Cahira called the women of Rathcroghan into the main hall and had them bolt the entry doors. Every single man had deserted the fortress to meet the enemy en route, and Cahira knew few of them would return. But Sorcha and Murchadh had slipped safely away with their precious bundle, and that was all that mattered.

In the thick silence of the hall, her mother sat in the king's chair, her hand trembling as she caressed the carved armrest that had supported a vast line of O'Connor kings.

"Fear not, Mother," Cahira whispered, bracing her shoulders as she walked slowly to the center of the room. "If the Normans reach us, God will give us the courage we need."

"Listen!" One of the maids lifted a hand, then brought it to her mouth. Cahira turned toward the high window and heard the dull rumble of hoofbeats.

They were coming. Her father's men—and Colton—had failed to hold them.

Whirling in the open space of her father's council chamber, she extended her hands to the women gathered there. "Courage, lasses," she cried, triumph flooding through her when the women ceased their quiet weeping and looked up. "Dry your tears, mind your courage, and remember that the grave is not our goal. Dust we are, and dust we'll be, but no man can touch our souls."

The hoofbeats grew louder, punctuated by the hoarse cries of men intent upon victory.

"Cahira?" She turned, and saw one of the young scullery maids standing before her. Tears stained the girl's oval face, but she bravely lifted her arm and offered Cahira a sword.

Colton's sword. Cahira would have recognized it anywhere.

"He gave it to me before he rode out with the others," the girl said, her voice whispery and tinged with terror. "He told me to give it to you."

As the sounds of horses quieted and Norman exclamations cut through the deep silence outside the hall, Cahira gripped the heavy sword by its hilt and felt the sharp stab of a memory. *Would an ordinary woman dress like a man to best Lord Richard's archers? Would an ordinary woman offer herself to stand as a human target? Would an ordinary woman slip away from her father's fortress to go riding with one of the enemy?*

Colton knew. He had heard her vow that their son would live, and he knew she would remain behind to defend her father's house. She was, after all, a warrior's wife and a king's daughter. Position required commitment, and commitment demanded obedience and sacrifice.

The barred door suddenly shuddered and cracked beneath a heavy blow. The still air of the chamber shivered into bits; a maid's scream scattered the last of Cahira's regrets. Death was only a horizon, and she would soon see Colton again.

"I beg you, Father God," she whispered, her heart like a drum within her chest. "Let me not be the last."

Rousing herself from the weariness that weighed her down, she lifted the heavy sword and pointed it toward the door.

❧ 30 ❧

M onday night, October 18, 1999
Ballyshannon

"SO WHAT HAPPENED TO CAHIRA'S BABY?"

Patrick lay stretched out on a rug before the fire while I sat next to him, my back propped against the easy chair. I had just finished reading the conclusion of Cahira's story, and Patrick had been a good listener, interrupting only twice for a quick kiss after declaring he couldn't bear not comforting me in the midst of such a moving tale.

I fumbled through my notes and pulled my stockinged foot away from Patrick's restless fingers. "Cahira's son, Aedh, grew up in his grandfather's household. After the initial invasion of Connacht, Felim O'Connor surrendered to Richard de Burgo. Felim lost his daughter, his son-in-law, and his wife, but he managed to keep his title. Richard, after all, needed someone who knew how to keep the native Irish in line, so the O'Connors continued to rule, but as subjects of the earl. Later, though, the O'Connors rose up against the English, and one or two gave the English a royal drubbing."

"Serves them right."

"More than thirty-five kings issued from the O'Connor line, but the last direct heir to the kingship of Connacht took Jesuit vows in the nineteenth century, so there the line ended." I leaned forward, planting my elbows on the carpet as I looked down into his eyes. "So what do you think of my ancestor Cahira?"

"I'm pure mad about her." His hand reached out and cupped the back of my neck. "Just as I'm pure mad about you."

Seeking another kiss, he pulled me forward, so I buried my face in his neck, breathed a kiss there, then playfully pushed him away. With Maddie and Taylor away on their honeymoon and Mr. and Mrs. tucked away in the back of the house, it wasn't wise for us to be by the fire, alone and in love.

He smiled at me, and the smoldering flame in his eye went far beyond the bounds of brotherly affection. "You've had time now, and plenty of it. What'll it be, then?" He pushed our bowl of popcorn out of the way, then rolled onto his stomach, and propped himself on his elbows. His eyes glinted as he looked up at me. "You promised me an answer days ago, and I'll be wanting to have it now. Will you marry me or won't you?"

I deliberately let my mind run backwards, thinking of a stony hilltop seven hundred years away from Ballyshannon. In an age when the risks were higher and the opposition greater, Cahira and Colton, a Gael and an outsider, had fallen in love and defied the odds, knowing they were following God's plan for their lives. I could see God's hand in the events that linked my life to Patrick's, too.

Colton, Cahira's beloved outsider, had entered an Irish family in a time of peace and died in the struggle that followed. I had entered an Irish family in a time of struggle, and in the resulting peace I was learning how to live. There was a certain symmetry to the situation, a completeness that appealed to me.

"I think," I began, looking into Patrick's eyes, "I've finally discovered what it means to be an heir of Cahira O'Connor. All my forerunners—Anika, Aidan, and Flanna—had one thing in common: They embraced life, its good and bad, with every ounce of their energy. Before coming to Ireland, I wanted only to observe life, to copy it down in neat, ordered paragraphs. I think the death of my parents made me pull inside myself, to avoid loving and risking again."

Patrick squeezed my hand when I hesitated. "Go on, love."

"To be honest, I always resisted the idea of being related to Cahira and her incredible descendants. They all did extraordinary things in unique circumstances, and I objected every time Taylor or the professor mentioned that I might be linked to them. I didn't think I would—I didn't *want* to do something *cataclysmic* with my life."

"And now?"

I looked toward the fireplace, where a chorus line of flames leapt and danced to the music of our voices. "Now I'm thinking that it's possible to be an ordinary woman with an extraordinary impact just by being faithful and unashamed. There aren't any wars here for me to fight, no continents to be discovered, but I think God brought me to Ballyshannon to help bring peace to a pair of warring souls."

A log collapsed in the fire, sending streams of sparks whirling up into the chimney, and Patrick squeezed my hand, understanding that I spoke of him and his father. Blinking back tears, I kept my eyes upon the fireplace. "God prodded me off my usual path—just like he did the others—and he set me here. I can help others, too, as long as I am steadfast. I think maybe I am destined to do great things, but in quiet ways."

"I love you, Kathleen O'Connor."

Leaning forward again, I parked my head in my hands, mimicking Patrick's posture. "'Tis my destiny to be yours, Patrick. So if your offer's still good, I'll take you up on it. But there are two complications you should know about. First, I can't remain in Ireland without my dog. But I think he'll love Ballyshannon."

Patrick smiled with warm spontaneity. "Shout would love a friend. What do you have, one of those wee foot-warmer pups?"

I tried and failed to suppress a giggle. "Hardly. Barkley was 240 pounds at his last checkup. And he's still growing."

Patrick stared at me for an instant, then his surprise vanished as he couldn't stop himself from laughing. "Well, then, maybe he'll give the calves incentive to grow. What's the other complication?"

I bit my lip. "My Aunt Kizzie. She's the nearest thing I have to a mother, and she'll have to come to the wedding. Trouble is, I'm not sure she can afford the airfare."

His hand tucked around my elbow with easy familiarity. "I'll bring her over. I can't be marrying you without your nearest and dearest relative."

"But can you afford it? I know things have been tight around here. Maddie's wedding wasn't exactly inexpensive, and there's the purchase of the new bull—"

"Things *are* a bit tight at Ballyshannon." His breath softly fanned my face. "But don't be forgetting my computer business, love. I could fly an entire flock of Aunt Kizzies to Ireland, so don't you worry."

I stared at him in surprise. "You're rich?"

"In many things." Patrick gave me a slow, almost drowsy smile. "In blessings, in love, and in cheek."

"Cheek?" I laughed softly and slipped one arm around his neck. "You'll have to explain that one, sir."

"Audacity," he answered, his touch sending fire through every nerve in my body. "As in, 'The cheek of me, imagining that a dairy farmer might marry an Irish princess.'"

"I don't know about the Irish princess bit," my fingertips moved to his lips as he sat up and pulled me into his embrace, "but I do know Cahira has brought me home."

EPILOGUE

Eighteen months have passed since Taylor's and Maddie's wedding—and seventeen months since my own. Patrick and I were married at a tiny church in Borrisokane, only a few miles from Ballyshannon. After the wedding, we settled straightway into the front rooms of the main house, knowing Ballyshannon would never again serve as a bed and breakfast. With Patrick's freelance computer work, my writing, and a new approach to the business of dairy farming, we're bringing in enough income to take the pressure off Fiona.

Besides, we needed the space. We're using one of the bedrooms as a nursery.

James was able to hold our son, James Patrick O'Neil, before he died. The baby came in December, and James went to be with Jesus three weeks later. I know he's with the Lord, for as he studied the changes in Patrick, he came to see that salvation was not a matter of belonging to a church, but of surrendering to Christ. He placed his trust in the work of Jesus alone, and he died in peace.

We hear from Taylor and Maddie fairly often. They have no children yet, nor plans for any, but Taylor has his doctorate and a wonderful position at New York City College. Occasionally Maddie sends clippings from the *Times* society section, and their names always seem to figure prominently in descriptions of receptions for the intellectual glitterati. They seem happy and content, which is all I ever wanted them to be.

Really.

As for me, I feel like a toddler who was led kicking and screaming to the table where a loving parent had spread the most delicious, nutritious, wonderful meal imaginable. (Sorry for the analogy, but my thoughts keep revolving around babies.) Through Patrick and the O'Neils, the Lord has taught me that the depth of joy I experience is in direct proportion to the pain I'm willing to bear. In giving up my predictable and ordered existence in New York, I am embracing all the pleasure and pain life can bring. I remember what Aunt Kizzie said: When we're walking close to the Savior, he demands more and more until our lives are given over. But with each burden he lifts from me, he bestows a blessing.

I'm not merely existing any more—I'm *living*.

Ireland, this beautiful emerald island, is my birthright and my destiny. I came here as an embarrassed believer, rather like Peter just after he had denied the Lord three times, but the Savior still had a purpose for me. Despite my shortcomings, I was able to fan the flame of salvation in Patrick, whose faith glowed bright enough to attract his father, whose changed life influenced the entire community of Ballinderry. James's confident belief touched everyone who came to see him in his last days, including the priest who showed up to administer the last rites.

"Thanks for the effort, Father, but I'll not be placing me faith in your words or the extreme unction," James told the priest, his eyes shining with steadfast serenity. "My faith stands on nothing less than my precious Savior's righteousness."

And so he slipped away from us and into the arms of the Savior. In that moment, Patrick stood by his side, as did Fiona. Little James and I sat in a corner chair, while a snippet of Scripture kept running through my mind: "Precious in the sight of the Lord is the death of his saints."

I know the Lord has a perfect plan for each of his children, and I know I've found his will for me. The Cahira stories *were* published, and nearly every week I receive letters from women who see a reflection of themselves in one of Cahira's heirs. I hope those books touch lives, and I know they touched mine.

I have to laugh when I remember the night Taylor taunted me by predicting that I'd end up getting married, driving a station wagon, shopping for groceries, and raising children. "Every night you'll fall into bed too tired from doing the little things to even *dream* about the big things," he'd said. "Is that any kind of life for an heir of Cahira O'Connor?"

I wish he could see—*really* see—me now. Every night I fall into bed with a man who adores me, and I'm so thrilled by the *big* things that I don't even think about the little things I might miss from home. A miracle sleeps in the room next to ours, and an exceptional man lies next to me. Words can't describe the beauty of my home or the people who fill my life.

Oh yes—Aunt Kizzie came for the wedding and never went back to the States. She now lives in the little house, and she and Fiona are like sisters. They've become prayer partners, and I am constantly challenged by their example.

There is much work to be done at Ballyshannon, but I'm working among lovely people who have warmed my heart with their goodness and charm. And though this isn't a battlefield or an uncharted territory, I've encountered many occasions where I needed to call on Anika's spiritual strength, Aidan's creative joy, and Flanna's raw courage. Being a good wife is a challenge, and motherhood is a daunting task. I pray daily for guidance so I can demonstrate the Truth.

Spring has come again, and as the pastures and hills around me grow lush and green, I find myself counting colors. I think I've learned to recognize twenty different shades of green. In a year or two, as my eye grows sharper and these hills more beloved, I'm sure I shall see all forty.

ACKNOWLEDGMENTS

The following books provided information, inspiration, or insight as I worked on *The Emerald Isle*:

Cook, Thomas. *Passport's Illustrated Travel Guide to Ireland*. Lincolnwood, IL: Passport Books, 1995.

Curtis, Edmund. *A History of Ireland*. New York: Routledge Press, 1995.

Greely, Andrew M. *The Irish*. Chicago: Contemporary Books, 1990.

Hewitt, Hugh. *The Embarrassed Believer*. Nashville, TN: Word Publishing, 1998.

Juergenson, Elwood, and W. P. Mortenson. *Approved Practices in Dairying*. Danville, IL: The Interstate Printers and Publishers, Inc., 1977.

Kaiser, Walter C. Jr., Peter H. Davids, F. F. Bruce, and Manfred T. Brauch. *Hard Sayings of the Bible*. Downers Grove, IL: InterVarsity Press, 1996.

Kelleher, Margaret. *So You Think You're Irish*. New York: Wings Press, 1988.

Morris, Mark. *Ireland: The Emerald Isle and Its People*. Lincolnwood, IL: Passport Books, 1995.

Roche, Richard. *The Norman Invasion of Ireland*. Dublin: Anvil Books Limited, 1995.

The editors of Time-Life Books. *What Life Was Like in the Age of Chivalry*. Alexandria, VA: Time-Life Books, 1997.

A special thanks to Bill Higgs, Hebrew scholar *extraordinaire*, and Liz Curtis Higgs, for sharing her husband's expertise!

Finally, I owe a world of gratitude to my editors Lisa Bergren, who helps keep me focused, and Rick Blanchette, who keeps all the details straight. I appreciate you both!

ALSO BY ANGELA HUNT

The Shadow Women

Magdalene

Risen

The Nativity Story

Paul, Apostle of Christ

The Jerusalem Road Series

Daughter of Cana, 2020

The Shepherd's Wife, 2020

A Woman of Words, 2021

The Apostle's Sister, 2022

The Silent Years series

• *Egypt's Sister,* Summer 2017.

• *Judah's Wife*, January 2018.

• *Jerusalem's Queen*, Summer 2018

. *King's Shadow,* Spring 2019

The Dangerous Beauty series

• *Esther*, January 2015

• *Bathsheba,* Fall 2015

• *Delilah,* June 2016

The Heirs of Cahira O'Connor Series

• *The Silver Sword*, January 1998

- *The Golden Cross,* October 1998

- *The Velvet Shadow,* January 1999

- *The Emerald Isle,* September 1999

The Keepers of the Ring Series

- *Roanoke: The Lost Colony,* 1996

- *Jamestown,* 1996

- *Hartford,* 1996

- *Rehoboth,* 1997

- *Charles Towne,* 1998

Legacies of the Ancient River series

- *Dreamers,* January 1996, Re-released 2008

- *Brothers,* March, 1997, Re-released 2009

- *Journey,* 1997, Re-released 2009

The Theyn Chronicles or The Knights' Chronicles

- *Afton of Margate Castle,* 1993

- *The Troubadour's Quest,* 1994

- *Ingram of the Irish,* 1994

Made in the USA
Las Vegas, NV
02 February 2023